HE
WASN'T
THERE
AGAIN
TODAY

HE WASN'T THERE AGAIN TODAY

A THIRD POSTMODERN MYSTERY, BY THE NUMBERS

An Epitome Apartments Mystery by

CANDAS
JANE
DORSEY

Published by ECW Press
665 Gerrard Street East
Toronto, Ontario, Canada M4M 1Y2
416-694-3348 / info@ecwpress.com

Cover artwork and design by Brienne Lim
Author photo: © Sima Khorrami

LIBRARY AND ARCHIVES CANADA CATALOGUING IN PUBLICATION

Title: He wasn't there again today : a third postmodern mystery, by the numbers / an Epitome Apartments mystery by Candas Jane Dorsey.

Names: Dorsey, Candas Jane, author.

Identifiers: Canadiana (print) 20230465528 | Canadiana (ebook) 20230465536

ISBN 978-1-77041-557-7 (softcover)
ISBN 978-1-77852-075-4 (ePub)
ISBN 978-1-77852-177-5 (PDF)
ISBN 978-1-77852-178-2 (Kindle)

Subjects: LCGFT: Novels. | LCGFT: Detective and mystery fiction.

Classification: LCC PS8557.O78 H4 2023 | DDC C813/.54—dc23

This book is funded in part by the Government of Canada. *Ce livre est financé en partie par le gouvernement du Canada.* We acknowledge the support of the Canada Council for the Arts. *Nous remercions le Conseil des arts du Canada de son soutien.* We acknowledge the funding support of the Ontario Arts Council (OAC), an agency of the Government of Ontario. We also acknowledge the support of the Government of Ontario through the Ontario Book Publishing Tax Credit, and through Ontario Creates.

ONTARIO ARTS COUNCIL
CONSEIL DES ARTS DE L'ONTARIO
an Ontario government agency
un organisme du gouvernement de l'Ontario

Canada Council   Conseil des arts
for the Arts   du Canada

Canadä

PRINTED AND BOUND IN CANADA

PRINTING: MARQUIS   5   4   3   2   1

"The future is there . . . looking back at us. Trying to make sense of the fiction we will have become."

William Gibson, *Pattern Recognition*

"As I was going up the stair
I met a man who wasn't there
He wasn't there again today
Oh how I wish he'd go away"

nursery rhyme (after — or before? —
William Hughes Mearns's
1899 poem "Antigonish")

"If you live in a place where you can't see the sky, you don't need to know the weather. But if the sky can get at you, you should have a personal relationship with it."

Harold Rhenisch, "Reading the Weather,"
Okanagan Okanogan (blog), April 19, 2021

YESTERDAY UPON THE STAIR,

1. NOT EVENLY DISTRIBUTED

On the top shelf of my bedroom closet, I have a box that sings to me.

When I say this, when I say that I have a box in my closet that sings to me (or, more properly, that I have, in my closet, a box that sings to me), I do not mean a music box, an automaton, a Victrola™, a phonograph, a record player, a stereo, a Discman™, a Walkman™, a television, a computer, an .mp3 player, a smart-phone with Bluetooth: I do not mean anything fantastical or even science-fictional except in the sense of that 2003 William Gibson quote in the *Economist*.[1]

The box is rectangular and deeper than it is wide, and it was carved by a lover, with love, to fit the shape of my hands, and in it is a sheaf of a technological marvel called smart paper that records in many ways — moving and still visuals, voices, text.

---

1. "The future is already here — it's just not evenly distributed." William Gibson, *The Economist*, December 4, 2003.

On those pages are the voices, work, and images of Nathan Bierce, who was the dearest love of all my dear loves so far, and the voices, notes, and a few images of Priscilla Jane Gill, who was a rediscovered college friend — and also, on some, there is the voice, work, and face of their killer, Lockwood Chiles, my worst enemy.

I am haunted by the voices of these dead.

I've already told the story of how I got the box, the paper, and a heartful of grief.[2] It's also the story of why on my bookshelf I have a very creepy dead-and-taxidermied cat yclept Micah the First, and why twining around my feet as this story begins were not one but two very non-ghostly, very living cats: my old tortoiseshell-and-white calico Manx buddy Bunnywit[3] and Micah Five, an elegant Abyssinian with a secret past.

Not-so-secret, actually, in these days of global media, but all three of us have long since had our fifteen minutes of fame. Our story is so last year.

Or so I thought.

Ha.

2. THE SECOND DEATH OF LOCKWOOD CHILES[4]

The first I heard of the second death of Lockwood Chiles, a.k.a. All the Names, a.k.a. the psychopath who killed my lover Nathan Bierce and my friend Priscilla Jane Gill and a bunch of other

---

2.   *What's the Matter with Mary Jane?*, the second of the books I've written about my adventures, the first being *The Adventures of Isabel*. If you haven't read them, please do that, okay?, because there is a ton of back-story there. I still must inevitably review in these early pages because people's reading habits, unlike life, are not always sequential — but we all have limited patience with expository lumps, amirite?

3.   Who used to be called Fuckwit until I decided I needed better manners. See *Isabel*, op. cit.

4.   And, retrospectively, the first strike. More on that later.

people last year, was when my pal[5] Roger, who is the head of the Major Crimes Unit in our city police force, showed up at my door.

This wasn't unusual given my life in the last few years. It *was* odd that he had with him one of his minions, yclept Dave (pronounced Daah-vay), whom I had met before, and their facial expressions were severe and serious.

"Rog!" I said. "Constable Dave! Come in! Welcome — I think?"

They came in. Bunnywit was attracted to the boots of the uniformed cop, of course, but Micah went straight to Roger and began to shed short golden-ticked hairs all over the ankles of his black dress pants, because that's how Micah rolls.

"Tea? Coffee? Iced tea? Hot chocolate with marshmallows?" The last two were a nod to shared stories in the past.

Roger didn't smile. "No."

Dave said, "No, thank you, ma'am."

"What's got your knickers in a twist today?" I said. Roger can be sarcastic, and he can be foul-mouthed, but he isn't usually rude. Well, not *that* rude.

"What would you say if I told you Lockwood Chiles was dead?" Roger said.

"I'd make you prove it," I said promptly. "He was dead once before, and look how that turned out."

"Well, he *is* dead."

"I thought he was in jail?"

"He's dead in jail. And I'm here because some people have suggested you did it."

Well.

My days in the last couple of years have had a way of changing state abruptly like that. It might be turning into a thing.

---

5. "Pal" is not quite the same thing as "friend", though there is probably a fairly substantial overlap in this particular Venn diagram. I mean, we have some fundamental disagreements, but isn't that always true?

But of all the things I thought might derail my day, this one would never have occurred to me.

I turned around and went into the bright, sunny living room. Roger and the other cop followed.

I had moved the big comfortable chair over the stain in the floor where, despite treatments by crime-scene cleaners of great merit, Lockwood Chiles's blood hadn't entirely come out of the old hardwood flooring.

I sat down in the chair, and shivered as Lockwood Chiles's ghost walked over my grave.

3. DAYS OF FUTURE PAST

So when, in its past, does a crime start happening?

The odd thing is that I was actually thinking this very question that day when all this began.

The future is rooted in the past. That's what they say, whoever they are. I suppose it's true.

Certainly at this point all my days were looking backward. I was backing into the future blindly, as some people say one does, while reaching my hands out to ghosts from the past. Finding reasons why things happen is kind of a hobby of mine, or, one might say, an obsession, but some things are pretty hard to trace. Yes, I know, people spend lifetimes and a lot of therapy dollars on this exact process, and despite my past as a social worker dealing with exactly that sort of quest, I was no different.

The deaths of my brother when I was a teenager and of my parents years ago, I had almost managed to leave behind, as much as one ever does one's dead.

But recently I had a new crew keeping me company, Nathan and Pris foremost among them. Now, apparently, Lock was going to join them.

Not on my being-haunted-by wish list, that one.

Nathan and Pris haunted me because of a set of criminal circumstances that had roots so deep I had not been able to trace them at all. Even while the three of them were alive, they were mysterious, and dead, they[6] were ultimately unknowable.

Or so I thought.

4. STRIP LIVING

The lot around the Epitome Apartments is fenced with hundred-year-old wrought iron in a classic "thou shalt not pass" design: pointy spears almost seven feet tall (over two metres, if you are not me therefore not stuck in the past), set in a line and strapped together with decorative twirly banding that theoretically can't be climbed (it was designed by people so optimistic as to be delusional). It's the kind of fence that bad guys and innocent victims fall on in the movies, and heaven forfend anyone should in real life[7]. There is some resident parking inside there, some raised garden beds around the inside edge that we are going to expand next year, and a few mature Dutch elm trees along the outside by the sidewalk and street.

Behind the fenced segment, there is a strip of land about fifteen feet wide and about fifty feet long, beside the alley. That is where the dumpsters sit, and some scraggly poppies and hollyhocks grow — and where Shayna and Ted were living, in a tent, with their dogs Killer and Fang (that's what I call them, in jest; they have real names, but this is fiction).

Fang is the ivory-furred throwback-Pomeranian, and, by looks, suitable to cast as some kid's sidekick in feel-good movies: Utility Dog from Central Casting. No glamourpuss, however,

6.   And, in the case of the insalubrious and psychopathic Lock, their crimes.

7.   Just to reassure you, this is not the-fence-above-the-fireplace.

Fang has a slightly-matted brush cut and is fairly grubby, but is well-fed, healthy, and well-loved — despite being hostile to every other being on the planet outside her pack of two humans, one dog, and three cats.

Killer is some kind of big yellow-brown Heinz-57, Central Casting ditto but probably for Generic Drug-Sniffing Dog in an international thriller. His smooth short coat doesn't mat, but ditto grubby and ditto well-fed. He's more amiable. He only alerts when people come too close to the camp, doesn't actually snarl or show teeth as Fang does.

Not only did these guys get their own food bowls and proper food, they get treats and rawhide chews. There was no way Ted and Shayna were letting houselessness compromise their standards.

The three cats comprised a black cat, a tabby, and some overly-fluffy kittenish thing I'd only seen at a distance, tearing around the vacant lot. Whenever anyone came by, it made for shelter PDQ and hid. I don't know the cats' names.

Ted and Shayna have a little tent, several shopping carts'-worth of their worldly goods, and a lot of blue and orange tarps with which they make a tidy cube about ten feet per side, opening toward the alley. Ted lost his cheap housing last year, and they have been homeless since then because Ted won't give up his five pets, and that puts him down on the bottom of the list. He supplements his meagre disability cheque by metal salvage, stripping wire and dismantling broken appliances and TVs he finds in the trash or maybe buys at the thrift shop. There's gold inside televisions — who knew? I know he doesn't steal, because Ted likes to pay his way. He once told me he's homeless because on disability he has a choice: pay for housing and steal food, or live rough and cover expenses for him, his girlfriend, and his pets.

I got to know them this spring as one does, by petting the dogs (or at least trying to in Fang's case) when they lived on the empty lot next door. When the bylaw enforcement started calling the owner of the empty lot and threatening him with big fines if he didn't kick them out, I offered the space behind the Epitome, and all the water they want from the outside tap.

When I got the same threat, I went to the city administration, to City Council, and to the media. I don't like bullying.

In theory, Ted and Shayna are on a couple of housing lists, but that had been true since the early spring[8] and nothing has happened for them yet. But Bylaw leaves them, and me, alone, for now, as we all wait for the mills of the housing gods to grind fine[9].

5. IT'S NOT HYPOTHETICAL

At the other end of the strip, Fleury and Dan set up six weeks ago — on the "open season on the Epitome of alley-strip-living" principle, I guess, and, on the same principle, I assume, Bylaw hasn't hassled them — yet.

I've known Fleury for a lot longer, though. He's been collecting bottles from the Epitome ever since I've lived there, which is getting on for thirteen years now. He's in and out of squalid housing, never getting ahead. Part of the winter he was in the shelters with Dan, so when spring came they got out into the air. They benefit from the temporary enforcement moratorium I negotiated, though they haven't really earned it.

But who ever *deserves* to have police and city workers swoop down and steal their belongings, no matter how disorganised their lives are? I mean, srsly, people, what is this civic desire to criminalise poverty and steal from people who have almost nothing to start with? Not to speak of the message it sends that homeless

---

8. Are you familiar with First Faux Spring, Second Winter, Second Faux Spring, Second Winter, and so on? This had actually been the case since First Faux Spring, in January IIRC.

9. They better grind fine — they are certainly slow enough.

people, like garbage, "deserve" to be swept up and tidied away, over and over again[10].

Dan and Fleury's camp is more than untidy, as are they. Years ago, Fleury had a workplace injury, and when the medical care ran out, he started self-medicating with alcohol. That was a long time ago. He lives — and drinks — with Dan, who's a squat, foul-mouthed, kindly old bird with long white hair and badly-fitting false teeth, and they're regarded as a couple by everyone. Whether or not they're lovers, they've still been beaten up for it at the shelters and called names, but that could just be generic bullying because Fleury's a nice guy and his name means Flower. They've been waiting for a year for an apartment in a harm reduction facility that specialises in combining housing with First Nations and settler healing techniques.

Dan's fat is the unhealthy, puffy, oedemic fatness of massive organ dysfunction and poor diet; his health is so bad now that he's been into Emergency three times in the few weeks since they camped behind the Epitome. Fleury is so thin that his bones bruise his skin from the inside out.

Neither of them would hurt a fly, but they smell pretty bad, which frustrates Ted and Shayna, who keep clean and present-able — but Fleur and Dan are so pitiful that Ted and Shay cut them slack, same as I do.

Last week when he was dumpster-diving, Fleury found a pretty little candle holder and brought it to me as a thanks for letting them stay out there. He was drunk, and when he's drunk he smells of urine and he cries.

---

10. Hot-button issue for me. I know some of City Council feels as I do, but the rest, the hardcore bootstrap-touting brigade, awfulises about crime and litter, making it hard to just get on with a quick housing-first solution. Hence Nathan's and my end-run effort with our Own Domains foundation and alliances with Gary and M2F2.

I held the gift in my clean, well-fed, non-addicted hand and felt like a shit.

If I were really kind, shouldn't there be something I could do? I can't bring any of them into the Epitome, not even the functional Ted. The Epitome is a fragile ecosystem. Some of its people have lived there for decades. Many are old, and many, old or not, are tired. Even knowing our area, nevertheless a large minority of them are barely willing to accept the need for the camp — they accept it at a distance, but no closer.

And face it, Fleury and Dan are not people I can get closer to, though I consider them neighbours. I don't have the resources to make them into a career project. It would take constant effort and a lot of funding to clean up after Fleur and Dan, in any of the meanings of *clean up*[11].

So I work on the big picture, feel small, hope for harm-reduction villages soon, and in the meanwhile give Fleur and Dan empty bottles and small change.

6. THE EXPOSITORY LUMP

I call these "postmodern mysteries" so that I can break the fourth wall — and the rules — and sometimes talk about things as if I'm the author, which I am. And because doing all that is trendy as hell[12], I actually got the first two of these both written *and* published. But now I'm into Part Three of my story, faced with the task of introducing myself and my increasingly complex life to someone who picked up this book first instead of third.

So. Here we go; hang on tight.

---

11. Including the bylaw officers', which we have established is institutionalised bullshit.

12. Even though postmodernism isn't even very modern any more. But its cachet hangs on.

A few years ago, I was a downsized social worker who'd been unemployed for a year and my cupboard was bare. I was literally down to one last package of fish sticks, food-adjacent protein which did not please Bunnywit my cat — who had until not long before been yclept Fuckwit. I had, as I still do, a born-again cousin Thelma, who had opinions about the cat's original name, so I had just changed it, but in those days tended to forget under pressure — or all the time really.

I already lived in the Epitome Apartments[13], but as a tenant, and I was in despair about the upcoming rent. At this crucial point my friend Hep's granddaughter was murdered, and Hep offered to pay me for my help keeping the police honest about young Maddy's case. Soon I discovered that first Maddy and then I had stumbled into a huge conspiracy — for real, not a tinfoil hats thing — to defraud the city of $28.8 million. Poor Maddy had been killed not over drugs or sex but because she had recognised the wrong con artist at the wrong time.

In the end: the baddies went to jail; I ended up with a better relationship with my cousin; my friend Denis gave up his lonely life for partnership and eventual marriage to a beau-laid cop named — I kid you not — Lancelot; I myself found a girlfriend, Jian, who afterward ran away to join the circus (with my help) — and I got a bit of a Reputation. Unlike my previous reputations, which whether exaggerated or well-earned had not necessarily been welcome, this one was mostly positive.

Life settled down, but Reputations don't ever really die, and the winter afterward, my former college roommate Priscilla Gill showed up at my door, complete with her life complications: her

---

13. Pronounced "EP-ih-TOME", no final "ee", by half the neighbourhood, half the residents, and the letter carrier. But not, yet, by me. Except sarcastically, sometimes, of course, because hey, me.

taxidermied cat Micah the First[14], her public life as an adventurer, her dangerous secret that she kept from everyone, and her best friends — a tech billionaire genius named Nathan Lockwood who was really two people (it does make sense, sort of, because who knows why computer people do *anything*, really, the way they do). One half of Nathan Lockwood was Nathan Bierce, who fell in love with me and vice versa. The other was Lockwood Chiles, whose greed and possessiveness over money and Nathan and Pris (more or less in that order) sent him on a little killing spree, at the end of which Pris was dead, Nathan was dead, some other nice people were dead, I owned Pris's living and taxidermied cats, and I had a box full of a marvellous invention called smart paper that spoke to me, when I touched it, in the voices of the dead. Eventually, after I became bait and he almost shot me, Lock was shot in the leg in a move worthy of *Person of Interest*, arrested, tried with surprising alacrity[15], and incarcerated[16].

He had now died suddenly and violently. So that was that. Well, almost that. If they thought I did it, it wasn't over, of course, but.

There was one other thing.

After all the other mysteries I'd unravelled at the time, and through no effort of my own, I'd finally learned that one secret Pris had kept from everyone[17] — a secret that maybe didn't need

---

14. I have also mentioned Micah the Fifth — the world's weirdest Abyssinian, which is saying something. But at least, alive. For my sins, Pris willed Micah One to me also, though that turned out to be a blessing in disguise: cf. the second book.

15. Considering his legion of lawyers and the waiting list of the courts.

16. Definitely not in a country-club prison, despite his fortune, but in a stern maximum-security cellblock where for sure no-one tangoed.

17. More on this soon, too, because, of course, rain=pour.

to be secret any more now, if Lockwood Chiles, or whatever his real name had been, was really truly dead.

Which is another reason why I tried to insist on ample proof, and why I eventually would show up to watch what was left of him cremated. An appropriate fate. There aren't many times[18] when I am willing to go on record with the hope that my cousin Thelma's born-again Christian beliefs might be true, but the idea of Lockwood Chiles burning in Hell for eternity certainly was attractive.

7. HOUSING, ENVY, AND DEATH

So.

This is a story about families, housing, corruption, envy, and death. It's about strangers and friends, community and solitude, brutality and kindness. It's about loss and value, particularly the value of any one human being. It's about how well-meaning people get screwed in the end. It features as its deus ex machina[19] a jailhouse murder and some Hands from Beyond the Grave —

Oh, and of course, it has cats.

Without cats, I couldn't have joined the Cat and Dog Mystery Writers of North America[20], but never mind that now. The point is, whether you like animals or not, get used to the cats who live with me.

They're here to stay.

Unlike, it seems, people, who come and go so quickly here these days.

---

18. That is, actually, none, up to now.

19. Or, more accurately, dei ex machinis, my editor tells me, since we had more than one of these. (I would have said deus ex machinae, but luckily there are people keeping tabs on me who actually *know* Latin.)

20. Of course, that happened after I met a Fool too, a later development that confounded the issue — and me.

I MET
A MAN
WHO
WASN'T
THERE!

8. HABEAS CORPUS, OR ELSE

After Roger broke the news, I tried to insist on seeing Lockwood Chiles's body[21].

Chiles had already faked his own death once — after he killed Nathan and Pris and some incidental rock climbers who weren't incidental to the people who loved them but were just bothersome collateral damage to an angry psychopath. He wouldn't have been caught, but he became progressively crazier and ended up targetting me as the last loose end between him and his main obsessions[22]. We entrapped him in a sting that drew him to my apartment, where Roger shot him non-fatally, just before he was able to follow through on his threat to shoot me *fatally*. All

---

21. Not that I have ever wanted to view a corpse in the morgue. It's a deeply insalubrious experience. You see it in the movies and on TV all the time. I have to say it's nothing like that, and, believe me, you never ever *ever* want to find out what it's really like. But I wanted to be sure.

22. Money and power, what else?

very Wild West, USian, and, for us Canadians, annoyingly over-dramatic — and also personally annoying to me in that it got more blood on my heritage wooden floor.

At least that time it wasn't mine.

However, seeing Lock's remains was not to be, and on this point Roger was obdurate[23]: "You are a Person of Interest[24]. Of *course* we're not going to take you to the morgue and show you the victim. Whose cause of death we are, by the way, withholding for investigative purposes, which is not gonna work if we just take people in there and show them the body."

"Which must mean you don't really think it's me, or you would believe I *already know* the cause of death."

"Immaterial. Not going to put you near that body and give some defence lawyer your get-out-of-jail-free card."

"Are you putting me in jail?" I asked brightly.

"Of course not. For fuck's sake."

"Just don't leave town," said Dave.

"People really *say* that?" I said. "I thought that was only on TV."

Dave glared and Roger tried not to show that one corner of his mouth had quirked upward slightly.

---

23. If I hadn't been so mad about it, I would have called him, oh, I dunno, steadfast, or even just stubborn, or something, but FFS, this was *me* we were talking about, and I fucking well hadn't fucking murdered fucking Lockwood fucking Chiles — nor even thought about it, though now that it had happened, it seemed like a good move on *someone's* part. Just not mine.

24. Not the TV series that I might have been binge-watching, but the real police thing. You knew that already, didn't you? Never mind, forget I spoke. In my defense, watching old TV and movies is what I do lately instead of having a life as I used to. Putatively used to, anyway — Denis begs to differ.

"Look," I said carefully, trying to sound serious for a change, "Chiles has done this before, and he had a lot of money, and he wanted to be out of jail a lot, so I want to be very sure."

"Best I can do is this," Roger said and whipped out his cell phone. The photo was not salubrious either, but the bulky, limp, yellowish-grey carcase with the roughly-repaired Y-incision had been, as far as I (or, Roger swore to me, anyone) could tell, the Lockwood Chiles I knew — all six-five (or -six) of former trouble now negated, with no facial mutilation to hide the blandly hand-some features now rendered in the unattractive marbled pallor of settled blood, part-jaundiced, part-liverish. Only his head and upper torso showed in the photo. Same blondish hair, in a jail-house cut now; same dead blue eyes, except they looked dead for real, this time, not just because of psychopathy. I moved to swipe to see if there were other pics, but Roger snatched his phone back.

"He must have lain for a while on his side, on his cell floor or somewhere, before being discovered[25]," I said.

"Don't be cute," said Roger. "You are not going to play detective here."

"Roger that. But I *am* going to ask my lawyer to verify Chiles's identity independently. Because I really, really need to know that he is not going to rise again, like the last time."

9. DOWNTOWN (NOT A PETULA CLARK SONG)

My lovely lawyer, yclept Mr. Spak, lives up to the folklore entirely. He is tall, neat, impassive, well-mannered, and has the ability to emulate the Welsh bedrock from which his first name, Dafydd, originates. I sometimes call him my tabby lawyer because of his

---

25. I hoped he suffered there, dying slowly, painfully, and with time to reflect on his manifold sins. Despite what that hope does to soul, my karmic balance, and my viability as a suspect.

hair colours, though I have to say since he met me he seems to be shifting from brown tabby to grey tabby. I try to hope it's not just the result of the problems and challenges that I, and later Nathan and I, have brought him over the last few years since we became his main clients — but I have no faith that it's not.

When I called Mr. Spak to tell him I was a murder suspect he said immediately, "Say nothing."

"Too late," I said.

"Say nothing *more*, then."

"They want me to go downtown for an interview. I feel like I'm in a cop show."

"You are. And what are the rules for a suspect in a cop show?"

I'd been binge-watching. I knew this. "Say nothing without my lawyer's permission?"

"Excellent guess. When do they want you there?"

"We're leaving my apartment now."

"I will be waiting when you get there." And he was. He even knew which door to come to. We went in through the perps' door. It was rather improving[26].

Mr. Spak stayed with me when they questioned me extensively. I have to admit, that event was much too much like TV and the movies for my liking.

The room we went into was not one of the nice conference rooms I'd been in before, but it wasn't as grotty as in the movies: it was a bit like a dentist's waiting room if the dentist was too broke to have a house plant or a magazine subscription. Or a new paint job since 1991.

I'd looked from the other side into some of these interrogation rooms, but I had never actually been in one.

"This is nice," I said, but Mr. Spak shook his head at me. "You mean I can't say *anything* anything?" I said, and he nodded. A

---

26. That is to say, not.

lesser being would have rolled his eyes, but this is Mr. Spak, so he didn't even deem my question worthy of a raised eyebrow.

"Sit," Dave said, and gestured to the side of the table facing the camera high on the wall. *Like he's talking to his brace of golden retrievers?* I thought but didn't say, in deference to Dafydd. It would have been a lot more fun if I could have talked. There are *many* ways to make fun of police procedure if the stakes are lower, even if it's not a good idea at times like this[27].

After he'd established the day and time and personnel for the recorder, Dave tried to go in for the kill. Metaphorically speaking. "You hated Lockwood Chiles. How did you arrange for his murder?"

I started to laugh, but Mr. Spak cut his eyes at me, and I buttoned it.

"My client categorically denies any involvement in the death of Lockwood Chiles."

"Where were you . . . oh, sorry —" he turned to Spak "— please ask *your client* to account for their whereabouts for the last three weeks."

Spak nodded to me, and I said, "Three *weeks*? What, was he starved to death with intent?" Oops. Now both of them were looking at me with gazes in which I could not find approval, though one of them thought I murdered Chiles by proxy and one knew better.

"Fine," said Dave. "I will be more specific. One month ago today, for the entire twenty-four-hour period, where were you and what did you do?"

I told him. Not without referring to my calendars, both paper and on my phone.

---

27. Though since when has that stopped me? I have a lot of respect for Dafydd Spak.

"Thank you. The next day, for the entire twenty-four-hour period, where were you and what did you do?"

I managed to get through almost six days before I reverted. "What the fuck is this anyway? Pretty soon you'll be asking how many minutes I spent taking a shit."

"Would that be of interest?" Dave said. "Do you talk on your cell phone at the time?"

So it was going to be war. Fine. And to think I'd kind of liked the guy when we first met, on that other case.

So over about an hour and a half, with the help of Spak and my Day-timer™[28], Dave started building up a database that would help him dig for dirt on me. We went through a lot — *so much* — of where-had-I-been and what-had-I-been-doing. I *so* was colluding in my own Person-of-Interest-hood, despite Mr. Spak's careful supervision. Charming.

"This would be a lot easier if I could just copy that calendar and the file on your phone," Dave said.

"Warrants or it doesn't happen," said Spak, and I looked at him sideways, but he seemed okay. Maybe he wasn't aware of the social media trope.

So Dave informed me what records were going to be sub-poenaed, and Mr. Spak and he spoke in legal shorthand, and I looked at the camera.

"You need a plant in here," I said finally, and, again, they both looked at me. "Or some *National Geographics* from twenty years ago. You can get tons of them at the EcoCentre."

I don't know if you know this, but folklore has it that if a vampire is chasing you, all you have to do is empty a bag of rice or barley in front of them, and they cannot, literally *cannot*, resist stopping to count the grains. I hadn't known I was testing Dave

---

28. I know, nobody calls it that any more, and it was a trade name. Whatever.

until I watched him try very hard not to pick up that conversation-starter — and fail.

"Weapons," he said grudgingly.

"Seriously, you are telling me that someone has used a rolled-up edition of The Valley of the Kings Special Issue to fight their way out of police custody?"

"Please," said Dafydd. "It was probably the Serengeti issue."

Were they *both* vampires? Was it just that Mr. Spak was *my* vampire? Wait, no, I'd seen both of them in sunlight. Never mind.

You probably get the idea, so I'm not going to detail the entire hour and a half. As an experience, it was both fraught and boring, a combination I don't get a lot.

Also it was repetitive and tiring, and when I got home I had to take a nap. Lockwood Chiles loomed at me in my sleep, startling me awake to the vociferously-expressed and claw-deploying disapproval of the cats using me as pillow and support.

10. CHANNELS

In short order after this difficult day, Mr. Spak also managed to achieve, through some lovely legal channels I didn't question, an independent examination of Lockwood Chiles's remains by another pathologist, and a second DNA test to verify the police's and ME's forensics.

Actually, our tests came back first, because: money. Our results matched the samples and records from the previous case. The body had all the right scars in all the right places, and, overall, there were no signs of trying to trick the hangman by sending a ringer to meet Death.

Inasmuch as it could be confirmed, it seemed conclusive.

I still had my suspicions, but I realised that at least half of them were about "seeing for myself", which was dumb even if I hadn't been a suspect: I mean, if Chiles could fool the ME and the corrections system and the cops, what would a traumatised glance or two from me really prove?

But every expert was telling us the same thing.

Lockwood Chiles was gone for good.

Why was that so hard to believe, right?

11. HERE'S A THING

My best friend's name is Denis. He is an awesome guy. But he won't appear as much in this book, more or less because he married a cop. Not just any cop, but Lance, a cop who works for Major Crimes, a.k.a. works for Roger. For Roger and with Dave.

So when I called Denis to tell him about being a suspect, intending to regale him with an utterance-by-utterance recap of my interrogation, he didn't respond with his usual snarky and supportive invitation to dish.

Instead, there was a moment of silence. Embarrassed silence? That was my guess, though I shouldn't put emotions into anyone's silences. But I know Denis. So.

Then he said, slowly, "I told Lance that was bullshit, honey."

"Of course you did!"

"Um, no, I mean, I *told* him. And he said there was nothing he could do. And that he couldn't talk about it. So, um, in a way . . ."

"In a way that means *you* can't talk about it?"

"Um, sort of, yeah. I mean . . ."

"I get it. If I talk about it, you have to choose sides."

"You know you would come first. I've known you since — well, a long time. I told Lance that. Don't make me choose, I said, because I'd choose her. And I would."

Another silence.

Unspoken: *Don't you make me choose either.*

I sighed.

All right, then.

"If it gets worse, I will need a friend to talk about it all with[29]," I said. "But for now, I'm gonna assume you support me one hundred per cent and we don't need to discuss the details. I don't want you to get stuck in the middle. That work for you?"

I'm pretty sure his return sigh was relief as well as apology. "Yeah. Sorry."

"Don't be," I said, thinking just the opposite. "But, you know, if things change, or you really wanna hear the gory details, you know where I am."

"All righty," he said. "Deal. So! Wanna forget it all and go to drag queen paint night with me?" Nothing like the giddy relief of dodging a bullet to make Denis ebullient AF.

"Say what?"

"Just what it sounds like, girlfriend!"

"Okay, end times be coming."

"No, really, it's a thing," insisted Denis, "and you gotta come with me, tonight!"

Usually I'm up for anything with "drag queen" in the description, but this? "I remember what my grade five art teacher said about my painting efforts, and it wasn't nice." That was one teacher I didn't remember fondly.

"Oh, get outside yourself, Grumpy-pants. Open yourself to new experiences!"

I had done that a lot recently, and wasn't feeling as if the consequences were exactly worth it. But in this very different second of silence, I could almost hear Denis tapping his foot, and I knew what that meant.

That meant it was up to me for the second time in two minutes to Be The Better Person and Put Aside My Feelings in Order to Save Our Friendship. Fine.

"Fine," I said.

---

29. Yeah, "with whom to talk about it all", I know.

"I'll meet you at the Art-op! You know where it is, right?"

I know where it is. "Sure."

When I hung up, I sat there for a long time with the phone in my hand, long enough that a couple of cats came and made nice.

From beyond the grave, Lockwood Chiles was still fucking up my life — and now my friendships.

I was so done with that asshole.

12. A NUMBER OF VALUES OF FUN (PUN INTENDED)

Drag queen paint night was fun, for an acceptable number of values of fun, and the art I made was indeed crap. Otherwise, think "Paint Nite"[30]. Think "drag queen". Think glitter and feathers, whaleboning[31] and cleavage, "Dancing Queen" and "Born this Way". I'm pretty sure you can imagine it for yourself. If not, we'll talk later.

I will also tell you, in confidence, that I hate making bad art, and this is why I don't have more hobbies.

Hobbies. Ha.

13. WHERE WERE YOU ON THE NIGHT OF . . .

If I had another hobby besides thinking too much, though, it wouldn't be murdering people.

You're probably pretty familiar with the concept of alibis, unless you were taken under a faery hill and have been away for a few

---

30. Yes, spelled n-i-t-e. End times coming for sure, and when they do, remember that I told you so.

31. Pretty certain no whales are harmed in the making of modern corsets. Steel has been substituted. Not inappropriate to the cited use of said corsets.

hundred years[32]. Of course I could prove I wasn't in the SuperMax correctional facility in person, shivving Lockwood Chiles with a sharpened toothbrush or whatever the hell killed him[33].

What was harder to prove was that I hadn't had a fixer take some of the money Nathan left me and pay some criminal (either one already in jail or one who would get himself arrested for a petty crime so he could mingle with the prison population) to carve a piece of plastic into a murder weapon. Or do whatever they did.

For several weeks I had seen Dave more than I had seen any of my friends. I had been through "Check my bank accounts!" and "My life is an open book" and was all the way to "You again!" Most of his surprise visits did not result in a trip to the little beige interrogation room, and many were so short I didn't have time to call Mr. Spak (though I did work out a protocol with Dafydd for dealing with Dave, which sounds like a kids' song but is no joke).

Maybe my hobby was thinking of creative ways to tell Dave that I hadn't killed the guy who had brought hate back into my life, just when I thought I'd gotten good at being all Zen-like and peaceable.

I didn't hate Chiles as much for re-introducing me to karma-compromising thoughts as I hated him for killing the people

---

32. Although, I would hazard a guess you don't know that "alibi" is from the Latin for "a plea of being elsewhere" and that any other reason one couldn't have done the crime is an "excuse". Also, since it's Latin, I'm gonna guess that alibis have been a thing for longer than the first recorded use of the term in 1743 or so. But cf. comment re: the amount of my Latin knowledge, which is Zero + Internet, No Limit.

33. Actually, they call it "shanking" these days. But since exact cause of death had been reserved "for investigative reasons", who knew how Lock met his end? I didn't much care, as long as he really had. Met it. You know. For that certainty, I was (almost) willing to give up my completist desire to know all.

I loved, but I have to say it was part of the mix. I found myself wishing I *had* been the one sharpening the toothbrush, and I could hear the whirr, so rapidly did my karma meter retreat toward the negative numbers. It's humiliating to think that evil can come and get you where you live that thoroughly, and turn you into a lesser person. It's embarrassing.

And yet, there I was.

14. AULD LANG SYNE

I go out for lunch with some people sometimes. Well, duh, of course, but I mean some particular people who work where I used to work. These are the people who were my best friends at one time when we were all trying to save the world from overdoses, child poverty, slum housing, and racial profiling.

These are also the people who didn't quit in protest when I was "downsized" — a.k.a., in this case, pretty much fired for being queer — but who's perfect? We've already established that instead of nice tidy boundary lines, there are huge grey zones in the world where we live and work and go to drag queen paint night. And *somebody* has to do the work. I like these people anyway, and they like me.

When I arrived at the Bistro[34], the conversation was already in progress. Since none of them knew I was a murder suspect, all I had to contend with was my established reputation.

"Hi, sweetie! Shot any psychopaths lately?" Mina grinned and patted the empty chair beside her.

I rolled my eyes. It was *Roger* who shot the psychopath. FFS, people.

"Only every second Thursday," I said. "You?"

---

34. There are many bistros where I live, but only one Bistro, which is the Bistro Praha, as everyone who lives here learns eventually.

"I'm just lining up the targets for you. I've got a cop who racially-profiles Muslim or Muslim-appearing men. How about a guy who ambushes women at bus stops and sprays paint in their faces? We haven't identified him, but there's a girl who's blind in one eye now, and the investigating officer told her she should have ducked faster."

"Oh, for fuck's sake!" I signalled Milan, the co-owner and waiter, to bring me my usual crab-meat open-face appetizer.

"Yeah, I've got seven complaints filed with the police service right now."

"And a blood orange San Pellegrino, and a small steak tartare with Jeremy salad for the main," I said to Milan, and to Mina, "Names and badge numbers and all?"

"For five of them. Still waiting on the other two. Not sure I'll ever hear. They deal with it all internally, they say."

"To be fair, sometimes they do," I said.

"And sometimes they don't."

"Yeah. Sometimes they don't."

"You work with them," she said. "Can you put in a word?"

"My guy is Major Crimes. But I can ask what's what."

"You do that. Don't forget us over here."

"Mina, as if!"

"Besides the seven filed complaints, there are more I can't file because there isn't enough information. What is happening to the police, anyway? First they were getting a bit better, and now . . ."

I sighed. "There's a new chief. He likes toys. New SWAT gear. A second helicopter. Helicopters in the plural, if you can fucking believe it — delusions of LA. Push bars on SUVs. Riot gear at sporting events, to control the high-spirited fans, just because they can. And he and the union are so in bed together that you could send in a PI to take dirty pix. My guy"— it was weird to call Roger "my guy" as if he were an informant who had to be protected, name withheld — "is from the old community-policing days when police services were actually *trying* to demilitarise their services, and he's swimming upstream now. Not that he would say any such thing about it to me. Or anyone. But I'm not clueless."

"Someone has to break ranks to make any kind of a difference."

"Yeah. But they don't. Everything is conditional."

Terry, on the other side, had been leaning in to listen. He's young and relatively new, so hasn't heard all my rants before. "What do you mean, conditional?"

"Look, this is just me talking, right? I look at these guys, these cops, and I see some of them are so upright they might as well have a rod welded up their spines. Or placed elsewhere, of course, but you know what I mean."

Mina nodded. "But then there are the others, the assholes with the flexible morals."

"Swimming in the same broth. So if you need a cop, for real, because crime, who ya gonna call? Is it a baby/bathwater thing, where the bad guys can be siphoned off and the good guys remain? Or is it shit soup, where you can't separate the nutritious from the toxic? I don't fucking know."

"But you spend half your time these days with cops." Mina wasn't stopping.

"A bit of an exaggeration there."

"Look more carefully."

"Look, it's true I have dealt with about, what, twenty or so cops lately? Out of a count of almost two thousand in the police service here these days, by the way, so mine are legit the one per cent. Of that number, I know about ten of them well. Four or maybe five of them I'd trust whatever the policing context. Two of those I actually like. But the rest? My ability to trust them is conditional. I can report a homicide and know that the detective will follow the evidence, but will they also card a Black guy and kick down a homeless camp? Some yes, some no. Conditional, situational, and really fucking annoying."

"You were always such an idealist," said Mina, and Terry laughed.

"Is it idealistic to expect equality of policing?" I said, momentarily sucked back into the same discussion we had ad infinitum, perhaps ad nauseam, back in the day I drew a salary there.

Mina laughed harder. "I do miss you!" she said.

"Yeah, thanks," I said. "So cut me some slack here."

"Maybe I get a little testy before my meal arrives."

"Yeah, sure, as if you aren't just as testy the rest of the time. You are just a hundred per cent testy as fuck. Sorry." Hardly sorry, but maybe a little sorry, I took a big bite of crab and caviar, which *had* arrived, because Milan has known me since I was a sprog coming to the Bistro because it was the cool place to be but still unable to afford anything but this exact semi-sandwich. "Anyway, you have it right," I said when I could. "I just . . . um, keep believing in, oh, you know, justice and the triumph of good over evil and that shit."

"How inconvenient for you," she said.

"I've found it so," I said, and she nodded.

Terry, who is sometimes a sweetie, but also sometimes a bit of a doughhead, said, "So, we haven't seen you since you got all lah-di-dah on us. What's it like being independently wealthy?" Maybe he was trying to lighten the mood in his way. His Very Terry way, which made me kind of glad I didn't have to work with him every day.

Before I could reply, Pamela leaned across the table. "For fuck's sake, Terry, show some manners even if you can't dredge up any compassion!" Ah, I see, *that* is how they manage to work with him every day.

"Never mind," I said, playing to the crowd. "I'm wealthy the way the cops are honest. Conditionally, in small numbers, and only enough to get by." I hardly felt guilty at all for throwing shade on my occasional allies and (two) friends. I was mad at all of them — and their boyfriends.

"Shades of Thomas Hobbes," said Mina.

"Who?" said Terry.

"You know, the guy who said life is nasty, brutish, and short, and people are only as ethical as they need to be under any circumstance," Pamela said.

"That's fucking harsh," said Terry. "We're not like that."

"Just wait," said Mina. "You will be."

15. MEANWHILE, IN SECRET . . .

I'm not going to talk about this very much, because it's sort of been my secret for a while, but I have made a little rule. Every working day I have to take out one piece of smart paper and try to figure out what's on it.

I am allowed (by my own rule, but I can be hella tyrannical, apparently) to spend as little as ten minutes on it, but usually if it's at the office, it's about half an hour minimum, for reasons you will discover later. So you need to imagine that all through this story I'm unfolding here, I am also scritching away a little tiny bit at the corner of the huge mass of data that is on both Nathan's and Lock's versions of smart paper[35].

Hmmm. Was *this* my hobby?

16. YOU AGAIN

When Dave showed up again — now wearing a suit, and this time, unlike the last four or five visits, with Roger again — I didn't even wait for the punchline. Nor did I let them into the apartment.

"For fuck's sake, there must have been two dozen people in that jail who wanted that asshole dead," I said. "And who could carve a shiv. Or a shank, or whatever the fuck it's called."

---

35. This will continue to happen throughout, with varying results of which I will keep you apprised, if relevant, I promise.

Dave glowered. He hated my constant sharpened-toothbrush references, but this time kept it at a full-body eyeroll, not a snide little lecture. But I've told him, that's what you get for all that pissy "cause of death is being withheld for investigative purposes" crap.

"Don't get your knickers in a twist," said Roger. "All you are right now is a question mark. You're hardly even a Person of Interest any more. We need evidence."

"Do you mean in general? Or that you need it against *me*?"

"There are various opinions on that," said Roger, which was nicer than he'd been since this began.

"You *are* in the habit of being around dead people," said Dave. "You aren't Jessica Fletcher."[36]

His tone was not recreational, or I would have taken the bait and discussed murder villages. Instead: "Seriously? You're going *there*?"

Even in the wide hall of the Epitome, Roger and Constable Dave loomed over me. Roger is very tall, and Dave is quite tall, though it's not that hard for a regulation-sized male police officer to loom over me, as most of them are in the upper range of the regulations, and I'd be at the lower end if I were the kind of person who tried to join the police force[37].

Dave loomed with intent.

---

36. Little did he know that at this point I had already written the first chronicle of my life in this particular bush of ghosts. So maybe I am Jessica, re-imagined for the twenty-first century. I wonder who will play me in the Netflix™ series? Uma Thurman, Charlize Theron, Halle Berry, and Tilda Swinton are getting on, and so is Noomi Rapace ... but then, so am I. Jenny Ortega, maybe? Anyway, maybe they can get Tantoo Cardinal for my friend Hep. That would be so cool.

37. Also, I'd be in the lower end anyway, even though I'm not the police-joining kind. In other words, I am Not Tall. This may be a problem where casting Uma Thurman or Charlize Theron is concerned. Maybe they could wear special shoes.

Roger just loomed, but perhaps a little wistfully. I knew he knew I didn't do it.

Speaking of tall people: "Should I be calling my lawyer again?" I asked, working hard to do a kind of reverse-looming and nearly putting my neck out trying to look upward down my nose.

"Do you need to?" That was Dave, of course.

"Unlikely," said Roger. "We will not be taking notes today."

Dave glared lightly at him, not me, which was a nice change.

"Oh, for fuck's sake, come in," I said graciously. "Have some tea."

As soon as they sat down at my kitchen table, Bunnywit, as usual, pretended that anyone else but me was water in the desert, and Micah concentrated on his slalom, figure-eighting around their ankles and shedding on both Dave's and Roger's dark slacks.

It was a hot, hazy day. The windows were open. Déjà vu all over again, but this time the air smelled smoky. The show tunes neighbour had moved to Toronto, thank goodness, but now it was rap.

What *is* the right music for sweltering, anyway? All the music described as "hot" is really for interior heat, and who wants to have sex when just sitting works up a sweat[38]?

I had iced jasmine tea in the fridge, and I poured three glasses and garnished them with sprigs of basil. Gracious Living Я Us.

"So, you are no longer taking apart my life," I said to Dave.

"It's been suggested —"

"Since he was promoted," added Roger pointedly, "to be a real detective."

"Ah," I said, "that explains the move to a nice suit. Do you have more than just the one yet?"

Dave ignored both of us. "— that I could use more of my efforts exploring other avenues as well as this one," he finished sullenly.

---

38. Some people maybe, but not me. JSYK.

Continuing my gracious streak, I jumped right in. "You mean avenues like catching the real killer. Excellent! And how's that going, anyway?"

Dave looked daggers (or maybe sharpened toothbrushes) at me, but Roger made one of his little hand gestures at him, and he subsided.

I did not. "I mean, someone in a cellblock of like two hundred people must have seen something, right?"

This did not make Dave happier. I could see there was a story there, so I made that little gesture with the moue[39] and the slight raising and spreading of the hands that means, do please enlighten me as to what the fuck that glowering is about. Dave does not understand subtle languages such as this, but Roger actually rose to the bait. I am positive I've seen *him* in direct sunlight, so maybe it isn't just vampires.

"Corrections," Roger said, meaning in this case the people who run the prisons, not Liquid Paper™[40] and its competitors, "have a different reaction to a death on a cellblock than homicide investigators."

Roger slumped in his seat and took a long gulp from his glass, which had already beaded up with condensation that dripped onto his adorably-crisp silk tie. He made his own moue (no, he really did! Maybe he doesn't like excessive heat either) and dabbed at the drip, making it worse. Take that, Zegna. "We knew we'd have to interview everyone on the block, so anyone with something to tell wouldn't look like a snitch. I want my crew in

---

39. Pronounced moué, dammit, even if it isn't spelled that way any more.

40. Did you know that Michael Nesmith's mother invented Liquid Paper™ in her kitchen, and that before (and after) he was a Monkee, he was heir to the Liquid Paper™ fortune, which may be why he could afford to make some great but weird early- and later-career albums? Well, now you do.

there scheduling interviews, working through the list, getting to the bottom of it, but. This is good tea."

"Thanks; it's jasmine mint. 'But'?"

"Corrections wants a peaceful cell-block more than anything, so after a death they shuffle a bunch of the inmates to other prisons. Some of which are on the other side of the country."

"So interviewing potential witnesses is expensive and complicated."

"And takes forever. And is also a fucking pain in the ass," said Roger. "Pardon my language." I'm sure he was excusing himself to Dave, as he and I have said worse in each other's hearing.

I had to wonder (and perhaps I might have wondered aloud) whether, in some eyes, Lock was just another dead felon, and did anyone in the system care who killed him, even if he was rich and all that? A little tabloid publicity might be worth it for the problem to go away for good?

Roger deplores this type of thinking, but he can't control the attitudes of the Corrections system, and he has superiors who have things to say about budgets and priorities. All this he now explained to me seriously, with Newly-Detective Dave looking on with equal seriousness.

"And you are telling me because?"

"I wonder that too," said Dave.

"Yeah, well," said Roger, "it's all public information, and anyway, we only stopped by because we knew you'd want to know the body has been released and will be . . . disposed of next week."

Those parts of it that weren't still on file with the ME, as is their gruesome but practical wont, would now be cremated. This was not to be a secret ceremony. I could, if I wished, attend, and I immediately decided I would go and cheer as Lock started his gig in the Lake of Fire.

From next door's hyped-up boom box, repeatedly, the word *muthafucka* hung rhythmically in the thick air.

I couldn't have said it better myself.

17. "AND THEN, OF COURSE, LIGHTNING COME OUT AND STRUCK ME . . ."

A long time ago, I saw an interview that David Frost, a talk-show host of yore, did with a guy who had made the Guinness Book of World Records for being struck by lightning a fuck-ton of times, or actually seven, which beats some mean-ass set of odds, since most of us aren't even struck once.

On top of his aggressively-ordinary-middle-aged-forest-ranger vibe, this fellow had a very flattened affect, which sort of made sense, and he told his story as if he were personally targeted by Nature, which from his perspective I suppose was true: aside from his forest ranger occupation, he had done nothing to attract lightning's undue attention.

He talked about the way clouds intentionally formed into storms above him much as if he were that guy in the old *Li'l Abner*© comic, or that kid in *Peanuts*©, both of whom are followed around by personal little grey atmospheric turmoils and seem to take it for granted that that is their life.

My recollection of what he said to Frost, while talking about his fourth or seventh lightning strike, was: "So clouds formed up right up above me and then, of course, lightning come out and struck me."

I think my reason for telling you this story may already be obvious. If not, wait ten minutes.

HE
WASN'T
THERE
AGAIN
TODAY,

18. THREE DEGREES OF WILLIAM GIBSON — AND NO MORE. I PROMISE.

The sky was the colour of a 21st-century television tuned to *Bladerunner 2049* on the June day a week later when we watched Lockwood Chiles burn. The north was on fire with eleven, or maybe sixteen, out-of-control forest fires. The temperature was sweltering, a hot wind was blowing the smoke in from the north-west, and the haze of the previous week had thickened into a soup of incinerated-boreal-forest particles. The sun was a brazen punctuation mark in a copper sky, the almost-tangible smoky air shone a dark burnished gold, and the Air Quality Health Index that morning had been 72 on a scale of 10. (Yes, 72/10, you read that right.) You could chew that air.

Nobody but me and some cops and a Crown Prosecutor came to Chiles's cremation, and I was mostly there for continuity of evidence: I wanted to be as sure as possible that he hadn't risen from the dead, and wouldn't be cloned.

That last is a joke, I think, but given the smart paper in my closet, and out in the world some household pets, a sheep, an endangered ferret species, and some weird kind of horse, I don't know any more. The future, we have established, is unevenly — but inevitably — already here.

Afterward, Roger, Dave, and I stood on the sidewalk outside the crematorium, while the nattily-dressed and bearded Crown[41] walked off with the other two cops. Clearly, that whole investigative concept of the bad guy coming to the victim's funeral wasn't happening, though Dave probably thought it had, from the way he still side-eyed me.

I looked at the sepia-tinged heat waves rising in near-invisible swirls above the crematorium chimney — and rejoiced.

I once had an office in a little historic building (gone now of course) overlooking a downtown funeral parlour (also gone now). Unless the burner malfunctioned (which it had done once, covering our windowsills and computers with a fine layer of cremains that resembled nothing so much as the ash that descended, even this far inland, after Mt. St. Helens erupted — of which my parents had had a container, swept off their cars at the time, which is why I know that), the chimney was very subtle.[42] Most people in the surrounding office buildings didn't even realise that when the air above that innocent-looking vent displayed that twisty, old-windowpane texture, it signified that a human body was going up in flames below.

Taking too much pleasure in that day's shimmer, in front of two Homicide cops, even if one *was* a pal of mine from 'way back

---

41. Crown Prosecutor, that is, and a pretty nice guy. Although he has only a cameo here, I'd actually seen a lot of him in the last couple of years. What with one thing and another thing. And now this thing.

42. I want you to note that was one hell of a sentence, and still grammatical. Thank you Ms. Lazarowich, Grade 10.

who had actually once shot the deceased (albeit in the leg), wasn't the wisest thing I'd ever done[43].

Dave didn't miss it. "Look at you," he said accusingly, picking up in medias res. "You hated the guy. At his trial you said jail was too good for him. Less than thirty minutes ago you spat on his cardboard coffin."

"True," I said. "But nothing in my history suggests that I operationalise my anger into murder. Even of psychopathic otherfuckers who deserve it. Quite the opposite, in fact — they try to murder me, as a rule."

When the topic seemed to hang in the air yet again, as the smoke was doing, I was fed up.

"So arrest me, already," I said to Dave, "or get the fuck off my case. Pun unintended."

"If it was up to me . . ."

"Roger told you to cast a wider net, yet here you are leaning on me again. What is *with* you?"

"Give it a rest," Roger said to us both. What he meant was, don't fight in front of the mortuary.

I might have turned my attention to his attitude as well, at that point, but I had a rule too: don't fight (with Roger) in front of the children, er, the junior detectives.

"I'll have you know," I said, "that you have wounded me, and I am going off in a huff."

I took a deep breath, which was also stupid, cf. AQHI 72/10. The convulsive coughing, and the need to take a couple of hits from my recently-prescribed inhaler, ruined my exit.

---

43. It wasn't the stupidest either, but that's another story — or another whole raft of stories. Someday when we all have a few months to spare, I'll tell them all to you.

19. RIDING OFF INTO THE SUNSET, EXCEPT AT MIDDAY (AND MORE LIKE GOING OFF IN A HUFF, WHICH I HAVE BEEN KNOWN TO DO IN THE PAST, BUT NOT SO LITERALLY)

I have a little car now. It used to be Nathan's, and I bought it from the executors fair and square, for actual money. It is a one-of-a-kind electrified version of a Scion iQ, and it is a convertible. I call it the Huff. It is cuter than most puppies, and I would love it unconditionally if I didn't have the 0.85 per cent discomfort I get from its resemblance to the weirdly-truncated little shoes some unfortunate people a couple of hundred years ago — I mean, of course, women, specifically — used to have to wear on their torturously bound and hideously-deformed feet[44].

Bunnywit loves this car, and I have bought a special safety seat with harness and tether — an open box really, which is fitting for a cat — so he can ride safely. The one time he convinced his pal Micah to tag along was no fun for any of us, as Micah deplores travel, and let us know this almost-continuously in his Siamese-ish voice. At an average rate of once every four seconds, he would have miaowed nine hundred times per hour, and we were out for an hour and a half, there and back to Denis's house. This strained Bun's friendship with Micah Five for some hours, and as for me, Micah is lucky he is still alive. He also did not endear himself to Denis and Lance once he got there, clawing Lance's ankle on the way by to take up a hiding place behind the wigs, which did the wigs no good either. Neither Bun nor I ever invited him for a recreational car ride again, and I returned the second safety seat to the pet supplies store. I now take them to the vet separately, where necessary, and am looking for a vet who makes house calls.

The original Scions got amazing gas mileage but this electric version is even better for the planet, especially since I charge it

---

44. I can't help thinking shit like this. It's my nature. I *am* sorry, if that helps.

with solar from panels on the roof of the Epitome Apartments rather than from the mains to which my solar array often gives back power — which gentle concern for our planet I would think proves conclusively that I am obviously not a murderer.

So leaving behind the small fuming cloud of cremains, suspicion, and cops, I was able to stride down the summer sidewalk in the funereal drag I'd donned to fit the ambience, get into a tiny car, and drive away. Going off in a Huff: obvious, right?

It was fun.

I like having the last word with Roger.

Anyway, I had to go. I was late for a meeting with the mayor.

20. OH, AND THELMA

The mayor, and Thelma.

I said my cousin Thelma was born-again, but really she's born-again born-again. During the time we were tracking down Maddy's killer, Thelma — who to be fully truthful had, despite her generally good heart, been something of a pain in the ass about behaviours alleged to lead to burning in hell vis-à-vis yours truly — got involved when the killers hid behind a creepy church outreach thing called Soul Patrol in which she had been enrolled. She was horrified to discover that not all Christians preached love and kindness. Some, who had become the radical arm of the Soul Patrol, liked to enforce their prejudices with sticks and fists instead.

She was so angry that she waded into the fray and straightened out her own church's affiliation with this ugly sub-group and, in the process, found a whole list of things: a new relationship with her faith (and me); new attitudes toward people she'd condemned before (and me); part of the answer about Maddy's death; a new friend (Vikki, a former sex worker who had been Maddy's life partner and who was now living in Thelma's nanny suite and taking care of Thelma's new baby, who has Down syndrome); and affordable housing.

Oh, not affordable housing for her. She has a house: a big, suburban, split-level, budget-straining mini-McMansion-type, and the less said about it the better. Affordable housing as a cause. One of her causes. Thelma was now on her church council, the board of a national Down syndrome support organisation, and the community advisory group of an organisation called M2F2.[45]

M2F2 is not a euphemism for the favourite oath of all of Samuel Jackson's characters, but is the Metropolitan Multi-Faith Foundation, an organisation that had united a whole bunch of charities that all used to provide a patchwork of housing in the inner city into one over-arching Force for Good. Over the years M2F2 had turned into a major influencer, both advocating for and providing good subsidised, affordable, and in some cases harm-reduction housing for not only the inner city but the whole metropolis.

M2F2 was the target of the big fraud attempt. I was able to warn the mayor, who is known to me as Gary.

Because confidentiality is forever, I'm not going to share *why* exactly I had had reason to deal with Mayor Gary and his family in my previous capacity as a social worker, but I *can* tell people that I did because the family all gave me permission. A while ago, Gary, his wife Leora, and their kids, decided to do a photo spread for the agency that introduced us all, with the message that there's no shame in family dysfunction as long as you fix it. His kids are happy, interesting, and only slightly rebellious[46]

45. Some might think I should ask for forgiveness to all these bodies for my part in bringing this about, but Thelma is a kick-ass board member, and I couldn't be prouder of her blossoming social activism.

46. In a good way: you and I both know the difference, right?

adults now, although, also like me, they have some tattoos they only show certain people.

So now in addition to his historical gratitude, he and M2F2 are both very grateful to me — and Thelma — for a brand new reason, and that reason has 28.8 million names[47].

But no good deed goes unpunished. Gary's method of giving thanks last year was to get me, my new sweetie Nathan, and my cousin Thelma involved in a big multi-use housing project in my area that was meant to house a range from my homeless and hard-to-house neighbours to swanky urbanites who wanted apartments close to work, the river valley, and the Downtown Farmers Market.

I got involved because I believed in the project. Nathan jumped in enthusiastically because he had a lot of money he'd earned by being a computer genius and inventing lots of cool stuff, smart paper only being the last of a long lucrative list, and he wanted to get rid of it. The money, that is, not the cool stuff. So he made a long-term plan to drop his fortune on the cause of eliminating homelessness, one city at a time, starting here.

His main vehicle was going to be huge housing initiatives, not as a developer himself but through donating big, earmarked, nine-digit-no-decimal chunks of change, with accompanying accumulated land parcels, to cities and non-profits who could then afford to actually build the homes, most of which would in the end be public and not-for-profit, and in some cases co-ops owned by their new residents. Mixed-use projects where possible, to de-stigmatise poor and/or homeless folk.

It was a wonderful plan.

---

47. I may have mentioned that number before. It's both impressive and easy to remember. I also may have mentioned the achievement of saving it from the baddies. I may mention that several more times. I'm annoyingly proud of it.

He had bought land, lots of land — joke absolutely intended — in the east and north of downtown. Most of it in my area of east downtown had before that been used for illegal parking or slated for infill — what urban planners call brownfield — and on it we had been poised to build some beautifully-designed multi-use housing villages — but then Lockwood Chiles murdered him.

Nathan's estate was now tied up in probate, probably until the hell in which Lock was roasting froze over, and several housing initiatives, including M2F2 and the City, were having to make new, less ambitious plans.

I was mad at Lock because of the Nathan part.

The mayor is not an indecent guy, and he hates murder as much as the next guy, but he was also mad at Chiles because of the housing part. Last year the homeless count found over four thousand unhoused people in our city, and that didn't include the ones who made sure they weren't found, nor the underhoused people living in squalid rentals owned by opportunistic slumlords (and -ladies. And -others. This kind of exploitive crime is not linked to gender performativity).

Nathan's and my company, Own Domains, was in limbo, and Roma, the woman who runs our office, was spinning her wheels or twiddling her thumbs or re-doing her fingernail art, or whatever her method was of putting in time while the whole thing was being sorted out. Knowing her, it probably involved three colours of hair product, three colours of highlighter, extremely high heels, and a side order of changing the world[48].

I was scheduled to meet Gary at that very office.

---

48. I think that covers the back-story. You can pick up the rest as we go along.

21. NOT A PHILANTHROPIST

Just to be clear. I'm not a philanthropist. Nor am I well off in the traditional sense, although I once had some rich friends.

My parents amassed a retirement fund and died instead[49], leaving to me just enough to buy the Epitome Apartments and fix the roof, the elevator, the locks, and the drains. Then I was broke again. Totally broke. Eats-fish-sticks broke.

This whole "land-rich" thing is bullshit. This little patch of land makes demands every month: property tax, utilities, repairs, routine maintenance, upgrades. My only hope is for the Epitome to break even — which it mostly does, since most of the suites are rented to long-term residents so there is a predictable base cash-flow[50]. Even so, some months are a bit fraught.

Against my protests, Nathan gave me a trust fund when we got together, which pays me about the income of an upper-level civil servant (but far below the level of a political flak). It seemed like a lot to me, given my habits, needs, and previous income as a social worker, but covering the Epitome's shortfall uses it up pretty fast — and it is definitely not enough to pay outright to house (in the Epitome or elsewhere) any of the thousands of people that the homeless-count volunteers enumerate twice a year.

So instead of running some sort of weird empire, I'm just a working stiff, and what I work on these days is mostly trying to persuade people with money to enter into fundraising "part-nerships", with all the persuasion that entails, and thus do the heavy lifting of keeping alive the dream until the estate gets sorted out and we can go back into high gear. (I also spend some

49. In an annoyingly flamboyant way, which I will not recap here, but see previous narratives op. cit.

50. Look at me using terms like "cash-flow", just as if I were a grown-up.

time every day trying to figure what-all is on that smart paper, but as I've said, that's more of a hobby really.[51])

These days we were aiming, scaled down, at a single harm-reduction village[52] of tiny houses around a larger building of multi-use suites, with support services therein, built on the only piece of land the title of which Nathan had, luckily for us, actually transferred to M2F2 before he was killed. The original idea was that services get decentralised where the people are, rather than burdening one neighbourhood with all the heavy lifting, and that we would someday build a lot of these around the city on surplus land, intending them to be unthreatening enough not to trigger too much NIMBYism.

But now we were all trying to figure out how to do it without Nathan's money at all, because Worst Case Scenario.

So you see, I definitely do have some personal reasons to get this stuff off the ground. Both in the past and the present.

22. IT'S AN ALGORITHM

When I got to the office, Roma and Mayor Gary stood in front of the SMART Board™, and she had the map of the city up. It had little hot-pink flags all over, many concentrated down-town and in the river valley. They matched today's version of her hair.

Thelma was also there, less backcombed than her wont, and taking notes in a jewel-embellished turquoise notebook with a matching pen[53].

---

51. Oh, shit, I *do* have a hobby!

52. Eventually to be, blah blah blah probate, the first of several such.

53. The Added Touch catalogue is a wonderful thing.

Roma was tapping at the flags with her pointer. An actual physical pointer, though with a scribing tip. Clearly, she had become dissatisfied with wheel-spinning.

Roma is the poster girl for a flamboyant style of attire I've heard referred to as "Kindergarten Grandma". She wears short nostalgia skirts and tops in plaids and patterns and appliquéd motifs, tightly cinched with wide belts over patterned leggings, all in contrasting colours and designs. Hair colour varies with her wardrobe, and her nails are always perfect constructs. I have no idea how she still manages to type. She looks like my flamboyant and semi-demented Grade 6 teacher did, and, like said Ms. Willron, she says smart things a lot. (Come to think of it, I'd loved Ms. Willron too.)

"So we accessed the tablets they use for the homeless counts, correlated them with the GPS data the tablets had in background, and downloaded them into the master database. Then I wrote this algorithm that geo-locates and rates the sites according to desirability and seasonal use. So when the Flying Squad goes out to offer housing, we can map a route that saves time and has a higher likelihood of finding the higher-risk clients."

"That's awesome," I said, coming up behind them.

Gary jumped and yelped.

Roma just carried on. "It's kinda obvious, though. Why didn't anyone ever do it before? I mean, it's just an algorithm. How hard?"

"Hi, Gary. Nervous much?"

"Hi back atcha. Is he really dead?"

"Spat on his coffin myself."

"For real?" said Roma. "Ew."

"If I believed in Hell," Gary said, "I'd hope he was roasting there."

"I was just thinking that," I said.

"Don't worry, I've got it covered," Thelma said.

Roma laughed, then sobered when she saw by Thelma's face that Thelma wasn't kidding.

Curiously comforted, I got a couple of pieces of smart paper[54] out of my folder, and we all got to work.

23. "... CLOUDS FORMED UP RIGHT ABOVE ME ..."

This is why I happened to be in the office when the call came.

---

54. Hey, I do hate the stuff, but it's useful, and all Nathan's notes and budgets for Own Domains are on it.

I WISH,
I WISH
HE'D
GO
AWAY!

24. GEESE, GHOSTS, OR CATS: TAKE YOUR PICK

You know, that "blah-de-blah walked over my grave" thing is a weird saying, right? First of all, you need a grave. Then you need a ghost, or a goose, or sometimes a cat[55].

Graves are rarer than you think. For instance, Lockwood Chiles the putatively dead didn't have a grave. They cremated him. Because who was gonna want to bury him, and where? In 20/20 hindsight, it might have been a good idea to have put him in a grave, for future exhumation and verification purposes, but the ME did store a lot of his organs and blood and so on, and that chain of evidence would unassailably prove that the dead guy was the dead guy. So that part was okay.

---

55. A cat or a goose is an improvement over a ghost, though I once read a great book where a ghost took the form of a goose, but never mind that now. I don't believe in ghosts as such; I don't have personal acquaintance with geese. OTOH, I have two cats — three if you count the dead-and-taxidermied one.

But even if they had buried him, I'm pretty sure my cats couldn't have been convinced to walk over his grave[56]. Geese, I don't know. Ghosts? If so, he deserved it.

That's Lock, though.

Me, at the moment, I also didn't have a grave over which any entity could walk[57]. And I wanted to keep it that way[58].

25. SUBJUNCTIVITY

As an aside, I don't think of myself as a crimefighter either — just someone in the Resistance who has occasionally been called upon to take a stand against barbarity and incivility.

If I thought of myself as a crimefighter, I'd have to either get a spandex costume (not my idea of an accessory), or take a middle-aged run at the police service (not my idea of a good time, despite Nathan Fillion's noble work[59]).

If you watch a lot of TV or USian movies, you might think a third path would be the private investigator's licence. I also thought so at one point, but my research revealed that in the real world PIs are pretty much limited to ferreting out minor industrial fraud, doing background checks, and skulking in the tiny — and often tawdry — world of infidelity investigations. Uh-uh, nope, and no-no — and not least because I am a stranger to sexual jealousy

---

56. Come to think of it, though, they *might* walk on anyone's grave if they thought there was dinner to be had. You can see, can't you, why the national bird might be preferable for omens and portents?

57. And if I *did* have a grave, my living cats wouldn't likely be accommodating enough to walk on *it*, either.

58. No doubt this will come up more than once. There is a lot of premonitory shivering in this story.

59. Don't get me started on the problems of policing. With my experience and my fast mouth, we'd be here all week. But the best of the police also catch bad guys, so we kind of need them. More anon on all this.

and can't really resonate with it as a motivation, so I don't want to be trapped in the simultaneously boring yet nasty underbelly of heteronormative monogamism gone wrong. So, no. Not a crimefighter.

As such.

I would really rather go back to being a clueless civilian, but that ship sailed a long time ago, even before I started having Adventures.

My attitude when this story began was exactly the same as my attitude now that I'm writing down what happened: Getting involved in any more criminal investigations is, to extend Samuel R. Delany's taxonomy of fictional states[60], *not ever going to happen.*

For that reason I tend to throw most of my snail mail away, or delete most of the messages from my e-mail inbox. I do read most of it first, though I hate to admit that in print, because I'll just get someone's hopes up. I usually don't even reply to these letters and appeals from people who've seen me in the news and mostly want me to investigate someone or something[61]. *Not ever going to happen.*

Really.

At home, I screen my calls and erase any appeals messages that have snuck through to my unlisted land line number, and as for the cell, everybody knows how that works. *Not ever going to happen.*

At the office, I have Roma, who, if she accidentally picks up on an appeal call, will clearly state, "*Not ever going to happen.*" (She filters out other annoying calls too[62].)

---

60. You can look up subjunctivity in *The Encyclopaedia of Fantasy.*

61. Or, less often, having read my first two books, they want me to write the book of *their* very interesting lives and they will generously share the royalties. Absolutely *NEVER* going to happen, though for very different reasons. (And by the way? Not that interesting. Trust me.)

62. Including business offers of various sorts, some of them far-fetched and some of them slightly reality-based, but all of them based on the delusion that because Nathan isn't around for them to importune, I might want to go into business with them instead. Roma puts her

I have a form letter that Roma sends for the paper letters. We send an automated reply to the e-mailers. They just both say approximately, as I said: *Not ever going to happen.*

Also, I retain, as I have mentioned above, the lovely Dafydd Spak, who tells those who enquire of him for help, "*Not ever going to happen.*"

Of course, that's what I said the last time, as Bunnywit and Micah Five often remind me, and look how that turned out. But on the day when this story began, I optimistically hovered in my chosen state of extended subjunctivity, designed to negate rather than enable narrative, and I was fighting hard to stay there. *Never again.*

The Universe has a way of punishing people who say "never". *Never ever going to happen.*

Ha.

Or, as Bunnywit and Micah Five would say, "*Ha!*"

26. OUT OF A CLEAR BLUE SKY

The office phone interrupted us in the middle of discussing some brilliant stratagem that was useless without money. Roma started into the whole screening thing, then, hearing something said on the other end, she stopped and shook her head, and walked over to me. Without a word, she handed me the phone.

This was so anomalous that I almost dropped it.

---

summaries of their calls in a file with all the weird letters, a bizarre collation that I have a look at occasionally when I want a laugh. True, not all of them are total crackpots, though the guy running the airplanes on electric current through a cord to the ground is a bit behind the times, nutbar-wise, great blueprints notwithstanding. But even among the credible threats, as we call them around the office, none — not one — of them is of the slightest interest to me: I am no more a business person than I am a crimefighter.

Then I recognised the area code, and felt a little shiver.

"Hello?" I said trepidatiously[63].

"Hello? Is this . . . um, sorry, I'm really nervous. Hi. Um. I'm calling about Priscilla? My auntie Jane, you know her as, maybe? Priscilla Jane Gill?"

Ah. Shiver justified.

"My name is, um, Kim? I met you before?"

"I remember," I said.

How could I forget?

Kim is the secret my friend Priscilla Jane Gill took to her grave. Kim is the hold-back in every one of the public, media-frenzied stories of Priscilla's life with Nathan Bierce and Lockwood Chiles. Kim is the hold-back in every story I had told to date about their murder.

If you have been reading these stories, you will know of Kim, but only because I wrote the last draft of the book about it after all this (including what I'm telling you about now) was over IRL, as they say, and Lock was dead, and it was safe, and even then, I changed all the names, and have not revealed the city even now[64].

But at this point in this story, only Roger and I — and Pris's sister, of course, who was the adoptive mother — knew that Priscilla Jane Gill had conceived a child by Nathan Bierce. By the time Pris knew she was pregnant, she had split up with Nathan and taken up with his best friend[65] Lockwood Chiles. She went away, and told no-one about the baby, and took the child to her

---

63. Do you know what Tom Swifties are? This is not one, but I wish it were. I do not have the Swifties gift. Alas, she said . . . what-ly . . . ? Feel free to suggest and insert any that occur to you.

64. Op. cit. *Mary Jane.*

65. And former lover, to add a layer. Nathan wasn't bothered, but Chiles always had been, seemingly a little at the time, but actually a lot. It turned out he had a vengeful memory.

half-sister for adoption. The half-sister was basically in stealth mode, unknown to anyone from close friends to distant fans of famous Pris, and she raised Kim as her third child. I only found out about this because last year, her sister, whom I've pseud-onymized as Mattie Groves[66] in this narrative, because she likes her privacy (as she likes to say), called to thank me for clearing Pris's name in the celebrated murder case.

27. LYING AND LOST SHEEP

Another aside.[67]

How do we really know that someone is lying to us?

We think we know, we think we can tell. Some of us say "I'm a good judge of character" or "I can always tell when someone is lying", but you know what?

We totally can't.

There's even research on it. We can't tell.

Criminal psychopaths and sociopaths can totally deceive us. Just ordinary liars can deceive us too. We believe both the social lie — the little white lie — and the big lies too — the colonialism-scale-white lies perpetrated by criminals, con artists, ticket scalpers, Ministers of the Interior, furnace-duct-cleaning

---

66. I agree, an odd choice if you know your Child Ballads, but JSYK, she doesn't end up with the real Mattie's fate, because the Lord Arlen of this story, if you map it onto the ballad, is Lockwood Chiles, and Mr. Chiles, he dead. (Probably.) (No, he dead.) (We are pretty sure.)

67. You might want to get used to these. Friends have told me I am a very elliptical person. Not in shape so much, I'm more narrowcast-zaftig: pear or hourglass — well, egg-timer — maybe. But in thought, yeah, I'm willing to cop to ellipses. Unlike many of my generation and younger, I actually *like* ellipses, which confuses those people on social media who, apparently, think ellipses are passive-aggressive . . . "Srsly?" she typed, passive-aggressively . . .

salespeople, libertarians, stump preachers, conspiracy theorists, populist politicians, and unfaithful family, friends, and lovers.

We are basically crap at systematically detecting good liars.

But sometimes, we get a little frisson of what is really going on, and then it's a question of whether we believe *ourselves* or not. What we are really doing is detecting anomalous input — data that, literally, give the lie to the falsehoods we're being fed. Whatever this process really is, perceptually, we *call* it instinct.

Pris had had good instincts, inasmuch as anyone does. She didn't know for sure that Lockwood Chiles was a murderous psychopath, or she never would have gone mountain climbing with him, but she did know that he was jealous and possessive — none of it good baby-nurturing behaviour, even had he been the baby-daddy, and definitely since he wasn't. So she asked her sister never to talk about Kim's real parentage, and to tell Kim about Kim's real mom only when Kim was legal. Mattie agreed.

When Kim was a teenager and Pris had begun to see how obsessive Lock really was — and that he could be as vindictive as fuck (in other words, when she came to understand he might be dangerous) — Pris then went back to her sis and extracted a further promise of complete secrecy as long as Lock was alive. Also promised, also delivered.

After Pris died and Lock was in jail. Roger and I had a short, secret, loose-end-tying, undocumented visit with the family, and we all agreed — except Kim, who was still in the dark at that point — that it would be best to keep to that strategy.

However, all these promises had become moot with Lockwood Chiles's death, so now only the natural reclusiveness of their normal suburban family was preserving the knowledge of Kim's existence from the world. Given that the world included a huge range of ravening, or at least ravenous, fandom and paparazzi of Pris's public self and of her countless books about her world travels, this was so the right thing to do.

What I didn't expect was to hear from the kid, or Mattie, ever again.

And now here was this rich but tentative voice saying into my ear, "I was wondering. Mom says that Auntie Jane was your friend since college, and you, um, knew my, um, birth father too? I've just, uh, it was my birthday, and I found out some stuff, and I was wondering, like, if we could talk. Or, you know, if I could visit you."

Okay, then.

"Sure," I said. "When?"

"Well, umm . . . ?"

A goose walked over my grave. Or a cat. Or something.

"What have you done?" I had controlled my tone admirably, I thought, but on the other end, there was a long silence.

"Well? What?" I heard my mother's voice coming out of my mouth, and if that didn't deserve another shiver, it should have. I waited.

I waited some more.

Finally, a small voice said, "Nothing! Well, not really. It's just I'm, well, sort of . . . at your house."

28. DO YOUR WORK AS WELL AS YOU CAN, AND BE KIND

"Stay right there," I said. "Do not move. It will take me forty-five minutes to get home."

I pressed *Off* and gently set the phone in Roma's hand. "Saatana perkele," I said, quite calmly I thought.

Both Roma and Thelma gave me a Look, probably for different reasons. Roma knows it takes ten minutes to walk home from the office; Thelma hates religiously-sourced profanity, no matter in what language. All justified.

"Do carry on," I said. "I am just going out, and may be some time."

29. COOL

By the time I trudged around the corner by the Epitome Apartments forty minutes later, I was carrying a couple of bags of groceries and, accidentally, due to propinquity (is propinquitiously a word?), a large flat of clearance-sale bedding plants from the rack in front of the neighbourhood grocer[68]. I could say "I was hoping it was all a dream", but I wasn't really; I'm too practical to waste time with that profound a fantasy.

Sure enough, on the doorstep of the Epitome sat a long, tall drink of water, with all the beauty of both their parents[69], clad in fashion-forward attire, and guarding a trendy woven backpack stuffed to bulging.

"Hi," they said. They had matured a bit since I had met them, and may have passed for adult to strangers, but their voice betrayed their youth and uncertainty.

"Are you here with anyone?" I knew the answer.

"No, I just . . ."

"So you'll stay with me," I said.

"I guess," they said. "Cool." Relief showed through the indifference, but I could see they weren't going to ever admit that.

"Until we get hold of your mother. Your, you know, your aunt who is your mother. I mean, Mattie. Take these," I said, and handed over the flat of pansies. I wiped off the potting soil that had gotten all over my hand, and put my clean-ish forefinger on the lock plate. The door clicked.

---

68. Pansies, not petunias. I loathe petunias. I also loathe pelargonium, if it ever comes up. Pun unintended.

69. Mattie called Kim "she" last year, but Kim is one of those fortunate people who looks a bit like everyone on the planet, in a youthful and attractive, if tall, way. And Kim told me almost immediately that they now prefer "they/them", anyway, which suits me fine. So I'll start as both Kim and I mean to go on.

I took back the pansies.

"Cool," said Kim. They picked up their pack.

"Yeah, cool," I said, but I didn't mean it.

30. LIKE IN THE MOVIES

Kim continued to vocalise as we wended our way through the historic hallway of the Epitome Apartments and into the elevator, which I used in deference to my armfuls of shoppage, the flat of pansies, and Kim's big backpack.

Kim had had a great trip. Kim had never been in an airplane before, and it was so cool. Kim went by *they/them* now, hope that's cool? Kim thought the city was amazing, especially the river valley to which my place was *so* close. Kim thought old buildings were cool. There were no cool old buildings in Kim's neighbourhood[70].

Kim liked the amazing hall. They liked the awesome bannisters. They liked the rad old plank flooring. They just *loved* the brilliant little elevator with the cool grill that has to be pulled across and clanged shut before the doors close and the car moves.

"It's like the movies!" Kim said.

"Yeah," I said. "Just remember, don't run *up* these stairs. You're in the wrong demographic."

They laughed. Okay, so Kim was clever, and in touch with pop culture memes. Did that help? No.

Kim had a hearty, unaffected laugh with top notes of Priscilla and a Nathan finish, which I found disturbing. I told myself that Kim *was* their child, after all, but laughs a lot like that laugh featured several times on the paper in the box in my closet, and Kim's were keeping that goose really busy.

---

70. That was so true. If I live in the Epitome of apartments, Kim and their adoptive parents lived in the epitome of a Ronnie Gilbert song. Even more so than Thelma, which hardly seems possible, but is.

The door of my apartment is old oak, and it has a transom above it, with a suite letter painted on the frosted glass of the transom, as well as two numeric versions indicated in brass lettering tacked to the door.

"Why three?" Kim asked, gesturing.

"Who knows? The Department of Redundancy Department, a.k.a. old building with lots of revisions to it over the years."

Kim had never seen such an amazingly cool thing outside of, you guessed it, the movies.

My twenty-first century security lock is set inconspicuously on the lath-and-plaster wall beside the door, and let me tell you, *that* had been an historic-preservation challenge. Juggling bags and a cardboard tray of plants, I unlocked the door and briefly held it from opening.

"Abandon hope all ye who enter here," I said. "Do you have pet allergies?"

"Nope."

"Don't let them out."

"Don't le— *oh!* It's *Micah!*"

Kim dropped their pack just inside the door and reached out. Micah and Bunnywit had come careering out of the living room into the hall. Bunnywit skidded to a stop but Micah kept running, and about six feet away from Kim he launched himself into a graceful leap that took him to Kim's chest, where he clung, purring, front paws around Kim's neck in an Abyssinian death-hug.

"You . . . know Micah?"

"Auntie Jane, well, you know, um, my — she left Micah with us most of the time. Not last time, but before."

Why not last time? I didn't ask out loud. I could guess, maybe. Pris was here, with us, that time, and starting to wonder why she was afraid of Lock, and she didn't want to risk drawing his attention to her sneaky trip to a city with nothing interesting in it, *la la la nothing to see here*, by taking the extra time to go home to

England and pick up her cat. Probably the same reason she had left Micah to me and not Kim.

Bunnywit looked over at me and miaowed. I shook my head at him. "I have no idea," I said. "Don't ask me. I don't know why *any* cats do *any* thing."

Kim laughed. "I taught him how."

Of course they did.

"That figures. Your parents could have sold camels to run the Iditarod."

"What do you mean . . . oh, like, high-key persuasive?" Kim buried their face in Micah's shoulder, and trembled slightly. I'd said it on purpose — I didn't know whether I was torturing the kid or not, but Kim had come here for information about their birth parents, and that I could deliver.

"Yes indeed," I said. "Pris persuaded me to be her friend again, despite her nature and mine, and Nathan persuaded me to . . . to love him." Again, may as well proceed as I meant to go on, and I meant to tell the truth, as much as I knew it.

Kim could be the nicest kid on the planet (unproven as yet). It was still going to be hell.

31. HELL

"This way. Bring these," I said, and shoved the tray of plants toward Kim. Micah was so firmly attached that he stayed put while Kim took the plants. Bunnywit stayed in the hall, investigating the pack.

"You eat meat?"

"What?"

"Meat. You eat meat?"

I dumped the groceries in the kitchen.

Kim stood there with the pansies, purring — oh wait, that was Micah.

"Kid! Put those out there on the fire escape."

Kim gracefully managed the challenge of cat, plants, window. The cat stayed on the right side of the pane, the plants didn't spill soil, and I shook my head. Kim had never met the father whose legacy seemed to be showing up in every move, and I had assumed they didn't really know Pris well enough to imprint on her. Genetics? Imitation of the admired Auntie Jane? Or just confirmation bias? My head told me it was confirmation bias, my heart did its own recognition dance.

"Meat? Fish?"

"Um, yeah? But not roast beef, that stuff's gross. All grey and stringy."

"Oh, my child, you have just not had the right beef."

Kim had been well-raised, and chuckled at my joke carefully, but I saw a kind of wildness around the eyes that did not bode well. This was a kid who was hungry, tired, scared, and wondering if they were way out of their depth.

"Sit down. Have some lemonade?"

"Um, thanks."

"Food allergies? Diabetes?"

"What? Um, no."

I surreptitiously sweetened the lemonade a bit more.

I then mustered my resources on the counter. I'd bought a pre-roasted chicken and the ingredients for a good salad. I had some leftover jasmine rice in the rice cooker in the fridge. "What's your favourite food?"

"Um, salad?"

"*Salad?*"

"Um, I can make it if you want. You're going to a lot of — I'm putting you to — um —"

"Kid! Kid! It's okay! Chill! You're here now. Just relax."

Kim swallowed, paused, and only slightly desperately said, "I can't relax. I don't know what to do. I didn't mean — well, yeah, I came, but I didn't know —"

I stopped, turned, and breathed slowly until, a few breaths later, in unconscious imitation, Kim did too. It's a useful trick you learn in crisis intervention class. Then I went into Full Social Worker, which, if you have never seen me do it, is an awesome thing. It's even awesome if you *have* seen it before. It was new to Kim.

"Kim. You want some answers. I get it. I can tell you what I know. It might take a while for us to get to know each other. That's okay. I assume it's summer holidays, so you aren't missing school, right?"

"What? School? No, I would never! I waited 'til after!"

Okay, I thought, I might even get to like this kid a little. Just a little.

"So we can take some time. Relax. We'll eat. We'll call Mattie. You'll sleep. You'll wake up. You'll hang around here for a few days. We'll talk. Then you can go home. Don't worry, for fuck's sake." Oops. Well, I haven't actually been *employed* as a social worker for some years. "Oh, and let Micah down. He's gonna have to use his own legs sometime, and he is not the boss of you."

Kim laughed slightly, and relaxed some, and put Micah down. Micah complained. Bunnywit heard the noise and came in to join the chorus.

"I can make salad."

"Okay, you do that." I piled everything salad-like that I had on one side of the counter. "Bowl here, knives there. Cutting board pulls out here. Go to."

Kim knew how to make salad. Surprising me, they even made it the way I like it, with all the pieces cut up very small so that in every bite you get a variety of flavours. This is rarer than you might think. Chopping lettuce has been unfashionable for some decades now.

I fed the cats, heated rice, set the table with the Bunnykins plates and mugs, cut up the chicken, put out a stack of paper napkins, and we ended at a dead heat, putting serving dishes on the table at the same time. We sat down opposite one another.

"So, kid. Talk. With your mouth full if necessary."

"Talk?"

Like, what the fuck are you even doing here? "Like, what . . . what are you doing here?" Don't ever say I can't exercise restraint. I can. Occasionally.

"I'm sorry," said Kim. "I didn't really think. I just, um, came."

"You must have thought on the plane."

"Well, yeah, I mostly worried. And I read one of Aunt — one of my, um, birth mother's books. That helped."

I passed the chicken and Kim passed the salad. We served ourselves and had a few bites. Well, I had a few bites in the time it took Kim to clear the plate and reach for more. Once, I thought, I'd been — wait, how old?

"How old are you again?" I said.

"Eighteen," said Kim. "Last month."

— I'd been eighteen. Though I had never been Kim's kind of eighteen, coddled in a suburban clone house, I know how food works at that age. I waited a bit, and ate a bit, while Kim ate a lot. It was rather peaceful, actually.

"How was the book?" I said when the feeding frenzy was settling down.

"It was really good," said Kim. "I felt like I was right there on the trip with her. She was having a real adventure. I mean, she was like deep-sea diving and stuff. I was just on a little jet trip. It really helped."

Kim paused and looked out at the glimpse of downtown skyline I have from that window. "She was a really good writer."

"Yeah," I said. "She was."

Still looking out the window, Kim said, "Did she love my dad?"

"She did."

Pinter would have been proud of this kid, but eventually —

"Did you?"

"Yeah," I said. "I did. A lot."

"She didn't mind?"

"They were just friends by then. She still loved him like a friend, and she wanted him to be happy. She encouraged us."

"She was nice."

"And smart. And strong. A good person. A bit weird, but good."

"He was nice too."

"Yeah. Very much so. Better than nice. Wonderful, really. And also good."

Kim nodded and went back to the salad, had a third helping.

After a moment, they nodded and I heard a quiet "huh."

Okay, then.

32. LOYALTIES

After dinner we adjourned to the living room and Micah reasserted his claim to Kim's full attention.

Bunnywit had treated Priscilla Gill as if she were catnip, and Nathan as if he were made of cashmere and to be lain upon (to be fair, he was often wearing it). I'd been a little jealous, which is unflattering but honest, of how my cat abandoned his grouchy, monosyllabic ways when they were about. I was slightly gratified that Bun didn't feel the same way about Kim.

I know, right? Kim was a kid and deserved All The Pets.

But this was Bunnywit. I had an investment. I was more than a bit gratified when Bun jumped up on *my* lap this time.

WHEN I CAME HOME LAST NIGHT AT THREE,

33. IF I'D KNOWN

I was wakened in the night by a phone call from one of the older, more nervous tenants. "All that shouting in the alley!" she said. "You let them stay there, *you* make them stop!"

"Did you call the police?" I asked. "I told you last time, just call the police."

"You do it," she said. "I'm fed up to the teeth with all them."

My bedroom overlooks the side lot. I got up and went down the hall to the window that looks out over the back.

"Naaw?" said Micah Five, speaking from beside Kim in the spare room.

"What?" said Kim sleepily, then fell back into sleep.

Bunnywit didn't even bother to show up. He's lived here as long as I have.

Outside, I couldn't see anything. No movement anywhere in the alley.

It was dead quiet.

34. AN ASIDE ON NIMBY VS. YIMBY

Some of my tenants don't like having the tents there. In one or two cases, as you saw above, they really *really* don't.

I do understand why other people's need makes some people, including these neighbours, mean. We humans like to hold on to what we have, what anchors us. If our fences give way and our anchors loosen, we fear that we could be swept away in a tide of need and powerlessness.

But fences can be prisons too. I spent the first decade of my social work career learning to have strong boundaries, and the rest of it trying to undermine them enough so I could remain a human being whom I was willing to face in the mirror each morning — and some days, succeeding, but not all the days.

When I was "downsized", I took my compassion fatigue home with me and nursed it for a year.

When my life took a turn upward again, I didn't get back my best, most giving self, even before some hoods beat me up, or Lock murdered Nathan and Pris and all. I'm just making do as best I can with who I am now — I'm most definitely not some kind of hero.

All I'm saying is, it's not hypothetical, this problem Nathan and Gary and Thelma and Roma and I — and all the other people working on homelessness — are trying to help fix.

For me, it happens every day, twenty-five feet down and fifty feet north of where I sleep[71].

---

71.   Yeah, not metric. Sue me. And, like all the other hope and need in the world, it would eat me alive if I let it. So you may have to get over it if I make some remarks that you find harsh. Just sayin'.

35. THIRD STRIKE[72]

Fleury rang the intercom early the next morning while I was making an effort at breakfast for Kim and me.

He was weeping, but this time, I was soon to find out, not drunk.

"Danny's dead," he said. "Danny's dead."

"When? What happened?"

"He's in the tent. He's dead."

"Right now? He's there right now?"

"Yes! He's dead!" He was sobbing so hard I could barely understand him.

"I'm coming down! Wait right there!" I said.

I grabbed my cell phone, keys, and inhaler.

"Stay here," I said to Kim. "Do nothing. Eat." I paused. "Forage. You can eat anything you find worth eating. Beware that lettuce, though."

The elevator is slow. I pelted down the stairs, ignoring the atmosphere-induced cough that any exertion caused. The halls and staircases of the Epitome were more than half as hazy now as outdoors, after several days of smoke, despite the hefty HEPA-grade furnace filters I was cleaning daily.

Fleury stood in the vestibule, leaning on the wall and his walker, still sobbing.

I didn't even try to calm him. "Show me!"

Instead of going back down and around the building, I led him through the dim hall to the back door, and down the iron-grated steps and ramp to the alley.

---

72. True, it didn't strike me. You could say the strike was just me-adjacent. That this wasn't about me, that I just got involved, out of guilt or an excess of Canadianism. But soon you will see why it deserves to be on the numbered list, and you will laugh at me, and not for the last time. Not a crimefighter. Ha.

The heat and the unfiltered air hit us like a wall. The ramp decanted us right beside the parking lot fence, only a few feet from their scruffy tent. The reek of unwashed clothes, urine, and spilled beer became more overpowering the closer we got to the tent.

Dan lay on his back in a tangle of dirty bedding. There was no question he was dead — he was the colours of stilled blood. It smelled as if he'd soiled himself, before or after death. But the swelling, bruising, and bleeding on his face and body were clearly pre-mortem: he had had one hell of a beating before he stumbled into his nest. His face was disfigured and even puffier than normal. One eye, wide open in death, had no unsullied white left, but was bloody and gruesome. The other eye's split and swollen eyelid was half-shut. His long whitish-grey hair and scraggly beard were tangled with blood, and his false teeth lay beside him, the upper plate broken.

"What happened?" I noticed that Fleury, too, had lacerations and bruising.

"In the night! I tried to stop them! They kept saying, 'Quit moaning, you fucking bum.' If they'da quit kicking him, he'da quit moaning! I tried!"

"How long ago?"

Before he could answer, I was on the phone to Roger. It says something that I have the head of Major Crimes on speed-dial[73].

"I need you," I said. "My apartment. Now!"

"What is it?" said Roger. "Ready to confess?" This was so not the time for him to get his sense of humour back[74].

"Shut the fuck up," I said. "This is real. Come to the back of my place. Bring the crime scene people. It's a homicide."

---

73. But I'm not a crimefighter. Ha.

74. Such as it was.

"They was like cops! Or soldiers! They had big boots! Real nice work boots."

Fleury gestured toward his own feet. He had found some black boots at the clothing swap at Neighbourhood Community Services. Docs, only just a bit large, and a menacing matte off-black. "Like these." He sat down on the concrete, a barely-controlled collapse, and began to pluck ineffectually at the laces. "Like these fucking boots, man! Fucking Nazi boots! I'm wearing fucking Nazi boots, man!"

He looked around wildly. "Little shortie jackets, like in the movies. Little fancy jackets. Tom Cruise, man, Tom Cruise!"

One of the Major Crimes cops was Lance. He crouched down on the heels of his own matte-black boots and reached out to hold Fleury's hands still. "What else, Fleury? What did they look like?"

"White guys. White! Short hair. One of them had that *Blade Runner* hair. Bleach, you know, dyed? Like that guy in the rain?"

All these years, and I had had no idea Fleury was a movie buff. Though come to think of it, his and Dan's street names were from a film. "Rutger Hauer?" I asked.

"Yeah. Like him, all blondy. Like her!" and he pointed to a young constable doing crowd control. Her hair was bleached to corn-silk paleness, razor-cropped-and-patterned at the sides, and she had just taken off her cap to run her hand through the curls on top.

"Their faces?" said Lance.

"I dunno," he started to sob again. "It was night-time! They was just fucking kicking his face, they was kicking his face! I tried to stop them! They had sunglasses! In the night-time!" Before Lance could stop him, Fleury threw himself down across the pallet where Dan lay, clutching the sides of Dan's jacket. "I'm sorry, Danny, I'm sorry," he howled. "I'm sorry! I'm sorry!" Fleury's fingernails were painted with glitter black nail polish and his hands were filthy, cracked, and stained with dry blood. "I shoulda got the ambulance no matter what you said! I didn't know! I'm sorry!" His words blurred into the wail of an injured beast, and he struggled blindly when Lance and I tried — unsuccessfully — to lift him up. The blonde cop came over but even three of us couldn't disconnect him.

In the end it was Ted who described the rest of the scene to the cops. Fleury was crying too hard. The paramedics had to help us pull him away from Dan's body. They sedated him and pressed him down onto a stretcher like recalcitrant dough.

I helped them convince him to go to hospital.

How?

By saying this: "I'll help them find out who did this, Fleury. I promise."

Well, shit.

That was a promise it was impossible to keep.

Lance rolled his eyes and snorted. I backed away from the stretcher and shrugged.

Ted stuck a word in.

"Don't worry, man. I saw the guys. Besides, the cops can come see you in the hospital. You just go on."

Fleury may or may not have understood or agreed. He really was incoherent, and the sedative was taking its time. They wheeled him away and put him in the first-response ambulance where Dan would have gone if he hadn't been waiting for the medical investigator's transport wagon.

The blonde cop actually burped the ambulance. Clearly, she hadn't been on the job long.

37. 20/20 HINDSIGHT

Ted filled in the gaps.

The gang had showed up at (or, obviously, just minutes before) the time my first-floor-rear tenant called me to complain about the noise. The noise, as it turned out, of five men with boots kicking a poor homeless drunk guy nearly to death[75], the victim grunting and moaning, and Fleury and the attackers yelling. Surely, I thought, surely that noise would have been . . . unusual in some way? Upsetting? Appalling? Enough for her to call 911, instead of me?

Also, I thought, I should have gone downstairs myself, but when I'd looked out the back hallway window from the top floor, everything had been quiet and there wasn't a soul in view. And from there I can see the parking fence, both camps, and all the way down the alley and out to the side streets.

Unshed tears and undone deeds: 20/20 hindsight.

Ted was standing by the garbage bins holding his dogs on leashes. Fang didn't like all the activity in her alley. She had a little rumbling growl going on that didn't let up. It sounded as if she could growl on the in breath as well as the out. I know classical singers who would envy her. She sounded like an idling chainsaw, but very quiet. Or maybe like a kettle on the boil.

Killer was sitting alertly, ready to defend Ted if need be, but he was bigger, and didn't need to rumble.

I asked Ted about the noise last night. The blonde cop came over and fished out her notebook, stacked it on her set-to-record cell phone. Ted waited for her to get ready before he answered me. Smart dude.

"It was the dogs barking what woke us up," he said. "They was going ape-shit. The little one was trying to get out under the tent. Shayna hadta hold them in. Then I heard Danny grunting. And them yelling at him to shut up. I come out and they was all around him. He was on the ground over there in the middle of

---

75. Kicking him to death? How do you say it when he died later as a result of the beating? I can't even.

the alley, and they was all around him." He shook his head, and bent it momentarily to search the verge at his feet for nothing that was really there.

"And then Fleury started yelling and trying to get them off Danny, and they turned on him. So I pulls out this cell phone, it was outta juice but they don't know that, and yell that I called the cops, to get off them, I'm taking pictures, yadda yadda, and I start to run over there, and Shayna come out with the dogs so they could see 'em. When I think about it, they coulda just beat the shit out of both of us too, we was fucking lucky, but they all turned and run down there —" he pointed toward the mouth of the alley that opens to the main street north of the building "— and around the corner, and I heard a truck rev up. I run down that way after them, which thinking about it now was pretty fucking stupid too, but I was mad. But I never seen them. They was out of sight."

"Did you see the truck?" asked Blondie.

"I seen three trucks go by after that, and a coupla cars. It's busy down there, all night. No way to tell if one of them was theirs, or all, or what. But I tried to kinda take note in my head. One white and two black trucks, blue car, silver car. Boring cars. I don't think these guys woulda drove boring cars. And the trucks was the same kind of trucks that's all over, right? Rig-pig kinda trucks, but all of them clean. One had one of them chain trailer hooks, I remember that, and some kinda detailing on the side, not flames but fancy line shit, I remember that, but they went by fast. I couldn't get no licence numbers or nothing. I never seen their faces in the alley, and I never seen who was in the trucks. It was all too fast."

"So then what?"

"I come back to those guys. Danny got up outta the alley, and Fleury and him was kinda leaning on each other. I said we could get Girl —" he jerked his thumb toward me "— you know, that's what they call her, to call an ambulance, but Danny, you know him, no ambulance, no, no, I'm okay, I just gotta lie down."

"What did he look like then?" asked the cop. "Was he speaking clearly? Was he . . . functional?"

"He looked like shit, man. His one eye was swelling up and bleeding, and he had his lip split, and he was holding onto his guts like he was gonna puke, and weaving all over and mumbling like he was drunk, but he wasn't, not very. But he wouldn't let me. No ambulance. He said even if they come, he wouldn't go. He yelled it.

"I told him, 'Man, you are fucked up big time, you gotta go!' He said, 'I'll go in the morning. I just wanna lie down with Fleur and go to sleep.' So after a minute I seen he ain't gonna budge, and I say, 'Okay, man, okay.'

"Oh, man, I shouldn't a . . . I shoulda . . ."

"You couldn't force the guy," said the blonde cop, now writing furiously on a statement form on a clipboard. "Not your fault. Anything else? Did anyone else see any of this?"

"There was that lady in that window there, she slammed her window shut while we was talking. Maybe she seen something."

He looked up at the building and then at me. "She don't like us, man." He chuckled ruefully. "She really, really don't like us down here." He shook his head. "But that's it. I went back to my place, and everything was quiet. Even the dogs quit growling."

"So what did they look like? Could you ID any of them?"

"Mostly I saw the backs of them. There was one with that hair like Fleury said, sort of like yours, officer, all shaved up in the back kinda ziggity. The rest of them had dark hair, but if I had to say, they was all white guys. Tall. Well, taller than me, which ain't saying a lot. They had these little short jackets. The blond guy had black leather, that I remember. But not like a biker, like some smooth guy on an ad or something. The others, a couple had leather and a couple had denim jackets. They was all mostly wearing jeans, that I saw, but maybe some was black and some was blue jeans. Hard to tell. There's a dark spot there between the street lights. I remember they all had fancy work boots though, dark colours. Clean boots. Except, you know, maybe not now."

He fell silent and rubbed his stubbly chin with the hand that wasn't holding the leash and the dead cell phone.

"That was a fucking awful sound," he said to the circle of cops and me, looking from face to face. "That thumping when they kicked him, and the way he was moaning. That ain't a sound I'm gonna forget too soon."

The blonde cop started to turn away.

"I'll tell you one thing," said Ted. "If that there bitch up there heard that noise and she never called 911, she is a fucking piece of work and I don't care who hears me say it."

But she didn't call 911. She called me. And I didn't see or hear a thing.

Ted walked back toward his tent, and the cop and I looked at each other.

I sighed, pointed, and gave her the back door code.

"Apartment 104, but it still has the old numbers on the door too. 1-D," I said. "Back, that side. Her name is Murray. Mabel or something. 'Nice' type. Pays her rent on time. Complains about noise and 'those people'. Good luck with her."

"Hey, you can't come in here!" someone said. I turned around, and there was Kim trying to get past the police line. Chip off the old block.

"It's okay," I said. "They're mine — er, they live here. I'll take them home."

38. CRIME SCENE

By then, a couple more plainclothes cops were there, Dave and an older woman wearing giant square wraparound sunglasses that hid most of her round, pale face. They were enlisting some constables who were struggling with poles and nylon to augment the crime scene tape by erecting some of those tentlike shelters they use to protect a scene — because unlike cops on TV and in the movies, real cops actually protect crime scenes and wait for the crime scene team to come before they look for clues. (Unfortunately, this crime scene was already so polluted that they might as well have taken their cue from the worst of the screen cops, but it's the thought that counts. Well, and also, police procedure for the win.)

They put a shelter above Fleury and Danny's tent that looked like the twin of a snap-up picnic shelter I bought ages ago at Canadian Tire and have used all of once. They put a smaller tent over the bloodstains in the alley. They had a lot to do before the ME's van could come in and take Dan's remains away, and they started doing it.

It was heartbreaking to see that their larger shelter covered Dan and Fleury's camp completely. Two entire lives lived in a twelve-foot by twelve-foot piece of waste ground.

"Should I . . . ?" I asked Lance, gesturing to the detectives.

"Go home," he said. "It's not as if we don't know where to find you."

True that.

39. HOT CHOCOLATE AND DRAMA

Kim was silent until we got into the apartment and Micah had applied himself like a medicinal patch. They stood in the living room. Micah was kneading paws on Kim's hoodie; Kim was shifting from foot to foot. Okay, so now I had *three* live cats.

"Was that man . . . dead?"

"Yeah, kid." I sat down heavily in the armchair and leaned my head back. "I'm getting too fucking old for this shit. Yeah, he was dead. He got kicked to death by some fucking upmarket goon squad."

I explained further.

"That's . . . awful!" Kim perched on the couch and detached Micah, who immediately curled up hard by the kid's leg and continued his attempts to comfort. Bun was probably still asleep on my bed. Clearly he didn't get the memo.

"Yeah, kid, it sucks."

"He was, like, a bum, though, right?"

"Even bums shouldn't be murdered."

"Oh my gawd, I didn't mean that! I meant, like, what they say in the papers, 'high-risk lifestyle' or something?"

"The streets are risky, yeah, but. Danny was a harmless old alcoholic who couldn't get his shit together, but at least one person in the world loved him. Lots of people who look okay on the outside can't say as much."

"I come from a pretty safe place," said Kim. "I know I'm kind of . . . ignorant here. I just don't understand. Why — ?"

I interrupted, "You know, kid, if I could answer all the whys, I'd be running the world. I don't know anything right now."

"It's really sad," said Kim. "The way that other man cried?"

"Yeah, Fleury, that was Fleury," I said. "It's really sad."

"Can we help them somehow?" Kim had been out of earshot behind the police tape, so this was all them, not them virtue-signalling after hearing me.

"Gonna do my best, kid. But right now, we both have to chill a little."

Kim got up, but stood irresolutely. "I don't know how I can. I've never seen a dead person before."

Okay.

"Okay, we'll have some hot chocolate first. With miniature marshmallows."

"What?"

79

"Very calming. Warm milk. Theobromine. Sugar. Good combo."

Nathan used to warm the milk for hot chocolate in a saucepan. He claimed the microwave somehow leached the special nature out of hot chocolate, as if it diminished the love. I wasn't ready for the saucepan method yet, though. May never be.

While we waited for a pitcher holding two mugs'-worth of milk to get warm in the microwave, and the chunk of dark chocolate in the little bowl beside it to melt, we leaned on the kitchen counter.

"Sorry your first day here is full of drama," I said.

"Everything in my life right now is drama," said Kim simply.

Oh.

"Do you know — well, of course you don't, but I'm going to tell you. The first thing your father — Nathan — did for me was make me a cup of hot chocolate. With his own hands. In a limo."

"In a limo?"

"It was a rented limo, and the hot chocolate might even have been instant, though it was in a vacuum flask so I can't be sure, but anyway he poured it out into a real mug and put little marsh-mallows in it. I had met him about fifteen seconds before, this smooth, pretty, well-dressed rich fuck, and here he was handing me a mug full of steaming hot chocolate, with marshmallows. Not just three or four. Plenty. Lots, actually. Enough. Which is rare."

The microwave beeped. I heard Bunnywit's paws thump to the floor in the bedroom. "It's not for you, you idiot!" I yelled, but he showed up in the kitchen anyway. I took the pitcher out of the microwave and poured the tiny amount of milk safe for kitty digestion out into a flat bowl for Bun.

"Knock yourself out," I said, putting it down. "Don't burn your tongue."

Micah protested, and Kim giggled. Mission accomplished, somewhat. I poured the same again into a twin bowl for Micah. Then I divided the melted chocolate into Kim's and my cups, focussing despite the blur. Yeah, fuck off, I don't need reading glasses yet. That's a fucking literary-device way of saying without really saying that I was crying a bit, again.

Kim handed me the sugar tin. Observant little beast. Kim also didn't comment on the tears I wiped away with the back of one hand. I stirred sugar in and handed one mug to Kim.

"I'm sorry —"

"Kid, quit apologising. We're here. It's going to be fine. There is lots of shit going down on this block that is far worse than our social discomfort here."

"I was gonna say, I'm sorry for your loss. Of my — of Nathan."

Oh.

"I mean, I sort of lost him too, but I never had him. So it's like hearing that Leonard Cohen died, right? It's real-not-real. But for you . . ."

"Yeah. Thanks."

I covered the top of the cups with a floating layer of tiny marshmallows, and left the bag handy, just in case. We leaned back on the counter edge and sipped at our cups. I'd used the Japanware, because I really *really* needed comforting. The marshmallows bumped against my upper lip, and I slurped in a couple and felt their half-melted stickiness against the roof of my mouth.

"You know what's fucked?" I said after a moment. "That woman downstairs. She heard it going down and she didn't call the cops. She looked out there and saw it happening, and then she called me to complain. She never called 911."

"Wow. That *is* fu— um, sorry."

"Go ahead, kid. I'm sure it's not the first time you swore."

"Mom is going to say you are a bad influence. She says there is seldom a reason for profanity."

"Yeah, well, your mom would have called the fucking cops." I licked the foam from my upper lip.

After a moment I added, "Either one of your moms."

40. DRESS FOR SUCCESS

Heather Wood, the homicide investigator I'd glimpsed below, and now in charge of solving Dan's brutal murder, was new to me. Without the sunglasses, she was revealed as a pudding-faced but intense white woman with brown hair. The sunglasses must have been on doctor's orders, because her dark eyes, behind a really nice pair of expensive blue-framed glasses, were reddened and her lashes were crystalline with medication. The glasses frames were the only individual note to enhance her navy jacket and grey slacks, white shirt, and the generic print scarf (with blue tints to match the glasses) that replaces a tie for businesswomen and female-identifying cops who are trying not to look too butch[76].

Detectives don't wear uniforms much. They spend some money on really good quality clothing which they then don't have to think much about[77]. In her case, I guessed she had read, maybe twenty-five or thirty years ago, a magazine article about how to dress for success, and hadn't felt the need to do more than trade skirts for slacks in the interim.

She looked as if she had been lean in youth and was still getting used to as small an amount of middle-aged spread as she could manage with relentless gym work and portion control[78].

I suspected she would be retiring in a year or two, seemingly too young but with twenty-five years on the job, after which it was the Serious Incident Response Team or private enterprise

---

76. Which some people in the world, alas, even in this day and age, think is a bug not a feature.

77. About which they then don't have to think much. Proof that I do balance my grammatical intensity with common usage.

78. These guesses proved out later, which briefly made me a little smug, also later, as in, "Ha, I can detect stuff too!" Call me Sherlock. If you want. No, actually, don't; I have a perfectly good name of my own.

for her. I picked SIRT. She struck me as the kind of cop who has kept their integrity[79] and would end her career helping keep the rest of the cops honest — which is a hard, almost impossible, definitely thankless job, but some of them do try. But that was just a guess.

Heather settled into the easy chair in my living room and opened her notebook. Kim sat out past the edge of the conversation, silently working at their laptop at the dining room table.

"Tell me," Heather tasked me. "Put in everything everybody said. We aren't in court here."

So I began. Fleury and Dan and their life: such as it was, but their own. Their hopes for the future. Their place in the economic life of the inner city, as bottle pickers. Brief aside to mount a defence of the bottle depot (across the street and up a couple of blocks from the Epitome) as a neighbourhood economic centre. Fleury's arrival at my door, weeping. His incoherent words, rendered as faithfully as I could. Leading him through the dark, smoky hallway and out into the unforgiving orange morning light to view Dan's body. All that was said and done there.

"But you didn't see the attackers."

"No. Fleury did. Apparently Ted also saw them. Fleury and Ted and Shayna and Ted's dogs between them seem to have scared the pack of them away. If Ted hadn't come along, Fleury probably would have been dead too — they gave him a good working-over, but they ran off when Ted and Shayna came out with the dogs. Killer's a bit intimidating, but Fang is the dangerous one. She's little and looks kind of cute, but she has a hate on for everyone who isn't Ted or Shayna, and if you get in her face, she will end you."

"Did she actually bite anyone?"

---

79. Keeping in mind that people can be bad and we can't tell, cf. earlier musings.

"Dave asked that at the time, but apparently not. Could you have gotten DNA that way?"

"Who the heck knows? Lab would know. Worth a try, though, wouldn't you say?"

"Absolutely. But no, alas, they ran."

"Are they really called Killer and Fang?"

"Hell, no. They're called, I dunno, Bobby and Sugar or something. Ralph and Sweetie. Nibbo and Grace. Whatever. I think Sweetie-Pie or Angel or something is right for the smaller one, but I'm not sure. Killer and Fang are their street names."

She laughed with me, her tired, responsible face momentarily lightening. "Fleury has a street name too — Donkey? What's that about?"

"Danny was Shrek."

"Oh." A beat, while we thought about that.

"Did you talk to my tenant? The redoubtable Mrs. M. Murray?"

She tilted her head at me.

"That's how she signs her cheques. I think her name is Marilyn or something."

"'Margaret, but please call me Meg.'" She made air quotes.

"She liked you?"

"Only until my questions got more pointed and I didn't take her up on her anti-homelessness stuff. Then . . ."

"She's a bit of a piece of work, our 'Meg', then, isn't she? I inherited her when I bought the Epitome. It was better before she found out I was the new owner, but now she's sort of at war with me. Looks daggers at me in the hall, that sort of thing."

"And you with her?"

"I wasn't until now. Now, I've been reading the Landlord and Tenant Act."

"Make sure you read it well," she said. "She heard the noise. She described it very well." We sat with that, too, for a beat.

After a moment, Heather: "I was thinking about his Rutger Hauer description."

"Yeah, me too. Are you thinking a haircut and bleach job like that would be easy to trace?"

She spread her hands and shrugged a little. "Among all of the salons in this town? We might try, but it's a needle in a haystack." I was glad to see that in Roger's absence, original speech wasn't threatening to infect the earnest detectives of Major Crimes. But despite her clichés, she seemed to care, possibly slightly more than seemed warranted.

"What about on the base?" I wondered. There's a big military base north of the city. "What if you went up to the base and looked at the guys? There can't be that many. Everyone seemed to get an off-duty-soldier vibe from those assholes. 'Cop boots' and so on. Either that or rich skinheads. But most of the skinheads I see who have too much drug money have spent it on tats and piercings and big motorcycles. These guys had invested in portable wealth. Personal grooming wealth. Soldiers do that, so they can travel light."

"That's a decent idea," Heather said. "We'd have to be fast and stealthy so he didn't know we were there for bleached-blonds. And he could have been deployed or rotated out or whatever they do."

She began to gather her pen and notebook into her sensible purse.

"This is the best description we have so far," she said. "Most of them won't talk to us."

"So far? Them?"

"There have been a number of similar assaults. You don't hear about them because the victims aren't considered newsworthy, I guess. This is the only time that there's any degree of unanimity on the description, but we have a kind of composite. It's a gang of five to nine males, short hair and short jackets, maybe leather and denim, definitely big boots, beating on street people. At first they left them alive. Lately they haven't."

"How many?"

"Seven attacks so far. This is the third fatality. Started with a guy leaving the liquor store with his cheap wine. He wasn't killed, and he was maddest that they busted his bottle, not so much that they busted it over his head. Couple of late-night attacks. Woman sleeping in a doorway. Hates the cops, won't talk. Couple others. First to die was another homeless woman. She was still alive, barely, when they left her in the same doorway as the one before. Arranged her there. Her pals claimed they saw nothing. She didn't make it. So that was the first homicide. Then there was the guy who liked to walk at night because people didn't bother him. Schizophrenic on meds, quiet guy, good neighbour, lived upstairs in a rooming house. He wasn't homeless, but he had shabby clothes and a beard, and he was strolling around at three a.m. Some residents yelled out their door and called 911, the attackers fled[80], and he lived, but a week later he checked himself out of hospital and went to the mall downtown, and his aorta burst. Bled out internally before EMS got there. Murder, now.

"It's the same as with Danny here. They don't kill on the spot, but they are escalating. Now they are violent enough that their victims die."

"Delayed homicide is still homicide."

"Yes. But they're all the same as this one, no way to ID the suspects. The residents only saw them from the back, same as here. Now Danny wouldn't go to the hospital or call us, and he's dead too.

"It's frustrating." She pressed her lips shut on that frustration, a habitual one I'm sure.

---

80. She really said "fled".

"It must be," I said. "Don't they want to know who killed their friends? Or even, don't they want to get the guys before they come back and get them too?"

"You'd think," she said. "Thanks for your time."

Kim looked after her as she left, then asked, "So, like, why won't they talk to the cops?"

I looked at them, but they actually meant it. So I explained a number of possibilities, and we had a Q&A afterward.

It took a while, but no biggie. After all, I had nothing else booked.

Also, it's possible I was getting used to this "shaping young minds" thing, but you didn't hear that from me.

THE
MAN
WAS
WAITING
THERE
FOR ME;

41. THE NEXT PLACE

Turns out Dan had had kids, three of them. Two daughters came to his memorial service with their own kids. A son sat uneasily by himself, fiddling with a cell phone. Aside from three street friends looking jittery and almost-sober, the rest of the people sitting in circle in the harshly-lit, tile-floored church basement were care workers and social workers — except for Fleury, who sat by himself, two vacant chairs on either side of him, sober and weeping, in ill-fitting dress clothes.

And except for me. I was there as a separate unit too, not by myself this time but with a notable but not necessarily comforting exception — I guess I would find that out. Denis and Lance were on a romantic getaway weekend in the Rockies, so not Denis (sans Lance since I wouldn't have wanted a cop there to scare the people likely to get scared by cops); I hadn't wanted Hep to come with me because the last time we had been in that room together was for her granddaughter's memorial; Jian had run away with the circus; Thelma had her kid's physical therapy.

In the end, I was there with Kim.

I hadn't wanted Kim to come with me, for unnecessarily protective reasons, but they insisted, and I realised I couldn't think of a reason why not that wasn't insulting. So there they were.

It didn't do to think who else might have or should have been with us, if life and death had gone differently.

The room was in the basement of an old settler Catholic church that has been renamed "The Church of the First Peoples". The priest was a local celebrity, and by local I mean in the neighbourhood. He didn't act, dress, or pontificate like a priest, but he lived his faith, probably better than Mother Teresa had, and the people of my neighbourhood adored him.

An Elder walked around the circle with sweetgrass, sweeping with a large feather to bathe us in its cleansing smoke. Eagle feathers were customary, but this one looked more like a snowy-owl feather. Was that a thing? Maybe I would ask him after.

I welcomed the smoke. Unlike the smoke of Lock's burning, it represented goodness and was kind, and unlike the forest fire smoke, it was savoury and gentle on the lungs. I like sweetgrass. I'm not much for formal spiritual practices, as cousin Thelma will tell you, but I am not averse to prayer, which I think focusses the mind on the health of one's soul. I just don't think it matters who prays for us to whom, or who we pray to. To whom we pray. I scooped the smoke across my face and body in the traditional way, and Kim imitated me earnestly and clumsily. The Elder smiled at them, and nodded, and they blushed under his approval more than they had under the stress of the unknown ritual.

I kept liking this kid again, despite my defensive intentions. Slippery slope.

The service was simple. The Elder spoke in Cree and English, and asked the Creator and the ancestors for help. Father Guy did the same in French and English.

Fleury cried.

Dan's daughter stood up, holding her baby, and said how much her dad had loved his kids. His other daughter stood up and said how much her dad had loved his grandkids. One of the grandkids, who was about four or five, had drawn a picture he said was of Danny, and put it beside the smudge bowl in the centre of the circle.

Fleury cried.

One of the care workers stood up and said how much Dan had loved Fleury. Father Guy went over with a little necklace that in the future would hold some of Dan's cremains, once his body had been released by the Medical Examiner.

"This is for you, Fleury, so that you can carry Danny with you," he said simply.

Fleury stood up, still crying.

"I love you, Danny," he said. "People like us aren't much. We don't do much. But I loved you and I don't know what I am going to do without you."

He sat down again.

I went around Kim to perch beside him, and took his hand. He was cleaned up for the service, wearing a white shirt with a collar too large for his fragile neck, puckered in by a thin black tie, and a shiny old black suit that fit well enough to look as if it might actually have belonged to him from before — though goodness knows where he would have kept it for some of those years — but he didn't fill it out. His hand was rough, but it was clean today, the only dirt on it ground in.

"What am I gonna do now?" he said to me, and began to cry again.

I knew if I said one word, I would say all the words. *I don't know, Fleury,* I thought. *If I knew what you were going to do, I'd know what I was going to do, and that would be a revelation.* I knew if I shed one tear I would shed all the tears, and that wasn't appropriate.

I hadn't known Dan that well. I'd be crying for me.

Dan's older daughter came by and I let go of Fleury's hand so she could take it. I moved back to my place so she could sit with him.

"Fleury, Dad loved you too," she said. "He did." The other daughter was hanging back. They both had the familiar (to me, in my past career) look of people who hadn't been able to prevent their father's life from becoming a train-wreck, but at least they seem to have loved him anyway. The son still sat immersed in his cell phone screen, two chairs away to my left, with an uncomfortable attitude of — what? I didn't have a clue.

Had Dan and Fleury been lovers, or deep friends? It didn't matter then and it didn't matter now. I could see from the reactions of the other two kids that they had some issues with something about the relationship, whether it was the same-sex nature of it, the beer, or the bottle-picking homelessness, but this daughter didn't hold back. She hugged Fleury, and said again, "Dad loved you."

After that the rest of the people in the circle were given the feather to hold and asked to share a memory if we wanted. Dan was generous with his beer (that got a chuckle), kind, never got violent. Dan loved his kids, even if he hardly ever saw them. Dan loved Fleury. Dan was a pretty good bottle-picker until his kidneys started acting up on him and his legs got so bad. Kim shook their head when the feather came around and gestured over to me. Dan had a foul mouth but a good heart, I said, which got another little laugh.

After my turn, I gave the feather to Danny's son, who looked up with a thunderous face, and shocked us all.

"My dad was an asshole when he was young," he said quietly, "and I used to hate him. I didn't know about the residential schools and Sixties Scoop and stuff. But he changed his mind a lot when he lived on the streets. I ain't gonna get my childhood back, but he ain't gonna either, and I turned out okay. I wish he'd hadda chance, himself. I guess he's in a better place. I hope the hell he is. This place ain't been much, here, especially for him, so I hope to hell the next place is treating him better."

After that, we all pretty much went home. What else could we say?

42. PTDS

The iced tea my friend Hep, Kim, and I were drinking was about the colour of the air. Hers was what's known as Long Island Iced Tea, meaning booze, and ours wasn't, but both were a robust golden-brown that helped soothe throats sanded into constant cough-triggers by the smoke — and by the tears I had finally shed when I was away from the crowd.

Kim was drinking regular iced tea because I was not going to lead a babe-in-the-woods astray. I was drinking it because I had recently, on another version of the slippery-slope principle, given up even the social use of booze — I didn't much like the taste and effect anyway, and anaesthetic these days was too damnably tempting. Also I had numerous examples, not the least of whom was Fleury, to remind me how that way lies rump of skunk and madness.

These days, any little piece of grief from anywhere can set me off. Post-Traumatic-Death Syndrome, I call it. Even if I see on social media that someone I don't know has had to say goodbye to their old, sick dog, I'm crying. When my brother killed himself when we were teenagers, I coped; when various friends of my youth died in weird tragic ways, I coped; when my parents died in their weird and spectacularly-tragic way, I coped. I even coped with Maddy Pritchard's murder and all the mayhem that followed it — but Nathan's murder, and Pris's, had finally pushed me past coping into this state of constant hypervigilance, in which I was just getting by. Feeling as dead as they were, but still walking around. The unnamed stage of grief: zombie.

Hep sometimes insisted I face reality — and humoured me other times, such as today.

We all sat in the swing chairs in her yard, under a big canvas umbrella, and said nothing, and drank our diverse beverages.

Every now and again, I would randomly and briefly break the silence: "I couldn't believe how stoic his kids were" or "Fleury — it was fucking tragic" or "I like it better when people smudge with sweetgrass than with sage" or "Dammit, I forgot to ask about that feather!" or "Pass the *real* iced tea, please?"

Kim had a couple of contributions too: "It was so sad what his son said" and "That little kid with the picture was so cute!" and "I never saw anybody do that, you know, with the sweetgrass and the feather?"

Hep explained sweetgrass and eagle (or owl?) feathers, so I didn't have to say a thing, and then they got into the Truth and Reconciliation Commission and the trauma of surviving the residential schools, and the Sixties Scoop and what it meant, while I lay back and looked at the leaves against the yellow sky, and thought about nature, nurture, and neglect.

Days are long at this time of year. We sat there until the brown sunlight was slanting in below the umbrella, but it was a long time before sunset even then.

"Let's get some food," Hep finally said.

"Good idea," I said.

"Double Greeting?" she said, and reached for her purse and her car keys. "I bet Kim would like Double Greeting."

"I'll drive," I said. "You're shitfaced."

So that's what we did.

43. ALSO COOL

Kim liked Double Greeting.

Thought it was cool.

While I was filling Hep in on events from Lock's death onward, Kim multitasked at listening, rubbernecking the prairie-café décor, and making friends with the servers. The world's most efficient waitress was not there, but she had trained her bevy of minions well. It was possible that in a few years one of them could assume her crown. Kim thought it must be cool to work here, and that it might be a cool summer job, and maybe they should apply. Kim also ate a huge amount, or number, of the Green Beans with XO Sauce, and was even persuaded to try half a thousand-year egg.

Just guess what they thought about that.

Yep, cool.

BUT
WHEN
I LOOKED
AROUND
THE HALL,

44. FOURTH STRIKE, OR, IT'S A HIGH FLY BALL INTO DEEP LEFT CENTRE FIELD

I was still asleep the next morning when the phone rang. I fumbled with the land line before I realised it was the cell. Yes, I know I am one of the last six people on the planet who also has a land line, but I Have My Reasons[81]. I checked blearily for familiarity, but alas, Unknown Caller can mean cops or weirdniks. I took a chance and answered.

"Meet me at the Nook, PDQ," said Roger, and hung up.

"Good morning," I said to the blank screen. "No, I don't have plans."

---

81. Mostly Luddite, as I was probably the seventh-last person on the planet to get a personal cell phone, only a couple of years ago. But also because, even though I wear no tinfoil haberdashery, I fear the failure of the digital grid because of the Global Electromagnetic Pulse (or, more boringly, the infrastructure breakdown) to come. Also, at the time of these events, 911 could track a land line call easier than a cell, and, in my non-distant past, that had been important.

Just as well, though.

45. INCANDESCENT

When I got there, Roger was ordering the grilled cheese sandwich of the day.

"I got yours," he said. "Sit." He pointed to the most private corner.

"With an iced chai latte," I said.

"We know," he and the owner said simultaneously.

When he turned, I realised that he was incandescent with some strong emotion that wasn't joy. I guessed rage, from the set of the small muscles around his eyes. Grief would be a different shape.

I've seen Roger angry, and it usually takes him the quiet way: cold, logical, crisp, and with perfect enunciation. This time, I could feel it from across the room.

When we got close enough to the table he'd chosen that we wouldn't be broadcasting, I said, "Roger, what's wrong? Are you all right?"

"*No!*" he said, then saw my face. "Oh, yeah, *I'm* fine, *I'm* all right, personally speaking. But . . ." He stopped and stood, silent, vibrating slightly.

Speechless? Hardly ever, if ever. This was something very bad.

I actually guided him to a seat at the corner table he'd probably picked for that reason. I put his back to the wall just in case. And he let me. Which was also really fucking weird.

Seated, he put his hands up on the table, palms up, and slowly clenched and opened them, gazing down and clearly holding himself back from pounding the table a little. Okay, this was scaring me.

"Okay," I said. "This is scaring me. What's going on?"

He shook his head. "Clusterfuck," he said. "Total fucking clusterfuck."

I put my hand over one of his. "Please. Explain." After a moment, I added, "Slowly."

He nodded. "Okay," he said. "I just don't know where to start."

"To the universal through the particular," I said.

He glared at me.

"Important rule of storytelling," I said. "To the universal through the particular. It means —"

"I know what it fucking means. Okay. Let's start near where we shit. You know the DNA and hair results that we used in Lock's trial? The pre-existing samples that we later used to compare with dead Chiles to make sure he was really dead Chiles and all that?"

"Er, yes . . ."

"Likely mishandled, possibly contaminated or compromised, maybe completely unreliable."

"*What?*"

"Because the deputy head honcho at the goddamn LAB[82] has been IMPROVING the goddamn TEST RESULTS to favour the prosecution's case, accidentally or on purpose, and we just caught it, and we think we might have as many as seven years of results at risk. Seven. Fucking. YEARS."

"Roger, shush. People are . . . concerned."

"What — of course they are concerned!"

"No, people here. Because they can hear you. At the other corner of the room."

He got up and began to pace our corner. Not attracting attention at all. No.

"Roger!"

"WHAT?"

---

82. Yes, that indicates he was shouting. Yes, I'm aware of texting conventions now. Not *that* much of a Luddite any more. You'd be surprised what I've learned about the digital world. Also, Bunnywit has his own Instagram page.

"If you must stalk your prey, go get our sandwiches or something."

He did.

"Now sit," I said, "and eat."

Amazingly, he sat.

After a moment, he picked up a sandwich, put it down, squirted way too much ketchup on his plate, picked up the sandwich, smashed it into the ketchup until he had achieved bloodspatter, and finally took a gory bite. I had a feeling he wasn't murdering the actual sandwich, exactly.

"Why didn't you come tell me this at home?"

"I thought memmmfìght . . ." He swallowed and tried again. "I thought I might break something if I weren't in public. Or scare the cats."

The *cats*? Scare the *cats*? What am I, chopped liver? (Except chopped liver is wonderful, so what is that idiom about anyway?)

"Scare the *cats*? What am I, chopped liver?"

"I've never understood that saying," he said. "Chopped liver is delicious." This kind of thing is probably why he is mostly my friend, despite everything.

"Eat," I said, and we did. The barista brought over our drinks: my chai and . . . "What *is* that?"

"Same again, with another round of sandwiches," he said to the barista.

"It's a decaf almond-milk latte, no sugar," she said to me, grinning.

"These *are* the end times," I said to her departing back.

"Last thing I needed was more . . . anything that would make my temples buzz even more. My head is about ready to explode anyway."

"Good thinking, I guess. But are you going to actually *drink* it?"

He sipped gingerly, then tilted his head. "Actually not too bad, considering."

"Considering?"

"Considering you don't wanna know."

"Fine, be that way. Are you better now?"

"No," he growled, and buried his face in his latte, coming up with his upper lip and the tip of his nose foamy, about which at other times I might have teased him. Oh, what the hell, live dangerously.

"You have reverse panda face."

He scowled and swiped at his face.

"You understand what this means," he says. "This is as bad as that FBI thing back in, when was it . . . 2015? DNA on dozens of cases is compromised. Hair evidence is a joke. Fingerprints? Maybe okay, but a work in progress. So half of what we have used to convict is suspect. Including Lockwood Chiles."

"What about my original independently-paid similar results last year, and Mr. Spak's new independently-paid results this year?"

"Comforting to us, perhaps, but two problems. One is that we are not yet sure whether an independent process passes the same high standard for chain of evidence that a judge would entertain, and the second is — this last time, what were you comparing it *to*? To what. You know. What was the base sample for your DNA test?"

"The gold standard. The one in your lab."

We sat quietly for a moment.

After a moment, I broke the silence. "Seven years, you said."

"Yep."

"Seven years when all the DNA and hair and print evidence in every case will be suspect and will need to be completely re-examined and verified."

"Every case that passed through her hands. Which is maybe as many as half, because she was the assistant head, so she caught a lot."

"Fuck."

"You. Have. No. Idea." I couldn't parse the mixture of fury, resignation, and hopelessness, but there was quite a spectrum in those four words. Roger *hates* it when bad guys end up back out on the street. He hates it worse when law enforcement is less than impeccable. He abhors dumb cops, bad cops, and dirty cops. And he has a side hate on for stupidity, of any kind. This was the perfect storm of all he hates.

"Seven years is a lot of bad guys," I said quietly.

"Yep."

"Including the putatively-dead Lockwood Chiles."

"Yep."

The owner came over with two plates holding two more sandwiches, and a cup of his . . . er, beverage. "Must be quite a day if you need a refill," she said.

"You have no idea," said Roger. Perhaps that would be his mantra from now on.

"Thank you!" I said for both of us, and made a circle over my cup too.

We were quiet while Roger murdered his second sandwich and I dispatched mine more humanely.

"So," I started, then lost courage. I cleared my throat — must have been a crumb, right? — and started again. "So, is Lockwood Chiles really dead?"

"I think so. I mean, yeah, pretty much I'm positive. But even if. Anyhow. I'm worried that good lawyers could get his offences pled down or his conviction overturned altogether. Then his money is in the wind instead of in seized assets, his evil empire is free and clear, and Nathan and Pris come back under suspicion. You too. Given you are the only one to come out of the whole thing alive."

"'Pretty much I'm positive?' Seriously?"

He made that eyebrows-up open-palms half-shrug at me, somewhat marred by some ketchup on his left hand.

The gesture that means *who the fuck knows anything?*
Great.

46. COFFEE-ADJACENT

After he was halfway through his second decaf almond-milk coffee-adjacent putative-beverage, Roger said meditatively, "Well, we have the confession. That's something."

"Kim is sleeping in my spare room," I said.

You could see that his head started hurting again by the way he grabbed it with both hands. Or maybe that was something else.

"What the fuck is she doing here?"

"Kim uses 'they/them' now. And they ran away from home to find out about their parents."

"Oh, for fuck's sake. Why now?"

"'So clouds formed up right up above me and then, of course, lightning come out and struck me'," I quoted.

"Don't be cute."

"I've told you that story."

"Same, same: cute. Don't."

"We need a real answer," I said. "For Kim if not for us."

"I know," he said. After a moment, he seemed to find himself in the dregs of his cup. "Wait a minute, what 'we'? There is no 'we'. Stay out of it."

"I always stay out of it," I protested. He snorted derisively. "Well, I try," I insisted.

"There is no try," he said.

"Real answer," I said.

He leaned back and stared at the ceiling instead. I followed his gaze with mine. The ceiling in the Nook isn't that interesting. So I stared at him instead, until I realised that he was actually thinking.

"That smart paper shit you have," he said. "Are you still messing with it?"

"On occasion. Sometimes," I lied. Always was more like it. "Why?"

"Do those weird SAS retirees still show up if you mess with Chiles's?" When Nathan and Lock had their smart-paper invention contest, Nathan invented nice paper (well, friendly paper, if you satisfied basic password protocols as required) and Chiles, in a spooky foreshadowing that should have rung alarm bells if anyone had been listening, invented paper with a level of security where if you try to pry into the contents of the paper and you don't have the right security codes, some people in the private-army version of tactical gear come to your door carrying automatic weapons and flashbangs, ready to Take You Down. I had had to have some quite careful discussions early in my ownership of the paper, and an uneasy but solid détente had been established.

"Um, yeah, if it's not at the office, they do. Unless I call them off."

"How do you do that?"

"There's a — pardon the expression — call centre."

"With round-the-clock staff. And on-call SWAT. Who get paid. By someone. Who?"

"You're getting an idea. I can feel the earth move."

"Just thinking, how much of himself did Chiles really invest in that paper? Do you keep them separate, his and Nathan's?"

How the hell did he know that?

I suppose it's not hard to guess that I wouldn't want the last remaining traces of Nathan and Pris — their voices, their laughs, their images, and their dreams — locked in a box with the last remaining same same etcetera of their murderer.

It wasn't logical. Nothing said there would be viral contamination if I didn't keep them apart. But yeah, I did. If I explored one of the pieces of smart paper and found out it was Nathanware, it stayed in the beautiful box he'd made me. If I happened upon some Chilescraft I hadn't already separated out, I took it downtown to the vault in my lawyer Dafydd Spak's office, where it was as cold and dark as Lock deserved. (Hell, not the Christian one but the real one, isn't hot, I'm sure. Hell is Fimbulvetr, but forever, not for just three years. "Hell is like a great lord's kitchen without fire in't." Hell is the cold space in my heart.)

Also, there are other, more practical reasons. Namely that I could work on it in the boardroom there, and Roma could help me.

I went with a simple, "Yeah."

He crooked his fingers in his minimalist-tasking sign for *gimme more*, and I said, "Spak's vault."

"I have an idea," he said. "Let's go over there."

47. BANK ON IT

Back when Nathan was still alive, he bought a beautiful old building right in the centre of downtown, and gave it to our foundation. It was designed in 1911 by the premier young architect of the day, Roland Lines (the same one who designed the Union Bank half a block away, which eventually became the little boutique inn where Pris had liked to stay). For a while it had a great Japanese restaurant in it where, at a very young age, I had my first sushi[83]. Then it sat empty, maintained, semi-restored, and saved by some heartfelt owners, but never leased. Those owners had to be convinced, before they sold, that we would love and cherish it, but that was easy, and thanks to their groundwork and a lot of love and money applied rapidly by Nathan & Co., it was now a heritage showpiece. Nathan then gave fifty-one per cent of the building to Spak outright and individually, and made him the trustee of the other forty-nine per cent, on the condition that he relocate his amusingly-named Kirk, Spak, and Lennie law firm into the place and take

---

83. As the twig is bent, so grows the tree.

a permanent retainer to be our lawyer. Oh, and work with me in perpetuity, or the mortal version of same, and keep Own Domains there the same kind of forever, and let Nathan have his workshop on the whole third floor.

Over time we had worked out how to distribute ourselves across the basement and the ground and second floors[84] in harmony, grace, and what seemed to me a huge amount of luxury, as a poor person used to living and working in small rooms.

I still hadn't gone up to the third floor — though I now owned everything in the workshop: by specific bequest, Spak had told me as he gave me the key.

The building used to be a bank, and it still has some bankish accoutrements, such as a huge walk-in safe in the basement, and, in another office in the basement, a big floor safe that looks just like the big black gold-trimmed boxes in cowboy heist movies. We'd had both of them refurbished.

Alas, Kirk and Lennie decided to carry on in their previous location, so unfortunately we couldn't fill their office with Tribbles for the opening[85], but luckily Dafydd Spak, who reminds me of a Rex cat and whom I call my multicultural poster child of a lawyer because of his excellent name, was made of sterner stuff and came over to our side, to be our lawyer-of-all-trades: for me and my business, for Own Domains, for various weird projects such as smart paper exploration, apparently now for accusations

---

84. In Europe, this would be the ground and first floors, but we are raw and rude colonials. Same note goes for the third floor, which I never ever call the second floor, even if it is the second storey above the ground floor.

85. Not that some of us *cough* me *cough* didn't think of it. I still have ten of the first twelve I bought. You can trip a switch and they vibrate and trill just like the real thing, er, the fictional thing. Bun and Micah Five really like them. Hence their diminishing population: I am propitiating the cat gods one Tribble at a time.

of murder, and to do whatever else he wanted to do. We like Dafydd Spak a lot, and we think he might like us, though he maintains a level of legal and personal sang-froid that is frankly exceptional.

Also he gets along with Roma as if they were twins separated at birth, which is a disturbing image on so many levels but describes their bond, which seems to include a private language none of the rest of us speaks, as well as a similar logical approach to problem-solving. Roma is the tech wizard of the two, and Spak knows All The Statutes. Between them, they give the impression that the League of Justice is real. Combine them in a room with Roger and you have every possible investigative option, though Roger tends not to see them as resources so much as ancillary nuisances to me, his prime nuisance.

Prime nuisance except when I own the world's entire supply of smart paper, half of it previously owned by a criminal mastermind, that is.

48. PAREIDOLIA

We spread the pieces of Lockwood Chiles's smart paper out on Mr. Spak's [86] boardroom table. There were more than I thought, seen like that rather than one at a time as was my habit. Several of them were the ones I'd tried to destroy by cutting, but except for being octavo instead of quarto, they looked — and were — just as pristine.

Nathan Bierce and Lockwood Chiles had set up a friendly side competition to invent this stuff. They had spent six months or a year, and scads of money, on it and had arrived at very similar points from very different directions.

---

86. I love calling him that. Even though I now have full permission to call him by his first name.

Nathan's smart papers varied as he refined them, but he seemed to have settled on a soft bright white with the feel of a fine hand-made cotton laid paper, a bit like an even-more-upmarket Arches, that held India ink and watercolour paint extremely well if you told them to, but never got an accidental smudge you couldn't wipe off with a tissue. They were easy to use and open to all, unless the user requested to activate a seamless password, voice-print, finger-print, or retinal-scan authentication protocol. Their programming was apparently quite elegant, which fits with who he was.

Lockwood Chiles had started his process with an almost militarised level of paranoia, so that it was necessary to remove levels of security to achieve any kind of normal access. I've mentioned that if they felt threatened, these pages called up — I mean actually summoned, via a signal-to-a-satellite alarm system — that private police force that Lock had created, theoretically for company security at Nathan Lockwood LLP[87]. These folks would knock on your door or break it down, depending on the perceived threat level[88]. As had Nathan, Lock had experimented with a range of finishes and tints, which made the earlier iterations hard to tell apart, but in the end he decided on a hard-pressed type of finish, and his final favourite had a slight grey undertone, very subtle, and a slightly greasier surface feel — in essence, IMHO[89], also a metaphor for his entire life: publicly a software inventor, secretly a greasy grey psychopath.

Metaphors abound if you look for them. Pareidolia of a sort.

We had tried. We really had. And we had tried not to talk much while we worked, because we knew that this stuff was listening.

---

87. Sometimes called Nathan Lockwood World in its prime, but it was really an LLP in all the countries that allow them. FWIW.

88. We now had an arrangement. To prevent property damage at least. Some of them are rather nice folks.

89. Perhaps not so humble.

Inside the copper room, that paper was probably lonely as hell, with nothing but other sheets of itself to talk to, but we were keenly aware that we were messing with stuff that was the tech equivalent of magical grimoires, and, like the ones in all the stories and movies, if given its freedom this stuff would as soon kill us as look at us.

None of the paper was activated at the moment, as far as we knew, so the overall effect of a whole bank of blank greyish-white sheets was a bit like those shiny grey-and-white interiors that are used as the sets of Russian TV crime series. Very crisp and ultra-modern, with an undertone of menace.

"Turn one on," said Roger. "Show me."

I had the security guys on speed-dial. My phone software had auto-coloured their little dot a hot pink, which was kind of strange, but unmistakeable. I stepped out into the hall to make the call, and put it on speaker so Dafydd and Roger could hear us.

"Marston," a manly-man voice barked. I love these guys. They're all like that.

Roger made a face[90], which I also loved.

"Vinnie," I said. "How are you? How's the kid's semester going?" I had made it a point to know some things about these guys, in case it helped someday.

"Paris," said Marston. "Sketching in the Musée d'Orsay. Scholarship." He sounded proud, in a laconic sort of way. I tried to imagine the family dinner table. Glock 19s and van Goghs? I knew he was a single dad. Perhaps the kid's mom hadn't been able to take the cognitive dissonance.

"We're gonna do some stuff with the paper now," I said. "For about an hour, I think. In the room, but something may get out. Just turn it all off at your end, okay?"

"I'll stand the guys down," said Vinnie. Their team was almost half women, but to Vinnie Marston, they were all guys. I grinned

---

90. *Almost* a moué.

at Roger and eyerolled toward the screen. I could do this because I have a little piece of leopard-patterned duct tape[91] over each of the lenses of my smartphone camera. I learned a few things last year about who can see what when and how. I try to minimise the risk, and sometimes the low-tech ways are best[92].

"Thanks, buddy," I said. "Say hi to Sharon and Bob and Hikaru for me." Those were the other shifts' team leaders for this bizarre call centre[93].

"Will do," he said, and hung up. I went back into the boardroom and tossed my phone on the credenza.

In that room, it becomes basically a brick that tells time.

Because here is a thing that we have done to Dafydd Spak's boardroom.

It's in the basement of a 1911 building, as I said, and thus has brick and concrete and stone walls that are a bit of a barrier to digital signals anyway, and by the use of some[94] of Nathan's money (technically, the foundation's money) and some interesting materials installed by some really peculiar people[95], we have made it into a self-contained Faraday cage. We can shutter the high

---

91. Properly "duck tape" (look it up), but not an argument I'm ready to have with my editor yet.

92. Why is it that it bothers me less that someone might illicitly hear me than see me? Humans are odd. Like how we shield our heads when it rains and then are miserable when our clothes and shoes get wet.

93. Did you know it takes a minimum of four people to staff a single shift 24/7? It's better with five, though. You learn weird factoids in life. I once had to make the schedules for a facility where I worked. Vinnie was old-school so he only had four crews. As a personnel policy it sucked for so many reasons, but it kept the family small.

94. Actually, really a lot, from my perspective, since I still think a good cut of steak is a luxury expenditure.

95. Who look as if I ordered them up from Central Casting, which I did, in a way.

little clerestory windows[96] that look out on the feet of people on the sidewalk, and turn off the land line with one flick of an inconspicuous switch on the wall back by the little fridge and amenities station, and be completely self-contained. There is some sound-baffling layer along with the metal mesh so that sound is, you know, baffled, and can't get in (sort of like that old joke about the soprano) or out. There is even the potential to isolate it from the electrical grid so surveillance can't use the wiring to monitor what's within, and the cage itself can be electrified[97]. I am told all this makes it da bomb in cybersecurity.

I like that.

After my last adventures with Lockwood, we all knew that there were levels of digital expertise that rendered ordinary privacy a joke, and I had a little PTSD[98] about that. We — which means I proposed, Spak and Roma disposed — had decided we needed one place, outside the secure command centre bunker room at the cop shop, where we could feel safe.

This room was as close as we could get without doing a Pratchett[99].

Now, the only risk was in what this paper was doing passively: Listening? Recording? It couldn't transmit for the moment, but

---

96. On the inside, with a gap before the actual windows, and made of a vibration dampening material, because we are paranoid as fuck, the peculiar people were even more so, and I go to the movies *and* read cyberpunk novels a lot. Also there is a vibration generator on vulnerable points which masks speech by a kind of white noise principle. And some other stuff that the weird little boffins thought of.

97. Don't ask me why. When I asked, I was told — in these words — by the weird boffins: "It's a feature." Okay then. Feature vs. bug — *that* I understand.

98. The real clinical kind and, actually, a lot. Also, it's not paranoia if the risk is real, right?

99. "DARK IN HERE, ISN'T IT?"

if it were ever released into the wild, we weren't sure what would happen.

"What do you want to see?"

"How it works," said Roger. "What's on it. Then we can put it away."

Put it away and talk freely, he meant. Because even before we'd talked about safety protocols on the way over, he had been just as worried about the stuff as I was.

49. RANDO

I handed Roger one of the octavo[100] sheets of Lockstock, the bisecting of which had proved to me that the full-sized pages are holographic enough to be cut in half a couple of times and still retain their data and functionality. After that, they toughen up and resist[101] damage. And believe me, I've tried.

This piece could at least be written on permanently, and it had a mark on the corner in teal Sharpie™ which indicated that we've found and transcribed contents (we think). Teal? That's Roma's work. It's colour-coded to the transcript, as are her paper clips. Teal, turquoise, purple, and royal blue. Roma doesn't like dull colours. Are we sure we've transcribed everything? Of course not. When you can get as many gigabytes of storage on a tiny little chip as is possible these days, imagine how many gazillionabytes that could be, under the right circumstances, secreted in something the size of a piece of paper. And is it recording *us*? Who knows. It's certainly capable.

"It bends," said Roger. "Those business cards Nathan and

---

100. Roughly. They riffed off North American paper at 8½-by-11 inches, so half here is 8½-by-5½ inches. Yeah, inches. Sue my retrograde ass.

101. And in Lock's case they call for backup. I really have to quit harping on that, but, like all of Lock's legacy, as well as being dangerous it is *so fucking annoying*.

Lock gave out, they were hard. You could clean under your fingernails with the corners."

"That's a salubrious image. Those were made to imitate card stock. This stuff imitates cotton laid paper, basically. Watercolour paper, or really fine stationery. There's a protocol that stiffens it up a little and another that makes it more floppy. And do not say one word of the joke you just thought of."

"Okay, take it as said. But it does occur to me that maybe Lockwood Chiles had some serious sexual performance issues in addition to his self-esteem problem."

Spak chuckled slightly. In a less restrained person it might have been a snort. Spak, however, does not snort. "You certainly get that impression when you look at this material and how it was linked to his security network."

"Do you have the transcript for this one?"

Spak handed it to him. "This one is business notes, mostly. Dictation to his staff. Instructions to prepare a legal agreement with some rando arms dealer."

"'Rando'?"

"I have kids, you know how it happens."

Not really, but never mind. I mean, I know how kids happen, but "rando"? Spak? I stipulate the concept of linguistic contamination, your honour. Moving on now.

"The thing to note," Spak went on, "is how sneaky a deal it really was. This guy Chiles was mean and smart. Dangerous even to the dangerous people. This one basically says that if there are issues with the armaments, he can return them, in pieces, by a shipping method of his choosing, including but not limited to loading little bits of them into projectile weapons and firing them back at a muzzle velocity of 715 metres per second[102]."

---

102. Or 2,350 feet per second. This is the muzzle velocity of an AK-47. See? What useful things smart paper can teach us.

"Seriously?" Roger sounded almost impressed. Hmph.

"Pretty close. It's one *seriously* effective indemnity clause, that's all I'll say about it."

"Do we have any idea whether the other party's goods failed?"

"No," I said. "Nor do we know why Lock was buying armaments. We think they might have been to bribe local warlords to leave a factory of his alone. Nathan thought they'd closed down any assets in war zones or totalitarian regimes, but we now think that Lock bought them through a shell company instead of dissolving them, and carried on with production as a kind of a side hustle."

"How did he explain the product?"

"He set up a shell factory somewhere else," I replied. "Paperwork in one of these other pages proves it. Nathan was paying decent wages and benefits to staff who didn't exist, while Lock had cheap sweatshops with machine-gun-toting guards. Collecting at both ends. Otherfucker."

"Piece of slime."

"That would be an understatement," said Spak. "Slime has an ecological function." You see why I love this guy. He knows how to do a drive-by slagging without even shooting his cuffs.

Roger thought up some clever tests for the paper. He tried piercing it with a red-hot pin. He had a lot of fun with crumpling it, then stomping on it before it sprang back flat. He microwaved it, as we had tried, and watched the subdued sparking, then I tapped the page and we listened to Lock Chiles's voice reading from a manifest of small guns and ammunition, just as if he'd never been disturbed.

Roger looked at the little bar fridge in the corner. "Have you tried freezing it, then hitting it with something hard?" We hadn't.

"I'll try that tomorrow," said Spak, turning the little fridge to maximum coldness to prepare. "Don't expect anything."

It was almost half an hour, though it felt like forever, before Roger got tired of playing with the pages and we started stacking them to return them to Spak's safe. We checked them off against the inventory and returned them to the proper cells in the accordion file where they were kept. That file folder looks normal, but it is hefty: it is made of solid copper sheets and copper mesh.

The safe is off the conference room. It's a big old walk-in, room-sized, with walls inches thick, and set in concrete. Even though a cell phone was already useless in there, we'd lined it with copper just in case.

That's where Lockwood Chiles's toxic legacy resides.

On that stack of paper is everything we need to know about Chiles's evil empire. It frustrates the hell out of me on an ongoing basis (cf. my secret hobby) that we can't get access to it all.

He died with his passwords intact[103].

50. THE RIGHT QUESTION

Paper safely shut in its box, and safe safely safed-up, we returned to the boardroom. Roger made a point of checking that a piece of the stuff hadn't got away from us, even though I rolled my eyes at him — as if we hadn't gone through our rigorous and annoying security protocols. There was nothing in that little freezer yet. The floor, desk, and chairs were clear.

"So, I've been patient," said Dafydd, "but what are we doing here, exactly?"

"I'll get to that in a minute," said Roger. "Listen, you two keep talking about how that stuff phones home like ET . . ."

"Yeah," I said at the same time that Spak said "Yes" with as much disdain as his soft, even voice ever conveyed.

Roger paused until he had our attention, and then a second more.

---

103. Cue the *Fistful of Dollars* music. But maybe in an ominous minor key? Make sure there's a tuba.

"Why?"

We looked back at him.

"Why?" he repeated.

We looked at him some more. My mind was racing, and I suspect Dafydd Spak's was too. When someone asks the right question in a room of smart people[104], there is often that moment of silence.

"Um, because Lock was a paranoid, psychopathic, violence-loving criminal?" I ventured, then held up my hand. "No, don't say it. It's not enough, is it?"

"No," said Roger.

"We took it for granted," Spak said slowly. "All this time."

"Well, yeah, we all did," said Roger. "Because it fit with Chiles's character. So no-one ever actually said, why would he bother?"

I nodded. "The paper itself has all the security it needs. It doesn't tell anyone anything it doesn't want to. At the risk of making it sound sentient. Sapient."

"I think we have to talk that way, for convenience. Because it is, sort of. The paper is a good soldier. It does what it is told."

"So it reports to someone. Because it was told to do so. Why, and to whom?"

"Exactly. Now Chiles is putatively dead, but —"

"Putatively?" said Spak, so we had to explain it to him.

After he recovered from the immediate shock, and we had the inevitable discussion about how "as much as seven years" was a long time and a lot of bad guys and all that, Spak went back to Roger's statement.

"So Chiles is dead, we think. We hope. But now, we don't *know*, is that what you are saying?"

"Yes," I said, just as Roger said, "No."

---

104. If I do say so myself.

We looked at him.

"I am not saying anything about the status of a putative victim in a room with a Person of Interest in his putative murder, and her lawyer. I am just thinking about the ongoing investigations into the criminality of his putatively-former empire."

"And?"

"So Chiles is dead. And before that he was in jail, with no Internet access by the judge's decree, and all his assets frozen pending a multi-year process of disposition of his estate. And yet, the system is still running. Has been all this time. Why?"

"The simple answer," Dafydd said, "is that the companies are in the hands of a trustee who is allowing them to run as per usual, to keep up the value of the estate for the heirs, or whoever gets it, once they are determined. So all the — shall we call them cogs? — are still turning as before."

"But that's not really true, is it?" said Rog. "All the real businesses, yes. All the legit stuff, yes. All the stuff that was joint with Nathan Bierce, yes. Everything above-board and known would theoretically be ticking over just fine. But shouldn't Lock's own little machinations, which were secret to everyone, which profited him secretly, and sometimes emotionally, have fallen apart by now? It is years now since Lockwood Chiles was putatively cut off from his assets."

"And yet," I said slowly, "the teams haven't been stood down. Vinnie and Sharon and Bob and Hikaru still show up, and get paid by someone."

"And Uncle Tom Cobley and all," said Spak unexpectedly.

For a few moments, no-one spoke — very literary of us.

51. REAL COFFEE

Roger wasn't done, so he soon interrupted our moment of intellectual satisfaction.

"So . . ."

"Wait," I said, having learned something from him just a little while ago. "Let me enjoy it for a moment more." I paused a little longer than rhetorically necessary. "Okay, go ahead."

He glowered at me. Back to normal, then. Good. I poured him a cup of coffee from the office carafe. He took it and swigged without thinking, then grinned.

"Yeah, I can handle the high-test now. So. Imagine, if you will, how to test a proposition that Chiles is or is not dead. Take your pick of which side you want to start. I am starting with the thought he may not in fact be dead and that all this is some kind of elaborate deception. I think the chances are low, but recent events have introduced more than a scintilla of doubt[105], and it is incumbent upon us to test it. People are depending on this.

"Then imagine, which is actually now true, that we mistrust many of the traditional pieces or types of evidence that we once thought empirically solid. Imagine, though it's also true, that some idiot at the lab was sacrificing objectivity for the sake of prosecutorial success, whether intentionally or by a kind of, what's that thing you natter about, that confirmation bias thingy?"

"'Thingy'. Is that a police term or a scientific term?"

"Shut up. So, imagine we are in this situation, and we have one thing that is solid. It's in that vault. It calls home when it feels threatened. It knows that somewhere out there is a network it can trust. Since it was built by a nefarious bad guy, we can assume nefariousness."

"Nefaricity? Nefarionism? Nefariosity?"

"Shut up," said Roger, and Spak at the same time said, "Is it actually truly possible to assume nefariety?" and smirked at us.

---

105. Yes, he said "scintilla". I *have* mentioned there are reasons I like him, right? Despite everything.

Roger glowered, but, "I'm serious, actually," Dafydd went on. "The police tend to assume that crime begets crime, and that anything a criminal does is by default criminal. Hammer, nail. But Lockwood Chiles was also head of security for a multinational. He had a lot of legitimate business activities. He had a girlfriend."

"Whom he murdered," I reminded them.

"The point is," Spak said patiently, "he did a lot of normal things too. You can't say that a criminal and a police officer who are both brushing their teeth are committing different acts of hygiene because of who they are. Some acts are neutral."

"Not helpful," said Roger.

"When it gets to court, these questions will be asked."

"Fair point. Ask away."

"What are you really testing?" Spak went on. "You yank a string. Don't think it's not obvious what string. A piece of that paper is accidentally removed from the Faraday cage after it has been told some disinformation. We then wait to see what happens. What you are testing is solely and only what happens when it 'phones home' as you keep calling it. Will a mothership of some kind come and take it away?"

We must have been giving him A Look because he said, "What? Everyone has seen that film!"

"Will Lock be driving the mothership?" I said.

"And if he's not," continued Spak, "because he is as verifiably dead as it was humanly possible to determine, what will the mothership look like, and who will be driving?"

"Forget goddamn *E.T.* And you *pilot* motherships, not drive them[106], for fuck's sake," Roger said. "Lock could be alive but not piloting ... er, he could stay behind the scenes and send minions."

"Fact. But it would be productive, wouldn't it? Or anyway instructive. No matter who is dri— ... who responds?"

---

106. Everybody knows that!

We enjoyed that thought for a moment.

"Dafydd is right, though," I said. "We're poking this bear to see what emerges. It's unlikely to prove anything unless Lock shows up, which is extremely unlikely, because he's dead and we're just being paranoid, and if he isn't, how stupid would he have to be to show up in person?"

"He showed up at your house when he could have sent an extraction team," said Roger.

"Point," I said.

"Extraction team?" said Spak.

"Roger watches movies too," I confided to him, and he let himself smile a little more, which for him was a guffaw.

"Well, it was an idea," said Roger.

"No, it's a good idea," I said.

"It's the only idea anyone has," said Dafydd Spak.

We couldn't deny that he had hit the nail on the head.

But it *was* a good idea. Especially measured, as Spak reminded us, against all the other ideas available, but also on its own.

"Now we just need a plan," I said.

"There is no 'we'," Roger said. "This will be a police matter from now on."

"What smart paper were you wanting to use again?" I said.

"Warrant," he said.

"Don't be an asshole," I said.

"I'm sure something can be worked out," said Mr. Spak.

I COULDN'T SEE HIM THERE AT ALL

52. A FUCKING STYLE EPIDEMIC

Everywhere I went, I saw dyed-blond hipster-Mohawk demi-skinheads. Cooking in the trendy vegan restaurant at the end of the street. On the bus. Shopping at the Downtown Farmers' Market. Selling phones in the mall. Playing with their babies in the playground of the community centre. In photos above bylines in online news services. Going into bars pretty much everywhere. At the photocopy shop. In fire engines and patrol cars. Even one of the phone techs who came to Own Domains to fix the wireless Internet had a fancy dye-and-razor job, though she wasn't white or tall or male enough to be a suspect. Apparently, guys of a certain build and age, and a few women too, feel moved to bleach their hair, get the sides shaved in patterns and perm the top, buy shorty leather jackets à lá Tom-Cruise-as-Reacher, and get a pair of black Docs. It was a fucking style epidemic.

Fleury came to the door every day. "Did you hear from the cops about Danny?"

Every day I told him something. Half of it was lies, though. Because truth?

Truth was there were no leads, and if there were, Heather would not be telling me anyway. She seemed to regret that moment of expansiveness at my place, and as the days went on, she got shorter and shorter with me. I began to wonder whether my initial liking had been some kinda Stockholm-syndrome thing. You think the good investigator is sympathetic.

But I called her again anyway. "Look, would you just drop in one day and talk to Fleury?"

"Come to Central Division," she said.

"Fleury's afraid of the cop shop," I said.

"Police Headquarters, we like to call it," she said. "I don't have time to go down there."

"It's two blocks away. I'll give you lunch across the street."

"I don't take gifts."

So there we were.

So I went to the cop shop by myself. The omnipresent smoke wasn't quite at *Blade Runner* intensity any more, but still, that morning, it made the whole city look like the Hell in some Gaiman TV show — hazy, brown, fragmented towers, all that. There was another bleached-blondish cop behind the counter, male this time. Fucking everywhere.

Heather came out to meet me and led me over to the chairs farthest from the counter. Her eyes were looking only slightly better. Maybe she had been suffering the forest fire smoke too.

"Can't we go in and sit in one of the meeting rooms?" I said.

"Protocol," she said. "No members of the public behind the shields."

Convenient protocol. I've been in those rooms a dozen times, as a member of the public, over the last couple of years especially. "What's the problem?" I said. "I mean, your problem with me. I can see something's eating you."

"I talked to Dave," she said.

Ah. Dave, who had just been promoted to detective a few weeks ago, a fast rise from being a gofer a few years ago, and was probably now her protégé or something (they *had* been at the crime scene in tandem). Dave, who considered me the prime suspect in hiring a death.

"The boss might like you, but Dave thinks you're crook. It's always the ones who hang around the cops. Try to insert themselves into the investigations."

So I was a fool who got involved, and she didn't like that I talked with her boss.

"Are you fucking kidding me? My boyfriend[107] and my best friend got killed. I didn't insert myself . . ." I trailed off, because I had. I really had. Gotten involved. I probably was a fool.

"How would I even do that?" I asked her. "How would I even find someone?"

"Crooked lawyers go in there all the time, along with the straight ones."

"Why would someone risk that? Getting caught? They'd be in there forever. What's the inducement?"

"Pack of cigarettes," she said flatly.

I looked at her blankly. "Seriously? That's off some crazy TV show. A cliché."

"Happens. Life's a cliché. Or somebody promises to take care of somebody on the outside — or threatens them. Promises a witness to lie in court to get them off something serious. Pay for a lawyer they can't afford. Bail. Whatever. Pack of cigarettes."

"Cigarette-equivalents. You think they measured out a life in cigarette-equivalents."

---

107. I usually say partner, but I was trying to speak the local dialect. '*Boy*friend', FFS.

Roger would have said, *Well, they sure as fuck don't have coffee spoons in there.* Heather said, "Dave says you hated the dude."

"Of course I fucking hated him," I said. "But if I did a fucking Lizzie Borden on everybody I hated, I would have started twenty years ago, right at the top, and the world would be a cleaner place."

Heather looked at me for a moment. "Okay, I'll concede that, maybe."

"And Lizzie Borden mighta been innocent, too, you ever consider that? It was all circumstantial." She gave me That Look. Seriously, why do people keep doing that? I probably shouldn't say out loud *everything* I think. I *really* shouldn't.

Bit late now.

"Fleury is starving to death from grief," I said. "Anorexia dolorosa. Give me something."

"I went to the base," she said. "That blond perm thing? Some hairdresser out there has been talking every second asshole into thinking that's the new macho hardass look, expensive bleach and perm to accessorise with their black boots and their expensive bomber jackets. There's a fucking brigade of them out there. Pun unintended[108]. We're looking into it."

"Yeah, I've seen the same thing all over town. Was there a movie or something?"

"Fucked if I know. I don't have time to watch movies."

She got up and prepared to escort me to the automatic door like the Martha Stewart of detectives. Just before we got into range of the electric eye, though, she stopped.

She stood for a moment, waiting for me to leave, and I stood for a minute, just to push a little. She reached under her glasses with a pinky finger and rubbed the corner of one eye, then the other, delicately and probably unconsciously, and looked away, toward

---

108. "But inevitable," I murmured in the background.

the armoured window where you went to make complaints, at the cops behind the armoured glass.

Front desk is the job they give to not-quite-suspended cops, on administrative duties because they wouldn't be good but the union wouldn't let them be fired. First you see their names in the papers, and then on the nametags at the front desk. Sometimes then SIRT[109] proves it on them and they go down, despite the police association[110], but more of the time they get away with it. Bear: eats/gets eaten. When they get away with it, I rant, sometimes to Roger, and he growls, bearlike, me-adjacent but not *at* me. Good cops hate dirty cops.

One of the three guys there was the blondie I'd noticed before, who had a lean and hungry look; one was tall and shaven-headed and handsome in that odd way where their face was widest at the back of the jawbones under the ears, and he looked half-asleep; one was a dyspeptic-looking plump guy who could have been the poster guy for one of those viral videos, shown with their knee on someone's neck, which probably meant he was the only good guy there, just to show me not to profile. I sighed.

Heather followed the direction of my gaze, and she sighed too.

"If Fleury wants to do something to help his buddy Dan get justice, despite front desk appearances," she said, "tell him to get those street people to talk to me. He shows up with any more witnesses, I'll come over in a New York minute, any time, day or night. You've got my card."

"So in other words," I said, "you've got nothing."

"Jack shit," she said. "Have a nice day."

---

109. Serious Incident Response Team.

110. Which is really a union.

53. A LEAF IN THE WIND

We didn't decide on a particular day for any systematic reason. We hadn't consulted any entrails[III], oracles, or soothsayers.

We just got antsy.

First I called Vinnie and asked him to come over for a meeting that morning. Once in the Faraday, I let him in on the plan. We weren't taking much of a risk: Roger had checked him out as much as he could, and found no evidence he was more than the guy we saw. WYSIWYG Security Co. Ltd.

"Just let them do what they would normally do if it calls," I said, "except please don't kick down any doors or shoot anyone."

"I never shoot anyone," he said. "Tempting sometimes, when the kid was a teenager." Perhaps Vinnie could be saved.

"And please don't tell the others," Mr. Spak said. "We want them to act naturally."

"Natural," I said.

"Whatever," said Roma.

If it were done, 'twere better it were done quickly. That afternoon we stood in an uneasy group outside Faraday[112]: Roger, Mr. Spak, Roma, and me, all united in impatience and foolhardiness.

Even Mr. Spak looked almost eager. He was changing. I suppose life does that to everyone. It was unsettling.

"Are you ready?" I said to Roger.

Of course we weren't ready.

"Sure," he said. "Let's do it."

Because why not risk life and limb and our fates and our futures. Hmmm? What else was new?

III. I am opposed to divination by vivisection, despite its popularity in ancient times. Although I do have a couple of cats to whom I sometimes say I want to do violence, I assure you that is only in the abstract.

112. The boardroom *and* the cage. Economical name, that.

"I should caution everyone —" Spak began, but Roger and I turned to look at him with That Look, and he simply nodded and opened the door.

Roma went to get the big file, and we spread out a few pages and started pretending to work.

The page we had chosen to release into the wild was one of the smaller pieces from our experiment with cutting the paper in quarters. We chose it because it had dozens of files that without a key just looked like lists of random numbers. Perfect for pretending we had found a key. I tapped it alive with a few of the others.

"What's on this one?"

"Check this out!"

And then the line I'd been rehearsing to make it sound as natural as possible: "Hey, guys, I think I found . . . hey! If you put that key over there to work on . . . wait . . . are these *passwords*?"

"Oh my god; holy crap! That's . . . !" Roma sounded completely natural. Later I would have to remember to ask her if she'd ever done any community theatre.

"Sorry," I said. "Look, we need to check these out, see what they're for. It looks like maybe . . . bank accounts?"

"Oh, wait, shhh, what if it's recor—"

"Oops."

"Let's put all this away and go upstairs," interrupted Mr. Spak, almost as if he hadn't been scripted to do so.

So we did, with more or less our usual small talk, and everything went back in the safe — but the quarter-sheet was "accidentally" shuffled up with Roma's papers, and carried up with us.

Hikaru and Bob both showed up, along with the bulky uniformed minion from Bob's shift, because we had caught them at shift change and Hikaru was curious.

"We have orders that a sheet of paper needs to be repatriated," said Bob.

Okay, *now* I could have some fun with this.

"Repatriated? What the hell does that mean?"

"We have to take it with us, ma'am." I didn't know Bob very well, and vice versa. Ma'am? Srsly.

"This stuff all belongs to me! I was given it!"

"Apparently, this piece is different," said Hikaru.

"Why?"

I could see he was wondering the same thing, and that it bothered him to say, "I don't know."

"But we have to insist, ma'am," said Bob.

After some searching, they showed us the innocent little A8 sheet that was the cause of their call-out.

We managed to act all surprised, nay, verily even shocked, and only resisted slightly when Bob put it into a thick envelope that I bet had a metal lining, just like in the movies.

Mr. Spak was brilliant. He made Bob sign a receipt.

We stood at the front windows of Own Domains and watched the three of them get into their black Hummer. Hummer, FFS. In this day and age. When they had safely left not just the building but the area, we grinned at each other.

"'Oops'?" Roma finally allowed herself to roll her eyes at me.

"Yeah, whatever. It did the job, right?"

"We should keep working on trying to decode what's on the paper," said Roma. "We have no idea how long this will take."

"You are getting wiser, Grasshopper," said Roger, who should have known better by now.

Roma just smiled at him sadly. "I'm so sorry," she said. "It must be tough to be so old and still have to work. Gambling debts, was it?"

In our state at that moment, we found this joke funnier than it deserved.

When I left the office, I admit I checked out the street, and looked behind me a few times, but nothing weird showed up. The next day, the others admitted they felt it too, that sense of some remote surveillance clicking in.

I never really lost that feeling over the next while. I remembered what it felt like to know that Chiles was stalking me, and to still have to give him the rope to hang himself[113]. It was a shaky, vulnerable place to live, and I didn't like having to be there again.

But days went by, and nothing happened — on that front, anyway. Front, haha, storm metaphor, get it?

Other stuff went on happening, though, because weather doesn't take breaks.

And when the other shoe dropped, we didn't even realise it.

54. "WHERE DID YOU COME FROM, COTTON-EYE JOE?"

Hep and I try to eat at this one hot pot place every month or two. Asian Express Hot Pot is in a little mini-mall hard by where I used to work. It is also remarkable for its single-pot tables, which allows people like Hep, with food allergies, to eat on a level playing field with people like me who can — and will — eat anything[114].

It also allows untrammelled conversation, because everyone is talking and, in the din, no-one is eavesdropping.

---

113. Metaphorically, of course — we don't have the death penalty in Canada.

114. Except crickets. Well, so far, anyway. If one of these days Kim talks me into following Pris's very public example in that documentary, and trying fried termites and cricket protein, I hereby declare, being of sound mind except for the crickets, that I leave Bunnywit to Roger so I can annoy him from the great beyond, Micah to Kim of course, my fine china to Jian, my books to Denis, all the smart paper to Mr. Spak, and split my entire wardrobe between Roma and Hep. I am still deciding who will get the Epitome. I promise to eat no crickets until I figure that out.

I filled Hep in on everything. Sometimes I did lower my voice to a confidential murmur, but when I was done, she knew everything I know. (Come on, I'm not even going to *approach* that obvious a joke; it's a figure of speech, right?)

Hep cut right to the chase. "Is Chiles alive?"

"Not that we know of."

"Is he dead?"

"They promise me that he is."

"But you still feel as if you are being followed, right? I saw you pick a seat where you can see the door, even though you hate facing the windows usually."

"Yeah, I'm a bit — unconvinced. But there isn't, as a pal of mine says, a scintilla of evidence that I need to worry."

"Right. And what are you doing to clear your name of that murder accusation?"

"Clear my name? I'm not a Person of Interest any more."

"And if you believe that, I have a lovely bridge in New York City that I will sell you cheap. Cheaply? Anyway, a very good deal, just for you."

"Cheap. Cheaply would refer to your manner of selling, and my dear, you are never cheap."

"Seriously."

"Come *on*! Roger *said* —"

"Has Roger come right out and said, 'Don't worry, kiddo, I know you didn't do it'?"

"Um."

"Isn't Dave still looking at you as if he's measuring you for an orange jumpsuit or whatever the hell they wear in the Max up here?"

"Um."

"And while you are being all co-operative and assisting police with their enquiries, has anyone actually offered you any protection or suggested that the risk you are taking might be out of line?"

"Um. Not as such."

"So you are being treated like a perp who is helping them with a sting, not like Roger's old pal of sterling character and provenance. Righty-ho."

"'Righty-ho'?"

"You need to actually be cleared. You need to be walking in the sunlight again."

"Such as it is," I said, gesturing out the window.

Hep just pursed her lips and shook her head. "So what can we do to make that happen?"

"As far as I can tell, nothing. Can't go interrogate prisoners all over the country. Can't go into the jail and ask the staff. I mean, I can easily *imagine* myself undercover as a trans man poking around a jail-like movie set, like the premise of some fantastic mini-series, but the real thing? Only in the B-est of B-movies. Can't see the physical evidence or the police file. Even if I weren't on the PoI list. Can't ask Dave because he does not seem to be neutral concerning me."

"Curious. I wonder why? One would think that your stellar character would overcome your hinky past —"

"'Hinky'?"

"— your hinky past, your tattoos and piercings, your peculiar parents, your strange good taste and luck in attracting billion-aires, your —"

"Attracting plural billionaires? I only had o—"

"— for good *or* evil, I mean. I don't blame you for Chiles. He was a natural disaster looking for places to happen. Speaking of which, add to that list: *and* your suspicious ability to benefit from disaster."

"Are you fucking kidding me?"

"Tell me that isn't what 'Newly-Detective Prasan Dave' thinks."

"Okay, I concede. He probably does see me that way. He has almost said as much, in fact. But I can't think of a thing I can personally do to change that. As you old people say, it is all happening in a Universe far far away."

"Oh, now you're just being cruel."

"Well, you *are* old. Compared to some. Of course, now that I have Kim, I am also old."

"You have Kim, now, do you?"

"You know what I mean."

"And *you* know what *I* mean. If it fits, I sits."

I did. And it did fit, but it itched like a tight wool sweater.

She laughed — right *at* me, not *with* me — and I shook my head. "You only do it to annoy, and 'cause you know it teases," I misquoted.

"I always hated that rhyme," said Hep. "I wasn't *beaten* when I sneezed, but . . . well, I wasn't beaten when I *sneezed*, I mean . . . Never mind, that was a long time ago, and besides, the witch is dead."

"And on that cheery note — there *is*, however, something I can try on Fleury's behalf. After lunch, let's go see Mina."

"Mina? Oh, right, Mina. Jeez, I hated when you worked at that place. Bunch of assholes. But I liked Mina."

"You will still like her, I guarantee."

55. SILVER THREADS AMONG THE GOLD . . . OR SOMETHING SOMETHING SOMETHING

The air was no longer hammered brass, but it was still almost the colour of the light broth we'd been using to cook our lunch — at the moment of its arrival at our table, I clarify[115], not after all the ingredients went in.

---

115.   See what I did there? I slay myself, sometimes, I really do.

It was also very hot out, also like the broth.

We strolled the couple of blocks to my old workplace, the name of which I am forbidden to mention by the terms of my settlement. Let's just say it is not one with a completely secular approach to charitable activity, and leave it there. It's actually as inclusive as it can stand to be, unlike the nearby Sally Ann, so it's a "from each according to their ability" sort of thing — and they do employ Mina, which speaks to a core of good sense in there. And to be fair, they hired *me* and kept me there for a lot of years, and I wasn't quiet during any of those.

Mina was hosing down the front sidewalk. She had given one guy, of the several hanging about, a big push broom, and he was sweeping trash and his buddies were helping put it into a big bin.

"Remind me to complain about bad urban design," she said by way of greeting. "When they built this place, all they could think about was getting the biggest footprint. They didn't think about staging our clients, comfortable outdoor spaces —"

"Speaking to the converted," said Hep.

"Mina, do you remember meeting Hep? Madeline Pritchard, actually, but we call her —"

"I can see why," said Mina, who never waited for redundancies to complete. "I remember you."

"Listen —" I said.

"She wants favours," Mina said to Hep. "She who only comes around here for favours."

"Seriously? I came and made sandwiches —"

"— last year," Mina finished for me.

"I . . . I've been . . . busy," I said.

"The dead are dead," said Mina. "We owe to the living."

"Is that a proverb?"

Mina ignored me, but "It should be!" said Hep.

"Am I going to regret re-introducing you two?"

"Probably," they said in unison, then burst out laughing.

"Yeah, very funny," I said, trying not to laugh myself. "Look, we need to talk about Fleury."

"Poor Fleury. That was terrible, what happened to poor Dan."

"What's terrible is that no-one but Fleur will talk to the cops. There must be people who have seen that gang of thugs, but they all play Three Monkeys."

"Three monkeys? You mean the Three Wise Monkeys? But that is a good thing!" Mina exclaimed. "Avoiding impropriety!"

"In the West, that idiom has come to mean turning away from seeing any evils, not abstaining from evil," Hep helpfully Hepsplained.

"Yeah, and it also doesn't work. Those assholes will just keep going unless they get caught, and they get caught only if their victims don't clam up."

"Clam up?" Mina grinned widely. She knew what I meant.

"Oh, for *fuck's* sake! You know what I mean. Why are you trying to derail this?"

Mina quit smiling and nodded. "Sorry. You're right, I am deflecting — because I've tried," she said. "Tried hard. But they're scared, and they have the right to be. Not all arrested people are held in jail, and angry people have been known to come back and intimidate witnesses. And this crew we're seeking —"

"— has a bad line in fatal intimidation. I know. So what would help?"

"What if there were a reward for information?" asked Hep.

"It's been on Crime Stoppers," said Mina. "It didn't get a nibble."

I gestured at the crowd lounging on the boulevard and the steps of the agency, in constant Brownian motion, swearing, arguing, in some cases kissing, in one case arguing *and* kissing, husbanding their belongings in packs and carts and rolling suitcases, wearing their spare clothing despite the heat, smoking despite the air quality, and waiting. Waiting, at this time of day, for the shelter to open for dinner despite lunch just being finished. Waiting for relief, waiting for housing, waiting for salvation, waiting to be anything but invisible. "Who here even *sees* Crime Stoppers? What about just putting up a poster and telling everyone when they come in to eat?"

"We could do that. It can't be too big a reward, however, or it's not safe."

"There's a bank over at BCSS."

"You know what I mean."

"Well, it's an idea," I said. "Pick a number, and I'll cover it. I'll meet them at the bank[116], even, so they don't have to carry it. But what else can we do?"

"I asked my workers to ask around. Ask everyone they talk to if they know anything. But if they do, and they tell our workers, it's confidential. So then we have to get them to tell the police, because there are only limited instances where we can break confidentiality without someone's permission."

"I'm the choir, remember? Offer to go with them. They trust you."

"I can do that."

We talked a bit more, but we didn't come up with any more brainwaves. We were just turning to go when —

"Hey! Girl!" It was Fleury. He wore his lighter parka today and only one shirt under it, in deference to the heat I guess. He looked like death warmed over, and smelled a bit like that too, but he managed to smile at us. "What you doing here? Come for lunch?" He laughed. "Too late, we ate it all!"

"What I need," I said, "is for your pals to give up what they know about those assholes who beat you up and killed Danny."

---

116. There's a social service agency nearby that houses a bank and safe deposit boxes for unhoused people: it uses retinal and fingerprint scans instead of ID. It's in conjunction with a real financial institution, and it's brilliant.

Fleur's eyes filled with tears, and I regretted my harshness. "Look, Fleury," I went on, trying to soften my tone, "you need to ask them. You know they'd do it for you. Some of them. Just ask them."

Fleur stood there crying and stubborn. "They don't wanna tell me. They just wish Danny wasn't dead. Me too."

"What's goin' on, Donkey?" The woman who stuck her face between Fleury and me was vaguely familiar, in that seen-her-around way that I know so many people after years as a social worker and further years living in east downtown. "These bitches giving you a hard time? Sorry, Mina, not you."

"Nothin', Debs," Fleury hastened to say. "Nothin'."

"I'm worried about those guys who attacked him and killed Danny," I said to Debs. "I mean, they *killed* Danny! Shrek, I mean. They could come back for Fleury. For Donkey. The cops need to catch them!"

"Cops. Ha. They just come around to kick us out of our camps. Fucking useless pieces of shit, cops."

"Yeah, they do that, and that's bullshit, we all know that. But they also arrest fucking murderers is all I'm saying."

"Goodness," said Hep. "Let's all just —" Hep was doing a language warning? Right now? For fuck's sake.

"Who the fuck are you, lady?" Debs was loaded for bear — until she got a good look. "Wait, ain't you Maddy's kokum?" Oh, I remembered her now.

"Yes," said Hep. "Yes, I am."

Mina stuck an oar in. "And this lady is the person who helped catch the as—, er, the criminals — who killed her."

"Well, yeah, come to think of it, I seen you at the memorial. I guess you'll do, then."

Gee, thanks.

She correctly interpreted my Look, which attempted admonishment and pleading in equal amounts, and probably just looked dyspeptic. "I know what you want. But look, you gotta know it's true. Nobody here ever calls the cops. Ever. Nohow."

"I get that, I do," I said. "But cops are all we have. Otherwise Fle— Donkey is going to live in fear, and so will everybody else sleeping rough. *Somebody* has to get that gang off the streets. Danny wasn't the first person they killed."

"Sure, I know," Debs said, "but you can't trust any fucking cop not to be like every other fucking cop. I can tell you right now, lady, nobody's talking to them."

"There's a reward . . ."

"Fuck the reward. Who needs it?" Wow. Hardcore.

"Not even for Donkey and Shrek and your other friends who died?"

"Well, there's friends, and then there's friends, you get me? Sorry, Donkey, sorry, Grandma, sorry, lady, but that's just how it is for most of us down here. See ya 'round, Mina."

Fleury was already walking away. I don't even know if he even heard.

56. AND ANOTHER THING . . .

"Well," I said to the air. "That went well, I thought."

57. HAVE A NICE DAY

I knew this harmless-looking white-haired apple-doll of an old lady once. At that time she was ten years older than Hep is now. When people said to her "Have a nice day!" she would say, "Thank you, dear. I have other plans[117]."

This was my life.

I try to have nice days, but the Universe has other plans.

---

117.   Sometimes they wouldn't even notice. It was awesome.

The next morning — late morning, with a side of Kim-making-breakfast — I got a call from Roma as I prepared for my walk into Own Domains. Seeing her name on the call display, I said pre-emptively, "I'm on my way."

"Good," she said, and hung up.

The skies were slowly clearing of smoke, but erratically, so on this particular morning, there had been a reduction in the number of the air quality index. My phone weather app said 32/10, which still packed a wallop. As a result, I was slightly late, and when I got to the building Roma was in the foyer looking simmery (no, not summery) and Mr. Spak waited beside her.

"So," I said. I couldn't help a reflexive look upward at the elegant tin ceiling ten feet above. No clouds, but that meant nothing.

"Took you long enough," said Roma.

"Not really, I — what?"

"There is a . . . lawyer here," said Mr. Spak. He managed to make his own professional colleague sound like a dead fish. Long dead. And not in a good way.

"A lawyer. A 'lawyer'. So?"

"He is known to me by reputation. He is primarily a personal injury lawyer."

"Ah." Was Mr. Spak prejudiced against all personal injury lawyers, or just this guy? I would ask him later. "And where is this paragon?"

"In Faraday," said Roma. Yeah, we had named the impermeable boardroom after its attributes. Sort of for fun, but not really. All our "break-out" rooms (stupid term) had ironic monikers. We were like a millennial tech company that way.

"My paralegal is serving him coffee."

Spak's paralegal is also the person he uses to conduct investigations, a tough, stocky, cowgirl-haired, weathered, parched, determinedly-blonde, handsome woman of a certain — or an uncertain — age. Imagine if you sent to Central Casting for a takes-no-nonsense, takes-no-prisoners, leathery-midwestern-barkeep type, and you got Frances McDormand crossed with Dolly Parton with a side of Jann Arden and a soupçon of Linda Hunt. Oh, and with some kick-ass-Sigourney-Weaver in there too. That's Gracelyn.

Gracelyn was not the person I would have sent to make a visitor comfortable. We went down to the boardroom post-haste.

The lawyer was also from Central Casting.

He also was of uncertain age, but not in the same way. He wore a shirt over his extended beer belly, but just barely. His suit had been tailored before the last of the weight gain. It was blue. Really very blue. His tie was diagonally adorned with wide gold and red stripes. His shirt had pink pin-stripes. The collar was too tight and the tie was askew[118]. He had jowls, which in the best tradition of their sort, had sweated into his collars.

He was stabbing a nicotined finger at the appliance-sized smartphone in his other paw, and as we paused before we went through the door, we heard him say to Gracelyn, "Why can't I get a fucking signal in this fucking place?"

Mr. Spak smiled. Then, as we came into the room, he shot his immaculate cuffs, indicated our visitor with a slight gesture worthy of Queen Elizabeth, and said, "Mr. Ulrich Dyck."

We have a lot of Mennonites in our part of the country. People don't laugh at this last name at all. Pity, because if there was ever a reason to think that God was an Iron, it was the totally non-Mennonite-looking guy with whom Mr. Spak was carefully not shaking hands. It was clear that all through Ulrich's childhood the other kids had called him Rick the Dick, and so — hoping,

---

118. On that guy who stars in *Brokenwood* this would all have been charming, but this dude did not look charming.

I assumed, that we would not do the same — he enunciated his name very carefully.

The two of them, side by side, looked like a class war, right there in our Faraday cage, the air sparking with the conflict between elitist privilege and stereotypical fat-shaming. I knew whose side I was on immediately, and that shamed me too, which made me more cordial. Willing to give him a chance.

"Hello," I said, walking to him with my hand extended. "I'm —"

He looked me up and down and ignored my hand pointedly — revenge for Spak's slight? — and interrupted, "I know who you are. I'm here to tell you that you won't get away with it."

Ah. Nope. Totally personal. But why?

"Ah. And by 'it' you mean — ?"

"I'm retained by Rosalind Brice Woodward, Anthony Brice, and Douglas Woodward." I looked back at him blankly. "Mr. Nathan Bierce's next of kin. His blood kin. His heirs. We are going to have your ass in court, you and your bullshit foundation, and you won't see another dime of his money."

This is why we can't have nice days.

58. NASTY, BRUT-ISH, AND SHORT

The meeting didn't last much longer. Mr. Dyck departed, leaving behind him a slight odour of stale cigarette smoke and Brut 33™, a few more threats, and some preliminary paperwork that Dafydd and Gracelyn took off to their office to air out and examine.

I followed them up the back stairs, to the Own Domains offices. We all try not to take the elevator, for health and environmental reasons, but with the air so smoky, I regretted that immediately.

"What are we supposed to —" I broke off for coughing and bronchodilators. "What should we —"

Spak interrupted me too, but with a better tone than his putative colleague.

"You are going to go home," he said. "We have to look at all this. We have to do research."

"Lawyer stuff," said Gracelyn helpfully.

"Also some investigation."

"That will be me," said Gracelyn helpfully.

"And then we will call you. Don't say anything to anyone that might have anything to do with this. Don't give anyone any ammunition."

"What about the money? Roma's salary? The bills? The —"

"Leave it to me," said Spak. "For now. As soon as I have a strategy to suggest, we'll have a strategy meeting. Until then, don't strategise. Don't even think about it, if you can manage that. Don't do anything. *Anything*."

"Anything," said Gracelyn helpfully.

I looked at them both.

"I know you," said Dafydd. "Please. Do nothing. I will call you. I absolutely will call you. This is why I have an office up here. This is what I do. For Nathan, and for you."

"Lawyer stuff," said Gracelyn.

"Too helpful. Dial it back," I said to her.

"Check," she said, and grinned.

After a moment, I grinned back, and nodded to Spak. "Nothing," I said. "But only because I can't think of what."

"Yes, I'm aware," he said. "I'll take that as compliance."

59. BENEFIT OF THE DOUBT? OR MAYBE NOT . . .

I wanted to give Nathan's brother and sister a chance.

For one thing, they looked just a bit like him. But not really, not where it counted. Still, I tried.

The sister — Rosalind, she said, Rosalind Woodward, "my married name" — was slender, the same height as Nathan (and, incidentally, me), and she had a hawk-nose and skin colour similar to the patrician profile and rich hue that had made Nathan so beautiful. But she held her lips tight and there was something odd about her gaze, which it took me a moment to figure out. Then I got it. She was wearing coloured contact lenses, maybe meant to turn her close-set eyes turquoise-blue. It wasn't quite working.

She was wearing a jacket with bulked-up shoulders, shades of my late mom's 1980s chic, and one of those weird crinkly tops that are dyed with a pattern while they're all crunched up, and then stretch across a person's body in ways that are almost never flattering. This was no exception. She was skinny and ropy, so her torso looked like a sack of rice with a distorted cat's face projected across it. The effect was as if she had stepped naked in front of an old-timey home movie projector.

The brother, Anthony Brice, had dark eyes, same colour as Nathan's but, like Rosalind's, set a little too close together behind a hawkish nose. He looked like a blurry photocopy of his sister — generation error — and only generically like Nathan. He wore a suit that tried to look expensive and failed, not because it didn't have chops but because Anthony shrank away from it inside as if it were made of steel wool. Under it he wore a thin crew-neck sweater that was slightly rumpled from within by his chest hair, of which he had clearly received the full family quota all for himself.

Nathan had been smooth. In so many ways, I was realising. But he hadn't been fake. When he re-made himself as Nathan Bierce, he'd used quality material, even when he was still very poor. I'd seen the photos of his rise to fame. These people looked as if they had shoddily modelled themselves on the paparazzi's blurry images of Nathan in the pulp tabloids, using off-the-rack options only.

Doug Woodward was the husband. It's tempting to say he looked like who he proved to be, but actually, he looked normal. Meek, even. Kind of a Bigfoot vibe, tall-ish but stooped, a little plump but not fat, not too flashily-dressed and not too dull: he looked as boring, vaguely-palatable, and harmless as the porridge Goldilocks ate. His suit fit, he had no annoying mannerisms, his voice wasn't whiny. The only disquieting note was that he had that flat, dead stare I associate with sociopathic politicians, family abusers, or murderers[119]. But since he thought we were the enemy, I wasn't really expecting him to twinkle. So, benefit-of-the-doubt time: maybe he wasn't a sociopath.

They weren't as averse to hand contact as Personal-Injury Ricky-Dyck, but none of them really knew how to shake hands, especially with a person wearing rings, or maybe it was with just a woman wearing rings. Or maybe that was their way of being passive-aggressive, whereas mine was to shake hands in the first place. It was with relief that I retrieved my digits from Doug and moved my rings out of the grooves he was the last of the three to grind into my proximal phalanxes.

Dafydd had made me promise not to speak if I could possibly help it (he's not an idiot, he knows I don't have perfect impulse control), and I had decided to start as I meant to go on, so I didn't yelp, swear, or give them handshake lessons[120]. I moved around the Faraday boardroom table, a classic of its kind, and established myself in the position of near-maximum dominance, at the foot of the table, Spak having already taken the catbird seat itself. Gracelyn stood behind Spak, at ease

---

119. Lockwood Chiles being the poster child for that look, the last few times I saw him.

120. All of which you will not be surprised to learn that I have been known to do in similar circumstances.

with her back to the wall, playing the Kimball Cho[121] rôle, her immaculate business attire only adding to her air of barely-suppressed menace. Or maybe that was just my impression, because I know her a bit. Mr. Dyck and his male clients seemed not to even see her, and Rosalind only turned slightly sidewise, so she could resolutely pretend that Gracelyn was not in the room, only to discover that from that angle she had to see more of me.

"So, we're here to discuss the estate of Nathan Bierce," said Mr. Spak, quietly enough that the Woodwards both leaned forward slightly. In attire, voice, and gesture, it was micro-expressions day in the Faraday as he brought his laptop to life with a tiny touch of the outside edge of his little finger.

"Brice," said Anthony.

"Shh," said Mr. Dyck.

"Dr. Bierce's legal name change is a matter of record," said Mr. Spak. Doctor? Later I found out that Nathan had been given an honourary PhD by MIT. But at this point I didn't even raise an eyebrow.

"May I ask," Mr. Spak continued, "what has become of Dr. Bierce's other sister, and is she a part of this action?"

They spoke all at once.

"No," said Rosalind.

"We aren't in touch," said Anthony.

"Shh," said Doug Woodward.

"That remains to be seen," said Ulrich Dyck, and, as he spoke slightly after the others, he won the speaking contest.

---

121. For those who haven't binge-watched as many old crime series lately as I had: Unsmiling, laconic, vaguely threatening without overt threat display, silent, attentive. Hands clasped loosely in front. Ready to star in a buddy cop show, chasing down and handcuffing bad guys. Ready for anything. I've gotta say, it's good that Gracelyn's on our side.

"That clarifies matters considerably," said Mr. Spak, and I saw Gracelyn duck her head slightly so any smiling wouldn't show. I didn't feel the need.

The contenders exchanged glances and were quieted with a little headshake from Doug Woodward. Gracelyn took this opportunity to hand out some multicoloured file folders and some stapled documents to everyone. I smiled and nodded my thanks but didn't bother pretending to read mine. If Mr. Spak could be a tranquil yet bottomless pool of restraint, I could too. Besides, I knew what was in them. Nathan had left his siblings some money — well, lots of money, in normal human terms — and the deeds to some houses in their home towns. Gracelyn then leaned back against the wall behind Spak, maintaining her Cho pose, and continued to loom at the contentious crowd.

Mr. Spak continued. "It is very clear that Dr. Bierce, Nathan Bierce, provided generously for his siblings — all of his siblings — in his last will and testament."

"Not sufficiently," said Mr. Dyck. "He has a huge estate. That provision is an insult."

"An 'insult' just into the nine figures might rather be described as a remarkable legacy," Spak said.

"And a generous one, given it is from someone who has not seen his birth family in thirty years, and in all that time, whose family never once tried to trace him," said Gracelyn, also quietly. "I know this latter fact because my investigative team has checked and ascertained without a doubt that this is the first time Nathan's family has reached out in any way. Please see the blue folder." She sat down, finally, and indicated with a flick of a forefinger the folders we all had.

"That is immaterial. The laws and principles of inheritance are clear. Blood comes first."

So not true, but to them, "immaterial". They wanted the whole enchilada.

Spak did not hesitate. "Dr. Bierce had clear intentions regarding his fortune. His will and supporting documents are unequivocal. He provided for his family, *and* for those *dear* to him" — I didn't imagine Spak's emphasis on the word "dear", and I saw Rosalind actually grit her teeth — "and then the bulk of his estate is disposed to his charitable foundation."

"Ridiculous!" Rosalind burst out. "He leaves his family out in the cold because this . . . this perverted . . . *honeypot* talks him into some stupid project for a bunch of losers and drug addicts?"

"*Honeypot*"? Had anyone said this anywhere anytime in my lifespan? I couldn't help a stifled "Ha!", but Dafydd checked any further hilarity with a side-eye, in a micro-tasking worthy of Roger. This stuff wasn't funny, true, but even if I had completed it, it still wouldn't have been that kind of laugh.

Also, "out in the cold"? Assuming they were who they said they were, they could take the win and start spending the money Nathan left to them — in fact, spend a lot of it, every day, and not run out in several lifetimes. For fuck's sake, what is *with* people and money? Lockwood Chiles's main reason for killing Nathan was that Chiles was pissed that Nathan was going to give some away. Money is mainly imaginary, and yet, people want the illusion of having it, like the emperor and his new clothes. I don't get it. As Tolstoy asked, how much land does a man need?

Ulrich the Dyck carried on, "We are of the opinion that remaking his will was done under duress. We want the court to revert to Nathan's former will."

"Are you sure?" said Spak. "You do realise that in his former will, which you reference, his family receives less? Dr. Bierce was considerably less well-off at the time it was made."

Doug Woodward dove for his turquoise file-folder. The others glanced from Doug to Ulrich uncertainly. Clearly, the fact that they had less in the former will, because Nathan hadn't been nearly as rich when he made it and had disposed of his wealth differently, hadn't really penetrated yet. If these were really his sibs, Nathan definitely got the brains in that family.

"We will have to study that," said Dyck, "but whatever the documents say, we are unanimous that the estate should go in its entirety to family."

"This meeting is over," said Doug. "Rosalind shouldn't have to sit in the room with the likes of *her*." He apparently didn't mean Gracelyn.

They all left, and I hadn't said a single word. If you don't count that snort of half-laughter.

"Well done," said Dafydd.

"What could I have said?" I said.

"You usually think of something," said Gracelyn.

"We are going to hand them their asses on a tray, right?"

"Oh, yes," said Mr. Spak. "Their legal proceeding has a snowball's chance in hell. If we are kind, we will not insist they pay our legal fees and court charges."

"Oh hell, why not?" I said.

"Because they are a trio of impecunious opportunists and that suit is borrowed," Spak said grimly.

"From a careless rental company. There is a stain on the left cuff," said Gracelyn. "Broke."

"I get it," I said. "Can you rent suits? I thought that was only tuxedos."

"We shall all try not to be petty," said Spak.

"And we will fail," I said.

"A righteous outcome will improve our ability to be kind," he said.

GO AWAY,
GO AWAY,
DON'T YOU
COME BACK
ANY MORE!

60. THE THREE-LEGGED RACE MODEL OF HISTORY (AND NARRATIVE) (AND LIGHTNING)

So, recapping The Big Picture, as they called it in a movie I saw at driving class one time:

- In the back of Dave's head, I'm still a suspect in the murder of Lockwood Chiles, and Dave's really the lead on that investigation now, even if Roger is the Major Crimes boss and keeps himself in the loop. As it were.

- In a public alley right next to my belovèd Epitome, a homeless man was swarmed and gang-kicked, resulting in his subsequent death, by some well-shod, well-jacketed neo-Nazi types with expensive haircuts who have vanished into the great rock and the great roll, leaving no clues behind.

- The mayor, Thelma, Roma, a bunch of other people, and I are trying to build a better city so that people aren't left on the streets (to be murdered, apparently), but we can't do it without Nathan's money. Nathan's now-contested will is already in a probate process that promised to be lengthy even without the upstart putative heirs. His money could be carrying out his last wishes, but it isn't.

- Lock died intestate — unless his will is undiscovered on some piece of that fucking smart paper — and his estate is tied up anyway until someone discovers how much of it was the proceeds of crime. All of it is sitting there passively accumulating via interest.

- On that front, we have a combination of uncertainties: 1) the terrifying prospect of Lock's second rebirth, whether in body or reputation, due to all that possibly-compromised evidence, and 2) a sheet of Lock's smart paper in the wind, on which we are also waiting to collect interest. The other kind of interest.

- Bear in mind that even before we sent out this unwitting emissary, Roma and Mr. Spak and I had been working regularly on the smart-paper content for months, and we had a lot of files in that safe to prove it, stored in Bankers Box™es[122] just like on TV — but we still had no idea what to do with the data or where it led, in part because Lock had been a cryptography maniac and we had no clue to his passwords. Despite what I had pretended for our charade.

- Let me remind you that right here in the Epitome Apartments, surrounded by cats, a gender-fluid teenager is trying to figure out who they are, after some surprising birth-parent disclosures.

- Now, a new problem — or a quartet of problems, taken as individuals — has come crawling out of the

---

122. Though the only place I have ever seen them used is in lawyers' offices, so why aren't they called Lawyers' Boxes?

woodwork[123], delaying all our plans even more, and
potentially derailing them completely.

In the way of things, each of those stories inches forward a
step at a time, and the whole narrative moves ahead in fits and
starts, as if a line of people decided to run a three-legged race but
nobody wanted to divide into teams, so everyone is hooked up to
someone on both sides, and the people at the end risk that the
game might suddenly change to Crack-the-Whip.

Complicated.

Because history is like that.

History moves as slowly as the slowest person in the line.

61. TRAIN OF THOUGHT

The next morning I watched Kim let Micah Five lick milk from
their cereal bowl. I was thinking that we are all really lucky that
Bunnywit only likes his milk warm. I was also thinking divers
other thoughts that would not, no matter how I wrangled them
around in the shunting yard, line up into a single train. Foremost
among them was that thinking is a mug's game and there have to
be better ways to spend time.

Clearly, Kim cannot read minds. "What?" they said defensively. "I was finished!"

"Too much milk makes cat poop runny," I said.

"I *know* that. But . . ."

"Yeah, but Micah is as cute as a honey bear. And so are you.
So *you* can clean out their litter box tomorrow. Finish up there. I
have an idea."

Kim left Micah meowing for more milk and took their bowl
to the sink and washed it, along with their toast-and-eggs plate,

---

123. Face it, they *were* a little creepy.

the plate where they'd sliced the apple and the orange, their juice glass, their coffee cup, their non-cereal-related milk glass, my cereal bowl, my tea mug, all the cutlery we'd used, the teapot, and the counter. I watched them as they brought everything in my kitchen to a restaurant standard of cleanliness, then dried and put away the dishes (I'm a "leave them in the rack to air-dry" person. You've heard of "it's a dry cold"? Well, it's also a dry heat. It's pretty dry most of the time on the prairies. So things dry fast. But Kim was clearly Well Brought Up[124]).

My idea was simple. Kim and I would go to every significant place I had been with Nathan and Pris in the time since Pris had come back and knocked on my door . . .

"Cool," interrupted Kim. "Let's do it."

. . . and, I added, I would tell every story I could remember about my time with them. And Kim could ask any questions. When we were tired, we'd quit. There are lots of days. This one day didn't have to do all the heavy lifting.

"Cool," said Kim. "I'm in."

Of course, this was me, so there had to be Discussions.

"Chronological or geographical organisation of data?"

"Data?"

"Events and visits. You want to have us retrace in order? Or can I just spiral around showing you where some stuff happened?"

"Like a jigsaw puzzle, and I put it all together in my head?"

"Just like that."

"Sounds good. I like that."

Of course it didn't work that way. It started out well at the bookstore, where we looked at Pris's books and I bought one for Kim, introduced Kim to the owner, and toured the crime scene out in the alley. But then we drove out to the acreage suburb where Lock and Nathan's first house had been and discovered

---

124. Possibly in a more humid place.

that the new owners had built a huge brick wall around their property. So I thought of trying to have a bar lunch at Little Flower, but it turned out Little Flower has been shut down for good[125]. So we came back downtown to try lunch at Double G, but it was closed for the weekend for interior painting and floor work, an unprecedented closure in my many years' experience. So we went to Madison's, but it was full.

So we went to the zoo instead, and saw the tigers, and there I told a whole bunch of stories, many of which had nothing to do with Nathan, Priscilla, Lock, or crime.

It was a hot, steamy, satisfying day, but the indoor pavilions were nice and cool, so we looked carefully at a lot of reptiles, small birds, and a slow lorus who happened to be sleeping out in partial view.

"You know, Nathan was always talking about the Night Zoo in Singapore," I said. "He wanted us to go there. He had lots of stories about it. It sounds really great."

"You could go," said Kim. "*We* could go."

I suppose it *is* that simple, in the very end. "That's true, kiddo. We could go."

We walked along to the aquaria and watched some attractive and some unattractive fish. What is an unattractive fish to me, you might ask? Well, beautiful and cannibalistic, mainly. I am unfond of angel fish, and said so, but Kim wasn't really listening, and, in a remarkable non-sequitur, burst out:

"What was my mother like? Out here, I mean, or when you were at university? At home, you know, our place, I mean, she would tell some stories but sometimes she just lay in a lawn chair

---

125. I'm sure you can imagine I Had Some Opinions about that. Kim received them attentively, that is to say, politely, but with little comprehension of the Deeper Community Issues.

out in the back yard by the pool and drank lemonade and slept. And sometimes she and my mom, I mean, you know . . ."

"Of course she was your mom. She *was*, in all but the one way."

"I know, but it feels weird."

"Call her your mom. Pris was just your mother. She didn't mom you."

Kim laughed out loud. "She sure didn't. One time she told me that it is better to be a dog in a time of peace than a person in a time of war. I was about eight. It took me all day to figure that one out, and then I asked my mom if that meant Auntie Jane was going to give us a dog."

"And the answer was?"

"Dogs shed. Muddy feet. When you are old enough to clean up after a dog, we can get a dog. But not now. Then she had a talk with Auntie Jane. Auntie Jane said she was just seeing to my education. She poured Mom a lemonade and made her get another lawn chair and they ended up really giggly. Later I figured out it wasn't the same kind of lemonade I was drinking. Sort of like the iced tea the other day. But then she brought Micah with her for her next visit. Well, that was the Micah before this one. And then when that one died, she took me with her to choose Micah Five. She said I was in loco parentis. I thought she meant loco like crazy, and I went around proudly saying 'I'm the Loco Parent!' until Mom and Auntie Jane sat me down and made me stop."

I laughed. "You probably had the perfect upbringing. I kind of envy you."

"Really?"

"Well, kind of. My parents were a bit strange. I'll tell you more about that someday, but it's a nice day out here. Let's go say goodbye to the snowy owl before we head home."

"Cool."

"Also, I don't think I can give you Micah Five back. I can live without him, but I'm not sure Bunnywit could."

"No big deal. One day when I have my own place I'm gonna get a puppy and a kitten both at once. Raise them together like siblings. It'll be cool."

"Cool," I said, thinking how I no longer would have the energy for a puppy *or* a kitten, let alone both at once. The cats and I are all perilously close to middle age[126], and that's fine with me.

We went past the tigers again on our way to the cool, pale, patrician owl, and both species' steady, assessing stares reminded us both of Priscilla Jane Gill.

62. DISCOVERY (NOT A SCIENCE CHANNEL)

When I was a social worker (or perhaps I should say, when I was *employed* as a social worker), I spent enough time in court to learn quite thoroughly what judges consider to be "proper and professional" attire. And clearly, so had Mr. Ulrich Dyck.

I was quite impressed to see the change in the clients he ushered before him into the examination for discovery, which was held, by our invitation, in the Faraday boardroom. This is a complicated proceeding in any case[127], and this one would take all day, recorded under the eye of a court reporter for later transcription. Everything that is said in a discovery can later be used in litigation.

Mr. Spak had prepared us well, but I was still nervous.

So were the plaintiffs, clearly, but the opposing team had, also clearly, decided to start as they meant to go on in full court later. I wonder if Mr. Dyck's vestiary advice had gone unheeded during

---

126. Depending on your definition thereof. I chose the WHO's.

127. Literally, any case, pun unavoidable.

our first meeting, or why exactly they'd arrived that time looking as if they had just come off an airplane. An eighties Aeroflot airplane. This day, they were transformed.

They still expressed character, but this time Anthony Brice wore a brown lightweight turtleneck with a tastefully-marbled cardigan over it, dark brown slacks, and loafers. Rosalind had a summerweight frock[128] with cap sleeves that flattered rather than satirised her thin frame, and her husband wore a summerweight suit in a neutral grey-brown with a casual white shirt open at the neck, no tie. They all looked far more comfortable. Whatever Mr. Dyck's own professional attire conveyed (and given today's cacophony of stripes and checks, I began to wonder if his image was deliberately chosen to encourage people like us to under-estimate him), he had taken charge of Anthony Brice and the Woodwards, and they were perfect court material now. Sartorially, at least.

Too bad a discovery isn't videotaped. They would have aced the audition.

"Anthony Brice and the Woodwards" sounds like a 1950s be-bop group, but their refrain was no more pleasing to the ear during their second engagement.

"We're family," said Anthony. "Nothing trumps family." Not at all original, but in law, often right.

"He wanted us to have his legacy," Rosalind said with a lach-rymosity she must have practised in front of a mirror. She even dabbed the corner of her eye.

Mr. Spak had me on a tight leash, or I might have remarked that perhaps if they had tried to get in touch with their brother any time in his actual life, their claims would have held more water.

"He told us that himself," said Douglas.

---

128. It wasn't a dress; it was definitely a frock.

"And when was that, Mr. Woodward?" Spak said mildly.

"Just call me Doug, everyone does," said Woodward. "It was the last time we saw him."

"Please remind us when that would have been, Mr. Woodward," said Spak (whom I know would have replied "Sure, and you can call me Dafydd" only if taken over by the Pod People). "And consider your statements carefully. A person with the business and personal profile of Dr. Bierce is seldom left unscrutinised. We have extensive documentation covering his whereabouts for the last several years of his life."

Ulrich leaned forward pre-emptively. "We have extensive proof, too, including DNA," and he fished a thick file from his briefcase. "A short-term and, frankly, exploitive relationship with your client was clearly not in the interests of Mr. — that is, of Dr. Bierce, and we will show that he was influenced away from his family during that time."

I know, because Nathan told me, that he had not seen his siblings for decades, learning about them from afar through the investigations that had found them, and that he had disguised his involvement when he tried to help them out. He had also told me they all had criminal records, though he hadn't said if those were minor or major. He had also said they all had family lives, but Mr. Dyck's representations as delivered to Mr. Spak's office mentioned none of this, and one sister was missing from the narrative altogether.

Gracelyn was serving coffee all 'round. Oddly, the usual mugs were nowhere visible: she had arranged some smooth, high-class, brightly-coloured designer plastic go-cups in rows on a matching high-concept paper tray, and poured them in situ, offering them in such a way that the recipient lifted the cup from the tray. It was quite deft and classy-looking, as befitted the environment. (That's a joke. It looked like break time at the Timmy's as imagined by a movie designer who had never seen the real thing.)

Luckily, all three of the lead singers in this particular hustle band liked coffee. Mr. Dyck refused, but we didn't need his DNA. We could safely assume he was who he had always been.

Yeah, Ulrich was going to hand us some DNA reports. But we weren't born yesterday. There *would* be private testing.

Of course Mr. Spak and Gracelyn and I also drank coffee from the same cups. We have seen all the right TV shows. Binge-watched in my case. It might be our first rodeo, but we knew enough about rodeo theory to proceed in a legal and methodical fashion. Including the chain of evidence forms we filled out at the end of the day, after Ulrich ushered out his little flock of fashion plates.

Meanwhile, we all sweated, metaphorically, through the questions of counsel on both sides, and Groundwork Was Laid. Or should that be Lain?

There were times Ulrich almost had us on the ropes, and many times I felt we'd scored some huge points, but a discovery isn't a trial. It's just putting everyone's case on the record. Now, we all had to go away and do something with the record, the transcript of which would be along in due time.

I have to say that my opinion of Mr. Dyck improved slightly as a result of that meeting. This wasn't entirely a good thing, of course — competence and virtue are two different things — but probably improved my karmic bank balance.

63. NO GOOD DEED GOES UNPUNISHED

Margaret Murray in 104 usually slid her rent under my door in an envelope, but that evening when she called as usual, redundantly, to say she was bringing it, I said, "It's okay, I'll come to you," and was at her door in a minute and a half.

I had all the best intentions. Bunnywit and I had discussed it at length, at night, in private, and I'd also talked with Kim. And Mr. Spak, to find out what my legal options were.

"Meg", as I never call her, nor have I ever been invited to, opened the door and stood back. She makes a point of saying she's a widow. I think she's in her late seventies, but she could be a well-preserved ninety-two, hard to tell. She's shorter than I am, almost as thin as Fleury, almost transparent, with crepey[129], powdered skin. Her thinning, wispy hair is determinedly coiffed into a bubble that surrounds her head like some strange sugar-candy dome. That afternoon she wore a flowered polyester top and navy blue slacks. Despite the heat in her apartment, which had no windows open, she had hung a cardigan over her narrow shoulders, its top placket edges held together with one of those cardigan clips, the kind with a small chain and a jewelled clip on either end. I haven't seen one of those outside period movies since I was four and visiting my great-grandmother for the last time. Central Casting was getting another workout.

A pair of cat's-eye glasses trailed around her tiny mottled neck on a chain spotted with coloured beads and, possibly, magnets. She wore clip-on earrings, both a brooch *and* a necklace, a lot of rings, and a tiny and vintage Timex™ watch on one frail, freckled wrist. Her hands are tiny and long, like bird claws, and her fingernails long and, that day, they were painted a daunting pink, clearly by her own hand. She wore matching lipstick.

She must have gotten dressed up for her trip upstairs and down the hall.

Despite myself, that bothered me.

I don't think she really wanted to let me in, but she's old-school, so she did.

Her suite was on the main floor, back, north side. I stepped down the tiny hall and into her kitchen, which was as full of tchotchkes as her attire. To the left, an archway led to her extremely-floral living room.

---

129. Not creepy. Also not, by itself, a bad thing. I like crepey skin, cf. Hep.

The view of the alley is excellent from both the living room and the kitchen.

There was a particularly good view of Fleury's tent.

That bothered me too.

She noticed immediately. "I suppose you are going to give me notice."

I was going to, but I hadn't actually prepared the letter yet. Cowardice? Bun thought so. He had had *things* to say to me. There are times[130] I'm glad I don't speak cat[131].

"Why would I?" I was being passive-aggressive, maybe, but I was going to make *her* say it.

"Because of that night. When I didn't call the police like you wanted me to."

"A man died that night."

"Do you think I don't know that? A man who would never have been there if you weren't so lazy."

"Lazy?"

She used one of her cramped hands as a pointer, repeatedly jabbing toward me at diaphragm level. "You're a lazy landlady. You never intervene. You should have had those two boys out of there."

I resisted defensive moves, or mirroring, and said, as calmly as I could, "On the contrary, I gave them permission to stay, just like the people in the other tent."

"Well, I should have known, I suppose. You are young and reckless. All the trouble you get into."

O-kay, then. That was how it was going to go. "Mrs. Murray, that gang who killed Danny went after homeless people as a hobby. If not here, someone would have been attacked somewhere else

---

130. Many, *many* times.

131. And so *few* that I wish I do.

that night. But you could have stopped it. By the time I looked out, after your call, it was all quiet again."

She side-eyed me. "You're young. You can run. You can fight back if they come after you."

At first I missed it. "But — they don't want to fight, they just want to be left alone until they find a place to live. That's the only reason I let them stay. They have nowhere else."

"People can do all sorts of terrible things. Just last year that elderly lady was attacked and, you know, raped at the Elder's Mansion. She died, you know! What if that happened to me?"

"But Fleur—"

"I didn't mean *them*. What if those boys with their boots had seen me calling for help and had come and broken into my home? What would I do? I weigh eighty-nine pounds. I already had one broken hip."

"But —"

"You have no idea. No idea at all, you with your fancy friends and your idealism and your good deeds. You think you know, but people could take advantage of you every day of the week and you would just smile and take it."

I opened my mouth, then closed it again. I don't think I'm *that* gullible, but she's probably right.

"I'm a mean old woman," she raged, both hands busy now, gaunt paws clawing the air between us. "I know that. That's what everybody says to me now. But nobody knows what it's like here. The violence. The fear. Out front it's all pretty trees and a nice fence, but back here? Anyone could climb up on those bins and get in here and do something awful, and what could *I* do?"

She abruptly turned away and picked up her rent envelope. As with every month, the envelope, with its War Amps return address sticker and floral decoration on the flap, and my name carefully written on the front in a small, crabbed hand, would contain her carefully-written cheque with its shaky signature. This one was just the same as all the rest, but she held it as if it were something strange. She looked down at it for a moment.

Then she put it down again, and leaned on her scrubbed wooden table, her breathing rapid. One of those bent canes hung over the edge of the table, the kind with the four feet.

Dammit, I thought, I refuse to feel sorry for her. She's a toxic mess.

I watched her stooped cardigan-shrouded back — her spine showing through in a knobby scoliotic S-curve — and her tiny desperate claws holding the table edge.

Some time went by. It wasn't long, but it seemed it.

"Look," I said to that terrible back, "there's a vacant apartment at the front, beside the front door. It's the mirror image of this one, but it faces the street, it's behind the high fence, and you can see downtown. The windows are higher in the front because of the sloped lot, and there are no bins. Nobody could ever get in your window. Do you want to move? Same rent."

"Why would you do that?" she said to the wall. "You don't like me." She paused. "I admit, I don't like you either." She made it sound like a virtue.

"I don't know you, Mrs. Murray. You're probably right. I probably wouldn't like you if I did, but who knows? Maybe I would."

She shrugged.

I went on doggedly. "It doesn't matter if we like each other. Everyone needs to live somewhere they feel safe. I wish you had said something before."

She remained silent. One hand went back to the envelope, but instead of turning and giving it to me, she clutched it until it bent.

I soldiered on. "If you want to move there, I know some people in the building would help you move your furniture. Everything would fit, just the opposite way. I just painted the place off-white, but you can paint other colours if you want. I see the pink in here and the yellow in the kitchen."

"I hate that paint," she said. "It was here when I moved in. I never drew attention in case my rent went up. That woman. She was worse than you."

She meant the last owner. "She certainly was. What colour do you want?"

"Off-white is fine. It goes with everything."

"That was my thinking."

She turned around and squared her jaw.

"I'll say thank you for that," she said, back on her game, "and I agree. I'll move. I'll even take the help you talked about, though heaven knows I can't repay their favours. But I'm too old to care any more."

"They won't care either."

"Well, good then."

We glared at each other. I held out my hand.

She put the envelope in it.

"I've lived here thirty-three years," she said. "Since my husband died. Longer than you have been alive."

Startled, I laughed aloud. "Seriously? You think I'm that young? You really do need those glasses!"

She just glowered at me some more.

"I get it," I said. "We're not friends. But I don't care about that either. I'll send you some helpers down to arrange a time, and I expect you to be moved by the middle of the month so I can paint in here and rent it next month, if that works for you."

"I can manage that," she said.

"Also, we will just move the numbers on the door. Maybe even switch out the whole door. Your key and your address won't even change."

"That's kind of you," she said, still with her jaw slightly clenched, as if my kindness were a greater sin than all my other shortcomings. "Good day."

"Good day, Mrs. Murray."

She watched me let myself out.

Dammit.

Now I'm stuck with the old bag.

64. PAPER THAT IS TOO SMART FOR ITS OWN FUCKING GOOD

I checked my cell phone when I woke up the next afternoon. A couple of nuisance messages from that one tech guy who just won't give up, which I deleted as usual. Nothing from Spak yet, but Roger had left a cryptic message asking me to come into the cop shop.

A dishy constable I'd met once ages ago greeted me and led me to one of the rooms Detective Heather hadn't wanted me to see. It was the secure room where the mayor and council would gather with their advisors to run the city in the event of terrorists or my old pal the Global Electromagnetic Pulse. I guess she thought it was Ultra Sekrit. Sucks to her: I'd been in there ages ago, when we had been concealing a conversation from Chiles's electronic surveillance abilities, way back before we caught him. In peacetime, it was also what we ancients would call the AV room, because it always had the best equipment.

Roger was there, drumming his fingers on the desk and bouncing slightly, in a senior-officer kind of way of course. The constable, at a gesture from him, went over to the media console, fiddling with it and muttering. Since Dave had been promoted, I guess she was the new gofer.

"You need to look at something," Roger said abruptly. "For identification purposes only, and you can't talk about it outside this room. Except maybe to your lawyer, in your Faraday board-room." Constable Cute didn't know what Roger meant, but I got a chill down my spine. A goose, treading lightly. A cat, treading normally. A ghost, treading poltergeist-heavily. Take your pick.

"Sloan. Go," he said to the minion, and she handed him a remote and left the room. As soon as the door clicked, Roger pressed two buttons, one that dimmed the lights and one that fired up a big flat screen and started a grainy silent movie on it.

I was looking at a room with empty walls, a table and two chairs. It wasn't the room Dave liked to question me in, but it was a near-twin: bland wall colour, bland furnishings, no sharp edges or potential projectiles. This one had obvious bars, rather than tempered glass, on the window set into the door.

In one of the chairs, facing the camera, sat Lockwood Chiles, wearing his prison garb as if it were boardroom attire. In front of him was a pad of lined paper, and he was taking notes with a long thin Bic™-like pen.

On the other chair, back to the camera, sat a man. Back of head said Caucasian, balding, perhaps (the colour was terrible) a blue suit, but that was all. Could just as easily have been Ulrich Dyck or Johnny Depp. (That's a joke. Ulrich is, as it has turned out, a lot better a person than Johnny.) Blue-Suit, too, had paper and pen, and a briefcase down beside his chair.

There was no sound.

"It's illegal to record a conference with a lawyer," said Roger, "but the camera stays on for safety reasons."

"What about lip-reading?" I said innocently. The video resolution was worse than a convenience store's security cam, for all that it was in colour. You could barely tell the people on the screen *had* lips.

Roger rolled his eyes. "Just watch."

We had clearly joined the episode in medias res, and it was running at about 2x speed. The lawyer talked and gestured. Lock talked and wrote. Their paper filled with notes.

"Now," said Roger, and with a click of the remote he slowed the playback to normal speed. In front of Lock was a sheet of closely-written notes. The lawyer put his briefcase up on the table and pulled another pad of lined paper out. It looked blank.

I was watching the lawyer and almost missed it.

Lock was still holding the pen. He seemed to sign his name on the page. Then he tapped as if dotting the *i* in Chiles.

He tapped not once but twice.

He handed the pad he'd been writing on to the lawyer, who put it in his briefcase. For a moment, they spoke, before the lawyer shut the case.

The pad of paper the lawyer had put in the case was completely blank.

The lawyer passed the other blank pad of lined sheets, the one that he'd just taken out, across the table to Chiles, who received it with a little nod of thanks. The lawyer picked up his case, turned around, hit a button on the wall, and the sound was back. "We're done," he said. In a moment, there was the sound of an unlocking and opening door, and the lawyer went out.

Chiles said nothing. He gathered his pen and the new blank tablet he'd been left, and lounged back in his chair, relaxed, smiling slightly, waiting for the guard to return and take him back to his cell. The guard asked for and received the pen, then ushered him out. The door snapped shut behind them.

Rog motioned with the remote, which turned off the system and restored the lights.

"Holy shit," I said. "That was smart paper."

"Yep," said Roger. "Going back and forth, right under our noses. He was allowed to have writing materials in his cell, under supervision, but they suppress WiFi at the Max to cut illegal cell phone use."

"Does it work?" I was momentarily diverted.

"It must, because look at them there."

"Yeah."

"He could run his whole empire from there."

"It takes dictation," I said.

"I know," he said.

"It phones home," I said.

"I know," he said.

"Fuck," I said.

"Yep," he said.

65. RUMP OF SKUNK AGAIN

So.

It was a very quiet room after the projector went off. Neither of us said a word, nor even tapped a pen on a page. We knew where that led: the ever-familiar skunk/madness.

What was there to say?

I mean, eventually, we would think of something. After all, he was Roger and I was me. Each in our own way, our mouths ran on our autonomic nervous systems. But for the moment —

Nope. I had nothing.

Neither, it seemed, had he.

66. STORMY WEATHER

Having Nathan's smart paper was like having lemon sandwich cookies in the cupboard. You don't eat them all at once, but you don't forget they are there either. My approach to Nathan's gift to me had already started to shift from melancholic dilettantism to serious exploration. As well, I had some long-term ideas starting to emerge, but I was steadfastly ignoring the long-term at the moment. Taking Anne Lamott's advice, I was going at it bird by bird: page by page, slowly, listening to Nathan in small, tasty, rationed bites.

But that was recreational.

The other stash was a clear and present danger.

Roger couldn't take the time for a consistent presence in the Faraday Boardroom, but Dafydd, Roma, and I upped our paper-cracking commitment from hobby to avocation. We spent time there as often as possible over the next couple of days, trying to crack the code on Chiles's poison pills. No luck, and the Universe was still sending us no weird responses to our stalking horse.

Roma and I also spent time with Nathan's files up at Own Domains, decoding his meticulous and lengthy accounting of his assets, much as we had previously decoded his meticulous and lengthy instructions about how to set up Own Domains, and just as easily, as Nathan had seen no reason to keep his plans secret from us. He had shared control of his password vault with Mr. Spak and me from the start, changing them all when he transferred all his sensitive business to Dafydd.

It was a day or so after Roger's revelation that Gracelyn came up and tapped on the door to one of the smaller meeting rooms upstairs where we were working, rooms shared by Own Domains and Spak's office. Roma had not put up the signs yet, so I wasn't yet sure if this one was going to be The Leonards or The Ursulas. They are plurals because our shortlist contained more than one of each name[132], and we got cute[133].

Gracelyn was wearing, in addition to bike shorts and a long T-shirt that showed all her muscle definition, a worried look. She

---

132. You should know already — right? But for the record: Cohen and Nimoy, Le Guin and Pflug.

133. Again. Or more. We are always cute.

was towing one of those boxy black lawyer's brief-cases (the ones that are an actual case for actual briefs, with the wheels and long handle), and carried a big laptop.

"I have an issue," she said. "Can you help me for a moment? Both of you? No, stay there, this is about what you're doing."

We stayed there. She came in and set up her big, wide laptop, with its spreadsheet-friendly screen, beside Roma, who was working at a desktop with a similar wide screen. She pulled some paper files from the brief-case.

"Here's the thing," she said. "You know part of my job is to do the forensic audit on Nathan Bierce's assets, to be submitted for probate. And for the lawsuit, now, of course."

I hadn't known, but if anyone besides Mr. Spak would be that person, it made sense it was lean and laconic Gracelyn, who was smarter than your average bear as well as being able to wrestle one.

"And you have the snapshot of how things stood just before his death, there, on your smart pages."

"We do," said Roma. "We have been getting them all in order. And printed, even though I think that's redundant. But *somebody* in this office has concerns about a global electromagnetic pulse[134] or whatever."

"Look —" I began, but Gracelyn wasn't in a bantering mood, apparently.

"I do too. Printouts are always good. But digital will do right now. Show me."

Roma pulled the file with the summary balance sheets up on her screen, and opened the spreadsheet with its multiple pages that added up to, in essence, Nathan's Last Annual Report, saved just before he went off on his death trip with Lockwood and Pris.

Gracelyn pulled up a similar file, and the two clicked until

---

134. Yeah, that'd be me. I told you about this.

they were on the same page (literally[135]). "This is the balance sheet for two days ago," she said.

Even I could tell how different the numbers were.

Just over a year after Nathan's death, his fortune was about . . . I did some rough math, not my forte, but in this case, fairly easy . . . two-thirds what it had been before he died. Which, given how huge it had been, was one hell of a difference. And, as we have established (which everyone knows anyway), you leave money like that alone and, like fruit-flies or mice, it goes about busily multiplying. It should have been increasing, not going down.

We sat and looked at it. Someone had been syphoning off Nathan's money, regularly, different but sizeable amounts every day, at a rate of millions — maybe even tens or hundreds of millions some days — at a time.

"If we were in the active accounts," said Gracelyn, "I guarantee you that we would actually be seeing the numbers turning over like a running counter, at a variable speed, a bit or a lot, cents at a time, but always decreasing. The accounts that Dafydd sees, the ones that Nathan's passwords open? They are completely different. Someone — some really *really* good programmer — has set up the computer equivalent of the 'two sets of books' in all those Mafia movies, so as far as the accountants know, everything is hunky-dory. And we know who was a really *really* good programmer, don't we?"

Hunky-dory? "Is this recent?"

"The process has been going on since Nathan's death," said Gracelyn, "but I only hacked into this file today. I got a hint it was there from something on the Chiles paper, and I went looking, which took some doing. I haven't yet figured out to what degree the rate was less or more in the last few months, and I want to figure out if it varied after Chiles went to jail, if it varied when we

---

135. Or, should I say numerically?

locked the paper into Faraday's safe, if it varied after we let the piece of paper out — but it's definitely still leaking."

"We have to call Mr. Spak," I said. "And Roger, in his official capacity." I was doing a Rod-and-Don[136], since Dafydd was the executor of the estate, and Roger was the head of Major Crimes, which includes fraud.

"Yes, that's the next step," said Gracelyn.

"Duh, Department of the Obvious, people!" said Roma. "Have you figured out who?"

"Who do you think?" Gracelyn said. "It may have slowed down since —"

"— since the death of Lockwood Chiles," I said.

"Yes," she said. "Or it may not have. To be discovered. There are tendrils. Traces, in these secret records. It will have to be proven without doubt, but I'm already convinced. Lockwood Chiles did this."

"Now we know what he was doing with his smart paper in jail," I said. "Still stealing from his dead friend. Whom he murdered, but apparently that wasn't enough. The utter, unmitigated, completely irredeemable asshole."

"But we knew he was one," Gracelyn said.

"Yes we did," I said, "but clearly, we underestimated his assholery."

"Is that a word?" said Roma. "I hope it's a word. I like it."

67. INTERESTING TIMES

You know, I'm just going to cut past the repetitive scenes where Gracelyn and Roma and I explained the issues to Dafydd Spak, and Dafydd and Gracelyn and Roma and I explained to Roger, and Roger and Dafydd and Gracelyn and Roma and I explained

---

136. See also "maid-and-butler dialogue", or The Turkey City Lexicon.

to two of the Fraud Squad (one detective and one civilian consultant), who threw their hands in the air in horror, but meanwhile sent Roger such a pleading look that even Roma noticed and said, "What?"

"This is worse," said Fitzdonald, the police member, young enough not to Dress For Success, so who wore generic geekgear, but the T-shirt was high-end, clean, and crisply new.

"'Way worse," said Sandhu, the consultant. Short and bearded, he had thoroughly crumpled a sandy-beige suit, and his shirt really did have a pocket protector in it to hold two mechanical pencils and a slightly-leaky, expensive, fat fountain pen (I knew it was slightly leaky because his hand rubbed a bit of ink off on mine when he shook hands). He wore an orange tie, and his matching hot-orange turban was so elaborately folded that it was fit for an art gallery.

"Worse than what?" I said, with trepidation.

"You should know," said Fitzdonald. "You caused the last one. We're still working on that one." She winked at me.

"Twenty-eight point eight million dollars," I said.

"That's the one," said Sandhu.

"Shame on you," said Fitzdonald. "Two in a row." But she was grinning. "It might be kind of fun, though," she said after a moment.

"Fun?" Sandhu squeaked. "I have a family! I have a wife. I have kids. I would like to see those kids grow up, from close up, not as some kind of absentee father. Fun? Sir," to Roger, "we need resources. We need . . . people." He was frowning. Together, they were like the masks of Comedy and Tragedy.

"'May you live in interesting times'," I said.

"Ancient Chinese curses are not useful here," said Sandhu.

"It's not Chinese," I said. "Big misconception. Some British diplomat family called Chamberlain probably invented it, in the nineteenth century."

"People that no-one has a clue who are[137] — you might as well say Mark Twain said it," grumped Gracelyn.

"Did he?" Roma leaned forward.

"For fuck's sake, no," I said, "and neither did Voltaire. For fuck's sake."[138]

"Children, please," said Mr. Spak. "Mr. Sandhu, you may take these diverse utterances as conveying sympathy with your plight."

"They didn't sound very sympathetic," replied Sandhu.

"We'll figure something out," said Roger soothingly.

"And besides, Lockwood Chiles is dead." Sandhu wasn't giving up.

Avoiding the slim possibility otherwise, Mr. Spak said grimly, "His estate isn't. Now that we know what has been going on, the connexions can be discovered."

"We'll have to check that he wasn't doing the same to Priscilla Jane Gill's estate," Gracelyn said.

Sandhu groaned.

"We'll get the Crown to freeze it all," said Roger. "There will be time."

"That should slow down those three-dollar bills that Dyck works for," I said, and after that had been decoded for the room, Sandhu groaned again.

"We'll figure something out," said Roger again.

"Methodically," said Dafydd Spak.

"Doable," said Gracelyn.

---

137. Notice I didn't correct her? I *am* getting better, I really am.

138. If you care to know, no Chinese proverb to match this saying has ever been found. The closest saying appears twice in a manuscript of vernacular short stories from the 1600s: "Truly, far better to be a dog in days of peace than to be a human in times of war." Familiar? That's because I also, like Kim, learned about this saying from Priscilla Jane Gill, once upon a time. I guess she really liked it.

Fitzdonald nodded.

Sandhu groaned.

68. MEN IN BLACK. BLACK-ISH. SUITS. MEN IN SUITS. PEOPLE. PEOPLE IN SUITS.

Gracelyn and Roma and Spak continued to worry away at the comparisons between the hidden books and the historic snapshot Nathan had left me.

We spent a few more frustrating hours in Faraday with Chiles's goddamn poison pill — all added to the fruitless previous hours and days that on my deathbed I'll be begging for because they were the very definition of a waste of life force[139].

Fitzdonald and Sandhu dropped in, carried boxes and copies away or brought them back, and came and sat with us as we worked.

It was like chewing tacks.

Because without passwords, our work was random as fuck.

Finally, during one of the hours that we were actually alone in Faraday, that is, without the outsiders, I threw down a still-blank sheet and looked at Spak and Roma, who were looking back at me.

"Let's lock it up," I said. "Now."

We locked the stuff up, and then Roma went upstairs and got us all some iced tea. She makes it from scratch and stores it in fancy old gallon jugs in the fridge up there. The jugs have little metal spigots and came from an estate sale. She brings it down the elevator on a little wheeled tea table, with some 1950s glasses that have cartoon characters on them. Today it was jasmine and hibiscus, and after Mr. Spak took my favourite, Casper the

---

139. Recently, oddly enough, I seemed to have started to care a little bit about my life force again. Huh.

Friendly Ghost, I had my pick of Betty Boop or the Monopoly Man. It was a hard choice until Roma *tsk*ed and took Betty Boop.

I'm not that fond of the Monopoly Man either, but the tea was fabulous.

I waited until we had had the first few sips, then I called Roger. "I'm putting you on speaker," I said. "Dafydd and Roma are here with me. Gracelyn is at the gym, or running up Mount Rundle in sneakers, or something. Fitzdonald and Sandhu have gone home with a bunch of Nathanware, but we've been with Chiles's paper all afternoon."

We all knew what that meant. "I'm listening," said Roger, cautiously.

"Okay, look," I said. "Every sheet of that stuff looks thin, but it's as deep as the ocean. We all want to know what's at the bottom."

"Beware, allegory incoming," said Roma to Spak.

"Too late," he said.

"All right, just for that, I promise to stretch it until it snaps. Chiles was deep in his way, same as the sea that swallowed the *Titanic*, or maybe as the Bermuda Triangle. Whatever. We've been thinking of ourselves as James Cameron looking for wreckage and sending drones down to try to record it before it dissolves."

Nathan had been Mariana Trench material too, but he was the ocean on a nice day, when Cousteau's crew jumps off the ship and takes a recreational swim in water seven miles deep. I kept that to myself. The metaphor was already too stretched, and I was sticking to it out of pure stubbornness.

Roma made a little interrogatory hand gesture, possibly encouraging, or I preferred to think so.

Mr. Spak raised an eyebrow.

"All right, fuck it, and fuck off the whole bunch of you. Everyone has been attacking this stuff — and as you once said, Dafydd, Uncle Tom Cobley and all got nothing on us. And the results? Fuck all. Cutting to the chase — we are not James Cameron, we don't have a sub, and that stuff isn't going anywhere as long as we keep it in that cage. Now Roger, you had the cunning plan to draw Lock's associates, or Lock if he really isn't dead, out of the woodwork, but we did that, nobody showed up but Vinnie's 'guys', and will anyone else ever show up?, and what will we do with them when we get them? We have fifteen boxes of file material and counting, full of Roma's transcripts, our notes, some bits of research that Dafydd and Gracelyn have dug up, and where does it lead? For us? No-fucking-where. For you and your Fraud folks? As close to nowhere as makes no never-mind, so don't even bother to sputter. You have two cops, one of whom is assigned elsewhere, and one civilian member on your Fraud Squad. You had to hire a consultant even to admit this fraud *existed*. Q.E.D."

Roger cleared his throat. We waited.

We waited more.

The silence crackled.

"Just what I thought," I said. "I'm trying to lead up to admitting something I hate to say. We are what my mother used to call too big for our britches. That's been the problem all along."

"Who's too big for whose britches again?" said Roger, sounding perhaps a bit more belligerent than he could enforce while disembodied and unable to task us, glower at us, or loom.

"Fuck, are you not *listening* to me?" I said, matching tone for tone. It's the only way to deal with Rog when he gets like that, right?

Also I was frustrated as fuck, and this is how *I* get when I'm like that.

I took a breath. Maybe two.

"Okay, trying again. This whole thing has been about processes on a scale we can't deal with. Sometimes I think that Nathan is now like the Man Who Wasn't There in that nursery rhyme — I keep seeing him everywhere, but not really. But this whole summer has been like that. Nathan isn't here. Lock isn't here. Oh, we can feel as if he might be, because he has left behind a huge engine that still runs, but he's dead and we all know it. Well, we *think* we know it, same same. As for the machinery, it has resolutely refused to go *sproing* and give up its secrets. Priscilla isn't here. That fucking gang beats up homeless people because the unhoused and addicted are invisible to most of the world, and they don't even get in the papers like serial killers usually do. You can't get in trouble for killing someone who has already vanished, right? If they had a place to live, they might be safe. Safer. And whoever those fucking idiots are who have been in our boardroom, I'm damned sure they are not Nathan's family, and we don't yet know where the hell the real ones are. Lockwood Chiles's murderer isn't here. And last but not least —"

I took another breath. This was going to be rough. "— I'm not here. I'm invisible too. I'll be back, but I need time for that, and no lightning strikes, and no paper that's smarter than I will ever be, and no Nathan's voice every day, and, even more urgently, no listening to the voice of his murderer witter on about shady business practices —"

I faltered, and couldn't start again.

Dafydd made a move to get up, but I stopped him.

"No. I may not actually exist at the moment, but I'm not dead. And I can still use my brain some of the time, and I have figured out what we need to do next."

"And you, as always, expect we will heartily embrace your idea?" Roger's voice sounded less heavy, despite the reflexive snark.

"I do," I said. "Here it is: we have to give up."

"Say what? Give up?" said Roger, and even Mr. Spak looked a bit shaken. Well, he raised an eyebrow, which is the same thing. Roma just watched.

"*We* give it up. We admit we need help. So right now, we get help. We figure out who *can* unravel an international criminal conspiracy, who *does have* the tech wizards to crack this fucking paper, and who really, really would *love* to have all of Lockwood Chiles's money in exchange for finding and giving us back Nathan's."

It was Roma who laughed first.

"We need the Men in Black!" she said delightedly. "Suits. Men in black suits, that is. Well, people in suits, they're probably not all men. And they probably don't really wear black, I guess — especially in this weather. But you know what I mean."

I nodded. I did know.

"I'm done treading water," I said.

GO AWAY, GO AWAY, AND PLEASE DON'T SLAM THE DOOR ...

69. ONE PARTICULAR PENGUIN

It wasn't that easy, and we all knew it.

After all, people like that are like the Bigfoot of law enforcement. They're dangerous AF, they live in the backwoods, they're legendary but no-one knows them, and they hide.

In the end, it was Mr. Spak who spoke up.

"Do you trust me?" he said.

"Unconditionally," I said at the same time that Roma said "Well, duh!" and Roger said "Maybe."

"Roger!" I said.

"Provisionally," he said.

"I know someone," said Spak.

"Get them to come here," I said at the same time Rog said, "Get them to call me."

"I can do that," said Dafydd. To me.

"Great," I said as if I hadn't heard Roger. "Dafydd, you call your someone. We'll meet here, of course. The paper is here. Roger, I just bet you know someone too, and you are itching to call them on some goddamn encrypted line."

"I do know some people."

"Good. So call them. We'll have a party.

"But first things first," I continued. "We've forgotten. We have some other allies here."

"Allies?" said Spak just as Roger said, "What are you going to do?" in the tones of deep suspicion that I was getting used to these days.

I grinned. "Don't you remember what happens when we let a piece of Lockwood's paper call home?"

70. ONE OF OUR PEOPLE

Mina called me that same afternoon.

"You have a guy you trust on the cops, right?" Mina thinks small talk is for ordinary people. She has a Higher Calling.

"Um, yeah . . ."

"I need a cop who can be trusted."

"What's up?"

A long silence. I leaned back in my ergonomic chair in my Own Domains office. I haven't mentioned that office, on a sort of literary need-to-know principle, but it's very small, cluttered, nice, and has one tall, narrow window that looks out eastward onto the front street. Inside, there is a wide windowsill I can sit on when I get tired of ergonomics. It's on the north corner, and Spak's rather more roomy office takes the other front corner, with windows facing east and south. The Ursulas Room tucks in beside his along the front, with one tall window. The Leonards Room, Roma's, and Gracelyn's all look out on the side alley to the south. But all of us spend 'way more time in the rear central atrium, with various windows facing out in three directions (including west into the other alley), because.

It was a long moment before Mina spoke. "One of our people has been beat up. By a kind of gang. With, you know, boots and brush cuts. She needs someone who —"

"I have just the thing," I said, and evoked Heather Wood.

Mina, chit-chat-free as always, thanked me and rang off, without sharing any details. Because FOIP, and also FOIP, and also other kinds of professional reserve. But my heart leapt, because here might be someone else who could perhaps ID some Persons of Interest. Which would help if said persons ever showed up. Not to mention that a long long time later, there might be another substantiated charge in a long list of charges against said persons, if etcetera etcetera.

So, one more three-legged step vaguely forward.

These days, that counted as a win.

71. SAIL ON, SILVER GIRL

I was short on sleep the morning of the big meeting, which often seemed to be the case.

I had spent a lot of time last night on a lot of mostly-pointless thinking. Finally I got up, made some hot chocolate, refilled the melting marshmallows a few times, and when morning arrived, early at this time of year, I got dressed in my most aggressive summer blacks. For this one, I left Kim sleeping in peace, with Micah curled on their pillow. Bun, seeing that I was getting ready to leave, ignored me and hopped up onto the foot of their bed and curled up into the bend of their knees. Very cozy.

Also cozily, Vinnie and Sharon and Bob and Hikaru and Gracelyn and Roger and Dave and Dafydd and I almost filled the Faraday boardroom. Spak's Someone I Know and two of Roger's Mysterious People, as well as Fraud Squad Fitzdonald and Consultant Sandhu and a deputy chief (Roger's boss, Danielle) completed the Compact Crowd.

Once everyone quit milling about, procured a bureaucratic beverage (in real cups this time), and sat down, the room settled down. There were two empty seats left at the big table, and I imagined Nathan and Pris sitting in them: though that was a fanciful conceit, it pleased me a little. I sat at the head of the table, flanked by Mr. Spak and Gracelyn.

"I guess you're wondering why I have called you all here," I said, then couldn't help cackling for a moment. A number of Looks from around the table got me flying right again.

"There is," I said, "going to be a Task Force, and I say that with capital letters. We've established that it will be co-funded by any assets of Lockwood Chiles's that were seized by the Crown, a small percentage of the recovered estate of Nathan Bierce should that come to pass, the extra-agency Law Enforcement Response Team[140], and diverse other agencies and governmental sources of income and resources. With any luck, Chiles will foot the whole bill, because we will find his dirty money, and it is forfeit for his crimes.

"We are here to get justice for those crimes. It is a big job, and someone's got to do it. We are going to seek out and prove Lockwood Chiles's criminal activities and try to bring all those involved to law."

"Excuse me?" said Vinnie, and stood up. He is tall and bulky and that day was wearing his serious outfit, to wit: camos, T-shirt and vest, utility belt of Divers Dangerous Weapons, and big black combat-ready boots. If Fleury had seen those boots, he would have shit himself. If Denis and his friends, who watch The Rock[141]'s movies for the fashion statements, had seen him, other bodily functions would have been triggered. I thought about his

140. Because we needed more LERTs around there, hahaha. I managed not to say this aloud — *that* time.

141. Who should, if there is any justice, play Vinnie in the movie, BTW.

kid and the Musée d'Orsay, and I smiled at him so sweetly that he unpuffed to almost normal-person size.

"Yes, Vinnie. Vinnie Marston, everyone. Security consultant."

"Why are we here?"

The other three crew chiefs of the Smart-Paper Flying Squad looked up, sullen and suspicious, as their glowering and suspicious boss looked around the room.

"You are here without prejudice," said Spak.

"Shhh," I said. "Skip the legal words. You are here because if anybody knows why that goddamn smart paper still calls for backup, and the backup still gets paid, and where that paycheque comes from, and where your orders might come from, you do. And if you don't, you can help find out. Also because Roger and his minions and these Mysterious People he has brought to us have all together found nothing to make us think that the four of you are anything more than dutiful, and honest, employees."

"Pawns," said Gracelyn helpfully, and unhelpfully.

"Fuck right off," said Hikaru.

"True, though," said Sharon, making her teammates glare at *her* now.

"Sharon is right," I said. "Honesty is the best policy."

"Horsepocky," said Bob.

"Hold up, guys," said Vinnie. "She's right, you know. The dude hires us, but he doesn't tell us shit, and then he's in jail, and now he's dead, and now all the evidence shows he was ripping people off left and right. Not the best look for us, I'd say."

I looked at each of his team as I spoke.

"I want — we want — everything criminal that Lockwood Chiles built torn down to the ground, and burned to a crisp," I said, "and you four are inside the walls. It's going to happen with you or without you. Without you, you're fired today and you sign NDAs that will apply for four generations — if you are still allowed to walk around, knowing what you know, which is not something I can control. With you, you keep getting paid those generous salaries, but you get to actually do what you trained for, and be more than a fucking call centre." Somehow, I can never manage not to swear. But this was Vinnie & Co., and they liked a lively oath now and again.

I grinned as I watched them all think it through. Vinnie watched them too. They're smart — Lock had always hired the best, back when he could — so it didn't take long. I waited, and slowly, each of them nodded.

Vinnie nodded last and, with his team settled, sat down. He reached for the tablet he'd set down in front of him and squared it up as well as he could against the uneven edge of the hand-planed table. I wondered what was on that tablet — the one that he had had the foresight to bring with him when the others came unarmed — except for the utility belts, and some suspicious bulges at the rear waistline[142].

"Ready," he said.

"Great," I said, and drew a breath.

At the back side of the table, midway, in what I can perhaps call the "anti-catbird seat", the one that is aggressively low-status, almost in a shadow despite the perfect lighting design[143] in the room, the Someone Spak Knew cleared her throat.

"Speaking of NDAs," she said.

I looked at her.

She stared back at me.

"You gave this away," she said. "You admitted that big fish need ocean trawlers to catch them."

"Very poetic," I said, as if *my* team hadn't already been on my case for the same metaphor. I gave it a moment, let the moment stretch, then sighed. "And true."

---

142. I never did find out, because Reasons, see later. A very short time later, don't worry.

143. It better be perfect. It cost enough.

"So it is *my* trawler, and *I* am the captain."

Roger's People and the Fraud Squad all stirred. She turned and simply looked at them, each of them, and that was the end of that. But the deputy chief did not look away, so the Someone spoke directly to her. "You know who I am," she said.

"Yes, ma'am, I do," the deputy chief said.

"I *am* the captain of this vessel."

The deputy chief is a very smart woman, but she's also a feisty fighter with a bit of a mouth on her. So there was a long pause, and a couple of twitches of her usual poker face, before she said, "Damn skippy, ma'am." Only then did she sit back.

"I am going to make a little speech," the Now-Captain Someone said. "You can even tell people about it. But it is the last thing said by this task force that will ever be spoken about without my permission."

She looked around.

"Seeing no argument," she said, "then hear this. I know about Lockwood Chiles. I know a lot about him. As far as I am concerned, he was a waste of skin when he was alive and now that he is dead he is going to waste a lot of good people's time. But I am going to go after him and his bullshit because everything that fucker thought and did is an affront to me and people like me. And because we will take his ill-gotten money and turn it to good use. You may not like me, who pays me, or who I stand for, but I am your only hope for justice. So you are going to submit to my judgment."

She paused, and looked specifically at me with her pointy gaze. "Yes, even you. I know you own almost all the smart paper in the world. You are going to give every piece Lockwood Chiles ever touched to me, and you are never going to ask me what happened to it. As far as you are concerned, it never existed.

"Do you understand me?"

72. THE BEGINNING OF THE END OF THE MIDDLE

There is a little meme stored on the Internet, a .gif of Nathan Fillion and heavily used, in which he starts to speak, thinks better of it, puts his hand over his mouth, and then the whole thing repeats[144]. I mention it because I, and most of the other people in that room, spent the next few minutes in that exact loop. Nathan would have been proud of our mimicry skills. Every time one of us thought of something to say, we thought better of it, sighed, and hit *Reset*.

It was almost funny. The room was filled with random sighs. It would have made a good comedy sketch if any of us had felt like laughing.

I have very little idea what the others were thinking, though some of us compared notes about it later. But others of us took the NDAs we signed three minutes later quite seriously and refused to discuss any of it, which by the way is annoying as fuck; Roger and Vinnie, I'm particularly talking to you. I do know that Vinnie and his teams got a new job, and I'm suspecting it's for Captain Someone, but he's not saying[145].

Here is what I was thinking. It is what had kept me up all night, but that didn't mean that the gerbils in my head had quit running on their wheel.

First, obviously, I hadn't thought this whole thing through when I said we needed help. (In my defence, I hadn't had the

---

144. It may still be at https://giphy.com/gifs/castle-nathan-fillion-favourite -Ow59copwTPruU, or not. The Interwebz ebb and flow.

145. Just like he never said what was on that tablet he gave to Captain Someone after the meeting when he thought no-one was looking. Vinnie's a good guy in his stickler-ish way, and if I ever need a stickler again, I know where to look. Although I generally don't mind that I don't see The Team as much since that day's events, I do keep an eye on Vinnie's kid, who's making quite a name as a mixed-media artist.

data I have now either.) Spak's Someone worked in one of those agencies that hide in the shadows even if the bright lights are on — why I saw the seat she had chosen as a creepily accurate accidental (*maybe* accidental) metaphor[146]. Roger's People worked for another, similarly-cloaked, branch of law enforcement (and I foresaw jurisdictional standoffs, but sorry, I can't tell you whether that prediction came true or not).

I tend not to like what those agencies do (understatement). When I worked with Mina and Pamela and Terry, we spent some of our time trying to shine light in those dark corners, with variable success. Sometimes what was crawling around there was disgusting.

I probably, on some idealistic level I didn't even know I could still achieve, had envisioned some kind of Justice League that would bring squeaky-clean ethics to bear on the wickedness Lockwood had promulgated and destroy his evil machinations with the Forces of Right.

But this is the real world. We were going to have to accept that shadow would fight shadow.

Was that even ethical? Did I have a responsibility to prevent that paper from falling into shadowy hands? And if I tried, could I?

I sighed, because, no, I couldn't. This Someone was within our gates, as it were. She knew what we had, and all she had to do was walk out with the paper, because I guarantee that no-one here, not even Vinnie & Co., would have been able to stop her if she really wanted to. She was that scary.

Yet without her, we were all at risk, just as we always had been.

As for our brave plan of letting the paper call home and seeing what happened, the answer appeared to be fuck-all. If there were processes, we weren't equipped to detect them.

I sighed again.

---

146. If there's ever a movie, they should get Susan Blommaert to play her.

I had asked for deus ex machina, and that's what I was getting. I had set it all in motion.

Had I done so out of tiredness? Well, yeah, but also, no.

In the same vein, was I just fed up? No there also.

So, excluding those, I had to trust that I had made the right call. I wanted Lockwood Chiles eradicated, and if it had to be posthumously, that's how this shit turned out, and I would have to deal with it.

Another sigh.

Unless, that is, we wanted to forget about Own Domains, Nathan's and my good work, and our entire futures, and instead spend the rest of our careers as investigators of one evil dude. Turn into a plucky little crew of Central-Casting crusaders, locked in small rooms with an ever-increasing stack of Bankers Boxes[147] filled with an ever-increasing volume of inter-indexed files, probably going nowhere in great detail because we had no passwords and no hackers — our best hacker being dead — and no real power in the shadow world where outcomes this big are decided.

We've all seen this movie. In the movie, there is victory. In the real world, not usually, and the process instead often leads directly to tinfoil hats and badly-designed websites full of poor spelling.

Subjunctivity again: not *ever* going to happen.

I sighed one last time.

I looked up from my interlocked fingers, and everyone else was watching me. I apparently was taking the longest to swallow this pill.

In my defence, it was a hell of a size. It was a fucking bezoar.

Lockwood Chiles was beyond my reach. Even dead, he would take an army to stop. And I didn't want my life to be about this asshole for one second longer.

---

147. ™ redux.

"Fine," I said.

The Someone got up, and with her own senior, captainy hands, she placed a thick sheaf of documents in front of each of us.

"You understand," she said, "that you are going to sign away a lot of rights you think you have."

"I *do* have them, until I sign," I said.

"You think you do," she said, "which is just cute. But most of the time, we are willing to let you believe that. Sign on this line, and you lose your illusions."

"What else is new?" I said. "My whole fucking life is that." Meaning: full of lightning, geese, cats, and ghosts, these days.

I had known this moment was coming, so I had brought something special from the trove I kept in Nathan's box. It was a fountain pen he had bought for me. It was one of the gifts that arrived after he died. It was therefore the most beautiful fountain pen in the world[148], and I had cleaned it, filled it with the very black ink that came with it, tested it, and put it into my pocket.

"Everyone should read them," Dafydd Spak said.

"Will that make a difference?" I sounded just as sour as I felt.

"Probably not, but humour me."

I pulled my sheaf of documents toward me.

"Wait a minute," I said. "None of this has to do with Nathan's paper, right? I still own that, and the formulae. And nothing to do with his activities, right? And if you find his money, it's in here that we get it all back, or actually Own Domains does, right?"

"That is our understanding," Someone said.

"Is it here, in these?"

"More or less," Someone replied.

---

148. And it writes on his smart paper, and later I found out a lot about this pen, but it is all immaterial to the narrative in progress, so just know that it was both the most beautiful and perfect fountain pen in the world, and as for the rest, it can be any story you want to tell yourself.

"I want it to be more *more* and less *less*," I said. After a beat, "If you know what I mean."

"I do," said the Someone to the Mouse That Roared.

I looked pointedly at her, and she nodded and said, "I'll show you all how to emend the relevant page. Pages."

"Okay then."

Had she caved too easily? Never mind, she had caved, and Nathan and I were safe. We all followed the leader, emended pages 26, 43, 45, and 139, with nods from Mr. Spak to reassure us, and then we all sat there for a lot of minutes, reading. Bob read second to slowest and Hikaru read fastest, but I was a close second — and I think Hikaru just skipped a bunch.

Mr. Spak was the slowpoke here. He kept leafing back and forth, and he did most of his sighing during this period. Several of us were done and he still had one hand slightly raised in the universal sign for "Hold up!" We watched him read.

Finally he nodded to us.

"Just cute," said Captain Someone again. "He approves. It's time."

For some reason, everyone stopped again, and now watched me.

I had primed the nib making the changes, so I knew the pen would work perfectly.

This was for Nathan and Priscilla.

I had always known I would sign a deal with the Devil itself to take Chiles down, and maybe that was what I was doing. If he was dead, that ship had sailed, but if, scintilla-wise, he wasn't, then that Devil We Knew sitting across from us would be meeting him in some kind of hell real soon now.

Any which way, I'd be free of him.

The document had little flags everywhere it needed signatures, and every page needed an initial, and twice on pages 26, 43, 45, and 139, but for symbolic purposes I turned to the last page, firmly wrote my name in black black ink, and gave away my revenge.

Take that, Lockwood Chiles, you murderous fuck.

73. "... FOR ALL INTENSIVE PURPOSES ..."

For all intents and purposes[149], I had just signed The Problem of Lockwood Chiles out of my life forever.

It felt right.

Once I broke the meniscus, there was a flurry of riffling pages all around the table. I signed in the other necessary places, and initialled the bottom of each and every page[150]. That took a while.

Meanwhile, in advance of the inevitable, some of the Someone's minions, who had been waiting outside, had started carrying the Bankers Boxes[151] out of the safe, which made Roma squeak quietly, once, before she subsided too. She and the deputy chief exchanged sympathetic looks.

When we were all done signing, Dafydd gathered up the contracts while I went into the safe myself, shouldering aside a surprisingly-solid minion[152].

I picked up the heavy accordion file and brought it out.

I couldn't quite manage to hand it directly to Captain Someone, so I put it on the table in front of her and patted it

---

149. And intensive purposes too. It's a joke, though, you realise that, right? One of my favourites, actually, as you might be noticing. Along with "a doggy dog world". Please don't write me letters. I'm on your side.

150. Twice on pages 26, 43, 45, and 139 ...

151. You *know* this, right?: ™

152. Solid considering that for the purposes of this story they are Plot Devices (not even red-shirts, as they had no names) and are barely dimensional. I am sure that they have Real Lives somewhere. Somewhere Sekrit.

twice, sort of like the blonde cop, seemed-like-forever ago, burping Fleury's ambulance. She nodded, reached out her left hand, and drew the file toward her. She gestured, and two of her more burly minions brought in a case that looked heavy. One of them unlatched and opened it. She handed the file to the other one, who placed it reverently in a special hollowed-out nest in the centre, just like the movies. It even fit that hollow perfectly, which in retrospect was probably one of the scariest things about the whole day.

He stepped back and his buddy closed the lid. Only then did Captain Someone move from her seat. She did something complicated with the lock, shielding it from us with her body. Then she nodded, and the minions hefted the thing and carried it out of the room and our lives. Stepping around the table briskly, her heels tapping on the old terrazzo and marble floor, she brought up the rear.

She did not slam the door. She did not even close the door. She followed the procession up the stairs to the foyer[153], and they all went through the front door and (as the alley-cams showed) immediately away in the row of rental cars that they had left illegally parked in the side alley. A bit of a surprise, those cars. Vinnie and his crew had brought their Hummers, ditto re parking but in the cross-alley at the back of the building, and I would have bet that Sekrit Departments would have had better cars than mere private security. But what do I know?

Never mind. The important thing was that it was done.

In the immortal words of Sellar and Yeatman, history came to a .[154]

---

153. Which we Canadians appropriately pronounce "foy-eh", with "eh" of course pronounced "ay".

154. That's "full stop" not "period", and definitely not "end" for anyone wondering if S&Y should have written an "an" there.

And I am now contractually forbidden from telling you anything else about what happened, at that table or anywhere else, that day or any day, regarding this part of the story.

It wasn't really the real end, but it was the start of the end. I am able tell you that in the very *very* end, the outcomes were mostly quite satisfactory, with exceptions that more or less followed any expectations you or we might have been forming. One outcome is shareable — what happened with Nathan's money — and I'll get to it later.

If that's too vague, too bad. I have a lawyer who reminds me from time to time of the documents I sign. And sometimes, when the stakes are high, I listen.

I can also tell you that in the moment, as I gently picked up the pen from the table and put it back in my pocket, I felt lighter.

And almost good.

AS I
WAS
FALLING
DOWN
THE STAIR

74. THE REST OF THE MIDDLE

That sounded like a nice conclusion, didn't it? But really it's just a second-act beat.

Because, as a well-known USian once said, it ain't over 'til it's over.

And it ain't over.

Not by a long shot.

Take a minute to remind yourself that Lockwood Chiles, though he tended to loom and worry us with his shadow, was almost certainly dead — speaking of which, if he isn't dead, I still have a problem, but if he *is*, we still have his unsolved murder hanging over my head — and also, in many ways the least of our worries. So all that Sturm und Drang was undertaken in pursuit of a secondary or tertiary goal. Cleaning up after a criminal incident, rather than solving anything.

Chiles's revenge, though, if he had planned one — now that might be another matter. After all, that paper was still in the wind. Nathan's fortune was still shrinking, albeit more slowly as

Spak and Gracelyn and the Fraud Squad and the Sekrit People plugged the holes one at a time.

We still have the unsolved murder of Danny.

We still have the rapacious heirs.

We still have the questioning teen.

We still cry for Nathan and Priscilla.

And there are still cats in the Epitome and dogs in the alley.

75. 23-SKIDOO

Which is not about the snow vehicle made by Bombardier. In this case, it is about our DNA, and the twenty-three pairs of chromosomes that make it up.

DNA evidence is the magic bullet of on-screen crime drama. Some detective scrapes up some blood spatter or steals a paper cup and five minutes later the results are back from the lab and they go after the bad guys[155] with one hundred per cent certainty of guilt, and quickly get a conviction.

In the real world, getting DNA evidence can take weeks or months, because of how backed up law enforcement is[156]. And although an expert can sound authoritative in court, there are limits — even before taking into account, in our case, that contaminating pathologist who had made our lives worse — to what DNA testing can do. Either those limits sound like waffling

---

155. As with Vinnie but for a different reason, "guys" tends to be an ungendered term to me when I'm in a crime-adjacent environment, and anyway I've gotten used to the copspeak — whether that's Stockholm syndrome or not. Given that I plan for my future to have a lot fewer cops in it, we'll be able to measure whether my usage changes. Some sociology-of-linguistics student could get a good paper out of it.

156. This is why Nathan's money could buy faster forensic results than Roger could get, because of these backlogs, which all deplore but apparently never enough to do something effective about it.

to juries, and some judges, and cause the reasonable doubt on which our courts are based, or people overstate certainties (which is sometimes called "confirmation bias", sometimes perjury, and sometimes downright lying) and get some really dubious convictions. So here's the real skinny.

First, you have to get a good ("good" meaning "not degraded") and uncontaminated DNA sample. Even on TV, that's hard. The behaviour of fictional detectives is laughable. Really, actual cops laugh at it, a lot[157]. And in the real world, all sorts of people (and other beings) tromp around a body before, at, and after discovery.

Crime scenes aren't pristine. After your body has been in the woods for a while, are you really your best DNA-contributing self? You're lucky if *you* can be identified, let alone whoever touched your sweater while killing you[158]. And a lot of crows, magpies, mice, skunks, rats, foxes, wolves, dogs, insects, raccoons (in some areas, not around here[159]), and other wildlife are implicated as well. So even if the people taking samples *are* their best selves, the samples aren't.

DNA fragmentation is a thing. You can look it up on Wikipedia, and get the full alphabet soup (RFLP, PCR, STR, miniSTR . . .) but for now, take my word for it that Mother Nature is an accessory after the fact to every crime against persons. An incomplete sample is hard to match, especially by the older methods that relied on having a larger amount of a better sample. So a kind of art form developed around DNA profiling, made of guesswork, intuition, and projection of a small amount of fact into a long string of conjecture.

---

157. So do I. I mean, srsly, why don't they pay *me* the big bucks to be their series advisor? I'd actually earn them.

158. Sorry, I guess that got a little personal. All I'm saying is, don't get murdered.

159. Yet. Thinking 'bout *you*, global climate change.

Though advances have made it possible to test smaller fragments, the mystique was developed before the testing got better, and labs and law enforcement and legal eagles had already filled in the unknowns on the map with handwavium.

Roger doesn't like this part, but he knows it's true.

Better testing is part of why cold-case investigations like the Innocence Project have success. They re-test with modern techniques. But they also look for the aforementioned confirmation bias, perjury, and downright lying, and they find a lot of all that.

Above all that, however, the real truth we hate to know is that the fewer points of comparison there are to start with, the more likelihood that even with the best available modern testing, there will be doubt. Or, in fancy terms, "reduced statistical weight of association in the event of a match".

But sometimes an expert will go on the stand anyway — as had happened 'way too many times in the USA before 2015[160], for instance, and as we had just found out had been going on locally — and swear that a match was made in heaven.

It gets worse with samples that are a mixture of two or more people's DNA. Nowadays this happens more because testing is getting better, which is a bitch for the prosecution and the defence both.

Bluntly, which bits go with which source? Is the "highly-trained forensic scientist" who sorts out the results actually that good? Sometimes yes, but sometimes . . . more handwavium ensues.

Some labs now have computers that will do this stuff, in the service of trying to take the guesswork out. But I wonder. A computer is only as good as its instructions, even nowadays when neural nets are helping with all sorts of complex tasks, such as DNA testing and inventing the messages on flirtation hearts.

---

160. DuckDuckGo™ will help you search for "FBI flawed forensics" and you will be horrified, as I was.

In conclusion: if you want your head to explode, just dive down this rabbit hole on the Internet. Soon, you will be throwing terms like "probabilistic genotyping" around at parties while you rant about justice, and your friends may stage an intervention.

If they do, ask them all, as they come in, to spit in a test tube, seal it, and sign on the label, in case things get out of hand.

76. OH, WAIT A MINUTE, I WAS MAKING A POINT THERE

My point wasn't to take us all into the weeds of forensic reliability and get us lost there. My point was that this process is hugely important, and subject to all sorts of pitfalls.

So every time you come to the table, you have to design a process to avoid as many of the pitfalls as possible. Some of this is arcane science, and some of it is common sense.

We all know that common sense is, famously, so uncommon it's almost a superpower.

But we try.

Achilles and the tortoise notwithstanding, we try.

We were already using DNA evidence in very direct ways. But as the science of DNA expands, there are many many avenues to try.

Here's one of the things we tried.

77. CAST YOUR BREAD UPON THE WATERS, AND IT SHALL COME BACK TO YOU AFTER MANY DAYS (ALBEIT SOFT AND MUSHY)

This idea wasn't that original, so it's a bit shaky for me to take credit. For one thing, it has become a much more common tactic of law enforcement, and is reliable as long as there are good investigating officers who don't make unjustified conclusions about the results. Also, the idea occurred to others almost simultaneously, so there is also that, invoking the "which triplet was born first" principle of primogeniture. But I did have it, while not in a room with others, unless you count a bus as a room, so I can at least record the circumstances thereof.

Despite my beloved little car, which I use fairly seldom (and mostly only when I need to reduce the hassle of getting to non-bus-able places like crematoria, veterinarians, and blue-grass festivals), I still have a bus pass — an increasingly expensive commitment to sustainable public transit, but I consider it an act of public good (and blind stubbornness).

So after I left the office, I went down a few blocks to get some groceries for my ravenous little growing family. I was on the #5 with my bulging reusable bags at my feet, zoning out as one does, ignoring the music that escaped from around the headphones of the kid sitting next to me, who was going to be *so* deaf by the time they were legal, and checking out the ads.

The ad above the back door was for "Ancestry and Health Testing" conducted by a public DNA business. Send them a cheek swab, and they will find your family and also tell you what your doctor should be testing for. These services are controversial for the loss of privacy involved, and for some commercial issues around stealing people's genotypes (this has definitely occurred in the past, particularly with people of colour), and for upset-ting racists by revealing that they are not pure-laine, and also for being inaccurate AF sometimes. But.

But they also have found kinfolk and reunited them, they have alerted people to congenital health issues, and they have traced criminals through running anonymous DNA at the state's request. We are a province, but did we do the same thing?

No-one knew who Lockwood Chiles had been. He met Nathan in a group home after Nathan had been made a ward of the Crown. Chiles had let slip that he hacked himself into the child welfare system and hid in group homes pretending to be younger than he was, hinting that he had done so to meet

Nathan and exploit his brilliance at game design and the genius that resulted in all the other inventions later. But that hadn't helped the cops or Mr. Spak or me find anything about his real past. He was a computer genius himself, too, after all, and lived up to the stereotype. He'd sanitised any record he could find, and he'd steadfastly refused to give any further information. Now he had taken that information with him to the grave — dead for good, we all hoped — but given our doubts, we needed to know more even just to track where he had been, let alone where he was if he was alive.

I fished my cell phone out and called Roger. "DNA tracing businesses," I said. "You know, find your cousins, find out which US president you're related to. They usually share with the DNA tracing projects. I know we are using the conventional methods, but what if we looked for relatives? Even a distant relative would give us a string to pull. That's another way we find Lockwood's real self."

"Good idea," he said. "But not new. Pretty sure we know how to do that. Maybe already did. I'll find out. Now hang up. I'm in a meeting."

78. IN A MEETING

So I called Spak.

"DNA," I said.

"The black dog howls at midnight," he said.

"For fuck's sake, what are those kids making you watch on Netflix™? I'm talking about the Woodwards, and Brice."

"We already got the official samples from their lawyer. And the samples from the shiny plastic cups in the boardroom. We're doing research on how we can use the latter, since we are not, technically speaking, law enforcement. Though I am an officer of the court. Takes research. Takes time."

"This is new. Different, I mean. I'm thinking of these private DNA testing places, like 23Skidoo or Roots Я Us, or whatever they're called. Could we send Nathan's DNA — and these people's, from our cups — to those registries and see if we get any other matches? Relatives? Maybe they are real, maybe they aren't, but if they aren't, who are they, and where are the real ones? And for Chiles, is there some other family connexion out there? Can we find it? I read online that most of them share with law enforcement, so Roger may have to do it, but what about us? Have we tried that with Nathan's DNA? Which I should be legally allowed to do, or you as his executor. And are we allowed to do that with Lock's and with the new samples?"

"Pretty sure those cups belong to us and we can do whatever we want with them. Roger might have to do it, as a law enforcement privilege thing. I'll check. But I'll call you back. I'm in a meeting."

So I hung up.

I sat there, phone in hand, glaring at my asparagus and eggplant.

The bus rattled as it turned the corner into my neighbourhood. On the left, a backhoe was in the process of destroying one of the last of the hundred-year-old single-family homes in the area. Because we are all poor, nobody really cares if some slumlord without a demolition permit wrecks a ramshackle house[161] where he has been renting broom closets to alcoholics and untreated schizophrenics, so that he can speculate on the land sale.

Nobody but us.

Nathan cared.

I care.

The people who live in those houses care.

---

161. Deliberately made ramshackle by targeted neglect and general malfeasance, BTW.

Own Domains and Roma and Thelma and M2F2 and the mayor and Mr. Spak and even Kim, bless their teenaged heart, care.

Yet the putative heirs were willing to steal that so that they could play out their cheap Kardashian fantasies.

That was the moment I realised how much it mattered to me that these pretenders not win. I have been poor before and I could be poor again — no issue. But the people of my neighbourhood needed those houses, those apartments, those harm reduction villages we had planned.

It's a good thing that I don't have superpowers or those vegetables would have been burned to a crisp right in their reusable shopping bags by my smouldering gaze. But the rest of the ride and the walk from the bus stop were just long enough that by the time I could see the Epitome's front door, I had almost calmed down.

79. OH, FUCK

My calm lasted until I walked in the door of my apartment and saw Kim there, and I had the realisation that you have had pages and pages ago. You were wondering when all the stupid people in the book[162] were going to catch on. Well, the answer is, right now.

I walked in and saw Kim's profile, with that beautiful arrogant hawk nose outlined so clearly against the bright window, and — and this is not to my credit — I said, ardently and involuntarily, "Oh, *fuck*!"

Unfortunately, in the other chair across from them, sat their mother (for all practical purposes) Mattie.

"I'm sorry," said Kim, jumping up. "She . . . you said we should call her . . . so I . . ."

---

162. Especially the ones who were saying how smart they were only a few footnotes ago, right?

"I wasn't swearing about that," I said, "and I'm really *really* sorry. Please forgive me, it was something else. It is *perfect* that she is here. Hello, Mattie, I am *so* glad to see you, you can't even *imagine*." To make the point, I tried to hug her, but grocery bags clashed around us. "I mean, I love having Kim here, love it, don't get me wrong, but . . . Oh, hell, I'm just going to stop babbling and — make a phone call. Sorry. It's really important." I set down my bags and stepped back into the hall.

Spak was still in the office.

"Um," I said, and stopped.

"What have you done?" he said, in a phrase and tone I recognised, and I realised he must have one goose, out of the flock that might haunt him, reserved specifically for me.

"Um," I said. "We have an heir. We have an heir here. Right here."

"What are you talking about?"

"Nathan's child is sitting in my living room. Nathan and Priscilla's child."

I explained further, with admirable brevity, Kim's immaculate and unassailable provenance.

"For f— . . . for exactly how long have you known about this?"

"Um, yeah, since, um, last year. Roger and I went to meet them."

"Them."

"Singular non-binary, and definitely theirs in the other sense of the pronoun, I mean definitely Nathan and Priscilla's, though they-single-non-binary Kim was adopted by Pris's sister, well, half-sister, Mattie, who also happens to be here. Kim. Just turned eighteen. Showed up on my doorstep, literally, a little while ago."

"I am horrified to realise that I understood all that. And you were going to tell me when?"

"Um, well, it didn't actually occur to me until this moment. I was thinking of them as a separate, er, bolt from the blue."

"And they came here because . . . ?"

"Because they were looking for more information about their heritage."

"And you didn't think. Of . . ."

"No, I didn't. Think. Of that."

"I tend to believe you are rather intelligent, you know. Despite your impulsive, er, risk-management style."

"Yeah, well, I think of myself as not too stupid either, but I'm re-evaluating that."

"DNA," said Spak.

"Yeah," I said.

"Today," he said.

"Send minions," I said.

"Gracelyn will be right there," he said, and hung up. Wow. He hung up on me. Of course I deserved it, but wow. This was Dafydd Spak we are talking about.

Of course I deserved it, but still.

I realised that Kim and Mattie had come out of the kitchen and were standing staring at me.

"We have to talk," I said.

"I think so," said Mattie. "Kim is saying that she — that they want to stay here."

"Not about that," I said. "They can stay, that would be great. Or not stay, I'm fine with whatever. Actually, more than fine. Kim is awesome. Kim is *cool*." I saw Kim grin at that. "No, this is something rather more serious."

I humped the groceries in past them to the kitchen counter. Something welcome to do with my hands, although seriously? I don't think quail eggs enjoy being treated that way[163].

Kim and Mattie came back through the kitchen door as if

---

163. Laid by quail raised locally in a home business not ten blocks away from the Epitome, so I *am* shopping local, JSYK.

drawn by magnets. I was tightly-wound enough to generate an electrical field, at that.

"You do realise, Kim," I said, my back still to them, "that your biological parents were rich."

"I guess," said Kim.

"Do you know how rich?" I turned with some butter lettuce in my hand. It was never going to be the same again.

"I dunno, I guess, kinda really rich? He was some kind of big deal in computers, right?"

I looked at them.

After a moment Mattie took pity on me. "We've explained Priscilla's will to Kim," she said. "There is about seven million dollars in a trust fund. Kim will learn how to take care of it and receive control of it at twenty-five. Until then, it will pay for schooling, amenities, a monthly allowance, everything."

"Unscheduled trips across the continent to visit honourary aunties," I said.

"Well, yes, I suppose."

"I saved my allowance for that," Kim said defensively.

"Some allowance."

"I was not consulted," said Mattie stiffly. "As for Nathan, we were not sure, so we . . . waited. That kind of money is a huge responsibility."

Kim is no fool, even though they as yet had no idea what Mattie had just meant. They hugged Mattie from behind and said, "Mom, don't worry. I am not going to get all weird, right? You know how I am. I just had to come here and do this one thing. I had to find out."

Mattie closed her eyes and leaned back against her tall cuckoo, and her voice was loving when she said, "I know, sweetie. You'll be fine. I just . . . worry." Her face, however, was pointed in my direction, and I could see the effort it took to choose trust. Apparently, no pun intended, I was seeing the exact moment every parent of any quality dreads and then experiences, when it is vitally important to open rather than clench their hands, and let the whole flying-free thing take its course. Mattie was making the right decision, but it was costing her.

Kim, oblivious, continued to hug, and said fervently, "I love you, Mom!"

I shook my head and smiled slightly, and Mattie, bless her, smiled back at me and nodded infinitesimally. Her courage gave me courage.

"This is not about your birth mother's money," I said. "I know, it seems like she had a lot, from the books and endorsements and reality TV and everything. But comparatively . . ."

They looked at me like owls on a branch in a *Canadian Geographic*™ photo.

I took a breath. Then I let it out, and took another.

"Nathan was —" I said, "your father, that is — was also rich. Much more rich. Um, exceptionally rich. In fact, he might have had more money than Bill Gates."

Pinter pause, then, "No way!" Kim let go of Mattie and recoiled a bit.

"Way," I said. "He made money in computers and technology. Then his money made money and that money made more money. It was driving him crazy, so he made provisions for everyone he knew and loved to be comfortable, well, rich actually, exceptionally rich by ordinary-people standards, and set up a sort of retirement fund for himself, and then he started giving it all away. He isn't the first really rich guy to do that, so he had some idea how. He had lawyers to help make it watertight. He had a plan, and I was part of that plan. It was all about ending homelessness. He was applying a housing-first model and there was enough money to do it right. We were starting here."

Kim looked around the apartment. "Here?"

I laughed, albeit a bit grimly, and circled my hand in the air. "Here, in this neighbourhood. In this city. All over this city, really. Oh, they are such pretty plans."

I tossed the ripped head of lettuce into the sink and sat down.

"But?" Smart kid.

"But he and your mother were murdered by Lockwood Chiles, and therefore the estate is tied up in probate, which is really *really* complex, especially since Chiles also set about stealing some of it while he was in jail but still alive, which is also complicated, and meanwhile, some putative heirs, some supposed siblings, have come out of the woodwork and are contesting the will. They want all the rest of the money."

"That's a lot of money," said Mattie.

"They have no idea," I said. "If they really *are* Nathan's long-lost siblings, which we have to verify and I frankly doubt, he had already left them enough money to live like B-list celebrities for the rest of their lives, but they don't seem to understand that. They want it all. They would literally do nothing with all that potential but sit on it like trolls."

"Dragons," said Kim.

"You haven't seen them," I said. "Dragons are nice. These are trolls. But —"

There was a silence no-one else had the sense to break.

I was steeling myself. I still hadn't gotten to the point. So I did.

"Nathan didn't know about you specifically," I said, "but you are his child. He provided for the eventuality that he might have one. You are his heir. Sole biological. Rock-solid. Beloved-by-law. Unmistakeable. Heir."

"Oh."

Yeah.

Oh.

80. REALLY FUCKING FAST

The doorbell rang. It was Gracelyn with a cheek swab kit.

That is uncanny for so many reasons.

Also, really fucking fast.

I MET
A BUMP
THAT
WASN'T
THERE;

81. IMMACULATE IN EVERY FEATHER

What to do now?

I asked Mr. Spak.

"Do nothing!" he said, the exclamation point being for him the equivalent of Roger shouting. Then he ruined it by actually being reasonable and explanatory, which, while welcome, was perversely disappointing: I was feeling stupid enough that I would have listened to his emphatic order without elaboration. "I don't know yet. I have to look at the will again."

"I seem to recall there is wording in there that covers this."

"You know perfectly well there was. But lawyers like to do more than 'seem to recall'. Give me some time to do the research. Say nothing. Do nothing. All right?"

"For once," I said, "I will obey."

"There will be a time," he said, "when I will look back on this day and gloat." He hung up again. This could not be allowed to become a habit, or the foundations of my world might just shatter.

If you can't trust Mr. Spak to be immaculate in every feather, who can you trust?

Mattie was exhausted from her trip. I took her down to the guest room and tucked her in to Kim's bed for the time being.

When I came back down the hall, I looked at Kim and Kim looked at me.

"I have no idea," I said. "Apparently, we wait and do nothing."

Kim grinned. Apparently, they already knew me well enough to find that funny.

I tried not to glower.

From now on I would be modest, I would stifle my ego, and I would try to get used to my new level of intellectual incompetence. It was possible I would have to give up the Oxford comma. I hoped it wouldn't go as far as saying those things like "it's a doggy-dog world" or "to all intensive purposes" for that matter, but I've read *Flowers for Algernon*.

When the decline happens, it can be fast.

82. DOING NOTHING, FOR SOME VALUES OF NOTHING

I tried to read, but I couldn't concentrate, not even on Sarah Smith. I lay back on the couch, which is a very fetching chaise longue actually, and tried to think.

Then I tried to not think.

Double fail.

Kim tried catching up with their social media, but clearly that was as unsettling to them as trying to think was for me. I closed my eyes, mostly, and from under my lashes watched them get up and restlessly cast about the room, browsing my life.

Finally, they picked up my autoharp and within a few minutes had placed it on their lap and had their tablet propped up with an instructional video playing, earbuds in, dark head bent and beautiful hands deft if inexperienced over the keys and strings.

After a while I got up to deal with the orphan groceries. On the way into the kitchen, I said, "Look up Bryan Bowers. That's the style I use. You will need finger picks."

Just saying the words hurt. Nathan and I had spent a lovely and loving afternoon in his workshop once, and he had used some moulding clay, a fancy 3-D fabricator, and far too much computing power to make me several personally-fitted sets of finger picks. My hands and Nathan's hadn't been that much different, which meant that likely Kim could fit those picks. I was going to have to share.

Irrationally, I almost hated that idea, as if Nathan's memory, and the loving acts he had done for me, were mine. But that kind of thinking was why Lockwood Chiles had killed him: jealousy and the presumption of ownership, dog-in-the-manger thinking that I don't really understand, deep down, and wasn't likely to be any good at if I tried to start now.

Not just to prove I was no dog in the manger, but also because I like Kim a lot, after I had put away the poor abused eggs and vegetables I went into my bedroom and opened the closet door.

I stood for a long time looking up at the dark box in the shadows of the top shelf before I reached up, fitted my hands into the contours made for them, and lifted down the soul of my lover Nathan Bierce.

83. OUT OF THE CLOSET

Bringing that box out of the closet, and believe me, the irony of that phrase is not lost on me, was going to be one hell of a distraction, but it was also the hardest thing I had done so far to introduce Kim to their parents.

When I finally came back into the living room, Kim watched me silently, I think more than a little taken aback by my inhibited tears. I wasn't exactly sobbing, but I also wasn't doing anything to discipline the ducts.

Still carrying the autoharp, but differently now, Kim followed me back into the kitchen. I put the box on the table, and it rested on the yellow Arborite™ like an alien spaceship, which I guess in a way it was. (Is. It is. It still exists; I still have it. And, absent the zombie apocalypse, always will.)

The same day we made the fingerpicks, Nathan had innocently given me another block of moulding clay to hold, and as a love-gift, in secret, from the resulting imprint of my grip, he had hand-carved the shape of my hands into some hand-cut pieces of a rich, dark, heavily-grained wood and made for me this perfectly-smooth, contoured, seemingly-seamless tea-chest-sized container. I call it a box, but really, it is so much more than a box. He left it to me in his will, possibly because he died before my birthday.

It's a box with an invisible lid. I had to place my hands just so and then press just so in order to open it, and to discover the gifts he had been assembling in it — most of which are none of your business now or ever, though I will admit they might have included dark chocolate. And real truffles, not the sweet kind. And it had since been filled to the top with all the smart paper in the world (and a few stealth smart-stock business cards) and the formulae for same, stored on cutting-edge media. The contents had rotated slightly over the ensuing months and, at the moment, were mostly smart paper, with a few other small items I will get to in a minute.

The most obvious of the pages had contained his will, which had a carefully-witnessed visible holograph on the page in addition to its spoken component[164]. Mr. Spak and I had had to play that thing to a lot of people and would have to do so many times

---

164. Which is how I distinguished it from divers other reports, and from all the "blank" paper with stuff hidden on it.

more, and I had hated every moment of that, because the message was in Nathan's rich, beautiful voice, and he had spoken intimately to me as if we had been alone together.

Taking pity on me, I suspect, as much as for legal reasons, Spak had taken it and kept it in his files, leaving me a notarised copy, which helped. When using it was needed, I didn't have to be there any more to have my chest cracked open and my heart pinned out on their official desks.

As you have already seen, I still haven't really found everything that is on the rest of the paper, but I can tell you that some of the pages contain light-hearted messages to me that also do serious bloody damage to my heart whenever I hear them. Others have all Nathan's notes for Own Domains, and still others a complex strategy for getting rid of all but a kernel of his vast fortune. Mr. Spak and Roma had some of those now — for ease of investigation — the second exceptions to my hoarding of the trove.

Most of the pages, including those, were not seriously password-protected, but I had still found a few blank sheets that might or might not have been truly blank; I couldn't get some of them to wake up, so I couldn't tell.

But never mind that now. I wasn't there for the smart paper, which made a nice change.

I was there for the finger picks.

84. BRYAN BOWERS STYLE

Because life goes on, because about two-thirds of the smart paper had gone to the Faraday's safe (and half of that had gone onward to bureaucratic oblivion, now), and for Reasons, there was room in the box, and I had now allowed it to surround — along with the notes and letters he wrote to me in life, and the key to his workshop — many of Nathan's other small-sized gifts, including my finger picks, and including small yet mighty things. Such as, op cit., that fountain pen featured earlier that he had ordered for me and which due to delivery-lag had arrived after his death. Such as other small pre-ordered gifts that still occasionally appeared, causing, as you might expect, new stirrings-up of grief. The thought of showing the box and its contents to others pained me then as it always did and probably always will — willingly exposing my most vulnerable self by sharing his.

But Kim's presence required me to get over myself now rather than later.

To play an autoharp Bryan Bowers style, you hold the sound-board against your sternum so that the sound resonates all through your chest cavity, and you hold the instrument as if it were a baby, or Micah when he's doing his thing with Kim. You can lean your head on the side if you like, and feel your ears ring and your skull hum along with the transmitted music[165]. You press the chord keys with your left hand, and on your right you don a full set of finger picks so you can pick out melody and chords and bass support, all at the same time, like a harpist.

These picks are shaped to surround your finger and thumb tips, and they hold on, which means you have to get them in exactly the right size or bend them to size. I prefer plastic to metal picks because I don't like a jangly sound. When I had used store-bought ones, I had submerged them in boiling water to make them malleable, then shaped them to my slimmer-than-usual fingers. I'd filed down the pick end of a couple to get a better angle, because they were really guitar picks I was repurposing. If Brian Bowers or his fan club had ever offered a set of custom picks, I don't know about them.

In the box there were several sets of the special picks Nathan and I had made. Once we had a suitable design, and by design I mean a 3-D modelling of the perfect shape for my hand and for

---

165. Also, co-incidentally, Auto-Tuning® your voice: pun definitely intended.

the picking angle of each digit, Nathan had 3-D printed them in all the colours of medium that he had, which were rich versions of the usual rainbow: a deep blood-red, a clear quinacridone red, a dark saffron orange, that deep yellow often called tiger-yellow[166], a less rich lemony yellow, a deep sap green (for Celtic music, obviously), teal, lapis blue, a dark intense magenta. He also did a set of grey and one of black while he was practising, but the samples turned out so well that we kept them.

So, eleven sets.

To deal with how attractive they were to the cats, I'd found — a classic Dollarama™ discovery — a little chambered Lucite™ box to keep them all in. It was divided into twelve compartments, which caused me some trauma, but I had decided on a reasoned arrangement to put eleven things into twelve spaces, and told my back brain to shut the fuck up.

I lifted it out and put it on the table.

"You will need a set of these. Your father and I made them."

"*Made* them?"

So I had to explain. Partway through I just quit talking altogether. Kim reached out and took my hands.

"Um," they began, "look, it seems like everything you tell me makes you feel bad. You don't have to keep on, you know. I get it that he was a good guy. A cool guy."

I sighed and squeezed those long fingers gently. "Here's the thing," I said. "Nathan isn't here. That's a source of great grief to me, and I made a promise that when I need to cry, I'll cry, whatever the circumstances. Except if I'm driving, of course, that would be stupid."

Kim snorted.

---

166. Or *marigold*. But I'm not fond of marigolds, and I do like tigers. Well, in the abstract. Micah is the closest I've come in the flesh, as an Abyssinian looks a little tigerish, if you squint.

"But," I went on, "for you, Nathan is just coming to life. The other day I was thinking it's like that rhyme 'As I was going up the stair, I met a man who wasn't there . . .'. You're just stepping up to meet him. You *need* to meet him. The best thing I can do here is get the fuck over myself, and help you meet both him and Priscilla. Maybe there will be a feedback loop, and I will get used to them being Not There. But this is not about me. It's about justice, peace, and hope."

I took a breath, and squeezed their hands gently, still doing Full Social Worker but now mixing in more than a little of my real heart. "Chiles needs to not get away with trying to erase them. That's the justice part. I need to get used to the reality. That's the peace part. And for you, knowing your forbears and their past will help you live a better life and aspire to great things. Which by the way, if for you 'great' means living well, being kind and good, and you don't care about fame or invention or wealth, that is just as great as anything else. You will figure it out and do whatever you want, but knowing who they were will help with whatever you do. That's the hope part."

After a moment, I said, "Thank you for coming to my TED Talk."

I shoved the little Lucite™ storage box over to Kim. "Pick two pairs. One is good, but two is prudent. Redundant systems. Try them all on. They are supposed to be identical, but I notice that they aren't, quite."

Kim opened the lid slowly and touched the tip of one of the picks gently. After a long moment, they said, "Which ones are your favourites?" and looked carefully at me.

I made one of those weird little moues that are accompanied by ambiguous tiny hand movements that may or may not indicate being completely at sea. But Kim wasn't letting up, and made a micro-gesture of their own that seemed to combine an encouraging look with an eyeroll. I nodded slightly and reached for the little box.

"My absolute favourite are these," I said, picking out the rich tiger-yellow set. "Pantone 123," I said. "If you are interested in that kind of thing."

Kim is young but has already figured out the power of silence. This wasn't the first time I'd noticed it.

"They were the first ones Nathan made. He knew my favourite colour."

"Do they fit best?"

"No, these lapis-blue ones do, just a smidge."

Kim began to try on all the other pairs. After the first set, they went to get the autoharp and began to try the picks with a strum. They seemed to get the idea of the Bowers style really quickly, and they carried on testing with little hums and subvocalisations.

Finally the grey and the lighter-yellow sets sat on their own, and Kim had put all the rest back in the box. By then I had long since stopped crying, and had become an advisor in the process, demonstrating the right angle of wear and giving a couple of impromptu autoharp demonstrations and lessons.

"Those two?"

"These two."

"They're yours."

Kim's eyes welled up now, and they looked at me like a deer in the headlights.

"Use them in good health. You'll need an autoharp. Do you want to borrow this one for a while? If you find out you like playing, get your own and bring mine back. If you get tired of it, give it back sooner. It comes back to me in two months, either way. All right?"

"O–okay . . ."

"If you decide to give it up entirely, I also want one set of these back. Keep your favourites, but one set is enough for memory."

"O–okay . . ."

I didn't really need them back, but I wanted Kim to be mindful. These were not fast fashion.

It was at this moment that Bunnywit and Micah, clearly sensitive to the need to break up a deeply emotional moment with cat bullshit, came caroming around the corner at a dead run. First Micah, then Bun chasing Micah, leapt up and across my lap onto the table, knocked aside the wooden box, scattered the fingerpicks and their box into an airborne shower of colour chips and a sound explosion of great complexity, and leapt from table to counter, where Bun cornered Micah beside the MixMaster™.

"Hey!" I yelled. "Get the fuck down from there! Leave Micah alone!"

Bun looked around, saw me bearing down on the hissing contest, and leapt to the top of the refrigerator. Micah skidded sideways off the counter and zipped out into the hall. Bun leapt down, using my shoulders and back as a climbing aid, and pushed off my buttocks with all his claws. He has many, many claws.

"Fuckwit, you asshole!" I shouted.

He disappeared down the hall with alacrity.

From the table, a voice spoke from within the box.

"I knew you'd yell at him at some point, mignon," said Nathan.

Kim jumped back almost as nimbly as Bunnywit.

I just stood there, my butt stinging and probably bleeding[167], and feeling gut-punched.

"Sorry for the arcane password," Nathan's voice went on, "but things are getting weird around here, and I needed something only you would say. Also, it may be apposite. If I haven't erased this, I suppose I'm speaking from beyond the grave. I love you, sweetie, and I'm sorry. When you are ready to hear the rest, just say 'Fuckwit' again, and then you can say 'Start' and 'Stop' to play this as per usual."

---

167. Yep. Bleeding. See next number. The little shit.

Then there was dead silence in the kitchen.

Pun fully intended.

And I'm not sorry.

Nathan had been security conscious sometimes — less often than Lock, but sometimes — but he had also had a sense of humour.

85. WHEN I REGAINED CONSCIOUSNESS, REDUX[REDUX]

It was some time, and a rather confused time, before I sat down to use the password again. First I had to calm down, which included assessing, cleaning, and dressing the cat-claw gouges on my ass. Also picking up, sorting, verifying the correct quantity of, and re-housing nine sets of finger picks. Their plastic box hadn't broken[168], and actually adapted better to nine than eleven sets, which helped calm me down. I found a nice little oblong tin for Kim's equally-verified two sets.

During this time I also had to explain that Kim had just heard their birth father's voice.

Then I had to calm *Kim* down.

Then I had to explain smart paper, and then I had to demonstrate it to Kim to make it make sense, and then we had to discuss how cool it was, and how it existed in the first place, and why there are two kinds in the world, and where the rest were, with proper vagueness in the case of the Chilescraft, and an elision of the whole fraud thing because I was too tired of it to want to get into that side wynd, and then Mattie woke up and we went

---

168. Which was remarkable given its cheapness. Pretty amazing, even, considering cat-paws propelled it across the room and into the fridge, and all its internal divisions had had to be settled back in place. I doubted this was an augur that the day would improve.

through the whole thing again, in even less order because Kim did half the explaining.

Then we had to eat, because those groceries had been brought home for a reason, but I abandoned my ratatouille plan as too complex, so we invoked eggs, fish, and frozen okra, with the help of a lot of butter and some herbes-de-Provence, and managed the whole thing from conception to clean-up in forty-two minutes. Which number, as you will recall, is the answer to life, the Universe, and everything, which seemed slightly appropriate in a twisted way.

Then I really couldn't put it off any longer.

"I'm sorry for the password," I said to Mattie. "When I was younger and stupid and so was my cat, I named him Fuckwit. I changed his name to Bunnywit a few years ago because I was trying to be a better person. Well, other reasons actually, because I have pretty much given up on being anyone else but myself, but that's another story. But I still backslide, especially at times of stress, such as today when a number of naked cat claws penetrated my skin in a delicate area. I guess Nathan knew that I would, sometime."

That was an understatement. Nathan had taken great delight in teasing me about Bunnywit's other name.

Now, apparently, he had placed huge trust in my fallibility when feline-provoked.

The three of us sat ourselves around the kitchen table. Nobody spoke.

I reached into the open box and extracted the sheaf of smart paper. Separating anything with something already on it, I fanned out the rest across the newly-wiped table. It looked beautiful lying on the rich marbled yellow of the classic Art-Deco Arborite™. I took a deep breath.

After another moment of silence, I said quietly (I was sure I didn't have to yell, despite that moment of discovery), "Fuckwit. Start."

A sheet about a third of the way through the fan developed a recording of Nathan's face, with subtitles for fuck's sake, as the voice of Nathan began to speak.

86. WHAT HE SAID

Hello, my sweet!

If I'm crazy, or imagining things, you will never hear this. I'll erase it and try to forget that I ever thought ill of someone who has been so important to me for decades. A boon companion and a co-creator, a lover sometimes, and a good friend before, during, and after that, I thought. Who probably literally saved my life in foster care, though I'm beginning to wonder about just how accidental that was. But maybe that's too paranoid.

Anyway.

I think Lock is going to try to kill Pris. And maybe me, but I'm not sure. Definitely Pris, out of some kind of weird jealousy. Possessiveness. I don't get possessiveness.

I found out that he was the one who got that guy to attack her last year, and when I just asked her about it, I found out that he somehow has her convinced that she was complicit in the murder of that guy behind the bookstore. Who may or may not be the same guy, she wouldn't say. This is bullshit, of course, but he has gotten into her head about it big-time. She is really fucked up about it, and she is terrified about this climbing trip we're going on, but she was even more afraid not to go. When I pressed her for why, she said, "Well, he might kill me, but if I don't go, I'm pretty damned sure he *will* kill you."

So I said, and I'm sorry I was so flippant, "Good thing I just remade my will then." And she said, "Better put in something ironclad in case some sprog shows up with your DNA." I looked at her. "I'm not saying anything," she finally said, "except I might tell you what year I got these stretch marks." And it took a hell of a lot to get her to say anything else, but she finally did, though she has sworn me to secrecy, so I can't tell you — yet. Food for lots of thought, when we get the time.

I can't convince her to go to the cops. She says Lock buys cops like other people buy cups of coffee, which is not inconceivable, when I think back. This all has me thinking back to a lot of conversations and events and situations, and maybe feeling just a little bit stupid and manipulated. Because even when we were a couple, and we were taking the high-tech world by storm, there has always been an edge. It's just that then, I loved him, and I accepted him, so I wasn't looking for where that edge was cutting too deep. Deeply. Whatever.

I have left a letter for the police, but I don't really trust Lock not to find it. If he's really going to go all the way to murder, he's planning it now. I can't even believe that these words are coming out of my mouth, but I also can't completely *dis*believe them. Looking at all that has happened in the last few months, it all seems to make a fair amount of sense now. Getting *proof* will take a lot longer, and meanwhile, I think Pris is right. Pris and I have to go through with this trip so he doesn't get suspicious.

If you keep exploring this piece of paper, there are a bunch of files here that will direct you to my various enquiries. Take them to your friend Roger. They may not add up to much in the absence of murder, but they should be conclusive if we're dead.

If it turns out I've been stupid, and Pris and I do die in strange circumstances, then I will have left you with an intolerable burden. I know that, and I am sorry. I deeply, deeply apologise. I still want to believe that Lock is angry and possessive, but not murderous. If I'm dead, I've just made a colossal blunder based on nostalgia, naïveté, and false confidence. I am not taking time for sweet nothings here, but please remember that you are half my heart and soul, and I would never want to contribute in any way to your suffering. Please don't hate me for eternity.

There's that other thing. This kid? I'm not going to go all breeder about it, but isn't it going to be great? I mean, really!

Okay, practical matters first. I have been clear enough in my will, but now I'm also telling you what I want. I want any child of mine who might show up (I have to say it this way because I promised Pris not to record the details) to inherit three times what I left each of my siblings, should they ever be found. Which is a hell of a lot of money, which is fine with me. And I want all those amounts to be kept separately, in trust, until a verifiable claimant shows up. Including the sibs. I want to be sure that they are who they say they are. Do the testing.

The rest of the money? You already know what to do.

That being said, if the child made by Pris and me shows up, I bet they will be something else again, if I do say so myself, and I hope you like them. No, I hope you *love* them. I've left them a message too. The password is, hmm, what would be unique enough? The password is "I am the only and awesome child of Priscilla Jane Gill and Nathan Bierce." Then add "Open sesame." That should do it. I mean, who would just say that out of the blue, right? I've separated those two phrases as I recorded them, so I don't set it off when you listen to this. What I have to say to them is private. If they want to tell you later, that's up to them. I hope they will share at least some of it. There's a lot on there. I did try to give them some ideas about what to do if they get suddenly rich. And what not to do. Speaking from experience.

Last, I hope that you are safe. If you find this and Lock is still around, be careful. And if he has killed you, too, and you never say "Fuckwit" again, I have been the worst fool in the history of the world, and sorry doesn't even begin to cover it.

I am working on how I could make sure that all this gets to Roger, but first, a little more proof.

Love to you, dear heart, and I hope you never get this message.

87. NOT FOR ETERNITY, BUT MAYBE FOR A WEEK OR SO

Oh, Nathan, I am so mad at you.

88. THE PLOT THICKENS

This tumultuous and eventful day was no longer a day, but a mid-evening — but this was an emergency. Dafydd Spak showed up about as fast as Gracelyn had. He lives downtown, too, as well as working nearby, but still.

In the meantime, Kim had spoken the words Nathan had left, and another piece of paper flared an image and spoke up.

"Stop," I said, and it sat quiet again.

After a moment of stasis, with both Mattie and me looking at them, Kim reached out and picked it up, then sat there looking between us with a slightly desperate expression. "Desperate" was what my parents had called it when someone had to pee, and in fact, the effect was a similar kind of anxious shiftiness.

"You can go," said Mattie at the same time I said "Go."

Kim bolted for the spare bedroom, leaving us looking at each other.

"The plot thickens," she said unexpectedly.

Suddenly, her resemblance to Pris, and the richness inherent in Kim's evidently agile mind, clicked, and I realised (too late of course, but at least I hadn't voiced my previous thoughts to anyone) why Pris had considered her child safe with her sister. It wasn't just physical safety she had been after.

"You are handling this well for someone who just walked into it today," I said.

"My sister was Priscilla Jane Gill," she said. "I have practice."

I laughed aloud involuntarily, and after a moment she smiled, grinned almost, and shook her head that way we do when we recognise something in each other.

"When this stuff calms down —"

"If it does," she murmured.

"— if it does, indeed, or even if it doesn't, I have to introduce you to some friends of mine. I think you will all get along. Tea?"

"Do you have any coffee?"

"Dark or medium roast?"

"Oh, medium, please. I need maximum caffeine."

So I made coffee. Medium roast.

After consultation, I made it thick, in Vietnamese style, in the little individual drip thingummies, dripping onto sweetened

222

condensed milk, Diamond brand. I had ice, so I went for the cold version, and I used the shiny carnival glass tumblers for the end product, just for fun. Mattie was testing the result and pronouncing it delicious, and that didn't seem to be just on account of good manners, when Spak signalled his arrival.

89. STRIKE NUMBER . . . WHATEVER — I'VE LOST COUNT

I have known Dafydd Spak for many years now, but I always see him in certain environments. In those environments, he either wears a suit and tie (or a suit, vest, and tie), or he wears perfectly-pressed, sharp-creased slacks paired with immaculate, expensive, one-of-a-kind sweaters (probably hand-knit by elegant and skilled people personally devoted to him) over a crisp shirt or a turtleneck.

It was a bit of a shock to see him in what was essentially a jogging suit — though I'm sure whoever designed, made, and sold it didn't call it that, and it was probably cashmere[169].

He was oblivious to my shock, but I did notice that as he sat down at the kitchen table with us, he gently lifted the knees of his pants as one does with dress slacks to prevent baggy knees and preserve creases, and there was a tiny arm motion as if he had started to shoot his cuffs, just by reflex, and checked himself. So it was a bit strange to him also, which was reassuring. He refused tea, also uncharacteristic, but said our coffees looked good.

This gave me something to do with my hands while I brought him up to speed.

---

169. What is it with cashmere? Everyone I know loves it. Including me. There are *so* many people who think the combed-out stomach hair of goats is the best textile ever — and it is. No wonder pictures of goats in trees go viral, or that Cronkshaw Fold Farm is funding its solar panels by sending goat videos to online meetings. We are all shopping for the best goat-bellies to comb.

Which didn't take long. I mean, all I had to do was explain how I'd convinced the paper to speak, first accidentally and then on purpose. No matter how I tried to spin that out, it took all of five minutes, and that included making the coffee *and* playing the introductory letter.

Spak sat there quite immobile and silent while I did so, and for some moments thereafter, apparently watching his coffee drip into its glass.

Mattie couldn't take it. She got up, picked up her coffee glass, and said, "I'm going to check on Kim."

"Migawd," I said. "We never got you settled! I'm sorry! You can bunk in with Kim? Or, um, take my bedroom, if you want privacy, no problem. I can sleep out here." Which was sensible, but kind of stupid, which tracked for me at that moment.

She didn't even blink, let alone ask for redundant directions, just extended the handle of the rolling suitcase she had left by the door hours ago and rumbled off down the hall to the spare room.

I'm made of sterner stuff. I've waited out Roger. Compared with that, Spak was almost amateur hour. Not quite, but almost.

Still, I was almost at even *my* snapping point, and all of his boiling water had slowly created coffee out of itself onto the thick milk and had quit dripping, when Spak finally moved. He gently moved the drip cylinder off the glass and onto the little saucer I'd provided. He reached for the coffee spoon[170] and gently stirred the milk into the coffee, past the "clouds in my coffee" stage and until it was an even light chestnut colour. When he removed the spoon, he tapped it gently on the rim of the glass with a tiny *tink*, releasing a last single drop back into the coffee. He then set

---

170. Because *I* have them, even if the cop shop doesn't. They were my great-grandmother's sterling silver coffee spoons, and they are the epitome of coffee spoons. If I am going to measure out my life in something, I am sure as fuck going to do it with the best tools available.

the spoon gently onto the saucer, not making a sound there. He had agreed to ice, so we both watched him gently cascade the thick coffee-and-milk over the ice into the carnival glass, where it animated the lustre finish with a swampy, oil-slick glint that would have been very pretty if I'd been wanting to paint it. All that gentleness was maddening — and also revealing, in its way.

"So," he said.

I stayed quiet. I really had nothing to add, and I had been making a list of the ways I was angry at Nathan ever since the first time through his message. The second time had just added a few bullet points.

"I cannot believe," Spak said, still *gently*, "that the man we knew, the man who could invent himself, and invent all that innovative tech, and make and run and grow an empire into the billions of dollars, who could think up Own Domains, who could have the good sense and good luck to fall in love with you, could also be — That. Fucking. Stupid."

I wasn't even shocked. It was true. I turned up my hands. What could I say? I was thinking the same thing, except about the falling in love. I was the lucky one there.

"The two of the both of you," said Dafydd. He ran his fingers over the pattern pressed into the glass before picking it up. "I'm at a loss for words. 'Idiots' comes to mind. 'Fools'. Even possibly 'nitwits'."

What could I say? I went with the obvious. Silence.

"In one day," he finished after a moment, and sipped his perfect coffee.

I took a breath. "'So clouds formed up right up above me and then, of course, lightning come out and struck me'," I said.

Spak looked at me. Why do people always look at me like that?

"In his defence," I clarified, "he had lawyers for that."

"For what?"

"For being suspicious, devious, and prepared for the worst. I do too. That's what you are for."

Spak tightened his lips, a waste of effort because he then had to untighten them to drink his coffee.

I sipped away at mine.

That stuff is dynamite in a glass. In a few minutes my temples were going to start throbbing with the excess sugar and caffeine rush, and sleeping tonight would be a crapshoot. But in the moment it would keep me from collapsing, so for now I tried to concentrate on the fabulous flavour, on the mindful act, and on working not to avoid Spak's glare.

You know.

Be Here Now.

90. LET ME COUNT THE WAYS

Perversely, in one way I felt better than I had earlier in the day. If Nathan, who had been the smartest person I knew — and I know a lot of smart people — had the capacity to be that willfully clueless and tragically misguided, my little bit of heir-forgetting shrank by comparison.

Just so you know, I didn't stop loving him, but being so blindingly, shockingly furious was probably helping kick my grief along its path. Whatever that path was. I have always known that I have to eventually mostly get used to him being dead. As much as is ever possible. The fury helped.

"He only had to tell someone," Spak said. "One person."

"I know," I said.

"Priscilla only had to tell someone."

"Yep."

"One other person."

"I know."

After a moment, as if he couldn't help it, he added, "Anyone."

"Anyone," I agreed, and after that, like Picasso and Gertrude Stein, we did not speak for a while. There had been a lot of Pinteresque pauses in this story to date, but none so fraught, so far.

This time I broke the silence. "I am *so* mad at him right now."

"As you should be," said Dafydd, which was obscurely comforting.

"I am counting the ways."

"I've only been here for minutes and my list is up to twelve," he said, with the hint of a sympathetic smile.

"Forty-two," I said, "but about thirty of those are 'Because you didn't *tell* anybody!' so we're probably even otherwise."

"Yes," he said. "I'm sorry."

"You know," I said, "I heard a story once about a guy who was organising one of those fancy parachute jumps. He was going to be one of the camera people. He'd made like a thousand jumps. He was a big deal in the fancy-parachute-jumps world. So he checked everyone who was going to be in the ring, and made sure their chutes were okay, and they all jumped out of the plane, and then he picked up his camera and jumped out."

Dafydd waited.

"He didn't check his own chute."

Another silent moment.

"It was still in the airplane."

Spak sipped coffee and watched me.

"One little lapse of attention," I said. "Two seconds. One little bad decision. That's all it takes. Sometimes it doesn't matter, and you survive. Sure, you forget to shoulder check on the highway, but there's nobody there, so the lane change goes okay and doesn't become a fatal fiery crash. You forget to turn off a burner, but you catch it before the pot boils dry and the building burns down. You step wrong on the stairs, but you don't fall, or if you fall you don't crack your skull or break your back. You're fine. But sometimes, one little moment . . . and boom. Nobody saw the guy in trouble.

Nobody did one of those in-air hug-the-chuteless-person stunt rescues that movies love. I heard that he filmed all the way to the ground. He left a message for his family. This was in the days of videotape. All they lost was the last few feet at the end.

"It takes several minutes to fall that far. He had time to be sorry.

"Nathan probably had time to be sorry. Maybe if he noticed Lock had messed with his climbing gear, he was sorry then. Or maybe when he saw Pris and the other climbers fall toward him. When he realised he wouldn't get out of the way in time. Maybe he thought, *Dammit, I should have called Roger. I should have made Pris tell.*

"Maybe he thought, *I should have told her.* Meaning me. Should have shared his worries. With me. Should have tried to capture his wisps of suspicion by talking them over with his lover, the person whom, as he has clearly stated, he trusted most in the world."

I could hardly say the next bit.

"But he didn't."

Dafydd reached forward and laid his left hand across my right. "No," he said gently. "He didn't. I'm so sorry."

"So am I," I said, and began to sob, and imperturbable, cool, lofty Mr. Spak gathered me into a gentle, softly-veloured embrace and offered me an immaculate handkerchief he conjured from an invisible pocket.

I would prefer to draw a curtain over the next few moments. They were noisy, messy, and 'way more than not-pretty.

Eventually, I was calm again, clutching a sodden square of linen. Spak let me go, went to the cupboards, and wordlessly opened drawers until he found a clean tea-towel, held it under the tap, wrung it out, and brought it to me to wipe my face. I folded it and held the cool fabric softly over my eyes.

"I really hate Lockwood Chiles," I said. "I didn't kill him, but I wish I had. To the detriment of my soul."

"It is not unreasonable to hate evil," Spak said quietly. "It is appropriate."

"Do you believe in the death penalty?"

"No," he said, "but as you recall, I did not object to the idea of Chiles burning in hell for eternity, once he got there. I wish he'd had longer to rot in prison. I wish he'd seen his empire stripped away. I wish he'd been reduced to a pathetic old lifer, a whiny little jailhouse-lawyer, with a combover and ball-point-pen tattoos, living out his years as some biker's bumboy —"

"Dafydd!"

He actually blushed. "I'm sorry. I'm not wishing sexual assault, at least I hope I wasn't. Just a grubby consensual relationship with some horrifying neo-Nazi gangbanger. Something as nasty as he was. He was a bad man." Never a truer word spoken, I thought, but he was still speaking.

"And I must say, I have observed over my life that evil keeps on giving. Even after the toxic flow has stopped, the scorched earth remains. I hate evil. It's why I'm not a defence lawyer. Hypothetically I believe that every accused deserves a just defence, but it won't be from me. Equally, I'm not a Crown Prosecutor. I don't want to mistake ordinary incompetence for evil, or condemn someone innocent. But perhaps someday I will be a judge, if I live long enough, and get wise enough, and they ask me."

Well. Sometime less fraught, I would have to remember and think about that speech, and decide if I had ever heard Spak utter, in all our acquaintance, as many personal opinions in total as he had this day.

But now was not the time. I couldn't even summon up a witticism, or tease him about his fervour. For the moment, I was pretty much done.

"We have to call Roger," I said finally.

"I'll do it," he said. "You go lie down in a dark room."

"I told Mattie she could kip in mine."

"Mattie is with Kim, and I will suggest to her that she remain so."

"Kim! You have to meet Kim!"

"I am quite capable of introducing myself. I will take care of it all. Go."

So he did.

I went, and Spak called Roger.

I heard Kim and Mattie emerge from their room and a light rumble of introductions and explanations to which I didn't even try to listen. I stayed in my room.

Roger was there in ten minutes, and Spak and Roger talked, a lower-toned rumble down the hall from my closed door, and I heard the paper speak again. I stayed in my room.

I'd had enough, and if now and again I was crying too hard to have spoken anyway, who's to know?

91. YOUNG PADAWAN, OR, LATER THAT SAME NIGHT

Fleury still had his tent out back, and I'd developed the habit of checking in on him every day. Also, I had noticed leftovers missing from the fridge, so I assumed that while I was out at work or dealing with the growing cohort of the invisible, Kim had been taking meals down to him.

I hadn't got to visit Fleury today because of Everything. After some hours, I gave up on trying to calm down enough to sleep, though at least I'd stopped crying. When the apartment got quiet, I came out of my room to wash my face and get a glass of pear juice. Kim leapt away from the fridge but stayed skulking in the kitchen, shifting from foot to foot, while I drank it down. Despite myself I had to smile — internally.

"What?" I said, innocently.

"Nothing. Nothing."

"Okay, then we might as well take Fleury down his supper. Not much left from tonight, but I have some canned ham we could slice."

Kim had the grace to blush deeply. I laughed in spite of myself. "You have to get up early etcetera etcetera, kid." At their look of incomprehension I shook my head. "It's a saying. You know? 'You have to get up early to put one over on me'? Oh, never mind. What else do you think he'd like?"

"He doesn't have many teeth. Soft things. Bread. Soup. One time he mentioned spaghetti ohs. I meant to look it up, but I forgot. What is that?"

It was nice that Kim paid that kind of attention. "SpaghettiOs® are an abomination unto good food everywhere," I said, "but most children love them at one point[171], along with their demon cousin Alphaghetti®, and I am deeply surprised they have never entered your world."

From behind me, Mattie said, "If any child of mine was going to have alphabet noodles in sauce, it was going to be made from scratch, just like all their other food."

Of course. Pris had known her sister was like this. Would be like this. Would do all of it right.

"Of course," I said.

Down we went, with no SpaghettiOs®.

Fleury was still wearing the suit he'd worn to the funeral, now somewhat the worse for wear. He was sitting on the back steps dozing, and woke with a start when we came out. "I'm just gonna go," he said loudly, then saw it was Kim and me and sat back. "Sorry, Girl, I thought it was that bitch down in the back there, pardon my language."

"Has she been giving you trouble, Fleur? Let me talk to her!"

---

171. I have always hated them, even as a toddler, but we have established that I am an anomalous individual. Haven't we?

"Never mind," Fleur said. "I know I don't smell too good. I can't just make myself go get a shower, you know, over to them shelters at night, man. Bad enough at meals. They remind me of Danny. Everybody talks to me about Danny if I'm over there. Did the police got anything yet?"

Kim, seeming to show no reaction though Fleur did indeed pong highly, sat down on the other end of the stair, spread out a napkin on the iron step between them, and we set down plate and tumbler and cutlery.

Fleury dug in.

"They need your help," I said. "I told you, you could help."

"Maybe," he said around a mouthful of bread. "I dunno, they kinda maybe won't talk to old Donkey, you know that. You heard Deb that day. They're all like that."

"You could ask again," Kim said. "You could go over, like for a shower, you know, pretend, undercover like, and you could ask them. Those guys have attacked a bunch of people, but nobody will talk to cops. If anybody saw their faces, and would describe them to that Heather, you know, the detective, that would be a big help. Maybe they could make some of those Identi-Kit® sketches, like in the movies, right? You know any of those people, Fleury? They go to the shelters too. I bet they all know about Danny, want to help, you know. I bet you could do it!"

"That's a good idea," said Fleury, as if I hadn't been asking him every day to do the same.

I gazed at Grasshopper in admiration. Perhaps Kim was a worthy young Padawan. Perhaps some day they would be running something like M2F2, or Own Domains for that matter, and I would be able to kick back and retire in the Epitome, saying I knew them when.

92. STORM TROOPS

That night, the gang came back.

Fleury had, we found out later, gone off to the shelter, leaving Ted to keep an eye on his stuff. The yelling in the alley started about two in the morning.

I know this because I couldn't sleep and I was at the back window, sitting in the window seat and looking at the brown moon, sash open to the breeze of dubiously-fresh night air. I heard the voices and I was already dialing 911 as I leaned out to see a group of men with tidy haircuts, nice bomber jackets, and big boots, looking weirdly foreshortened from the fourth floor, storming through Fleury's camp, stomping the aluminum arcs of the tent supports, kicking the sleeping bags and plastic bags of belongings all over the alley. Five. No, six of them. I have always hated the number six, don't know why. Kim crowded beside me as I gave details to the 911 operator.

Two of them headed toward Ted and Shayna's camp. Ted was already out of his tent with the cell phone, charged this time, I hoped, as I had given him access to an outside outlet in the parking lot. Shayna was halfway out of the tent, wearing not much but a long T-shirt, holding the dogs back by their collars.

"I've called the cops!" I yelled down, just as Shayna released the dogs.

I'm pretty sure the gang didn't hear me, but that could have been because Fang was snarling and Killer was barking — baying, really, like a bloodhound out of *Down by Law* — as they barrelled down the short length of alley that separated them from the gang members.

93. ME AND DAN BRIGGS AND OLD BILL BROWN

I don't know if you listen to much Buffy Sainte-Marie. If you don't, you should, because she is fabulous. But why I bring this up is because of a song she recorded quite early in her career, on her album *I'm Gonna Be a Country Girl Again*, called "They Gotta Quit Kickin' My Dawg Around". I sing this song sometimes with the autoharp, and after this was all over I taught it to Kim, for obvious reasons.

The Interwebz say that this song was written by Cy Perkins and Webb M. Oungst, who may or may not have been from Iowa, and who may or may not have put their names to an already-existing folk tune. It was first recorded in 1912, which is some considerable time before Buffy sang it (and even longer before I first did). The "dawg" in the song is named Jim, and he doesn't react that well to a gang of bullies who try to kick him, viz.:

> *Well, Jim seed his duty there and then*
> *He lit into them gentlemen*
> *He sure messed up that foot of square*
> *With the rags and the meat and the hide and the hair . . .*

Fang and Killer had seen their duty, and they did it, and it was a thing of beauty to watch them light into "them gentlemen" and put six grown men to screaming, yelling, bleeding, swearing flight. I wish I had not found it so splendid. I have my already-compromised karma to care for, and it takes a beating at times like these.

As I watched, though, I was also in action. Once 911 was done and I'd described what I could see, I headed down the stairs, my cell phone in one hand and in the other a handy piece of sturdy wood by way of weaponry[172]. On the way down, I called Heather. She'd given me her card and put her cell number on the back, so

---

172. If it matters, it was the thick old hardwood dowel I'd taken out of the back hall closet — not Bunnywit's boot closet, but the other one — when I converted it to a linen cupboard.

she was in my speed-dial now, and I had no hesitation waking her up at two-whatever in the morning.

"Hello?" she said sleepily.

"Can you get DNA from a dog's teeth if they bit someone?"

"What . . . who . . . wait. It's you! Um . . . if you test quick enough, maybe . . . What's —?"

"Get down here with an evidence kit. Our little gang of thugs came back for a second helping, and Ted's dogs handed them their asses on a plate. Teeth were embedded in flesh. Blood was shed."

When I got outside, Ted and Shayna and the dogs were trying to pin three of the guys into the corner of the wrought-iron fence, but just as I came out, loaded for bear with my impromptu ninja staff[173], their quarry broke away and hot-footed it into the shadows. This time we saw the big four-by-four pickup with a crew cab — generic black, some little decal trade-name along the side, also generic — that they piled into. The whole unit peeled off in a hurry. I tried for a photo of the truck or its licence plate with my phone. How the hell do people do that? Just as in one of those stupid anxiety dreams, it took me ages to press all the right buttons, and the truck was long gone by then. Ted's is a flip phone, so no joy there.

The first cop car skidded up about ninety seconds later, then, after our quick briefing, peeled away in pursuit, but they had no luck either. Heather was only about three minutes after, in a civilian car with a chaotic interior that didn't match her work persona, and, after her, the forensics people were on the scene PDQ as well.

It was very turbulent in the alley for several hours after that.

---

173. I *have* been watching a lot of kung-fu films. Before you judge, remember that guy from sometime in the sixties who was mugged on the New York subway and he subdued his three muggers so they could be arrested? He was just some ordinary office guy and they asked him how he did it. His answer? "I just tried to do what Mrs. Peel would do." Now those were the *real* Avengers.

I stayed down there briefly, but although watching the lab folks try to get Fang to sit still for mouth-swabbing was entertaining as fuck, I was exhausted.

I still had to tell some cops what I had seen. I went over to find Heather Wood, leaning on my closet rail like a cane as if I just happened to have found a sturdy one-and-one-quarter-inch dowel lying around somewhere. What, weapon? Not me, Detective!

She was wearing her tinted glasses again, even though it was night. But apparently, she could still see. "You look like shit," she said.

"Happens to us stupid civilians who insert ourselves into police matters," I said.

"Well, I might have been a little hasty there. Thanks for the rapid call. We might get something out of this."

"Can I write a statement in the morning? It's been a day, and I don't have any more spoons."

"Sure. Here's a couple of forms. Bring it by my office."

"Will do."

"What the hell is that thing?"

This thing I wasn't recently prepared to swing with intent to do grievous bodily harm? "Um, a clothes rail?"

"Well, I suppose I have to give you credit for initiative. Bringing a clothes rail to a boot fight."

I just looked at her. Was that a snide remark, or a sense of humour?

Wait," she said as I started to turn away. "One more thing. Do you know who the other witness was, the one who made the other 911 call?"

"What other call? Ted managed to call it in?"

"Yeah, him too, but this one, it came in first, before either of you, and it was a female."

I looked up at the window of 1-D/104 in wild surmise. Mrs. Murray's move wasn't until the upcoming Saturday. She still looked out over the alley, for now.

Heather was sharp, I'll give her that. "No, really, her?"

"I don't know, but why don't you pay her a little visit?"

"I'll do that tomorrow — well, later today. I'll have the info from the call centre by then to verify. I'll give her our thanks."

All the way up in the elevator, with what small amount of brain I had left, I marvelled at bread cast upon water and all that. I never did find out if it was her, but who else would it have been?

Kim was still looking out the back window, this time with Mattie beside her, both of them looking almost as tired as I felt.

"Is Fleury all right? Are the dogs okay?"

"Everyone is fine. Fleur appears to have taken your directive. He wasn't there."

It had been the longest and most bizarre day of my life, and proved out the research that says if you are busy with new events, it will seem as if time has slowed down. I seemed to have lived several, many, a lot of, a hundred years in that day. I pushed away from the window, nodded at Mattie, and tapped Kim's shoulder. "Go back to bed. Go to sleep."

Surprisingly, we all did. How does that even work? I would have thought I'd be awake for hours more, but no.

IT MIGHT HAVE PUT ME ON THE SHELF

94. ". . . CLOUDS FORMED UP", REDUX

Fleury was at my door the next afternoon.

He smelled very strongly of booze, but not so much of stale Fleur[174]. He hadn't been in the alley last night, and he was wearing different clothes, so I deduced shelters and showers.

"I was thinking we could go by the cop shop there," he said. "Just, you know."

I knew.

I called Heather, and she was in. Major Crimes have their offices in the downtown cop shop, which is pretty close to the Epi-TOME and to our heritage offices, which is why Roger and I spend a lot of money in the neighbourhood cafes. It is a five-minute walk for me, absent smoky side-effects, but I wasn't sure how quickly Fleur could walk and whether he would change his mind on the way, so we went in the Huff. I had been wrong

---

174. EfFleurvia?

about the odour. There was still an underlying tang that got a little overpowering in close quarters, but the ride was only about five blocks. The outer air had actually substantially recovered from the forest-fire smoke, and this day a fresh west wind was blowing more of the haze away every hour. Otherwise, I suppose I wouldn't have noticed Fleur's aura at all.

I parked in the little visitor lot of the downtown station.

I've mentioned the lobby there before. It's a mid-century-modern concrete building, and you come up to the entrance on some wide concrete steps that are almost like escalating patios. From these steps, if the light is right, you can see in to the front desk through some big plate glass windows. Even now, when a bulletproof Lexan™ wall has been built atop the counter, you can see the cops working Reception, as through a glass darkly.

Fleury was walking just ahead of me up the steps, picking his way carefully and unsteadily, when he looked up. He gave a little shout, wheeled with surprising agility, and started back down the steps, running right into me and almost knocking both of us ass over teakettle onto the pebbled approach patio. We grabbed onto each other like long-lost relatives and reeled back toward the parking lot.

"I'm not goin' in there now!" he said, whisper-yelling. He dragged me along, one claw-like hand on my arm.

When we were back at the car and out of sight of the front desk, I was able to stop him.

"Fleur! Fleury! What is it? What's the matter?"

His face was deathly pale, and he was sweating. For a moment, I thought he was having a heart attack.

But he wasn't.

"He's in there, man! Black boots, Blade Runner, he's in there. He's behind the desk! He's a fucking cop!"

Suddenly I was shifting my grip so I held his upper arms. Whether I was steadying him or myself is unclear.

"Are you sure? Fleury, are you sure that's him?"

My thoughts were cascading horribly into a nasty, yet logical, pattern. I knew exactly the cop he meant. He'd been on the front desk several times, and I'd noticed the haircut, but just because of the ubiquity of it.

"I saw the guy! He was right here in my face that time! Same distance as you right now! I'm never gonna forget that face, man! And that hair! He has that zigzag in his hair, razor cut? It's that guy! I gotta get out of here!"

"No," I said. "You are gonna stay right here with me!" I unlocked the Huff and half-helped, half-pushed him into the passenger seat. Then I leaned over and spoke gently.

"Fleury. If that's the guy, he's a bad cop. He has to go to jail. You understand that, right?"

Fleury smelled urgently of urine and terror. "He's gonna kill me!"

"Just let him try," I said. "I will knock him into the middle of next week!" Bravado of the most ludicrous kind, but it made Fleury snort and grin, scared but amused despite himself. Yeah, I know, I would have made quite the hero, Fleur, thanks a lot. And me without my clothes rail. But it had worked.

"Please," I begged him. "Please help, for Danny's sake. You were brave going up against him when he attacked Danny. Please be brave now."

His hands were working against his jeans, plucking and twisting them, but he slowly nodded. "I ain't goin' in there." He stood up, which could only do my upholstery good, but made me nervous as to his flight risk.

"No, you aren't. You definitely aren't." I pulled out my cell phone. "We won't go in at all. I'll call Heather, and she will come out here."

I was careful to stand where Fleury would have to go through me, but he held fast, wringing his hands, watching my face with desperate fear and trust.

"Heather," I said. "Fleury and I are in the parking lot. Come out here now. Please bring Roger if he's there, and Dave. You have to come out immediately."

There was some of that *Peanuts*©-teacher squawking for a moment, but I just said, "Now. Five minutes ago, if possible." It was an eternity about two minutes long before a little mini-phalanx of three cops came out the front door, and the two tall ones craned their necks over the rose bushes and found us by the Huff. They hustled over.

Fleur shrank back slightly into the V of the open car door, but Heather was great. She signalled Roger and Dave to wait and came up slowly. I stepped away, and she reached out and took Fleur's hands in hers.

"Thank you for coming," she said quietly, smiling at him and nodding gently. "I know it's hard."

He nodded back, and I could see his shoulders come down another inch. He clasped her hands desperately.

"I seen the guy," he said. "Blade Runner. Boots guy."

I moved back to Roger and Dave.

"What's the name of that guy on the front desk with the blond dye-job?" I asked Roger. He looked puzzled.

It was Dave who said, "Edwards. Jason Edwards. Why?"

"Oh, him," Roger said, a world in two words, and then, because Rog is smarter than the average bear, "Oh, no. No. Really?"

"Really," I said.

Rog looked across to Heather, who was speaking quietly with Fleury. Fleur was gesturing with one hand to the door of the building, and as we watched, he repeated, "Blade Runner guy.

Blondie. Black boots. It's him there! It's him!" His voice got louder, and Heather shushed him.

I said, "Fleur talked to some of the other people who were attacked. He had something to tell Heather, but goodness knows what, now, because when we tried to come in, he saw that guy and freaked."

"He's on administrative duties," said Dave, who took four words to convey the same disdain Rog had in two. But then, while Dave was smart, he was green, and Rog, when I met him at the same point in *his* career, had already been twice the cop Dave was.

"Well," I said, "he's going to be under arrest now, and how much do you want to bet that other people besides Fleury will pick him out of a line-up? And how much do you want to bet that he has a healing dog bite on his ass cheek, and another one on his hand?"

"Beating up homeless people? Who the hell would do shit like that?" Roger said.

Surprisingly, Dave had an answer. "It's some kind of stupid club. You see it all over the country. They film the attacks, and they used to put them on YouTube™ for a while, until the complaints started, so now they have some kind of secret website. It's cops and armed forces, off duty. We've been following a line of enquiry."

"In my house?" said Roger. "In *my house*? This is *over.*"

And oddly enough, it seemed almost that easy, to start with. Heather stayed with Fleury by the car, and the two tall guys walked back through the door. I followed at a discreet distance, undeterred by Roger's glare and micro-tasking hand motion.

Edwards looked up, saw who it was, and routinely buzzed them through the security gate into the secure area. I remained in the lobby.

There's a sort of corridor people have to go down before they can enter the front desk area, so I lost sight of them for a moment, and turned to check out the two cops at the reception desk.

Edwards was well-put-together, even in uniform, with his dyed hair impeccable and the fancy razor cut looking crisply new. He was playing Walmart-greeter beside a dark-haired, fair-skinned, slightly-sloppy guy who had three pens in his shirt pocket, a woven friendship bracelet on his right wrist, and a shaggy, barely-regulation haircut. Their body language was interesting. They were barely five feet apart at their stations, but they were turned about fifteen degrees away from each other, in what looked like a habitual two-solitudes silence. I wondered what the back-story was.

When the door behind them opened, the two guys on the desk barely glanced up — until Roger, so quietly I barely heard him, said, "Stand up."

Edwards looked around, but yeah, Roger meant him. Rog saw me watching and lowered his voice until the blond asshole almost had to lean in to hear himself arrested.

It took less than a minute. Dave turned Edwards around, and I noted that he indeed had a Band-Aid™ on one hand. Dave cuffed him, despite token protests, and immediately took him away through the back door and into the bowels of the station, leaving a gobsmacked colleague to watch them go.

Slowly, the guy, whose nametag said "GASSLER", regained some sang-froid, and in a moment he was able to turn to me and say, "Ma'am? May I help you?" I noticed his correct verb with approval.

"No," I said. "I just tagged along to watch the show." I gestured. "Are you on administrative duties too?"

"No, ma'am," he said fervently.

"I don't suppose I can solicit your opinion on what just happened?"

He narrowed his eyes. "Are you a reporter?"

"No way," I said. "A concerned citizen. Just asking."

"No comment," he said. But he shook his head and cut his eyes toward the door, and I thought, *Here's a guy who is going to have a lot to say to someone when he gets home tonight.*

"Talk to Roger," I said.

"Say what?"

"Talk to him," I said. "He's actually one of the *good* ones. It will help."

He shook his head, not dismissing the idea but definitely done with me. "If that's all, ma'am?"

"That's all," I said.

Heather was leading Fleury in as I left. "He won't see you," she was saying to Fleur. "I promise."

We stopped to face each other in the sliding doors.

"Fucking cop boots," he said to me. "I shoulda known. No offense, ma'am," he said to Heather.

"None taken," she said. "It's a bloody disgrace. You can trust me to pursue this. I'll take all the help you and your friends can give me."

"Yes, ma'am," said Fleury. It was a love-in.

"Um, I'm gonna go," I said. They both nodded at me perfunctorily. They almost carried on, then Heather turned back momentarily.

"Don't tell anybody about this yet," said Heather. "We have a lot to do and I don't want you to muddy the water."

"Well, right, then," I said.

"Promise me!" she insisted, not kindly.

"I said all right, didn't I?" She turned away without answering, and I shrugged and headed out. The door whooshed shut behind me.

But as I walked down the steps, I heard the door again, and Fleur shouted, "Girl!" I turned back. "Thank you, Girl," he yelled.

I nodded. He nodded back. Heather nodded at me too. I nodded back. We were all getting good at that.

Then he was occluded again by the sliding door, and I was left in the wind and sunlight, under a smoky-but-cloudless, gamboge-washed-over-blue, only-minimally-toxic sky, staring at the cop shop's blank façade.

After a brief interval with a wet-wipe I found in the glove compartment and used to sanitise my passenger seat, I got in behind the wheel and, with great pleasure, and yet again, drove off in a Huff.

I may even have been smiling.

EXCEPT
I WASN'T
THERE
MYSELF.

96. ENTER MISS VIKKI

Heather came around the next day to talk with Ted and Shayna. She had one of those photo-lineup files where she had assembled some pictures of dyed-blond guys with jackets on. She probably just had to walk through the fucking mall, or the cop shop, and she could have found ten. But one of these was Jason Edwards.

Both Ted and Shayna were sure of their identification of Edwards. Heather made them sign statements right then and there. Good for her. Dotting and crossing the appropriate alphabet elements.

After Heather left, I stood with Ted and Shayna for a while, talking about the surprising turn of events.

"They won't do nothing," Shayna said. "Cops takes care of their own."

"You never know," I said. "Good cops hate dirty cops too. Maybe that will prevail."

"It's the fucking police union," said Ted, somewhat surprisingly, and with some accuracy. "Thin blue line crap. They defend each other 'cause they think if one cop goes down, they lost their authority."

"Not entirely wrong," I said. "Tarred with the same brush, and all that. But one would hope even they can't turn a blind eye to murder." We all looked at each other, thinking about whether I was an optimist or just an idiot. At least, I was thinking that, but their expressions were kind enough to feel patronising.

"Hey!" I said. "We can hope, right?"

They nodded those maybe/maybe-not nods that are more lateral than vertical. Clearly they thought I was a dreamer. Then Fang did me the honour of bumping against my leg, and I got almost a whole pat in before her ears went back and I found discretion to be the better part of valour.

"Sweetie-Pie likes you," said Shayna, optimistically. Sweetie-Pie. Hmmm.

"She do," said Ted. "Much as she can like anybody. She's kinda fu—, um, she's into tough love, you might say."

"So, I got another call from Bylaw," I said. "I told them you were on a list, and you needed at least until the end of the summer. She said she'd tell the bylaw enforcement officer on this beat to, and I quote, 'take it easy'. Which I assume is their way of saying they told the dude to back the hell off and quit being a jerk."

"Great, that's . . . oh, here's my worker right now!"

"Hi, Ted," said a familiar voice.

I turned. "Vikki?" Standing behind me was a tiny blonde woman in high heels and business attire that was only stressed slightly by her Dolly Parton . . . profile, if you take my meaning. Last time I had seen her, she had been wearing sweats and dandling my cousin Thelma's baby on her shoulder.

"Vikki? What the hell are you . . . ?"

"I'm Ted's new housing worker," she said with dignity. "I work for M2F2."

"Why? I thought you worked for Thelma."

"Sorta. But I needed a real job, for tuition, like, and Lucky needs a better worker for daytimes. I'm only in first year. I don't know really jack-shit yet about special needs and making the most of his potential. So Thelma saw that M2F2 had this vacancy, and they needed somebody got some street-smarts, which is me for sure, right? So luckily I got the job. I'm still with Lucky on the weekends, and we got a proper aide for the weekdays from some program."

We. "We?"

"I still live in. I guess I kinda . . . live there now. I guess Thelma kinda adopted me. Like a puppy."

Had I known then what I know now, when I heard the word "adopt" I'd have made the *avert* sign to whatever dark gods control the future.

97. LANGUAGE

Instead, I pulled Vikki down to the other end of the lot.

"This is Fleury," I said to the lump of blankets. Despite crime scene tape and revisiting hoodlums, Fleury had been back in his home as soon as it was no longer guarded, and had managed to reassemble his nest of possessions in the wake of the gang's depredations but in no particular order.

"Fleur! Wake up! This is Vikki. She works for M2F2 and she's an old friend of mine. She's gonna help you find a place to live."

"There's a helluva long waiting list," Vikki muttered to me.

"Fuck the waiting list. His friend was murdered here, and he's sleeping on dried blood. He needs to get a safe place yesterday. A cop just got arrested for killing his buddy, but he's part of a gang. They've already been back once. What if the rest of them come again? He's a sitting duck."

She glared at me, and there might have been an eyeroll, but when Fleury emerged from his odiferous cocoon, smiling his sweet hopeful smile, she smiled back at him quite genuinely.

"How can I help?" she said, commendably. "Where would you like to live, Fleury?"

"I just need a place where they don't cost all my AISH[175] and they don't come in my place all the time and steal my Ensure™," said Fleur. "We was gonna go to that Indigenous Harm Reduction over there —" he gestured vaguely west and north "— but Danny was the Native one, not me. Besides, they was expensive."

"You get all your meals there," said Vikki. "It's a good deal, somebody cooking good stuff for you."

"I got Girl and Kim for that," Fleury said, and laughed. "Kidding. I know they can't do that all the time. I just can't afford it in one of them places. Even with the money from the empties, I wouldn't have nothing to spend after I paid all that."

"We will find you something," Vikki said. "Definitely. Give us a minute. You got a phone?" She wasn't being mean. Lots of the underhoused and homeless I know have cell phones. They can charge up at the social agencies in the day, and it gives them access to the day labour services and social agencies. Fleury, though —

"Nope, I lost it, well, those guys at the shelter took it that one time they beat me up. But I'm usually always right here."

"Okay," said Vikki. "I'll see if I can get you a new phone, and here's my card anyway. And I'll start looking for a place."

"Thanks, Girl. Thanks, Miss Vikki," said Fleur. He grinned at us. Grinned. I grinned back, but as soon as he turned away, I found I was shaking my head, not at him or Vikki, but at my own thoughts. Vikki caught me at it.

---

175. Assured Income for the Severely Handicapped. Assured hella small income, a bit better than trying to live on dumpster-diving, and helps prevent petty crime of the food-stealing variety — if one doesn't have to spend it all on housing. Which often is the case. It all comes back to housing, in the end, doesn't it?

"Don't worry," she said. "I'll put him up top the list. Poor bugger."

"Language," I said, channelling Thelma.

"You'll put a spear in that if you want any more favours," she said, but she was grinning too. Fleury tends to have that effect on people when he's lucid. It pains me.

"I'll work on it," she said. "I'm on the bottom rung over there but for some reason they listen to me a bit."

"Thanks," I said. "I bet you won't be bottom-runging it for long. You're perfect for them, and I'm sure they know it."

"You should see me when the assholes start up on me. Thinking their worker is a little blonde bimbo they can con. Fuck that noise, I say."

I could imagine the scene. Blunt force trauma and the flinging of bodies may have figured in my imaging. Miss Vikki. Ha.

My phone rang.

"You might want to get over here," said Gracelyn. "Fast. But in a good way."

LAST
NIGHT
I SAW
UPON
THE STAIR

98. NOT A DICK

Mr. Dyck was in the Ursulas, watching traffic as he waited for us.

If anything, today he looked worse. The bags under his eyes were pronounced, and his mouth drooped. Today's shirt was rumpled as well as stretched, and had an odd sort of greenish-grey paisley underpattern, and to match it, putatively, today's tie was a seventies number[176] with purple paisley[177] on red-and-orange brocade. And the blue suit. It was terrifying.

Gracelyn, showing no sign of sartorial distress, ushered us in, and Mr. Spak gestured to Mr. Dyck to have a seat. But apparently, actually sitting down was too slow for this. Ulrich carried a file

---

176. To clarify, the nineteen-seventies. Not Victorian.

177. If paisley is the name of the overall pattern, what is the name of the individual little yins or yangs that make up the whole? I say, "Paisles," pronounced PAY-zulls, with the singular being "a paisle" (PAY-zull), but my editor does not agree. We have conversations like this often. (Doesn't everyone?)

folder (ordinary buff, which ruled it out as one of ours), which he immediately opened; he handed one of the pages in it to Dafydd Spak, one to me, and one to Gracelyn. Before we had a chance to peruse their 10pt Times New Roman[178], he said abruptly, "This is my letter stating that I'm withdrawing from representation of Mr. and Mrs. Woodward and Mr. Brice."

Spak tilted his head inquisitively and said nothing. It might have worked better if I hadn't done the same thing in the same direction, accidentally I swear, so there was a chance we looked like a pair of defective bobbleheads, or the leads in an Iditerod team. But it did work well enough.

"Obviously I am not at liberty to give you details, but there were some ... irregularities ... that led me to believe it would not be in my best interests to remain as counsel. I wanted to bring these over in person so you didn't waste your time on the requests I've sent you."

Mr. Spak is a fine human being and an excellent lawyer. I certainly hope he does not, secretly, play poker professionally, but if he does, he will get rich. He quickly scanned the letter, then moved forward with his hand out. "Thank you, Ulrich," he said. "I appreciate the heads-up. And your principled stand."

This was a bit of a shock to all of us, and Ulrich's hand came up slowly, but he completed the handshake to a better standard than that of his erstwhile clients. I knew this because I lined up behind Spak to do my own handshaking, and apparently I was no longer Jezebel or whatever, because he gave me a decent Toastmasters pump (with no pressure on my rings) and even a small nod.

Gracelyn saw him out politely. I watched his rear view — as unprepossessing as the front — with some bemusement as he trailed behind her and vanished into the foyer, and was reminded

----

178. I really hate Times New Roman. And 10pt? Srsly, who even.

of admonishments about books and covers, good in even the worst, and all those other clichés that elderly relatives tend to throw around. Hmph. Who knew they would be right so often, and so annoyingly, as life went on?

The security lock on the door to the elevator foyer clicked shut behind them, and Gracelyn did not return. We sat down at last, and I stared at Dafydd across the charming little asymmetrical artisan-made table that graces the meeting room. A friend of Roma's makes tables from wood reclaimed from architectural demolitions. We have one in each of these shared "break-out rooms", and a few scattered around the rest of Own Domains and the lunch room. They are all different, and very pretty, but they are in no way square, hence Vinnie's issue with his tablet the other day and my constant satisfaction with the symbolism of something with no straight edges. I let my hands stroke the smooth re-finish on what had probably once been part of a warehouse door or something before it got gentrified.

"'Irregularities'," I said, my hands finding none.

"A surprising development," he said. "I have known him to take some cases where irregularity would be a kind description. And often win them. And yet this."

"Stranger things have happened," I said primly. "So it's not likely that Ulrich Dyck was Chiles's jailhouse visitor?" Accepting Roger's specific permission, I had told Spak about my movie date with Roger[179]. Confidentially, of course. That's why I pay him a dollar a year[180].

---

179. I would have told him anyway, and Rog knows that. Is there such a thing as pre-emptively opening the barn door after the horse is assumed to have been ready to be going anyway? If so, whatever its verb tense would be, Rog excels at it.

180. That's a little joke. He is paid almost commensurately with his value, "almost" because he is priceless.

"I actually asked him the last time we met if he acted for Chiles. He said no. He was able to satisfy me that was the truth. It's a matter of record, but sometimes the firms send in seconds, articling students, that kind of thing. When the visit is routine. He could have gone as someone's agent. But he says not, and his, er, well, alibi, not to put too fine a point on it, stands up. And he is known for working alone. For obvious reasons."

"But he actually has ethics. Who knew?"

"It is gratifying," said Dafydd, "if somewhat unexpected. I will have to reassess some of my prejudices."

"Just what I was thinking. I'm kind of pleased, though. I did move him up a notch after the examination for discovery, when he had groomed his clients so effectively. As you know, I started out thinking he was the Utility Sleazeball from Central Casting[181]. I'm internally apologising for that right now, and re-casting him with a minor name actor instead. That guy with the pear-shaped face and the naturally-marcelled hair? You know that guy? You know him. He's in everything. Not that it is going to completely repair the karmic damage."

"I am sure your karma is still in a net-positive position. They will soon have another lawyer, though. They are probably briefing someone even as we speak."

"So we have to buckle down and make progress on our own detection of 'irregularities'."

"Straight up," said Dafydd, who Has Children: only explanation.

"How old are your kids?" I asked him.

"Thirteen and fourteen. Why?"

"No reason, really. Curious." This explained it. When we first met, his kids were safely pre-teen. Now, they were actively embroiled in the great sea of linguistic evolution that is teen culture

---

181. There was a lot of Central Casting in this movie, actually.

online. I now saw that from this point on, I could expect anything from Dafydd Spak. Sad about the perfect Spak-as-was: I would have to accept he was actively evolving. Teenagers destabilise, it's what they're for. Another reason we can't have nice things.

"I am going to get in touch with the DNA people," he said. "Enough time has passed. Any more is just laziness."

Not too destabilised, then. Good.

99. EXCEEDS EXPECTATIONS

Spak apparently still knew how to motivate boffins. It was only a day later that Gracelyn called me in again.

Kim and Mattie and I had spent that day in a combination of conversation and action. Kim wanted to stay here with me for a while and soak in the last known ambience of their parents, but they also wanted to get on with other parts of their life. After a bit of research, they discovered that there were computer game programming courses and folklore specialties at one of the local universities, and forensic science at another. A veritable cornucopia of life choices.

Meanwhile, I had a vacant studio apartment at the Epitome, on the second floor at 2-K/205, as well as the upcoming one-bedroom vacancy in what had been 1-D/104 and was now 1-A/101[182]. If Kim decided to stay, they could be autonomous

---

182. I suppose I have to explain, since I've alluded to all this a few times. It's another Epitome Special Instance. There will be a quiz later. Each floor in the Epitome has either five, six, or seven suites, for a total of twenty-four bachelor, one-, two-, or three-bedroom suites. On the transoms, the ancient painted suite designations are actually black-and-gold-painted single letters, running from main floor front A to fourth floor rear X. (Y and Z are in the basement, not suites but the furnace room and an old office in that order. Who knows why? Nobody living.) Then a long time ago someone added floor numbers

but nearby. Mattie approved that, but she also wanted Kim to remember their other plans, made before the Big Reveal, and make good choices. By the end of the afternoon, they (both of the theys, not just Kim) had decided that Mattie would stay here with Kim until the initial legal stuff was resolved; then Kim would go home for the rest of the summer but would rent a place here and plan on coming back, if only part-time. The rest would settle itself in time. We had also gone to Ikea™ and Kim had bought basic furnishings for the studio suite (they thought the bigger apartment was a bit too much house for a first-time move-out, which was smart, or, as they said, cool). Apparently, lemon yellow and grey really were their favourite colours, not just in finger picks, and luckily, those were the featured colours at Ikea™ that summer.

---

and employed letters for the suite locations on each floor, using brass letters held to the door with little brass round-headed nails. There was a sort of logic: 1-A and 4-A started in the same relative location (until the events of this story). Finally, a few years ago, with no consultation, the previous owner, who was a pain in the ass in so *many* ways, changed all our suite numbers arbitrarily to numerals one day, with the hundreds-digit as floor number and the ones digit as suite number, and a zero in between because WTF, right? Some of us didn't like that, kept using the number-letter combos, and wouldn't let our doors be changed, so her workers added tacky new stick-on numbers below the nice brass ones. *Very* sticky numbers, and still there. When I bought the place, I decided to leave all the numbers — all of them — on the transoms and doors, and let residents choose. Nobody uses the letters alone because I don't know why. More than half use the second set: like Mrs. Murray, some of them had been getting their mail there for a long *long* time, and/or like me, didn't want to be bullied. So Mrs. Murray still used 1-D, while on the same side of the corridor, newer tenants use 102 and 103. I did move Mrs. Murray's door, as I promised, so now the corridor has this progression from front to back: 1-D/104, 102, 103 and 1-A/101. 'Way more than you wanted to know, but all of it chaotic good in action, IMHO, though I wonder what the letter carriers think.

We woke up late, and moved around the apartment with the ease of old friends, which was both odd and comfortable. Mattie made waffles. Actual waffles. With my parents' waffle iron that I didn't even remember I had. She had done something magical that cleaned all its rust away. Hmm.

I was polishing off the last of the maple syrup on my plate — literally polishing — when Gracelyn called. I left Kim and Mattie to wait for the Ikea™ delivery and walked slowly through an even more clear day. I didn't have to use the inhaler once.

100. A FINE EXAMPLE OF A PETARD

When I came into Faraday, Dafydd Spak was in the catbird seat at the head of the big table. He'd tilted back his ergonomic wonder chair and his feet were up on the desk. His smooth, immaculate handmade shoes had fancy coloured soles scored and stained with some kind of elaborate design that would be completely invisible were he in his usual posture — by which I mean, dignified and upright. I bet he left really pretty tracks on a wet sidewalk. Assuming it ever rained again. His fingers were steepled above his trim Brioni-clad torso. I was about as surprised as if I had surprised the queen of England[183] in the same pose.

"Whoa!" I said. "Who are you and what have you done with my lawyer?"

Spak smiled slightly, then tilted his head toward the other chairs. He was, if possible, getting better at this micro-tasking thing. Also, he hadn't unbuttoned his jacket to take the strain off the button. I wasn't sure if that was good or bad. Bad, I think, from the guy who always, always lifts his pant legs at the knee when he sits down.

---

183. Who was still living at the time.

"I have been thinking about crime," he said. "And the proceeds thereof, of course."

"Of course?" I said slowly, meaning, of course, *What the fuck?* I sat.

"One of the things we have been fighting," Spak went on, "is, of course, the legal definition of crime. Our challenge has always been and will continue to be proving the criminality of Lockwood Chiles. Aside from the murders, that is. And the fraud. That has helped, but only in that area. What about his other activities?"

He made a minuscule adjustment to the crease of this pants, then looked at me directly. "His pervasive venality, of course, is clear and unquestionable."

"Of course." I was on more solid ground here.

"It's not illegal to sell guns. It's not illegal to buy them. In the countries where Chiles had his sweatshop factories, he was actually operating according to the labour laws of that country."

"Yeah. Nike™ does that too. But the workers still can't afford the shoes they make."

"Nor, by the same token, could those wage slaves afford the intricate computer devices that Nathan Lockwood LLP, the corporate entity, was making at those factories, but that's not against the law. Yet. Yes, he misled his partner about the labour practices, and yes, armed guards with guns aren't a good look, but nonetheless, on all these fronts, Chiles was usually, or almost, within the law, and could have talked himself out of the exceptions."

"Which sucks."

"Indeed it does. But they got Al Capone on tax evasion, as you might recall."

"Yeah, I saw the movie. But Chiles wasn't . . . didn't . . ."

"Unfortunately, not that simple. Luckily, also no longer our headache. So, if you recall, we all asked each other that day about how we prove . . ."

"Nefareity?"

"Just so. How we prove it for him, in relation to us, and similarly I have been concerned about how to prove it in our putative heirs."

Spak swung his feet down gracefully, sat up, and subtly settled his attire, much as a cat ripples its skin to get its fur in order[184].

"I have some news," he said, and reached to his right to snag a file from the credenza there.

"Is this going to take a while, this reveal? Should I get coffee, or maybe order in some sushi or something?"

Spak smiled.

Broadly.

Mr. Spak smiled broadly. It was as shocking as his namesake's behaviour in that weird-spores episode of *ST:ToS*.

"The DNA tests came back," he said.

Okay, *that* might be something, if he would only hurry to the point and tell me what.

"You will be delighted to know that neither of those people is related in any way to Nathan. Our claimants are indeed pretenders. The samples they *provided* to us have a family match to Nathan Bierce. However, the samples we got from the coffee cups in the boardroom? Different DNA, and that proves fraudulent intent. So Nathan's siblings are out there somewhere, probably oblivious, but somehow these people procured samples of their DNA.

"We will have to find out if they were put at risk during the process, but sufficient unto the day is the evil thereof. Right now, the bottom line is that the claimants we met are not relatives.

---

184. Well, a normal cat, or even Micah Five. Bunnywit goes through life looking like an unmade bed, an expression of my mother's. He does lick himself, but only to get the raw material for the hairballs he loves to hork up onto my pillow, or onto manuscripts. The digital revolution has done one good thing anyway.

259

"However —"

"Oh, for crying out loud."

"As I was saying. The lab was intrigued by the similarity of one of the coffee cup samples to another sample we had provided not that long before."

Spak leaned forward, elbows on the table, and did that fancy thing where people fold their hands together except for the index fingers, which they place pad to pad and use to prop their chins.

I have to say, I hate that move, and what's more, Dafydd knows that. He was fucking with me. And enjoying it.

Two can play at that game. I breathed quietly and deeply, then leaned back in my own seat and swung my Fluevog boots up to the slab of wood between us. I made sure not to point the bottom of my feet at my pal. I then mirrored his hand position, tilted my head slightly the way Bunnywit does when he's thinking (or when he has an ear infection, which may have a similar uncomfortable effect inside his tiny skull). My return message was clear. I now had all day.

The grin stayed, despite a little headshake of acknowledgement.

"The Terrible Twins? Not even related. But the husband?"

One last pause.

"He's related to someone whose DNA we have recently verified."

I waited. My goose, ghosts, and cats were busy, but not in a bad way. More anticipatory than apprehensive.

"The DNA," said Dafydd, "shows that our Mr. Woodward is a relative of Mr. Lockwood Chiles. Despite our efforts to find family, so far he is the *only known relative* of Mr. Lockwood Chiles."

"He was — what, now?"

"He won't admit exactly what relationship so far, but he's likely a half-brother. Not only that, but his day job? He has a vague administrative title, but we think he's one of Chiles's fixers.

Vinnie recognised his name. A couple of their directives came from him."

"How are we allowed to know that, after all those signatures?"

"It's not in the remit of those black ops types. This is simple criminality."

"Nefariety."

"Just so. I told all this to Roger earlier today, and he got onto That Woman —"

"I call her Captain Someone."

"Indeed. And after some jurisdictional discussion it has been determined that their team is able to share with us any material evidence pertaining to Lock's simple civil crimes. This is a great gift, as Roger says our information fits with some scraps of smart paper found in Chiles's cell — once they figured out it was smart paper, which you saw in that video, not just some random scribbles on a yellow legal pad. So with, er, Captain Someone's, and more specifically Vinnie's, help unlocking those specific sheets, they have discovered quite a few transactions that can now be traced to Mr. Woodward.

"So, now we have him. If he had applied on his own behalf, 'way back at Chiles's death, he could have had all of Chiles's legitimate money. But he wanted a faster outcome. Chiles's money was tied up until the investigation was over, so he went for Nathan's using the fake-heir scam — but with the resources he had from Chiles's operations. In doing so he has implicated without a shadow of doubt the entire Lockwood Chiles — *oeuvre*, as it were."

"Boom."

"Indeed. He has unequivocally committed a crime and is legally not permitted to benefit in any way therefrom."

And Mr. Spak, my darling, unflappable multicultural poster lawyer, unbuttoned his jacket, folded his hands behind his head in the traditional pose of relaxed satisfaction, and began to laugh and laugh.

101. THE THIRD AND FINAL DEATH OF LOCKWOOD CHILES[185]

Not long after this delightful meeting with Dafydd, Roger came to the Epitome Apartments with Prasan Dave, and they took instructions from the note on my door and found Kim, Mattie, Denis, and me in apartment K/2F/205, surrounded by cardboard, bubble wrap, piles and little plastic bags of tiny metal puzzle pieces, sheets of wordless and vaguely threatening instructions, and the birch components and melamine-veneered boards that Ikea™ has used to conquer the known world.

The two cops stood, tall and aloof, in the open door, looking into the little "studio suite" with its one bay window and one small above-the-kitchen-sink windowlet, all the windows open as far as their hundred-and-eleven-year-old sashes would let us open them, and a valiant fan on one windowsill doing sweet-fuck-all to move the hot air.

We sat sweatily and grimily on various parts of the lovely old wood floor, surrounded by the inevitable confusion that comes to four people with four approaches to flat-pack furniture who were each dealing with a different module of Kim's New Life™. The rest of the floor was littered with packaging, hardware, and tools of various sizes and efficiencies.

Roger may or may not have been grinning. Sweat was dripping into my eyes, so I gave him the benefit of the doubt.

"What?" I was trying to hold a join together while turning a big Allen key, and I may have snarled slightly. "There's iced tea in the fridge. What do you want?"

"Lovely to see you, too," Roger rejoined, "and congratulations on a delightful DNA result!"

"Oh, you heard?"

---

185. And some strike or other, but do they still count as lightning strikes if they are *good* news for a change? Anyway, I've lost count.

"How not? I *am* the head of Major Crimes, and fraud is still a —"

"If you are here anyway, take off those suit jackets, you must be sweltering, and help us out here."

Roger was indeed grinning. "Not a chance," he said. "I have done my time in Ikea™ hell."

He did, however, seek out the cold beverages and pour two glassfuls into the new set of tall, clear tumblers that were going to be Kim's moving-out glassware.

Dave, however, already had his jacket off. He hung it carefully on the one assembled chair of the putative dining set — and then sat in the chair. Hmm. I had had hope for him for a moment.

"Detective Dave has something to say," Rog said portentously, though he spoiled it by chug-a-lugging his glass of tea. He handed the other one to Dave.

Dave sipped at his glass, which was already slick with enviable condensation.

I wanted more of that cool draught. I picked up my own tumbler from the mess beside me and struggled up from the floor, shedding an Allen wrench and a few of those assorted jigsaw-puzzle-piece widgets that look like factory sweepings until you insert one into slot A and the other into slot B and they turn into a clever assembly method.

Dave raised his hand, and I stopped despite myself and set my glass down on the counter. Damn. I had been tasked by my arch-enemy. Yet I did notice that he was surprisingly relaxed for someone who, not long ago, had shown all the signs of hating me for eternity.

"I regret to inform you," he said, "that Mr. Lockwood Chiles is dead."

We all looked at him.

And then a bit more.

Then I tipped my head and spread my hands slightly in the universal sign for *What the fuck, Dave, are you talking about?*

Dave just drank another sip of tea.

Clearly, he didn't speak my dialect of Hands. Fine. "What the fuck?"

Roger finally couldn't help it. He laughed, which broke the meniscus. "As you know, we have to retest all the lab results from that seven-years-of-bullshit fiasco, which is going to take until hell freezes over, but never mind that now. The important thing is that because of this investigation, we prioritised the Chiles samples. I am happy to report that Mr. Chiles, he dead."

Now Dave looked at Roger as if *Rog* was crazy, but hey, guy, now that you're a detective you will have time and energy to read some goddamn books, right? Or at least watch a movie or two.

Roger didn't react because he was pouring iced tea into my tumbler.

Dave decided to step in, one might guess to save his boss from further bad grammar. "We went right back to the original preserved samples. We sought out new samples from Nathan Lockwood LLP headquarters. We didn't trust any existing test result. It has taken quite some time" — Yeah, no kidding! Though in fact, it had been damned fast for police results, which often take months or years to get tested and verified[186] — "but we are now completely satisfied that the evidence is unassailable. We linked the man we saw cremated with his former life, crime scene evidence, and post-mortem tests. The man serving the sentence was indeed Lockwood Chiles, who indeed committed the crimes for which he was convicted, who was indeed murdered, and whose body was indeed correctly identified. The chain of evidence is now re-verified. Mr. Lockwood Chiles, convicted felon, is dead."

---

186. Ask Mina and me about rape kits some day if you don't have much to do for a couple of hours.

"What I said," said Roger. "Get off that damn chair and let your boss take a load off."

"What the hell," said the hitherto unbendable Dave, and he slid off onto the floor beside Mattie and said, "You're doing that all wrong." In the moment of shock that followed, he took up an Allen key[187] and a handful of hardware, pulled three pieces of wood toward himself, and set to work disassembling a dysfunctional connexion.

He did notice us staring.

"What?" he said. "You just have to follow the bloody instructions!" and he tapped the sheet of diagrams with the bent end of the tool.

"Right," I said. "Simple."

"Exactly," he said.

"So did I kill him?" I asked, trying to actually sound as if I were curious.

"Bloody hell, shut up," he replied. "You never know when to stop. You were ruled out weeks ago. Hand me that thing there, will you?"

And that was that.

Cross one item off our list.

Lockwood Chiles was dead.

And apparently, I was the first, and last, to know that I, at least, had not been the one who killed him.

102. OUT OF OUR HEIRS

The meeting was in Faraday, where we had all our best meetings these days.

Mr. Spak sat at the head of the table, with Gracelyn as usual holding up the wall behind him. I took the seat to his left, to keep his sword arm free.

---

187. It's a wrench. It's a key. It's a wrench *and* a key . . .

Kim sat to *my* left, studiously looking down at the tablet in front of them, as if they were just a paralegal or articling student. Leaving an empty seat to the right of Dafydd, Mattie sat across from Kim.

Four tall, suit-clad lawyer-looking types had chosen seats nearest the door, so when Douglas Woodward, Rosalind Brice Woodward, and Anthony Brice arrived with their new legal team, they all had to file in past this quartet.

How deceiving suits are. Roger looks very official in a suit, but official *what* is context-dependent. He had brought with him Dave (who was proving yet again that, despite my rude joke, he *does* have more than one suit); Fitzdonald, out of her usual geekwear and into a very smart asymmetrically-jacketed dress suit; and the other Fraud Squad cop, the one I'd never seen before, who rocked a grey pinstripe three-piece with a blue shirt. His remarkably complexly-patterned and, I think, Gaultier tie still managed to look completely neutral. I didn't even know Gaultier *made* neutral ties. The guy was damn near invisible, and nobody introduced him either.

I thought four of them was a bit much, but Roger wanted a minion to nab each miscreant, without having to disturb his own sartorial equilibrium. He settled himself carefully to avoid creasing.

Because of that empty chair[188], Gracelyn had to squeeze in the chairs for the two real lawyers. Finally everyone got settled, the five of them all in middle seats at the table, as intended. The Faraday is in the basement, but as with our Sekrit Meeting with the Someones, having a full house does take the chill off the room pretty fast.

"Welcome," said Mr. Spak. "I suspect you are wondering why I have taken the unconventional step of calling you here, when normally we would not be meeting until court."

---

188. Technically hers, but destined never to be used. Though I imagined Nathan in it, the ghost at the feast.

How come when I make a joke like that, I get a Look, whereas Spak always gets away with it? I know, I know, Dafydd is a cat and never ever loses his dignity. But what does that make me?

He did get looks, but they were more the polite-but-hostile looks of legal opponents, and not at all admonitory.

Everyone cordially waited for him to continue, though I saw one of the new lawyers, a tiny sharp pointy woman in an expensive black suit who looked as if she would turn into Margaret Murray when she got older, with her birdlike hand on "Rosalind"'s wrist, cautioning her not to react. By the way, I think we can safely add the quotation marks now, right? Because we've established that whoever this was, it sure as fuck wasn't Rosalind Brice.

Mr. Spak did that thing again with the hands and the steepling and the chin[189]. Oh, he was enjoying this.

"I will, of course, be recording this meeting, if no-one has any objection. For the microphones, please agree verbally, repeating your name as you do."

There was a murmur of agreement and name-calling.

"Of course, we all know that we have issues with who are the legitimate heirs of Dr. Nathan Bierce."

The hand on the wrist had to tighten slightly in response to "Rosalind"'s tension, but the other two didn't stir.

"However, I think we can settle a good deal of this today, when I introduce you to Kim Gill Johns —"

He paused to indicate Kim, who looked up and smiled with surprising grace and sang-froid. Wait, why should I have been surprised? I already knew they had been on the debating team, in the model parliament, and in the drama club. And they had been raised by Gills. What was I even thinking? I was *so* going to be saying I knew them when.

---

189. Later, I might suggest on whom he is and isn't allowed to deploy it. But this was an appropriate deployment, for sure.

"— who is the only child of, and the legitimate heir of, Nathan Bierce and, might I add, the only blood relative of Dr. Bierce in this room."

Wow. It was *Jurassic Park 2* in there for a while. With the running. And the screaming.

Well, due to some many cops, not so much running.

But there was a lot of screaming, in various registers. A lot.

As I had already experienced when I watched Jason Edwards cuffed, it does not take very long to actually arrest someone and tell them what they are charged with. It was really only about fifteen or twenty minutes until the Faraday was half-empty again, with cops and criminals gone, but those minutes were strenuous.

First, all of the heirs, and their lawyers, leapt up with protests. Roger and Dafydd handled the main exposition, with paper-work. Remember that old expression about "reading the Riot Act"? This was sort of like that, but quieter, and about fraud. Mr. Spak had prepared some succinct accusations, and Roger had the actual charges to correspond with them. Handcuffs were invoked.

"Anthony" just said "Goddammit to hell" and sat down, but the others, not so much.

The lawyers were flexible. Each one of them picked a Woodward who was expostulating and advised them to shut up and take counsel. That was their rôle, after all, and they did it well.

"Rosalind" stood over "Anthony" and screeched, "What did you get me into?" "Anthony", it proved, was really her husband, and she dished out recrimination with a side of insult. As he tried to calm her, it became evident that her first name might be Sherry. Whatever her name, she could not be propitiated, and I suspected that the separation of jail time would end up acting as protective custody for the man formerly known as Anthony but now being called "you stupid asshole".

After the first outburst, Douglas Woodward fell silent, and his cold eyes stared at first Spak, then me, then Kim with alarming intensity. Gracelyn, noticing, stepped in and ushered Kim and Mattie away, and they went upstairs to wait in Leonards.

Woodward glared.

Roger arrested him formally, and Dave handcuffed him.

He glared some more. I didn't like this guy's glares. Suddenly there was a family resemblance to Lock.

"Mr. Woodward, if that is indeed your name," said Dafydd, "you do realise that with patience, you could have had the legitimate part of your relative's estate legitimately."

He broke his silence. "Fuck you and the horse you rode in on."

I couldn't resist. "The horse is innocent."

Schadenfreude is bad for the karma, but sometimes it soothes the soul.

"Shut the fuck up!" Woodward was red-faced and he thrashed around alarmingly in Dave's capable grasp.

Damned if I would, now that I didn't have to. I was too curious. "Crime doesn't pay," I continued sanctimoniously, because I could, and Mr. Spak didn't even twitch. Neither did Roger, which was even more fun.

Woodward was handcuffed and in Dave's grasp, or I would have feared for my life in that moment.

"So much you know, you fucking bitch. I already have more of Nathan's money than you'll ever see!"

"Sir, I must advise you," said the lawyer valiantly, at the same time as I said, "What the fuck do you mean?"

"Oh, Doug, be quiet," said You Stupid Asshole, but his tone was fatalistic.

I moved closer to Doug, just out of headbutting reach, another kind of micro-tasking that every street fighter knows, and asked, "Did Lock send instructions from jail on that smart paper?"

"Of course! None of you had a fucking clue."

Ha.

"But it didn't work."

"Because all his paper went off the grid! You fucking locked it up. I know it was you because I heard you."

More ha.

"Doug, for Chrissake!" yelled Sherry. She was still resisting being handcuffed.

"Shut up, you bitch," Woodward said, just as the lawyer tried to *shhh* him again. "And you, get the fuck off me!"

It took some work to separate Sherry from her surroundings without anyone suffering bodily harm from her fingernail extensions. She yelled the whole time, and the lawyer, the woman of the two, whose name I also hadn't learned, cautioned her fruitlessly. I never saw that woman again. (Later, in court, Sherry was represented by a different legal team, yet again, and managed to parlay her injured innocence into a plea that she had been led astray by love. Yeah, that old saw, but apparently it still cuts wood, as she got a lesser sentence than You Stupid Asshole[190].) But in the moment, the other fraud guy, whose name turned out to be Andersen, bundled her out of the room firmly but without excessive force, which certainly can't have been easy, with all the provocation.

Next to go was You Stupid Asshole, who said not one word after his attempts to calm Sherry and silence Woodward failed. Fitzdonald was able to lead him out in cuffs with no challenges to her authority, which, given that she was more of a computer nerd than a street cop, was a Good Thing.

Spak, Roger, Dave, and I were left with Douglas Woodward — or whatever his name was — and the other lawyer, who also acts as a spear carrier in this narrative, given he was never introduced and — for reasons you will soon see — was never seen in proximity to these jerks again.

---

190. They threw the book at him. And threw a bigger book at Woodward. But that was then. We are still at Now.

I kept leaning into Woodward's personal space. The recorder kept recording. "When exactly did you hear me, asshole?"

"When you let that sheet of paper out. We finally got access to the data we needed, and you'll never see a cent of Lock's. Congratulations, idiots." This was getting better and better.

"Sir, I really must — sir, please, for your own good —" The young lawyer still had a brotherly hand on Woodward's arm.

Woodward shook him off, and moved to strike him, struggling in his cuffs. "Leave me alone, you cretin! You're fired!"

Later I would treasure the next moment, though it passed quickly at the time: "Thank you, sir!" said the lawyer involuntarily, and I am damned sure I heard a sigh of relief, just before he fled. Good for you, dude, whoever you are and wherever you may be.

"Come along," said Roger, but Woodward wasn't done with us.

"It doesn't matter," he said angrily. "We've got half of your damn fortune already anyway. Try and find it."

Try *to* find it. Schools these days.

103. YOU CAN'T GET GOOD HELP

After they were all gone, Dafydd and I joined Kim, Mattie, and Gracelyn in the Leonards.

"They were so low rent," I said in wonder. "With all his resources, Lock couldn't afford a better class of grifter?"

"Based on that peculiar remark he made," said Spak slowly, "I think that when we put the smart paper in the Faraday safe, we somehow cut off all the access Chiles had to his account numbers. Suddenly he lost a lot of his source files. So perhaps he lost some or all control of the criminal part of his empire. He might not have actually been able to get to his criminally-acquired funds and his contacts, and his legitimate business assets were all frozen. Maybe he didn't have the — well, shall we say 'bandwidth'? — to get through those firewalls from jail.

Especially since the jail damps down on unauthorised signals to prevent the use of contraband cell phones. So he had to do some serious plotting, and that's where the first fraud came in."

"'If you can't be with the one you love, love the one you're with'," I said.

"Just so. He must have had some fun writing that set of routines."

"We know Woodward worked for him in another capacity," Gracelyn put in. "Did the others?"

"There's a thought," said Roma. "Maybe 'Rosalind' is actually on the accounting side, but the dark side of the accounting."

"But she was mad at her husband for letting her into it. Maybe it's him who is in dark accounting. And do we know what Woodward actually *did* for Lock?"

"I'm just getting the info on that," said Gracelyn, flicking at her tablet. "Yep. Woodward was his fixer in several shady areas. And here — looks like the fake brother does something — did something — in HR with third world sweatshops. Mean, but involving mostly taking orders, not original sin."

"Copycat sin. I like that. Explains a lot of the world's ills," I said. "Well, Woodward may not look like much, but he has the same furious narcissism Lock had, and after that last little scene, I can certainly imagine him being a partner in crime. I suppose we are never really going to find out more than we know right now." I was thinking of certain disclosure agreements.

"Well, we'll get enough to convict, and the rest is going to keep some acquaintances of ours busy for a long time, I think." Dafydd was clearly thinking alone the same lines, but stopped there, obviously because Kim and Mattie were out of that particular loop.

"But not us," I said.

"No cap, not us," he said, thus falling off his pedestal permanently and forever.

I had made certain suggestions the last time the alley had been the site of gang violence, but I wasn't sure if anyone was taking me seriously. I certainly didn't *see* any unusual activity for a while, and I had had other things to think about for the last few days.

So I didn't notice at first, the third time the gang came back, until Kim came and said, "Something's up in the alley again."

A brief glance out the hall window showed us the same old foreshortened view, but this time lit with flashing cop-car lights, and crowded with people in uniforms, SWAT jackets and vests, with various weapons, busy bundling some handcuffed, crop-haired dudes in dark jackets, jeans, and big boots into police transport vehicles.

When we got down there and popped open the Epitome's back door, Heather was leaning on the railing of the back porch, watching from an elevated vantage as various people got into various vehicles and drove away.

"Well!" she said when she saw us.

"What was *that*?"

"We thought we might just stake out Fleury's tent in case there were reprisals."

She was smiling slightly.

I grinned and clapped her on the shoulder. "Thanks for that. And for taking me seriously too."

"Looks like it was a good idea. No matter who had it."

In other words, you can get a lot done if you don't care who gets the credit. We contemplated the scene with mutual satisfaction.

"Sometimes you eat the bear," she said. "Five arrests. With Edwards, that's probably all of them. Let's see who turns on whom."

"Like on TV?" asked Kim eagerly.

Heather looked at them, then at me for just one second (perhaps a little helplessly?), then back at them. Then, reluctantly, it seemed, she cracked a broader smile and nodded. "Yeah, kid, just like on TV."

"Cool," said Kim.

105. ALSO COOL, REDUX

Vikki found Fleury a temporary place the next day. Kim and I were bringing him a sandwich when she came by.

"It's only a room in a rooming house," she said to him.

"That's okay, Miss Vikki. I like that."

"We'll find you something better later," she said.

"I don't mind," he said. "I don't need a big space. I'm not much of a housekeeper." He gestured at his messy tent.

He grinned, and Vikki and I did too. Kim looked between the three of us, then grinned slowly.

"'Sometimes you eat the bear'?" Kim ventured.

"You got it, kiddo," I said.

"Yum yum," said Fleury. "'Cept with my teeth I can't chew it that good any more."

"We'll puree it for you," said Kim, and Fleury laughed out loud.

"Cool," said Vikki.

106. SWINGS/ROUNDABOUTS

The New Tan Tan was very quiet, despite us being there in the prime dim-sum-eating hour. I'd gone to meet Roger and Heather Wood, who apparently now was willing to drink tea with me[191]. I

---

191. Literally. Going to eat dim sum is called going "yum cha", which is Cantonese for "drink tea", and is a pastime that combines many of my favourite flavours and vices. Pu erh is a taste like no other, and yu chu gao, which are not made with shark fin any more, are IMHO among the best of the "heavenly morsels" on offer. Crap, now I'm hungry again.

wasn't sure why, but a chance to eat with Roger is usually good. When I was poor, he used to pick up the tab. Now we get separate checks. Progress (and ethics).

"Um," said Heather, after we'd done with the little flurry of tea-pouring, socialising with Mary, and general anticipation, and were waiting for the first shipment out of the kitchen.

Roger was looking out the front window and his leg was doing that weird little piston thing that isn't usually one of his nervous mannerisms. I have told Roger many times that being in upper management has not been good for him, and this new tic was more proof.

"What?" I said. I put my hand on his knee and reefed down hard. His heel hit the lino and stayed there. He glared at me, and I glared back. "I hate shit like that," I said. "Stop it."

"Jason Edwards is out of jail," said Heather.

I forgot any intention of curing Roger's jittering via tough love. "You gotta be fucking kidding! I thought the judge wasn't going to allow bail!"

"His lawyer and the police association lawyer argued that jail was a dangerous environment for a cop," said Roger.

"World's tiniest violin," I said. "And not even playing. A page of rests."

Heather shook her head, but Roger nodded. "The judge agreed to set bail, but at an extremely high figure. Against the objections of the Crown."

"Okay, but doesn't that happen a lot? Why the meeting?"

"Key figures in the police association posted the considerable bail within minutes," said Roger. "We are management, so we can't verify this, but it is possible bail came from a fund within the union itself. Deep pockets *somewhere*, anyway. Edwards is on the street, thanks to his — supportive professional organisation or certain of its influential cheerleaders."

"Fuck a duck," I said with my usual suave elegance.

"Exactly," said Heather Wood.

"Are you going to melt down?" I asked them, halfway between polite interest and duck-and-cover.

"Been there, got the T-shirt," said Roger.

"Not again," said Wood at the same time, and they stared at each other briefly before turning identical burning glances toward me[192].

107. "BEEN ON THE JOB TOO LONG —"

My father was a bona fide crackpot, and he died as he lived. While still alive, he was in the habit of writing letters to the newspaper. Often he rehearsed his arguments at family dinners, which were grim affairs anyway, even before I came out or my brother died.

One of his favourites, usually undertaken while reproaching me for my chosen career, was about how crime was ruining society, law and order was undermined by commie tree-huggers like me who wanted to let drug addicts take over our streets, and that these days jail was just a revolving door and it was hardly worth arresting criminals if they were going to be out on the streets ten minutes later.

I know many people who sympathise with him.

I had never before had any time for those particular arguments. I'd seen too much of how remand and jails are used punitively to punish poverty, addiction, and mental illness. I prefer police stick to investigating actual crimes and catching actual criminals. I haven't had to argue with Roger too much about this, and I've been careful not to test Lance, for Denis's sake, but over the years there have been . . . er, discussions . . . with other police and police-adjacent people, some of which have taken place while

---

192. Oh, Detective Wood was *so* going to SIRT when she retired. No question, that was SIRT-level outrage.

physically standing between police and their targets, others of which have been bureaucratic, such as my recent resistance to the bylaw officer who had been so eager to ticket my back-alley tenant-equivalents.

However. There are times. This was one.

"This is bad," I said. "This is very bad. First the lab, then these guys. Revolving door, hm? Add all the carding going on around the 'hood."

"We don't call it carding any more," Wood said gloomily.

"Same same. This is very *very* bad," I said.

"Yes," said Roger.

"They will never trust us again," said Wood.

"They don't trust you now, Heather," I said.

"Exactly. What. I. Said."

"Sorry, but, it's true. What about the other five?"

"Two are out, same bail deal but private lawyers — we don't know where they are getting the money to pay. We suspect a group like the Proud Boys, given the lawyers are known to work for them," she said. "The Armed Forces have asked that the other three be transferred to their custody."

"Well, that's something."

"Maybe. Unclear."

"How the *hell* —" Roger exploded suddenly, slamming his hand on the table, setting up a slight vibration in the plate glass window beside him, and frightening the youngster who was bringing us a tray of (among other things) chai sui bao, yu chu gao, sticky rice, and custard tarts.

"Shhh!" I hissed at Rog, and "Sorry," I said quietly to the kid. "Just got some bad news. Would you mind bringing me some red vinegar, please?"

"No problem," he said, placed our food, and scuttled away. There was a silence. In a moment, Mary brought the vinegar.

"Thanks," I said. "Tell the kid everything's okay, really."

"I tell him," she said, but she rolled her eyes over slightly toward Roger as she sidestepped away.

"That big tip is on you, big guy," I said.

"Fine," he said. "But they will not get away with it."

I gestured quizzically at Mary and the kid. Roger did his growl. Of course I knew who he really meant, FFS.

"They might," I said.

"I know," he said.

And, in one of the Pinter pauses that pepper (and possibly even characterise) this narrative, we began to eat. Usually, that would have made things better.

Not that day.

Does anger mess with the taste buds? I'd like to see a scientific study on why food almost-literally feels as if it turns to ashes of chagrin in the mouth sometimes. Even though everything was delicious, because, duh, New Tan Tan, still it was wasted on us.

It wasn't a day for eating bear; in fact, we were feeling decidedly snacked-upon.

I returned to the office to spread the bad news, and I resigned myself to having an old murder ballad about Duncan and Brady playing in my head for the rest of the week.

108. ALL WE HAVE IS MEANS

It wasn't one of our happiest days at the office either. Dafydd and Roma plummeted with me into the funk that Roger and Heather's news brought. Then, halfway through the afternoon, I got the news that a big housing grant I'd been hoping would rescue part of Own Domains had been awarded elsewhere. It was a long shot, really, and too many projects had been vying for not enough money, so I wasn't mad at the project that *did* get it, but still.

So I had a few millionaires who had signed up for a total of only a few millions in donations, but I needed a full match of the City's money[193] before we could go ahead with even a modest project. And we had nothing near that until Nathan's estate was probated, which was going to take even *longer* because of the goddamn fraud.

Also, I needed not just capital funding right fucking now, but endowment funding. The projects had to sustain themselves with all their services, because you can't take people, especially folks like Fleury, from unhoused to housed without transitions and supports. Otherwise, the hope of housing just becomes another empty promise, another revolving door, and thus provides no hope at all.

Spak and Roma and I just looked at each other when I told them about the grant, did our own versions of that little shrug and mouth-twist that means, "well, fuck!", and we all went into our offices.

My chair at the office is very comfortable, and I like to sit with my feet up on the desk, resting my eyes — and my mind, especially after the double-whammy of the day. I have the kind of view that people who like cities like and other people find boring. I was taking a few moments not to be bored with it, wondering if that peregrine falcon sitting atop the building across the way was ever going to swoop down on a pigeon when I could see it.

This has been a hobby of mine since I came in one day and found the remains of a pigeon on the windowsill. I can't say I was sorry. Pigeons are rats of the sky. What are they even *for*? But now I wanted to see it happen. Today, I *really* wanted to see it, and I would even name the pigeon Jason Edwards or Doug Woodward as I watched it being torn apart. I guess I needed two pigeon victims. At least two. After all, there is always a special pigeon named Lockwood Chiles.

Roma tapped on the door. "You busy?"

---

193. Repeat after me: "Twenty-eight-point-eight million dollars . . ."

"Yes, but for you I will interrupt my nature watch," I said, without otherwise moving.

She came around where I could see her. "Still no hawk murder?"

"Falcon. Alas, no. What do you need?"

"What do you want me to do with this?" She held a sheaf of smart paper, the stuff with Nathan's notes on Own Domains. We had gleaned everything we could from it all, but Roma knows I like to keep the originals together (cf. box, nostalgia, grief, and obsessiveness op. cit.).

With them were two digital storage keys. "What's this?"

"Oh, you brought them in for Mr. Spak to do the trade-marking validation during the audit. The keys with the formulae."

What *did* I want her to do with all this?

Suddenly the answer bloomed like fireworks in my brain, dazzling me with my own brilliance.

For a change.

"What do I want you to do with all that?"

"Why are you looking at me like that?"

"I am pondering the many reasons I value you. One is that you can use 'formulae' in a sentence. But you do many other important things."

"Um — yeah — ?"

"Including field all those importunate phone calls."

She made that little moue that means "Get to the point?", complete with question mark.

I looked back at my hands, one hand with a sheaf of That Paper, the other with two storage keys.

You know that Le Guin quote about how there are no ends, only means? Maybe true philosophically, but there are times when ends are also important. I had two handsful of means, and for once, an end that could be quantified.

109. THE END OF THE END OF THE MIDDLE

I looked up from the paper into Roma's intelligent face, which was starting to have that look she gets.

"You know that guy?" I asked her. With my usual precision.

She tilted her head.

"You know, the guy that keeps calling. With the money."

Oddly enough — or not so oddly, this is Roma I'm telling you about — she instantly knew who I meant. This was a hungry tech guy, smart and, in his way, very nice, but pushy, who had caught a whiff of smart paper coming from my direction, and he called a lot. A lot. He had even hacked my cell number and annoyed me at all sorts of weird times until I told him off about it, but even after that he kept leaving messages with Roma on the regular.

Annoying as fuck if you don't want to admit you have any smart paper or that any adorable tech billionaire had left you the means to make it.

But oddly endearing on a day when a great big shitload of money would come in handy.

Roma didn't pretend she wasn't following my line of thought. "I'll get him on the line for you. It might take a while. He's got a lot of layers." Yes, she said "layers", not "lawyers". She meant protective ones. He has lawyers, too, which would be handy for later.

"For this, he'll answer."

I then went looking for Dafydd, and indeed I had hardly dangled the computer keys in front of his nose and said, "You see these?" before Roma was patching through the call to his desk.

"Tell him to hold, please, Roma?" I turned to Spak.

"You know what these are?" I said.

He nodded.

"You know what it's worth?"

He started getting one of those looks *he* gets.

"All of the funding for Own Domains," I continued.

Our mood was definitely changing for the better, second by second. He inclined his head slowly, thought surrounding it in an invisible but tangible aura.

"Possibly forever," I said. "A huge down payment. A permanent royalty. A constant income," and I set down the Own Domains plans and tapped their surface with the keys.

The paper woke up, which serves me right for posturing. I tapped it again to shut it off.

Dafydd reached over and stopped my hand. "Are you sure?"

"Yes. It's time," I said. "On the phone? It's that guy."

He nodded and said to Roma, "Okay, put him through."

We put it on speaker.

"Hi, Omar," I said. "You've been wanting to talk to me."

I know these people are Our Hope For The Future, but they all sound twelve years old[194]. "Sure, yeah!"

"Do you know what I have in my hand here?"

"I'm guessing it's bigger than a breadbox."

"Do you even know what a breadbox is?"

"A lot like a cornucopia, which is what I think you have, if I'm right."

"Tell me what you think it is, for real."

He told me.

He was right.

"So, Omar. Do you have a lot of money?"

"Maybe."

"It is going to cost you a lot of money. A lot."

"At the beginning. Then I will be the richest guy on the planet. You can have some royalites out of that, if you want."

---

194. This is happening to me more and more as I get older.

"Ah ha! A rich guy who has learned the share lesson. I'm here with Dafydd Spak, my guy. I'm sure you have your guys with you. It's time to make a deal."

So we did.

And *that* is the end of the middle.

A LITTLE
MAN
WHO
WASN'T
THERE.

110. ENTER A NUNCLE

"There's a guy here," said Kim into my ear a few days later. "Says he's . . . my uncle?"

That caused some commotion. In other words, I said "Wait there!" and hung up without another word, and got busy phoning others.

But when Dafydd and Gracelyn and Roger and I got to the Epitome, more or less simultaneously, it wasn't the fake Mr. Brice, magically escaped from custody, who sat peacefully in the padded chair, his feet up on Nathan's ottoman, drinking tea and looking as peaceful as he could manage, given our stares at his ripped sleeveless black vest, his jailhouse biceps and jailhouse tattoos, and his really bad haircut. This was some other guy, a stranger.

He stood up awkwardly, looking surprisingly shy, and held his hand out to me. He was small, wiry, swarthy, and had a beaked nose. He had slim, long-fingered, capable hands under the tattoos, and he shook hands like a proper person. I immediately knew I was looking at Nathan's real brother, even before he spoke.

"Hi," he said. "I'm Tony. Tony Brice. Anthony Brice, I guess, but I go by Tony, always have. Good, you brought a cop. We'll be needing one, later."

111. SPOOKY ACTION AT A DISTANCE

Kim did a double-take and the rest of us did the original single-take.

There was a small amount of chaos, at the end of which hospitality had triumphed over good sense and we were spread around my living room: on the couch, Kim and Mattie (who unobtrusively put down the blown-glass orb paperweight she'd been holding when the cavalry arrived); Tony back in the armchair; Mr. Spak in the other chair; Gracelyn making beverages and keeping an eagle eye out through the doorway from the kitchen; me making do with a dining room chair.

Roger stayed on his feet, leaning on the bookcase, his head perilously close to the taxidermied cat, and looming. Another activity of which we had had a lot recently.

All of us were staring at Tony.

"I guess y'all are wondering why I showed up," Tony said, then laughed nervously. I noticed a small kitbag over by the door, and a surprising absence of cat. Then I realised that the kitbag was moving slightly, but before I could panic, a thin Abyssinian tail briefly lashed out of the open zipper and then retracted. All right then. Bun has boots and Micah has . . . luggage?

"We've been talking about my . . . father, when he was young and all that," Kim ventured, also tentative.

"He always was a pistol, which makes you a son of a gun," said Tony, and Kim stared at him with complete incomprehension. Gracelyn and I were the only ones who snorted slightly with laughter.

Then we all fell silent for a moment.

Someone was going to have to take charge, and dammit, it was *my* living room.

"Okay," I said. "This is my living room, so I am taking charge of what is clearly going to be one of the weirdest conversations that will ever have been held here. Let me warn you that the bar is high on that."

Now they were all looking at me, which was not really an improvement, but it was a change.

Gracelyn handed out a trayful of various beverages, hot and cold, and went to bookend the room by leaning against the kitchen doorframe, more or less across from Rog, and flanking Tony at a similar angle. I noticed that she had used my grandmother's old round stainless steel tray to serve, and she had kept it in her hand, just in case. I've *so* watched that scene in more than one movie and TV show.

Okay, might as well just jump right in.

"You are clearly Nathan's brother," I said. "For real, unlike some asshole who has been pretending to be for the last few weeks. Congratulations. You will be rich."

"Won't do me fuck-all good where I'm going, pardon my French, ladies." *So* not what anyone was expecting him to say.

"What? Why is that?"

"Well, that guy holding up the wall there is going to arrest me in a little while, and I won't be seeing the sunshine for a long time. Well, I'll see sunshine, but, you know, truncated. In hour-a-day segments." Yep. Nathan's brother, albeit with a different adult life arc.

"So you are here, now, because . . . ?"

"I just wanted to see the kid. I mean, I only just heard about the kid, otherwise I woulda kept myself scarce, but I had to see for myself that Nathan had a kid. There's no doubt about it, is there?"

"Oh, none at all," I said.

"One hundred per cent DNA verified," said my dear Mr. Spak in his edgiest voice.

"I suppose you'll want to do that to me too. My DNA's in the system, though, so never mind that right now."

Mr. Spak seemed to be taking notes on his phone, and Mattie had an arm protectively behind Kim, who sat forward on the couch alertly, tight-focussed on Tony. Forget about waiting for the other shoe to drop. We were waiting for the *first* shoe to drop.

"Just tell us," I said, "what the *fuck* is going on here. And never mind the fucking language apologies, which would offend my French friends, and the 'ladies' shit, which offends *me*. Just start from the beginning and spit it out."

"Okay, fine. So, I guess I gotta go back to when Nathan and us got apprehended. I was, what, like nine years old. We had a couple of little sisters, Rosie and Leenie. Rosalind and Arlene[195]. They were cute as fu— . . . cute as buttons, and they got fostered right away and then when our parents bought it, the girls got adopted by those people right off the bat. But me? I was a little pain in the ass. I wanted my big brother, and I wanted my house, and nothing else would do. So I yelled and kicked a lot, which meant my adoption didn't exactly stick, not that they were saints either, and I ran away a lot, and so then I was stuck in the system, and you know what happens to a kid like that, pretty soon he's boosting cars and carrying dime bags on his bike for the neighbourhood aristocrats, if you catch my drift, and that was that.

---

195. I wondered why The Pretenders hadn't included sister number two, but I think it's because they didn't have a henchman — henchwoman? Henchperson? — they trusted to play the role. Or maybe they couldn't find her to get her DNA. They never said. I later, eventually, met the other sibs, and they indeed had taken many different paths in life, but despite their sometimes-poor choices, none of them was anywhere near as bad as their impostors had been.

"Then at a certain point I got into the con business, you know, fresh-faced kid can do no wrong. I learned the ropes from this couple, and they took me in and trained me up, and that was working out okay, but I kind of got into the substances too much so they had to drop me. I ended up in the . . . um, in jail a few times, petty stuff, but no more juvenile court at a certain point, right? I ended up doing some short time in the provincial system, you know? Theft under, that kind of thing. Nothing violent.

"I got dried out in jail, which is a fucking miracle given the amount of shit you can get in there, pardon my language, easier than outside, anyway I managed to straighten up a couple of times. Also I got some kind of legacy from my parents for some reason, pretty fucking weird given they didn't have a dime when we got apprehended, so it was a hell of a surprise[196], but I wasn't gonna complain. But I burned through it a little faster than I should have, you know what I mean. And I even got married once, to a nice little Somali girl who had a kid and needed her immigration sorted out. That worked out kinda how you might expect. I mean, we hung in a few years, but I'm shit at learning languages. I signed over the last of the moolah to her when we split."

I noticed Roger also had phone in hand and was texting rapidly. Tony noticed too, but he didn't seem to care.

I gave him a minimal encourager. "Mmm?"

"I was still on the legal side at that point," Tony went on. "Had almost fifteen years clean and sober, and more than ten out of jail. I was working autobody, I mean, doesn't everybody, it's like everybody in jail smells the Fordite and wants to go sand some fenders, I mean, it's a fucking cliché, isn't it? But there you go.

"But then —" He broke off and sighed. "Then I went to some parties, you know how it is, and one time you just can't resist

---

196. That was Nathan, of course. Remember?

doing a couple of lines just before you get laid, like, for old time's sake. Like. Sorry, kid."

"Don't say sorry to *me*," Kim said acerbically. "You were the one who got wasted."

He huffed in amusement. "Yeah, I did. And I was in that condition when I got sucked into helping my buddy out with a convenience store thing, right? Stole a car, a stupid little Dodge Neon, went out in the burbs, waved a water pistol around, and what did we get? Not even two hundred bucks, some cans of Coke, a couple of packs of beef jerky, and we left all the Cokes in the car when we abandoned it, so what was it even about? Only turns out that my buddy didn't have a water pistol like me, and he lets off a shot — thank Christ it didn't hit the clerk, I get nightmares about that sometimes. We get caught on the traffic cams, and he stood right in front of the cam in the 7-Eleven, the fucking idiot, so now it's armed robbery, and off I go to the Max. Him, they declared him a dangerous offender and threw away the key, but me, I got five years less time served so I just got out last week. Took me a while to get back from where they transferred me."

"And in jail," I said, as all the foreboding of all the cats and all the geese and definitely all the ghosts of the past few months came together in one fell swoop, "you met a man named Lockwood Chiles."

"That's right," he said.

112. MICAH DOES HISTORICAL RESEARCH

There was a thumping noise over by the door, and we all started. It was Micah Five, backing out of the kitbag, pulling something out.

Tony laughed. "What is that, some kinda cat detective or something?" He moved to get up, and everyone got tense. "I'm just going over and take that before he does some damage," he said to Roger, who nodded infinitesimally but still put his phone down on a bookshelf and stood ready.

Tony went over and gave Micah a pat, while with the other hand he took a small booklet out of Micah's mouth.

"I like cats, but why the fuck do they love chewing on photos?" he said. The booklet was one of those little cheap five-by-seven-inch photo books that you used to get at the drugstore when you processed your film, that would fit the prints from one roll and had ads for Kodak™ or Fuji™ on the covers. You could put the new photos in them for ease of viewing. Anyone who needs a translation for the last two sentences can apply to the Internet.

"I brought this for you, kid," he said. He handed the booklet to Kim, who took it as if it were an ancient artifact, which I guess it is, in digital-age years, which are sort of like dog years, except in centuries per year.

"I couldn't hold on to much," he said, "but I managed to keep that. That's us in there, before, like, with our folks. Rosie and Leenie, Arlene that is. And me. And Nathan."

113. AND AFTER THAT[197], WE DID NOT SPEAK FOR A WHILE

Kim looked through the photos of her father's family while the rest of us — well, speaking for myself at least, while I — tried not to crane our necks to see also. Later, I was given a set of scans of the photos, as was Kim and everyone else involved who seemed to deserve them. Nathan and Tony are unmistakeable, and the two little girls are poster children for gender-normative kids' outfits, but, I will admit, also cute. There's no new data in those photos, exactly, except the faces-to-names thing, but they sure do pack an emotional wallop.

But that was later.

---

197. Thank you, Gertrude.

To pass the time while Kim looked at them, I said, "How did you know Kim even existed?"

"I got a pal who's in Remand, and that asshole that was pretending to be me is in there now. My pal, he knows I wanna hear anything now that has to do with Nathan, so he gimme a call yesterday. And he mentioned the kid."

As easy as that, after all the secrecy. We would have to get used to being visible. Kim would, anyway. I think I've already grown all the protective skin I'm going to have. Which is never enough, but that's how we get wise, right?

Tony leaned forward, elbows on his knees and hands dangling. Aside from the tattoos, they might as well have been Nathan's fine, beautiful, maker hands.

I couldn't bear it.

"Why does Roger have to arrest you?" I blurted.

Tony looked at his own hands, turned them over to look at his palms, turned them back.

"Well, I done it, didn't I?" he said. "Before I got out. I killed that motherfucker Chiles."

The world went very still.

"He killed my brother," he said.

And after that, we did not — any of us — speak for a while.

HE
WASN'T
THERE
AGAIN
TODAY

114. A CAT IN DRAG

The sky was clear, the air was breathable, and there were tarps laid out on the vacant lot. I went around behind the wrought-iron fence and found Ted packing up.

"What's up?" I said. "Problems?"

"No problem. M2F2 just came by. Our suites just came empty and got cleaned. We get keys after the weekend. Taking some stuff over tonight to start."

"Suites?"

"This worker's smart. She got me and Shayna to apply for a place each. Shayna don't always sleep here anyway, you know. So say we each got two pets, that's within the limit, and two places happened to come open on the same building. Same floor, even. So I got the dogs in a one-bedroom and Shayna's got the cats in a bachelor."

Vikki. Of course she would find an answer.

"But aren't there three cats?"

He looked around. "Nope, just Ebony and Tiger there." The black and the tabby cats were lying tranquilly atop a tarped shopping cart.

"What about that kitten that's always running around and hiding?"

"Kitten?"

"That little fluffball."

Ted began to laugh. "Kitten! That's a good one. If that fool's a kitten, must be in drag!"

"Um . . . catch me up, here?"

"Fool's a dog. A Pomeranian. One of them teacups. Fool, get out here!" A tiny brindled cat-toy of an animal bounded out of the half-deconstructed tent and made a tiny urring noise like a Tribble. It was that shape, too, but with shining brown eyes and a tiny snout at one end, an extra puff of fluff at the other end, and tiny paws sticking out the bottom, as if the Tribble had been crossed with The Luggage.

Close up, the beast proved that indeed, my species meter was almost as faulty as my give-a-fuck-about-gender meter. It was indeed a dog, but its body was blurred under the most fur I'd seen since Denis sorted his boa collection. It bulked in at about the volume of a small cat, but when Ted put it into my hands, I couldn't believe how light it was.

"Not even four pounds," said Ted. "But it's fully growed. It's kinda a rescue. This lady bought it to be a breeder, but there's stuff wrong with it, not serious but makes it not show quality, like, so she gave it to Shayna. But Shayna don't really like dogs, she likes the cats, and we can only have two pets each in the new place anyways. Nice little pup though. So, I was wondering. Well, I was thinking. Fool gets along real good with cats. Socialised and all. Housetrained, sorta, if this here is a house. Make you a nice addition to the family. Kinda a thank-you for what you done for us here."

"Oh, no, no, I couldn't!" What I meant was, *never going to happen*[198].

"He don't bark. Don't know why. Just makes that little burbling noise, and he's got kind of a whirr he does when he has to go out to poop. But he goes in the litterbox half the time anyways."

"But I don't —"

"I still got most of a bag of that small bite food, and he likes them liver treats, I got a bag of them too. You gotta give him only about a third of a cup a day max, or he puts on weight."

"I don't have —"

"His records are in that East Downtown Vet Clinic, place where the vampire vets is."

"Vampire vets?" But I knew who he meant. Three vets practice there, and they're all from Transylvania. They're my vets too.

"They're my vets too!"

"Great, makes it easy for y— oh, here's my worker."

"I brought you your keys," said a familiar voice. "You sorted out that puppy yet?"

"Vikki," I said. Vikki. Of course she would have her fine hand in this too.

"Just doing that, Miss Vikki."

Miss Vikki. For fuck's sake.

"Awesome." She turned to Ted. "Here are your keys, and you need to take all this paperwork over to your social worker to get them to deal with the security deposit. If you can do it right now and get it back to me today, that's the best."

Ted pulled out a file folder from one of his big plastic totes. A file folder, for fuck's sake. I told you this guy had his shit together. He put it in my hand, under the tiny dog. "Chip, records. Bill of sale, kinda. I already filled it out. Just you gotta sign here to get

---

198. How is this subjunctivity shit working out for me these days, anyway? Read all this, and let me know what *you* think.

the chip registration reassigned. Fair warning, he still hasta get fixed — we couldn't afford it."

I was still looking at Vikki, and I took the folder automatically.

"Cute puppy." She nodded at the dust-bunny in my hands.

"Vikki . . ." I began.

"Just a sec," she said. "Ted, wait up, you gotta sign this thing."

115. WHO'S THE FOOL NOW?

The scrap of fluff in my hands wriggled around until it could put its tiny paws on my chest and stretch up. Okay, I admit, I was sort of cuddling it by then.

Kind of.

It licked my chin. Fool dog.

"I'm not tak—" I looked around, but Ted had taken his housing paperwork and vanished.

In one hand I had a file folder and the handles of a plastic carrier bag with dog food and treats bags in it. In my other hand, about four pounds of fluff on a small solid core. I had been left holding the bag. And — the dog.

"That thing is so fucking cute!" said Vikki in passing, as she tapped back toward her car.

The dog stretched up as far as it could, which wasn't far, and licked my chin again.

"Yeah," I said. "Cute."

Some necessarily-small interactions ensued. They might have been described as patting.

When I got control of myself and turned around, Vikki was gone. The M2F2 car was ten feet away and accelerating.

Fuck. I was stuck.

Which is why I now have a one-and-a-quarter-year-old, three-and-three-quarter-pound Pomeranian named Fool.

Although there is some doubt who's the fool in this scenario.

116. WHICH IS WHY . . .

. . . I can now join the Cat *and Dog* Mystery Writers of North America. I told you so.

Just sayin'.

117. KNOCK, KNOCK. WHO'S THERE?

The knock on my door was quiet but a little scary. Who got to my door at that hour without going through the security system?

I looked through the complicated electronic peephole that didn't show an inside watcher's tell-tale shadow.

Out in the dim night-time hallway stood a very tall man with bulky shoulders in an overcoat and hat, his back to the door.

I wasn't scared, exactly. I knew it wasn't Lockwood Chiles. He was three times dead.

Chiles had favoured a sheepskin jacket, anyway.

I was holding Fool tucked into the crook of my arm, in case he barked at the door, but he wasn't the concern. As Ted had told me, he never yapped. It was Bun and Micah Five, making more noise than Fool had ever made since I'd met him, who were producing the ruckus as they both miaowed at the door. Micah, who has one helluva miaow, was even patting the door with his front paws.

The man outside turned at the sound.

I was going to give Roger shit once I found out what the hell he was doing showing up in my corridor on the stroke of midnight dressed like the guy in *The Maltese Falcon*.

118. I QUIT

I thought that until I saw his expression.

And until he said my name, once, quietly, and nothing else.

"Roger! What the fuck? What's the matter?"

He shook his head at me as he came in, shrugging out of his overcoat. He took off the hat, a blue fedora which made him look like a private eye in a black-and-white movie, one of those urban but rugged manly-men of the nineteen-forties, half of whom had turned out to be gay[199].

He knows my place. He opened the front-hall closet where Bunnywit keeps his red fuck-me boots, and carefully hung up his attractive and stylish overcoat on one of my fancy wooden hangers with the carved metal hooks shaped like cranes'-heads. He hung his hat carefully on one of the brass hooks inside the closet door. Every move he made was calculated, calm, and contained the coiled energy of an explosive device.

"Would you like tea?" I said.

He nodded.

"Go sit. I've just boiled the kettle, it'll only take a moment."

He nodded and we went into the living room, where I set the microdog on a chair and went through into the kitchen. The kettle belied the watched-pot adage and really only did take a minute to come back on the boil, and I made my best tea, a Jasmine Dragon Tears green tea, the pearls of which would unfurl in its special clear pot while I listened to him tell me what was wrong. For full comfort-mode I brought the Bunnykins mugs, though my hand hovered over the Japanware.

I had some ideas about what might be coming, not all good, but I was trying not to think ahead. He would tell me. Eventually.

Roger was standing in the bay window, looking down. From that vantage, he had a pretty good view of a slice of the river valley, including a nice full moon — and even a few of the brightest stars were visible toward the south.

Micah, as usual, was twining around his feet. Bunnywit had leapt onto the little table that I kept in the window now, and was

199. Roger is not gay. So far.

picking his way delicately around the plants there, about to reach out and snag the immaculate sleeve of an expensive suit I'd never seen Roger wear before. When I came in, Bun jumped down guiltily and tried to pretend he liked me best. Fool, sitting pretty on the chair, silent and alert and minuscule, watched us all with his round dark eyes open wide.

The suit was one of those ambiguous designer fabrics that might be purple, might be green, might be navy, and for all I know had a thread of hot pink in it. In the light from my lamps, it looked dark silver. Micah was rubbing against Rog's leg, but on that suit, his ticked Abyssinian hairs were hardly going to show.

On Roger, the suit and its contrasting shirt and tie did not look at all ambiguous. Like many cops, he has a great wardrobe. He cleans up really well. I hardly ever, any more, imagine cracking him out of the shell of his designer suits and seeing whether the meat was still as sweet as it was all those years ago — and this was not one of the times I did either. Tonight, that suit was unassailable.

I was carrying the mugs and teapot in on the little liqueur tray that had been my mother's, and I set it on the coffee table (which, when you think about it, is a very weird sentence with a lot of beverages in it).

"You're in armour," I said. He turned, and leaned back against the wide windowsill. He nodded.

"I made the Jasmine Dragon Tears. It has to steep for a few minutes," I said. "You may as well tell me."

"I've been . . . Well. Today I sent the last of the cases to the Crown Prosecutor. Edwards is still out on bail, and the union rep was in my office half the day. I think Edwards is in the wind, but the rep assures me the asshole will show up when needed. Like I believe anything that otherfucker says after the union posted bail. Anyway, I didn't know at that point if the Crown would go ahead. There's a lot of pressure."

"Shit."

"Yeah, well, we knew that was a possibility. But it burns my ass."

But that clearly wasn't all.

"What else?"

"And then I was called to a Police Commission meeting tonight. I just came from there."

"The in-camera kind of meeting?"

"Yeah."

Oh, Roger.

"Oh, Roger."

Then I waited for the bad news. He was going to be told to drop it.

"I was already on my way when I got the call. Crown took the cases."

"Wow."

"The Commissioners wanted to know everything. So I briefed them. On all of it. Then I . . . I quit."

What the *fuck*? *That* wasn't what I had been expecting, not by any means. I had thought his flattened affect meant that the Crown had decided not to press charges, but that hadn't been it. Then I thought the Police Commission had gotten on his case. Nope.

Instead, I saw it had been him calmly holding in some strong emotion.

"Say *what*?"

He grinned suddenly, and I thought, *Is that glee?*

"I quit. I gave them my letter of resignation."

"Not to the chief?"

"The chief will be resigning tomorrow. He may not know that yet, but he will be. I saved everyone a little time."

"So why the hell did *you* resign, if that boys-and-their-toys bullshit artist is going to be gone?"

He looked at me and laughed out loud.

"I can play games too," he said. "Tomorrow, I'll either be out of a job, or they'll make me an offer and I'll be the Interim Chief of Police."

I just looked at him. That was something, all right.

"I don't know if I can do it," he said, "but if they let me, with the help of the people I can trust, I will clean those otherfuckers out of my house."

"The Police Association is going to try to fuck you up, you know that, right? They are all about the Thin Blue Line."

"Let them fucking try," he said. "I am the *real* Thin Blue Line, and I am *done* with their cover-up bullshit. No more biased labs, no more brutal cops, no more profiling, no more recreational boot-fests. We need *decent* policing. Human-scale. Honest. Trustworthy policing again." That was some speechifying. Wasted on me, but a promising framework for future media conferences. "Availabilities", they call them these days.

"Now *that's* the Roger I know and love," I said. "Have some tea." I poured it out, and after a moment we sipped. Gawd, I love these mugs — thin bone china with cavorting, retro, anthropo-morphised, heteronormative rabbits stencilled on. The first designs were painted by an Anglican nun. Go figure. The tea was great too.

After a while, though, I had to say it. "I want to believe in Good triumphing over Evil, Quality over Shoddiness. I really want to. You know that, right? But Evil abounds in that house you call yours. You realise you are up against the odds. They are legion and they can Fuck. You. Up."

"It helps that I don't give a tinker's dam what happens to me. Even if it means I crash in fucking flames, I will not accept their way any more."

"To the High Road?" I raised my cup to him in a toast.

"To the High Road!" He repeated the gesture. "As much as I can take the high road, at this rank. You lie down with dogs, you know the saying. There's a lot of shit to shovel. But I'm going to call them on all of it that I can. And fuck 'em if they can't take a joke."

Then we both jumped, and I almost knocked over the teapot, because across the room, someone, sharply but approvingly, said, "*Yep!*"

119. THE LAST WORD

We looked over to see the tiny Fool sitting alertly on his chair.

For the first time since I had seen him, he had barked.

OH,
HOW
I WISH
HE'D
GO
AWAY . . .

120. LOOSE ENDS

This has been a story about people and things that weren't there. It has been an empty box that yielded mysteries. It has been defined by voids, by shadow outlines: of people and actions that used to be; of operations deep in shadow and therefore unseen; of ghosts; of impostors; of pretenders; of fakers and fakirs; of lost people who could return and lost people who are gone forever.

Now you know how most of those lost stories turned out — but you are already saying it to me. I can hear you. Yeah. There are a bazillion loose ends here.

Because loose ends happen, and stories just keep unrolling — because that is how the world works in real life. You can't deal with this level of nefareity in a tidy little shoebox — or even, similarly-sized, a beautiful custom box hand-carved by a lover.

At the start of this story, I was thinking about when a crime starts happening. The crimes of Lockwood Chiles, and the terrible damage he did, began long before I knew him, and probably well before Nathan and Priscilla knew him. His ability to deceive and manipulate took him to the top, up there in the upper percentile of the one per cent, and yet it still wasn't enough for him. His hunger began before he chose grift, lies, fraud, theft, exploitation, assault, and murder to try to slake it. The crimes for us began when they were committed against us, but Chiles was already a nexus of destruction, a perpetual negatively-charged storm-cloud, a hurricane (as Hep had said) looking for places to happen. No wonder lightning struck all those around him.

There are consolations to offset the terrible swathe Chiles cut through the world.

First and best: Lockwood Chiles is dead. And though he has been as troublesome in death as he was in life, soon his empire will be dead too. The legit business will be sucked into the same void where the illegitimate transgressions created their vortex of deadly greed, and all of it will be inaccessible to the forces of evil that Chiles gathered around himself[200].

There are going to be forensic accountants and lawyers and Crown Prosecutors — and Uncle Tom Cobley and all — all over the money, the smart paper records, and all the long tentacles of the business Lock and Nathan built legitimately and Lock built illegitimately, until basically hell freezes over (or melts, depending on your hell-related ideology). Either way, dead, and good riddance. But even in the areas I can still legally talk about, that's not gonna be me.

If I had kept my fingers in the untangling of the Lockwood Chiles mess, I'd be living in an eternal Now, a place of endless thinning where Lock kept killing Nathan and Pris again every moment, trapped in a stasis of maximum anger, loss, sorrow, shame, and guilt. I didn't want to spend my life there. As I'm sure

---

200. It did him no good to be a control freak and a loner, either, because apparently that meant he didn't have very high quality evil minions — given that "Douglas Woodward" and his cronies were a reliable sample.

is more than obvious, survivor's guilt was haunting me when this story began — guilt, and shame that I didn't save Nathan's life, and Pris's, and those of the other people who died with them.

Oddly enough, knowing that Nathan was just as sucked-in as anyone else, and just as unable to prevent his and Pris's murders, is comforting. I don't lie awake nights torturing myself any more about what could have been different. I have almost become reconciled to being a fallible human being who loved — loves — another fallible human being, and have almost accepted that whatever the best intentions, shit happens.

Almost. Almost.

Almost is as good as I will be able to get, I suspect, given how much I respected as well as loved Nathan, how much ego accompanies me through life, and how much I hate entropy.

I have temporarily given up being the compulsive fixer that I always deny I am. For once, I'm taking Mr. Spak's and Roger's and everyone else's advice and *not doing anything*. Except what I was going to do anyway.

Which is live in the Epitome Apartments, and go to work at Own Domains whenever I feel like it — if I feel like it — and help build really *really* good, really creative housing for homeless people, and do lunch with my old workmates, and drink iced tea with Hep, and go to Drag Queen Paint Nites with Denis and Lance, and maybe go see my girlfriend Jian — I think her Cirque troupe is somewhere in Europe now — and (takes breath) in general have the life Nathan and I wanted to have.

But without him.

Which I will eventually get used to.

As I must, because he is dead and I am still alive.

Because I sold the smart paper formulae to Omar and his band of boffins, Own Domains broke ground five months after Tony's confession. The central village, and the tiny houses throughout seven neighbourhoods, are going up fast — because they are small, neighbours don't freak out about them, and they are easy and quick to build.

Sometimes, you eat the bear; sometimes, there are no clouds, geese, cats, or ghosts to fuck things up.

Nathan's estate was bilked, but when you have money on that scale, it's all kinda hypothetical anyway. Over time we are discovering how to plug the leaks, and there will probably be plenty left, thanks to a few people, nameable and not — including Tony Brice, who killed Lock before Lock could finish bleeding Nathan dry posthumously.

Nathan's will has been proved — with much celebration by his friends, heirs and assigns, and our lovely multicultural tabby lawyer Dafydd Spak — and in the fullness of time Nathan's legacies will be settled on his family — his real family, including Kim — and eventually on Own Domains, and to a very small extent on me.

Before that ever happens, still, here, already, some homes will soon be ready for people like Ted and Shayna and Fleury. Phase one, all down to me letting go (again), and to Mr. Spak's canny bargaining.

Even without a dime of Nathan's.

But *with* his dimes, when all is said and done, his work will go on, and, eventually, go on all over the world, we hope. His remaining fortune will soon crumble not by graft and grift, but in the positive way he intended, as a bevy — perhaps an army, or even a flood — of functionaries, under Mr. Spak's capable leadership, takes it apart and spreads it around.

Roma has a larger staff now, and is spinning off satellite offices. I may or may not stay involved. The work is in good hands.

Kim, the child of Priscilla and Nathan, can emerge from secrecy as much as they want, and live as they please, with the love and support of their family — including those that until they turned up on my doorstep they didn't know they had, such as for instance me.

Priscilla is dead, but her fame outlives her, and her books still encourage people to take small risks in her large shadow. Kim will have to grow into her legacy, which ought to be interesting.

Also, Jason Edwards and his heavily-shod pals aren't there. They played brutal, deadly games with people that they thought were invisible. They discovered otherwise. We're still waiting on court and sentencing, but they aren't cops and soldiers any more, and their boots were taken away for forensic examination, and some of them are in jail while they wait[201]. Cops and jail do not mix, for which I feel an unworthy schadenfreude.

Mrs. Meg Murray wasn't there at first, and as a consequence someone died, but even though she felt as if she had vanished long ago, somehow I accidentally — and by that I also mean despite myself — saw her anyway. As a result, she stepped up the next time she was needed, and she is still here, the auld bezzom, a mosquito in the Epitome ecosystem.

The impostor heirs were *never* there, of course, and now they, too, are decomposing in prison, which is another way of vanishing; Chiles's co-conspiring cousin Doug, ditto.

It's only a matter of time until Captain Someone, who also isn't there, susses out Chiles's real identity through his DNA link to the grifter Douglas Woodward and decides whether to tell us what went on there — or not. And since we now know what part of Nathan's holdings were swindled by Chiles, that might help decode the transactions.

But most of that is not our job, and I'm just as happy in that case that some other people who aren't officially there are going to do it for us.

Nathan's missing brother, Tony, came out of his shadows to be our deus ex machina, and now, in prison, has chosen another

---

201. Because Edwards *did* try to rabbit, and got caught, and the police union lost their bail surety, and some of us are not very sorry about that.

kind of invisibility. But I write him letters (the real, old-fashioned kind), and I think Kim does too. And he has some money in the bank now, for when he gets out. Let's hope he spends it well, but after all, it's his life, and he makes his own decisions.

Danny isn't there, but his memory has gotten Fleury into a harm reduction place, where he's already looking healthier, and soon we hope he'll have a tiny home of his own in our first village, close to supports and helpers — as will Ted and Shayna and all their dogs and cats. Done and dusted and on to their next adventure.

Except Fool: I'm stuck with Fool.

I suppose you could also count as characters those aforementioned gravewalkers: cats, geese, and ghosts. The shivers were certainly real. And there are still three cats annoying me, two of them trying to lie on my keyboard as I write this and the other, moth-eaten, resting on his laurels on the shelf above us.

They get along with Fool just fine, in case you wondered. Almost too well. I am now thoroughly outnumbered.

But it's the emergence of the people that thrills me. Beyond all the recognised dead, there were these invisible, insubstantial, "unimportant" people who weren't there — and we found them anyway.

Now, they *are* here. In all the ways they can be or want to be or have to be, they have made their mark.

And finally, last but I hope not least, I wasn't there.

But I grew back. Or maybe I have always been here, at my centre, just thinned out a bit, as one does get — if one isn't a psychopath — when things are tough. People can put up with a lot and still exist. I have discovered that I still do. Exist.

I exist.

I'm still here.

And maybe, someday soon, I'll take that skeleton key out of the box Nathan made me, go up to the third floor of the office building, and see what's in the workshop.

— 30 —
[a.k.a.]
finis
[a.k.a.]
... the end
[a.k.a.]
— fin —

THE MAN WHO WASN'T THERE: THE POEM(S)

"ANTIGONISH" (1899)

— William Hughes Mearns (1875–1965)

Yesterday upon the stair,
I met a man who wasn't there!
He wasn't there again today,
I wish, I wish he'd go away!

When I came home last night at three,
The man was waiting there for me;
But when I looked around the hall,
I couldn't see him there at all!
Go away, go away, don't you come back any more!
Go away, go away, and please don't slam the door . . . (slam!)

Last night I saw upon the stair
A little man who wasn't there.
He wasn't there again today
Oh, how I wish he'd go away . . .

Note:

This poem is in the public domain, has many slight variants of wording and punctuation, and "(slam!)" is or isn't included (I chose not to include it in section titles), depending on where it is quoted. Its original inspiration was an account of a haunting in Antigonish, Nova Scotia, Canada. It was first written for a play that is long since forgotten, and Mearns wrote many parodies of it, which he called "Later Antigonishes", including the very tempting and genre-appropriate "Alibi", which I have added to the section titles:

As I was falling down the stair
I met a bump that wasn't there;
It might have put me on the shelf
Except I wasn't there myself.

I haven't been able to track down whether the nursery rhyme variant, quoted in the epigraphs and below, is derived from "Antigonish" (or one of its variants) or vice versa.

When I was going up the stair,
I met a man who wasn't there!
He wasn't there again today,
Oh, how I wish he'd go away!

ACKNOWLEDGEMENTS

My homeless and underhoused neighbours in Boyle Street neighbourhood, in east downtown Edmonton, continue to occupy my thoughts. No billionaires are constructing harm reduction villages here yet, alas, but I wish they would.

I thank my neighbours Emile Foisan, Daryl Hendricks, and Misty Dawn Dudac for giving me permission to adapt certain elements of their stories in certain parts of this book. I also thank a number of people, left nameless here, whose experiences, whether adjacent to my partner and me or recounted to us, helped me to deepen this narrative; I hope I have done them the justice they deserve. I specifically recognise (with his sister's permission) the late Denis Beaudoin, a neighbour who was attacked near our home many years ago by a gang similar to the ones in the story, and who died of his injuries. The attackers were never caught.

Although the characters of the dogs themselves are based on two real street dogs, the street names Killer and Fang are the street names of our own recent dogs. Fang was a rescue, a toothless throwback-Pomeranian, much missed, who had the same attitude Princess does and, given teeth, would have behaved much the same, while Killer, unlike the fictional version, is also a Pom: charming and beautiful, only four and a half pounds, and he wants you to know that if you challenge his people or his safety, He. Will. End. You.

Thank you to the FBI crime lab for its very-public meltdown in 2015.

Thank you for the invaluable help of John Wilson (retired, formerly of Alberta Serious Incident Response Team) and other members/former members/associates of ASIRT who prefer to remain unnamed. Before I even wrote this book, I went to them with an untenable premise and said, "This would never ever happen, right?" and then over the course of a couple of amazing hours, we discussed the rules of crime fiction, what happens in the real world, and where they overlap. Things I thought were TV nonsense turn out to be true ("pack of cigarettes"), and stuff that seems true is totally fiction, and often nonsense (DNA is handwavium, and no cop ever "burps" the ambulance). This meeting was extremely helpful and I so appreciate their gener-osity with their time, but any nonsense remaining is All My Fault. They tried.

Thank you to Sean Beckett and everyone involved in Crime Minds, a remarkable periodic event Sean and I organise where working members of detection and law enforcement meet with crime/mystery writers for Q&A and stories.

Crime novels are written from a deep call for justice. John Gardner called them "moral fiction". Even when the bad guy wins, the reader knows what should happen. Recently, the problematic aspects of police over-militarisation and brutality have come to the fore in many jurisdictions. I know there are still good cops. I've met some. But as a whole, they and their Police Commissions and police unions need to break ranks, quit standing up for the bad ones among them, and clean up their houses. Dashiell

Hammett said, "Down these mean streets a man must go who is not himself mean." Allowing for sexism, that's still the goal, isn't it — not to be mean, or take power as permission? As well as just laws and clean courts, we still need people — specialists — to call when there's a crime, who can be relied upon for ethical behaviour and equality of policing. I worked for seventeen years on a citizen committee on that very issue, and saw some hard-won positive changes beside a lot of negative crap, so the recent trend for the negative to win is heart-breaking as well as infuriating. The answers? A very *very* long conversation, and not here. But it's on all of us to make it right.

A couple of pre-emptive thanks: To Barb Galler-Smith for a joke I didn't use — yet (JSYK, birds may be dinosaurs, but so are we. Sort of.). Also, to reviewer Dan Burke of *Crime Talk UK*, who called Nameless's home the Epiphany Apartments. I haven't been able to work that in yet, either, but I will, someday. I promise. It's awesome.

Thanks to my first readers, John Park and Timothy Anderson.

When I was younger, I tried to keep Real Life and Fiction more separate, but recently, I amuse myself by mixing them up wherever it's safe and fun. So again I have namechecked in this narrative some people I really like. A few appear as themselves, but some have their names attached to characters who bear them no resemblance. Mr. Prasan Dave was my travel agent back in the day, and a gentleman, a community pillar, and a wonderful person. When Detective Dave needed a first name, I used Prasan's, but then the plot took Detective Dave into a darker place, so I want to stress that the Prasan Dave I knew would never have held an obsessive suspicion of murder against anyone, and was one of the most positive and kindly humans I've ever met. He also introduced me to ragamala music, and for that I also am grateful.

I also named someone after my dog. Gracelyn had not yet died at the time but "is now late" as Alexander McCall Smith might write. Still, there it is. I have stooped to that level. And I am not sorry. My remaining dog wishes you to know that any resemblance between him and Fool is accidental (as he is fully a pound heavier and some years older), and that he is no fool (debatable), and that he knows how to bark, thank you very much, and will do it at will — which is often. Right this minute, in fact, if provoked. Or even if not provoked.

I do not thank the mouse. Any of the mice, who have shown me that my own savage nature is not far below the surface. It is war between us now.

Thank you to my agent, Wayne Arthurson, now an associate of The Rights Factory. Thanks to everyone at ECW Press, including but not limited to Jack David; David Caron; Jen Albert; Jessica Albert; Rachel Ironstone; Jen Knoch; Jennifer Gallinger; Sammy Chin; Kenna Barnes; Emily Varsava; Neta Rose (who did the audiobook of *Mary Jane*); Brienne Lim, who has made all the awesome covers for the series; and Caroline Suzuki, who does the awesome @ecwpress Twitter. Thanks to Pushkin, my UK publishers of *Isabel* and *Mary Jane*, and Surhkamp Verlag, my German publishers, who have been great with *Isabel/Drag Cop* and who will, if they are sensible, go on with *Mary Jane* and this book too.

My family and several of my friends love/loved and read/read mysteries and thrillers and spy novels, and so have I since I was a sprog. Lists of authors or titles are too long to include, but anyone who aspires to write in this genre needs to read books from about 150 years of tradition, love what's right about them, acknowledge what's wrong, and try to do better by the genre, in the name of literature. Meanwhile, to Mom, Dad, Jaclyn, Betty, Mary: thanks again for all the recommendations: wish you were still around to read these. Also thanks for recs to brother Michael, who I am glad to say is still here to let me know if I've lived up to history!

Thanks to my friends for their love and support.

More than thanks, much more, to my partner Timothy, for everything, including men's fashion advice for my characters.

Someday I will have a website that actually works, and I will put its URL in here.

Finally, thank you to all of you who have come along with Nameless and me on our journey through the crime fiction genre and its tropes. So far, so good.

© SIMA KHORRAMI

CANDAS JANE DORSEY is the award-winning author of *Black Wine, A Paradigm of Earth, Machine Sex and Other Stories, Vanilla and Other Stories, Ice and Other Stories, The Adventures of Isabel,* and *The Story of My Life Ongoing, by C.S. Cobb.* She is a writer, editor, former publisher, community advocate, and activist living in Edmonton, Alberta.

This book is also available as a Global Certified Accessible™ (GCA) ebook. ECW Press's ebooks are screen reader friendly and are built to meet the needs of those who are unable to read standard print due to blindness, low vision, dyslexia, or a physical disability.

At ECW Press, we want you to enjoy our books in whatever format you like. If you've bought a print copy just send an email to ebook@ecwpress.com and include:

Get the ebook free!*
*proof of purchase required

- the book title
- the name of the store where you purchased it
- a screenshot or picture of your order/receipt number and your name
- your preference of file type: PDF (for desktop reading), ePub (for a phone/tablet, Kobo, or Nook), mobi (for Kindle)

A real person will respond to your email with your ebook attached. Please note this offer is only for copies bought for personal use and does not apply to school or library copies.

Thank you for supporting an independently owned Canadian publisher with your purchase!

This book is made of paper from well-managed FSC® - certified forests, recycled materials, and other controlled sources.

MIX
Paper from responsible sources
FSC® C103567

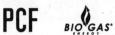

PCF

BIO GAS
ENERGY

PERMANENT